the Mountains of Channadran

Susan Dexter

A Del Rey Book

BALLANTINE BOOKS • NEW YORK

A Del Rey Book
Published by Ballantine Books

Library of Congress Catalog Card Number: 86-90870

ISBN 0-345-31976-1

Manufactured in the United States of America

First Edition: September 1986

Cover Art by Greg Hildebrandt

Encounter with a Shape-Shifter

There was a ripping sound, and the Sword of Calandra tore free. Tristan caught the hilt, then felt the blade lift his hand to guard position. Cheris almost ran onto the point.

"Oho!" the shape-shifter exclaimed. "The cub has teeth. You'd bite me, would you?" He sprang forward.

Tristan lunged to meet him. Then he was frantically turning the blade aside, trying to stop its thrust, as the figure before him was no longer Cheris. Now it was his old master and foster father Blais! He couldn't kill Blais! But the sword still pulled his arm, slashing for the figure's throat.

Cheris shape-shifted again. Below the aim of the sword, a tiny, fanged ice-lizard appeared. The red sac at its throat sent poison spewing.

Tristan collapsed onto the ground as the spray hit across his face and into his eyes. _____

By Susan Dexter
Published by Ballantine Books:

THE WINTER KING'S WAR

This book is for:

Jerry Zona, who first showed me an *Illustrator's Annual*, wherein I first saw a Ballantine Adult Fantasy cover, which started me reading this stuff, which started me writing this stuff. And for all those creamstick doughnuts, too.

Charles, who gives great haircuts and bought copies of *The Ring of Allaire* as Christmas presents for all his friends.

Patti Ramsay and John Sloat, who were not only kind enough to read this book in manuscript, but to comment thoughtfully upon it.

And for Baron.

Contents

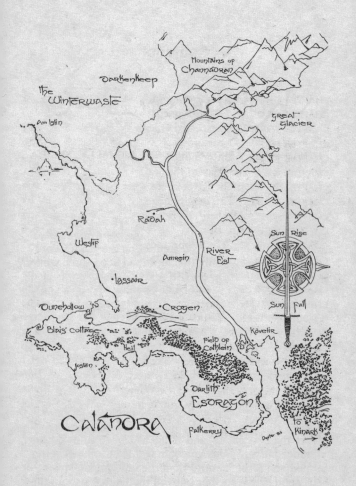

the Winterwaste

Am Islin

Mountains of
Channadran

Darkenkeep

Great
Glacier

Radah

Westlif

Amrein

River
Est

Sun Rise

Lassair

Dunehollow

Crogen

Blais' cottage

Kôvelir

Sun Fall

Hel

Field of
Cathlein

Josten

Darlith
Esdragon

CALANDRA

Falkerry

Oskar '83

to
Kinark

A Rumor of Storm

It had been, Tristan thought dismally, such a promising sort of day.

The dawn had been lovely, the sky the shifting color of pearl, and the air refreshing as new ale. He'd risen early to give Dickon a promised lesson at fencing before anyone else was around to use the practice yard or call him away to less enjoyable duties, and Tristan had been pleased that all his master's teachings on the art of sword-play had come back easily to him. It had been some while since he'd lifted a blade even in practice, and he was glad of the excuse Dickon lent him to sharpen up.

Just as they were finishing, Tristan was hailed by the old woman whose dried-up cow he'd been doctoring. She had walked all the way from her home, one of the lean-tos on the far side of Crogen castle, just to tell Tristan that his spell casting and herb lore had done the job better than he had hoped and that the cow was much improved. Besides a half dozen new-laid eggs, the woman gifted Tristan with a kiss.

Tristan didn't suppose she had the faintest idea he was her king. His everyday clothing tended farther toward comfort than regality—and if he had been allowed his preference, no one in his kingdom would have been better informed about his identity than the old woman was.

His good spirits further buoyed by the news about the cow, Tristan headed for the kitchens, hopeful that he could manage to cook the eggs in peace and maybe even snatch a bit of bacon to companion them. These might be the last moments all day he could count on having for his own use.

The respite didn't last even that long. Taking one of the less-frequented routes to the kitchens, he passed through a narrow courtyard whose sunward wall had lost so much of its mortar that it was more of a stone screen than a proper wall. It still stopped vision well enough, but sound carried through with ease—conversation best of all.

Tristan paid little heed at first—beyond the wall lay only the stables, where merchants and messengers arrived and unloaded goods or possessions. Then a word arrested his attention and his feet.

"King—oh, aye, 'tis fine to have a king again! Let's see how you feel about that come harvest time, when the taxes fall due. Kings don't fathom that they can't take a lord's portion of nothing. Indeed, it'll be worse than the lords—at least your own lord can see that a harvest's failed."

"But, Larkin—the harvest hasn't failed. There'll be enough for all, surely, if not plenty—"

There was a bitter laugh for an answer. "You try to harvest a field of barley that's been hail-flattened into the mud. Or dine on a late lamb that was stillborn in a blizzard."

Tristan froze between one step and the next, as stunned as Larkin's companion sounded.

"Hast gone so ill for Westif, then?" the unseen speaker finally asked, very low and slipping a little out of the common tongue. "Darlith has been plagued by cold rains off the sea, but we seldom get weather much better. There's hope to bring in at least part of a crop."

"And did this King you champion not promise you'd bring it all in? Give us a better season than we're used to? As if he could command that! Don't be such a fool, Trevare, if your lord sends you here to deal at Crogen. Canfors can't afford that."

"My lord supports the King," Trevare said carefully.

"So say they all—and swore it at the crowning. But there's rumor it was forced on them. And who can say what will befall this winter? It will be hard times, man."

"Does Danac of Westif hope to ease them by plotting revolt, then?"

"You'll not trap me so easy, Trevare. What need revolt, anyway? What's this King got for an army, except Polassar's men? That won't be enough. Best if he and Polassar realize that and spare us bloodshed, at least."

Tristan found that he was trembling—not at the open talk of treason in his own supposed stronghold, though that properly disturbed him, but at the thought of hail and blizzards in Westif, when he knew full well that Elisena was doing her utmost to marshall warm winds and soft rains to nurture the ripening crops. Her work had seemed effective—the weather at Crogen was fair, and they'd had no bad reports from the outlying districts, unless no one had thought such usual calamities worth reporting—or the disasters were too recent for word to have come yet.

Tristan walked on, no longer anxious for his breakfast nor eager to be about his next duty, which would involve his sitting with Polassar, listening to and attempting to resolve whatever ridiculous disputes were to be brought before the King's justice that day. Or perhaps Polassar had in mind for him to spend the day reviewing military tactics—again.

He'd reached the point where the wall became the back of the stables and the courtyard became an alley. No doors or windows broke the masonry—except one, high up, which let into the hayloft at about its floor level. The bricking seemed to have been laid with climbing in mind. Jutting edges promised easy footholds.

Tristan considered. If he went round to the front of the stable, the risk of running into Polassar was great. And his commander certainly would not approve what he presently had in mind. Best not to encounter him.

He had to use an unlocking-spell on the shutters, which proved more difficult than the climb itself, but Tristan was soon inside the loft. Brushing chaff out of his hair, he got his bearings and walked around the piles of hay to the far end of the space. There was a trap in the floor, meant for throwing hay down to the horse in the loose-box beneath. Tristan lifted the wooden panel and whistled softly.

The black stallion turned about in the stall, lifting its head toward him. *My lord?*

"Just didn't want to startle you," Tristan told Valadan, as he dropped lightly through the trap door to land beside the horse. He rubbed Valadan's broad forehead, then turned to fetch the horse's gear.

As he tightened the girths, Valadan plucked a bit of hay he'd missed out of Tristan's hair. *Do we go swiftly today?*

"Very swiftly." Tristan did up the buckles. "We're not just hiding from Polassar this time. I need to go to Darlith for a while. And then Westif."

Not a state, visit, I trust?

Tristan gave a start and dropped the bridle just as he was about to offer its bit to Valadan. The reins tangled badly as it fell, and he swore alternately at that and at Thomas as the cat wound about his ankles, purring and pleased at having surprised him.

"I'm glad I haven't lost my capacity to entertain you," Tristan said bitingly. "You can repay the debt—if Elisena comes looking for me, tell her I'll be back very soon. And she's not to worry."

Is there any surer way of getting her to worry than by telling her not to? Thomas asked.

Tristan put a boot in the left stirrup. "No time for games, Thomas." He swung into the saddle. The stall door, more courtesy than necessity with a horse like Valadan, was not latched. It swung out when Tristan spoke a minor word of opening at it. Valadan danced through, and they left the stables and Crogen castle itself so briskly that they might as well have been cloaked with invisibility.

Night was falling. Tristan was soaking wet, chilled to his bones, and expecting a good scolding just as soon as Elisena set eyes on him.

He had found Darlith under a siege of storm, its apple crop past anything save remembrance. In Westif, where less fruit was planted, the few trees had fared better, but the barley fields had all been plowed under. Perhaps Danac's yeomen had still hoped to save the wheat—sturdier, it had risen a bit after its beating. Unhappily, it could not withstand the ice that now loaded it. What harvest there was would be made one seed-head at a time, and the salvage would go for the next planting's seed, not food.

Near Falkerry, ice had jammed the Fal, flooding fields so that the potatoes planted there rotted. There had been farmers afield there too, trying to glean what they could.

Tristan didn't know which would haunt him longer—the stench of the fields, or the memory of a young wife resolutely wading through the frigid pools, grubbing in the mud while the child strapped to her back whimpered at the sound of the wind.

Neither recollection would quite let him go as he rubbed Valadan slowly dry. He hardly felt he was back in the stable at all.

It was not cold at Crogen. No sleety rain fell. And Valadan, having his speed by magic, needed less care after travel than a merely mortal steed. Tristan worked on him till he realized that neither Crogen's climate nor Valadan's close warmth could banish the chill that was wrapped around his bones; then he got the horse food and water and decided to seek out Elisena.

Thomas came pacing carefully atop the wall of the loose-box. *You'd better hurry. She's been waiting for you.*

The stillroom door was newly made, plain cross-bound wood, unpainted and undecorated. Inside, the room's walls were freshly whitewashed and broken up with odds and ends of planking collected from all over Crogen. Most of the shelves and half of the big table were covered with a miscellany of jars, bottles, and old books. The jars on the table bore neatly penned labels—medicines for ailing folk living in the countryside about the castle. Bundles of dried herbs hung from the ceiling, and a flowering branch stood in a pot of water by the bull's-eye window. A fire burned cheerily in the grate, with a fat-bottomed silver teakettle hanging over its flames. The whole room smelled of herbs, spices, and dried flower petals, like a just-opened potpourri jar.

Elisena was stooped by the hearth, unhooking the steaming kettle from the fireplace crane. She straightened with it in her hand, turned, and saw Tristan.

"Some tea? Or would you rather I magicked this into brandy? You look chilled right through."

Tristan was thankful he never needed to keep secrets from Elisena. Plainly, he'd be terrible at it. He crossed the room, began to lean against the table—then shifted hastily when he felt it begin to tilt. He belatedly recalled its weak leg and removed himself to the bright cushions beside the window. "Tea's fine. Thomas said you wanted to see me. I didn't expect to be away so long. Things were ... worse than I expected."

Elisena smiled ruefully. "You aren't alone in the experience." She set a pair of porcelain mugs on the table and dropped a palmful of cailon flowers into each, then added water from the kettle. "I had a messenger from Radak today."

Her eyes motioned to the corner of the room. Tristan followed her direction. At first he saw nothing not ordinarily found in the room. An herbalist's clutter passed description. Then there was a soft flutter, and firelight reflected from the red eye of a white ringdove. Its neck feathers were stained with blue, affirming its messenger status and place of origin—Radak.

Elisena's ringed fingers brushed Tristan's. "This was the message."

He took the rose from her hand. It had been white, but the bud was blackened, frost-kissed. Tristan turned it over slowly.

Elisena lifted his cup and scooped the soggy flowers out with a spoon. "You want honey in this, don't you? I sent Radak a gentle rain, the last before the harvest. I'm told it froze even as it fell. And I think Radak is not the only holding so troubled?"

"No. I went to Darlith. And Westif. The storms were done, so there was nothing I could do. The crops are gone. Or nearly."

He cocked his head as a faint but persistent sound of fluttering came from the other side of the window by his ear. Tristan fingered the catch and pushed the casement open.

Minstrel came through the opening with a whirring of wings, spread his tail, and executed a neat landing on Tristan's right shoulder. He chirped brightly and began to preen himself. Tristan brushed the canary's tail with a fingertip. "Where've you been? Out chasing sparrows again?"

Minstrel bit his finger, then turned to scold at the ringdove.

Elisena put the honey jar away carefully on a badly overloaded shelf.

"Can't we do *something*?" Tristan asked, not distracted by Minstrel.

"Certainly." Elisena turned her mug slowly between her hands. "For a time. Bit by bit. I've stopped the rain at Radak. It's possible to break any storm Nímir sends."

She sounded quietly certain. So why did Tristan feel no leaping of hope at her words?

"Nímir is going to harry us as the sea harries the shore, and we can withstand him a while, as the shore does the sea. We can break his storms, moderate the damage—as weather-witches here have always done. And as they have done, we will age and die. Then Nímir will have his victory, for the price of a little patience."

Tristan wondered to himself what a plant felt when frost touched it just as it came into bud. A desolation that could match his own?

"Why doesn't he just let us be, then? Why attack us?"

"Calandra has a crowned king now; that, along with these rings, is a threat to Nímir. He knows there's another answer—if we're brave enough to take it."

"Another answer?" Tristan raised his eyebrows.

"Wait till Polassar gets here."

"He's coming?" Tristan thought he'd missed a move in the game.

Elisena set her mug aside. "He will be." She poured from the kettle again, gestured over the mug elaborately. The water frothed and became ale. Not even Calandra's Queen would dare to offer Polassar of Lassair *tea*.

The doorboards shivered with the blow Polassar probably considered a discreet knock, and Polassar himself entered at once when Elisena spoke. Lassair's lord was clad in a short tunic of grass-green velvet, over trews checked with scarlet and murrey. The effect, especially when coupled with the fluttering yellow of the cloak he'd thrown over all and the brassy glitter of his armbands, was unusual, not to say painful.

"Lady, there's wild talk in the Hall! Some fool just in from Josten swears the Cold One's Hounds have been heard—" He spotted Tristan. "My lord, I've been seeking you these past two hours! I was beginning to fear—"

Tristan reminded himself that it was unseemly for crowned kings to cringe.

Elisena gestured impatiently for Polassar to sit. "Reports from all sources agree," she said calmly. "We were just discussing the problem of Nímir."

A Secret Council

POLASSAR LOOKED PUZZLED, THEN RELIEVED. "YOU know all about the matter, then." Plainly, he expected everything would now be easily resolved.

His broad forehead furrowed as Elisena demolished that belief by relating the report from Radak and what she'd seen in her scrying crystal. His brows knotted as Tristan went on to tell what he'd seen at the other holdings.

"If it were possible to hold back Nímir's storms piecemeal, the High Mage would have done so long ago," Elisena said. "Obviously, that is no answer. For every storm we break, Nímir will simply send another to the other side of Calandra. He'll wear us down and ruin the land at the same time. He's served us so before this."

Polassar's gaze traveled slowly to the corner where Tristan's sword was propped upright. Its blade glowed gently, echoed by the gleam of the silver rings on Elisena's clasped hands.

"Aye, but do matters not stand different now, Lady?"

"One skirmish seldom ends a war, my lord. Not with men, neither with Nímir. Our fight still lies before us."

A spatter of sleet clattered against the dark windowpanes, and Elisena looked up sharply. Her hands gestured commandingly, rings flashing, and her eyes narrowed. The noise ceased as suddenly as it had begun.

Elisena raised a hand once more to brush a straying tendril of hair away from her nose. "I shouldn't even bother. Nímir will but toy with us here now. He only wants us to know that we are not overlooked."

Minstrel stirred sleepily on Tristan's shoulder, pulling a foot up under his feathers as he prepared to nap. Save for the firelight, the room was dark. The sleet had delivered them up wholly to thoughts of Nímir, of ice and death, and the faint glow suddenly seemed the last light in the world.

"Say it out, Lady," Polassar whispered, scaling his voice to his surroundings for once. "What are we to do?"

"You have no memory of that time when Nímir did not have the teeth of his winter locked on Calandra's throat. Nor have I, really—I was a child then and not privy to the councils of the great of the land. Later, when I had been chosen to receive the rings, Nímir prevented the Council that was to have instructed me. I know there were many questions asked in those days; but, while long years have been sufficient to turn those times into dim legend, they have brought few answers."

Polassar settled back.

"Nímir's nature will have been much debated. But whether he is an elemental, a god, or some unthinkably puissant sorcerer, I no more know now than did the High Mage in those far-off days."

The kettle, left hanging over the flame, began to hiss, and Elisena moved to quiet it. "This is certain: Nímir tore the heart of this land to shreds. A third part of what was once Calandra now lies under the Winterwaste, and each year Nímir's winds spread the desolation farther by leagues. Yet when this kingdom was beaten to its knees and his victory seemed certain, Nímir hesitated in his attack. Perhaps he needed to do no more and preferred to save his labor. Perhaps he *could* do no more. We can have no answers. We have barely knowledge enough to shape questions—and that little learning is hard-won at the cost of many lives."

Tristan, remembering the chronicles of wizardry he'd read as an apprentice in Blais' cottage, knew exactly how much that information had cost. He tried to swallow, but found his mouth was far too dry. The tea left in his cup was cold and bitter under the sweetness of the honey. He put the cup aside.

"How long do you think we have?" he asked.

"All our lives. The greatest danger is far from immediate—ice is a relentless tool, but it is slow. And the land seems to resist Nímir's will more strongly since your crowning. Nímir will need to work hard to bring his winter early and hold it late. He will seek to entangle us and keep us too busy to see beyond the present day."

"So the less time we waste, the better off we are," Tristan said.

Elisena swung the kettle gently, so that the firelight flickered on it. "Ice and chaos are Nímir's strengths, now as ever. Darkness is his element, and the little I know of him does not suggest that he will abandon such weapons. Our one advantage is this—to an attack gauged against centuries, we can move with what must seem impossible swiftness, like gnats before a glacier. And so we must. We may surprise him."

"Attack?" Polassar asked, not so eagerly as Tristan might have expected of him—not that he blamed the man for his caution.

"If we do not, we lose all. Nímir has only to wait. We few are perhaps the last who threaten him, and our days are like grass, soon withered. We must strike while we have the weapons and the strength to lift them."

This, then, was Elisena's other answer. Her rings glowed softly on her fingers, and Tristan was surprised to see that his sword was answering them. A glimmer of fairy-light leaked out of the heavy leather scabbard.

Either Polassar had grown used to such things or he refused to be overawed by the magic. Discarding the fey mood, he was all business—the sort of business he knew best of all.

"Where and how do we strike, Lady? I'd not half trust those men Danac and Kerrgis left here, but my own arrays are ready enough."

"We won't need an army. Not where we're going."

Cold bit sharply at the end of Tristan's long nose, though the fire in the grate still burned brightly. He sensed what was coming.

"Nímir will not come to us—no more than he must, if he hopes to keep us occupied here. If we would fight him more than that little, we must choose the ground we will meet him on. Perforce it must be Nímir's own—the oldest of legends place his origin in Channadran. It is my belief that he is there still, a spider mastering his winds from the center of the web he has spun. If we would face him, force him to fight, it will be—must be—there."

"We carry the war to his very face?" It was more a statement than question from Polassar.

"To Channadran," Elisena said.

Tristan closed his eyes tightly, as if the mountains he so dreaded were actually before him. Of all possible places . . . Channadran had a worse reputation than Darkenkeep and was reckoned to be more perilous than even the Winterwaste, in spite of—or perhaps because of—the fact that no observer had ever come out of the mountains alive to make a report. Many had tried. He'd read their names in Blais' books.

Channadran. The very name was ice in the blood. It would be healthier, less paralyzing, to stop dwelling on such fell thoughts, but Tristan couldn't. He felt as if his mind was blackening at the edges, like the frosted rose.

Minstrel was a warm puff of feathers beside his ear, sleeping, safe and content. That was a comfort to draw on and use to hold the blackness at bay. Tristan began to attend to the conversation once more.

"I still hold that 'tis work for an army! At least a troop of picked men," Polassar rumbled. "Begging your pardon, Lady, but I've never yet met a wizard with sense enough to watch his own back. Did your folk learn nothing from all those that went alone into Darkenkeep and were never heard from more? And if you're set to go into those witched hills—"

How long the two of them had been going round on that point Tristan could hardly guess, but it must have been a considerable while, to judge by the exasperated look Elisena tossed his way. He glanced from her to Polassar.

"An army couldn't have taken Darkenkeep," Tristan said. "And the case is no different now. Magic defeats magic, steel bests steel. That old saw is nonetheless true. We have the rings and the sword. That gives us two powerful weapons. And how would we feed an army in the mountains, if we thought we needed one? Where would we get firewood to keep it warm? If we need help with this—and I'm not too proud to suspect that we may— we must look to those having magic for it."

Elisena laid a gently hand upon his arm, and Tristan

saw that he'd also guessed wrongly. "Kôvelir won't send anyone. You were there, you should know that best of any of us. And a Calandran mage? When was the last time you saw one?"

Tristan couldn't quite remember. "Even if we found a few, they wouldn't be trained as Blais trained you, Tristan. He schooled you in the High Magic, and he was one of the few still fit to do so. For a dozen lifetimes, Nímir lured Calandra's wizards to their deaths or worse. He set his traps to catch the best, leaving only the ignorant and backward behind to pass on their mislearned knowledge. The average mage in Calandra now is a wandering conjuror, competent enough with the small magics and able to do a bit to keep the land alive, but blissfully ignorant of those greater spells so far beyond his grasp." Elisena shook her head, making the crystals in her hair ring together. "There's none of them I'd turn to for this. They'd but lose their lives for a help they cannot even offer."

Tristan had never thought much about the extent of his master's power. Could gentle old Blais, fond to foolishness of birds, bees, and herbs, busy with his books and simple philters, have been a great mage like those of Kôvelir? Nothing Tristan remembered discredited Elisena's version, though he found the import of it all hard to accept. And the old man had, at the last, even taken on Nímir in single combat, though Tristan thought he probably hadn't intended to. Tristan's eye fell on the flames in the grate, curling red and yellow, white and gold.

"What about Reynaud, then?" he asked reluctantly. "*He's* no petty conjuror, whatever else he is—or isn't. Where does he fit in?"

"Reynaud is of Kôvelir. Once they sent us many promising mages—in the old days when every lord had his master of magic. Kôvelir has long forgotten us—so it may have been Reynaud's own choice that brought him here. He's a bit of an adventurer."

Polassar called the man something even ruder, then made a hasty sign behind his back, as if to avert Reynaud's absent malice. Tristan shrugged. For all any of them knew, Reynaud was yet in Kôvelir where Tristan had seen him last. And thank the Est, even Reynaud's ears couldn't hear over that distance.

"You're sure the Wizards' City can send no help? If

we fall, will the Cold One not be at their walls next? Who'd come to their aid?" Polassar asked.

"Men find it hard to believe in a danger not continually before them," Elisena excused. "Nímir has shrewdly lulled them into false ease, and they will be slow to rouse from it. Would it were not so, but we must depend on ourselves alone."

Polassar nodded heavily. "Where and when, Lady? And how many men will you let me take?"

"None, I fear." Elisena smiled sadly at Polassar's protest. "Consider! Channadran is too high for forests to grow. It is a dead place of bare rock. Horses cannot travel its trails past the foothills. We will have no food save what we carry on our own backs. How many mouths do you want to try to fill? There had best be only the three of us, I think. As to when, we must have a few days to make preparations and leave things orderly here—but not too many days. I had hoped for more time. There is still so much to be done."

"What are the lords to be told?"

"As little as possible. We are fortunate. Crogen has yet to regain its place as the hub of the country. And Tristan has very little to do with Calandra's actual governing. We are set free to act as we must."

Suddenly, Tristan didn't feel so guilty about being slow to take up his kingship. But the thought couldn't warm the chill he got when he looked farther ahead than Polassar was doing. The picture he saw in his mind's eye didn't really bear thinking about.

It was suicidal enough to consider confronting Nímir on his very doorstep; but even to attempt that they must cross leagues of frigid, lifeless waste and then find passage into impenetrable, impossibly high mountains for which no map was known to exist. Had Elisena considered that they could not afford aimless wandering while they conducted a search, limited by the amount of food they themselves could carry? How could they quickly seek out something without knowing where to look?

Elisena plainly had given the matter thought, but she still paused to consider it again.

"One man may know the mountains well enough to help us," she said finally. "Though whether he *will* help us or no, I fear to guess. There is a tower called Am Islin beside the Frozen Sea, and there dwells Royston Ambere. All the birds in that country look to Magister Ambere as lord, it is said. Birds fly over Channadran and return— the only creatures that do so. I think Royston Ambere will know the way to what we seek, if I can convince him to help us."

"Why should he not?" Polassar asked, baffled.

"I find it difficult to predict the actions of a man who seems certainly something more than a man. Ambere has been in that tower since time began, or at least since before the mages began to write the chronicles of this land—all alone in his high tower with his beloved birds. The legends reckon him to be as perilous to deal with as Nímir, though he is not inherently evil. The legends may exaggerate—or they may not. We will try him. We can scarcely miss that great tower. It will be a fine landmark, pointing our way."

The fire flared brightly, sending a shaft of white straight up the chimney. It stood for a moment in the semblance of a tower, with flames licking at its base like waves. Through the afterimage of it, Tristan saw Polassar making the sign against evil again. The man would have his fingers worn out, if he kept that up. Tristan lifted up his mug once more, and drank down the bitter dregs.

"To Channadran." he said.

Unexpected Guests

PACKING WOULD BE SIMPLE. TRISTAN WAS TAKING THE warmest clothes he possessed, as many of them as he could get on his back, and his magical gear. Polassar had pressed a cobbler into service and had boot soles studded for surer footing on ice and ice-covered rock. Tristan's had been delivered that very morning. Food, herbs, and medicines were Elisena's realm of expertise, and Tristan was quite sure that she was dealing with them with her customary dispatch.

At least I hope she's dealing better than you are doing with this court of complaint, Thomas told him.

Tristan was rudely dragged back to the present moment. The Throne Hall was very still, but far from empty. Somebody had just summed up the case he'd been presenting, and Tristan hadn't heard more than half of it. He stifled a groan and hoped that his presumably vacant expression might have been taken for deep judicial meditation.

You should be so lucky. It's not that dark in here.

Tristan swallowed, wet his lips, and firmly stated his royal opinion that the sheepdogs ought to be allowed to settle the question of which sheep belonged to which flock. After all, were not the dogs in closer touch with their charges than the shepherds?

He'd been afraid of his solution's simplicity at first; but for a wonder, it was accepted, even marveled at as an example of good sense and fair dealing—the sort of thing one came to a king for.

You'd trust a dog's opinion? Thomas asked, aghast.

"Very few shepherds keep cats. I didn't have much

choice." Tristan watched the last of the onlookers exit the Hall. The clerk who'd begun recording the morning's proceedings had gone off in search of a fresh quill—two hours past—and hadn't returned. "That's the last of them, then."

"Not quite."

Tristan froze, staring to see which shadow spoke. He knew the voice, though he'd last heard it leagues distant from Crogen. Its inflections were etched deep into his brain for reasons which also made it impossible to mistake.

Reynaud stepped forward, his elegantly draped black cloak scarcely stirring.

"How did you get in here?" Tristan asked in the whisper that was all shock had left him of his voice. The instant the words crossed his lips, he wished he might call them back, but he couldn't hope to creep away either unseen or unheard.

"In a puff of smoke?" Reynaud suggested as he took another step toward the throne. "Actually, I walked in through the front gate. Now that Crogen's no longer under siege, that's considerably easier than you might suppose."

Confronting Nímir himself might not prove more harrowing. Tristan had no means to judge. The pit of his stomach grew cold, and his mind scurried desperately. He could only recall being thus alone with Reynaud once before in all the times they'd met. If anything, he was more terrified this second time. He knew the man better now and had fact as well as instinct to go by.

Tristan's fingers ached to wrap themselves around the hilt of his dagger, even while his brain was calmly insisting that such a paltry weapon would be useless against a sorcerer of Reynaud's class. His sword might have offered him surer protection, but it was just out of his reach, propped beside the throne, handy enough for inspiration in adjudicating, but too far off to grab quickly. Crogen was home; it was safe ground. He hadn't thought he'd need to go armed here.

"When did you get back from Kôvelir?" Maybe, if Tristan could find means to delay, Thomas would have time to run for Elisena. The cat could surely slip out of the Hall before he was noticed. Tristan fought to keep his voice steady.

"The weather this side of the Est was inclement. I lingered on the coast till the storms passed." Reynaud was smiling.

Tristan felt he'd been shown a trap he could neither avoid nor comprehend. How fast could he expect Thomas to run? Only seconds had passed. He must hold out a good while longer, before he could expect reinforcements. He hoped Elisena was in her stillroom and that Thomas wouldn't need to search her out—

There was a small movement by his foot. Tristan looked down in horror as Thomas settled himself, his tail wrapping neatly about his paws. The cat all too obviously hadn't realized that he was being depended upon to effect a rescue, and there was no way to tip him off to the plan under Reynaud's quick eye.

"But I have forgotten my manners," Reynaud said.

The words and an eye's-tail glimpse of movement brought Tristan's head up as his heart leaped in his chest, and his fingers grabbed for his useless dagger. He stared at Reynaud, growing more amazed by the instant.

Reynaud had dropped to one knee and was elegantly poised with his back straight and his right leg bent respectfully to Tristan. He spread his empty hands at his sides, like a dancer offering a performance.

"My service to Galan has been terminated, my lord. I've come to sue for permission to enter yours."

If Reynaud had expressed a desire to be flung into what remained of Crogen's moat, Tristan could not have been more surprised.

Reynaud's dark eyes drank at him, but the man's face gave out nothing beyond his words.

Tristan, certain he was being mocked in some way he would doubtless soon understand, felt his temper flare accordingly. Good! Rage fought his panic down nicely. He wouldn't be played with, whatever the danger. Anger wiped out fear and burned it away, scattering the ashes.

"Get up, Reynaud. Humility doesn't become you and it doesn't deceive me."

"Such mistrust of so simple a request? Surely I can't be the first to make this offer. I had heard that even Baird of Amrein was welcomed here." Reynaud rose smoothly to his feet, coming closer to the throne without seeming to take a step. Tristan resisted an impulse to draw back.

"You must know you've no reason to fear me. What would I dare attempt on you here in broad day and all your friends within call?"

It was Tristan's turn to smile—bitterly. "That sort of thing never stood in your way before this. You betrayed me to Galan. You betrayed me to the Council. I'd be just a bit simple if I trusted you now, wouldn't I?"

"Ah." Reynaud stroked his neat beard. "That! I have," he pointed out thoughtfully, "a certain pride in loyalty. It bound me to Galan when he attempted your life. I would rather have acted otherwise, perhaps; but my duty to him left me no choice, you will agree."

Tristan laughed, more because his nerves were tight-stretched than because Reynaud's notion of duty amused him. "Don't pretend to be noble. You betrayed me to Galan for your own reasons. No man could bind *you* to something you didn't want to do."

"Betrayed is rather a strong charge," Reynaud countered. "It suggests that I had your trust at the time—which is certainly not true. I do not disclaim my guilt, but neither will I shoulder more than my share. In any case, I had left Galan's service by the time we met in Kôvelir."

"And the Council?"

"The Council had you in their hands before I arrived in the city. I was as startled to see you there as you were to see me. I might have been able to secure your release where Cabal was failing—but of course your escape prevented that."

"So you claim you would have asked the Council to set me free?" That was far enough past belief to be truly laughable.

"I wonder why I should bother making claims you so obviously won't believe? But, since you insist, I will attempt it. My lord, surely you've spent enough of your day in this dismal hall. Can we not venture somewhere more comfortable for our talk?"

"No. I don't expect this to take long." Tristan was beginning to suspect that there was some reason Reynaud could not touch him where he was. He didn't trust the feeling fully, but he was determined to stay where he was.

Reynaud shrugged. "As you will, my lord. You may have guessed that I came here from Kôvelir many years ago. Elisena knows that, I think. What she does *not* know is that I was posted here by secret directive of some who were then members of the Council. They felt the situation in Calandra needed close study, for various reasons I won't bore you by detailing."

"Thank you for your consideration."

Reynaud ignored the interruption and proceeded with his explanation. "As a means of survival, I attached myself to the only lord I found with sense enough to appreciate the sort of use a wizard could still be. The craft was not in high repute here in those days, and there were not many choices open to me. At that point, Galan looked likeliest to come out on top of the power struggle. If he did—and I could do much to ensure that he would—I would have my safe spot at the heart of events, and that was an advantage I badly needed. A long-range plan, with fruition many years off, but such was what my masters in Kôvelir had expected and prepared for. Events moved much as they had anticipated and as I had steered them. And then you popped up."

"That must have been galling for you," Tristan said nastily.

Reynaud arched his brows. "It scarcely mattered to my mission, except it took me a while to get free of Galan. There were certain pacts to be considered. He knew a bit about sorcery—enough to write binding oaths. I see you still do not trust me. That will, I think, be a far greater difficulty than Galan."

"I'll shed a tear for you."

"You may have cause to," Reynaud rejoined sharply. "I could be very useful to you. My lord, there's no proof I can offer for your inspection—not about the Council, anyway. With the climate there what it is, secrets will stay so."

"Convenient that way! What brings you to me now? How is it the Council didn't lock you up before you spilled their little secret?"

"They're a touch busy at the moment. A frightful storm rolled down the Est's valley a week past. Crops were ruined for leagues about the city. There are some who believe Nímir's power now, but their struggle with the rest of the Council only rouses impatience in me. There's more good to be done here now than in Kôvelir."

"And that's what brought you to me?"

"When I was but an apprentice, I swore that I would fight Nímir with all my strength and with all my life. I will hardly turn about and aid him now, whether through Galan or those dolts who form the present Council." He looked sharply at Tristan's face. "Does none of that move you? What then of wizards' brotherhood?"

"If you seek brothers, I suggest you go back to Kôvelir," Tristan said rudely.

"I'm posted *here*, you—" Reynaud checked himself with an effort that Tristan was both surprised and delighted to note. He went on, more smoothly. "We're both on the same side of this. Can't you see that? Whatever our personal differences have been—"

Tristan stopped listening. He had more important thinking to attend to. He'd hoped at first that he could offend Reynaud enough to send the man away. The last thing he wanted was Reynaud hanging about Crogen after he and Elisena had gone. He couldn't leave something like that at his back, and Allaire was going to have enough to deal with. But Reynaud was not cooperating. Tristan would have to try something else, having no means to enforce banishment.

"All right. Spare me the long words. You can stay."

What? Thomas hadn't expected that decision.

Reynaud looked as startled as Thomas. "My lord—"

Tristan cut him off with a gesture. "You have my leave to stay in Calandra—but not at Crogen and not near me."

Reynaud was frowning, but Tristan paid no heed to his expression. "I don't want to see your face again," he went on. "You might try Radak. You ought to feel right at home there, and it's a nice distance away from here."

"Yes. I might just as well be in Kôvelir."

Tristan smiled. "Yes. You might, at that."

Reynaud's cape swirled. Tristan was reminded of Thomas twitching his tail when something crossed him. "I don't care much for your conditions, my lord."

"I didn't suppose you would."

The cape switched again. "I'll take leave of you, then. Taking service is a wearisome thing."

"And it's a long ride to Radak," Tristan said, his tone one of dismissal. He wondered if Polassar would have been proud of him.

Reynaud, a few paces off, stopped and turned back toward the throne. "Oh. I've something else to offer you besides my service," he said offhandedly. "You'll find it in the kitchens."

I'm surprised he took it so well.
"So am I, Thomas."
What if he hadn't? You have the oddest way of handling situations—and it's worse since Polassar set to work on you. All force and no craft.
"Thanks. If you'd gone for help, I wouldn't have had to do that in my own inimitable way."
Was I supposed to? Thomas flicked the tip of his tail as if surprised. *Dear me, I was too curious about the turn of the conversation to think of that. Whose help did you want?*
"The point is, I *might* have needed some. Reynaud doesn't pay purely social calls, and I didn't know he wasn't with Galan any more. I really don't know it now."
You could have guessed. The man doesn't back losers—which ought to hearten you considerably. What was that bit about the kitchens?
"I don't know. Maybe we ought to go see."
It is almost dinnertime.

The kitchen fire burned hot, and there was a sizeable clot of people grouped about the long trestle table that filled most of the workspace before the ovens, but a meal was neither in progress nor preparation. Tristan halted uncertainly, one hand still on the door-latch. He wasn't quite sure what he was seeing. He hadn't known what to expect from Reynaud's words, and he needed time to work it out.

The crowd focused into three adults and a child. No, that one was surely a stripling boy, the one Elisena was tending with what Tristan's nose told him was a bit of comfrey-leaf salve.

"Just a touch of frostbite," she was saying. "Very mild. It won't trouble you. If you're sure your feet aren't in like case. Any of you—" She wiped her fingers on a bit of cloth as she spoke, looked up, and saw Tristan hesitating by the door.

Elisena smiled with either welcome for him or relief.

Every other head except the child's turned to see where she was looking—in such weary, furtive ways that Tristan still didn't recognize any of them for a long moment.

Then a hood slipped back, revealing tangled red hair and a sharp, pinched face. "Your weather's a bit chancy, for summer," a voice said acidly.

"*Crewzel?*"

"A new start, he promises me. In a fair land. And we nearly die in a midsummer blizzard. After nearly starving and almost drowning in the mother-of-rivers, mind you! Serves me right for trusting—"

The figure seated beside her put a hand on Crewzel's arm, either to calm or silence her. "We're safe here now. That's all that counts."

"All that counts to *you*, maybe—"

The man shook his head wearily, then turned from Crewzel to Tristan. "You look surprised to see us, my lord. Did you forget you invited us, or are you maybe regretting it?"

Tristan finally managed to move and cross the flagstone floor and clasp Jehan's muscled forearm warmly. "I didn't forget! I just didn't think you'd manage to get here so soon—"

"We were scarcely across the Great River when we were hit by the worst storm I've ever fastened my eyes on, even in the mountains of Kinark. Sleet like a mail curtain, wind wild as wolves, and cold to shrive your bones swept down on us before we knew what was happening. It was dark as night, and the day barely past sunhigh." Jehan brushed away crumbs from his meal.

Tristan nodded. "I know. Nímir caught me with one of his storms not long after I left you in the city."

"We sought shelter, but we were barely ashore when it hit—I didn't even know which way the port lay, if there is one there. Next thing, we were back by the Est, and I swear it was freezing over. Looked like black glass. And the wind was blowing fit to tumble us right back over the bank, with sleet cutting our skins right through our cloaks. I thought we were on our way past the Gates for sure, and I was cursing the foolishness that brought me to such a mad land, especially since I'd brought Crewzel here as well—and the boy and that girl."

Tristan glanced across the kitchen to where Kitri the dancer sat beside the fire, watching Delmon dangle a bit of yarn which Thomas condescended to bat a paw at. They seemed little the worse for the ordeal of the storm and the journey inland to Crogen, but Tristan could well imagine how frantic Jehan would have been, as leader of the enterprise and responsible for all their lives. Safe now or not, they had been in real danger.

Crewzel was deep in conversation with Elisena. Elisena asked a question, and Crewzel looked slowly toward Jehan before answering. It was the most notice Tristan had ever seen her take of the smith, and he was reminded that much must have happened between the pair of them since he'd left them—more than Jehan's freeing Crewzel from her undeserved bondage and collecting Delmon.

"You found her, then," he said to Jehan.

"Aye. Just where you said. Then we went for her boy. That little dancer was a lot of help. Didn't seem such a high price for all that she did, her coming with us." He said it as if uncertain Calandra's welcome extended to Kitri, too.

"I've never seen you make a bad bargain," Tristan assured him. "And I suppose a king's court can always use a dancer."

"That's just what *she* said." Jehan laughed and lit his pipe. "As to bargains, I'm not so sure what I've got at the moment. But that's for another time, I think."

Tristan nodded slowly, glancing at Crewzel again and wondering how to get to the matters pressing worst upon him. "How did you get here, then? What happened in the storm?"

"We were rescued. By you, I thought at first."

Tristan's eyebrows shot up. "*By me?*"

"Well, 'twas dark," Jehan explained. "The river was rising, and so was the wind; as I said before, I thought we were done for. And then the man came out of the gloom, dark-cloaked and riding a great black horse. I saw his hands move in the air, and they left trails of light, as if his fingers were candles . . . I could still hear the wind, but it wasn't ripping at us after that.

"I knew he was a wizard then—and what else was I to think? It wasn't till I spoke your name and he didn't answer to it that I started to wonder. He put his hood back for a moment, and I saw I'd been mistaken."

In the excitement of reunion, Tristan had nearly forgotten that Reynaud had known the smith and his charges had arrived. That was one trouble he couldn't put off any longer. "What did he say?"

"Not much, then. We were busy with trying to get through the storm. He wouldn't even say where he was taking us—I think I wasn't certain we were safe until you walked in here. Though your lady made us most welcome, considering how we surprised her."

Elisena, whose approach had certainly inspired Jehan's turn of phrase, squeezed herself onto the bench beside Tristan.

"Surprise is not a bother. Well met, Jehan of Kinark. There are rooms being readied. You can judge our hospitality better when you're rested."

Jehan agreed with that politely, while Crewzel said something to Delmon about folk being tired enough to sleep on a floor didn't mean they'd have to, and where did he think he was? Delmon's response as he curled up beside Thomas on the hearth did not suggest that he took his mother's harshness any more to heart than the cat would have taken it. Jehan tacked back to the earlier topic of discussion.

"You know the man, I take it?" he asked Tristan.

"Oh, yes," Tristan admitted. "Better than I'd like. His name is Reynaud."

"And no friend of yours, by your tone."

"No."

"I wonder why he troubled to help us."

"I wonder myself. It's not what I would expect of him. Did you tell him you were coming here?" Would *that* explain Reynaud's game? Was buying Tristan's favor a simple enough explanation? And how would Reynaud have known or cared?

Jehan frowned and shook his head. "Now you mention it, no. We scarcely spoke. Too busy trying to steer clear of the storm. And he didn't seem to invite talk. I must ask Crewzel if she said anything to him."

Tristan grinned, his mood lightening at the notion of what Crewzel might have had to say to Reynaud. That sharp tongue of hers might have been a sufficient goad to whip Reynaud along to Crogen.

And Reynaud's little trick had gained him nothing but sore ears. His good deed had aroused only suspicion—and Tristan would not call him back.

Departure

SETTLING THE NEW ARRIVALS IN TOOK TIME, MADE problems—and solved a few as well.

The question of whose hands to leave Crogen in had been much simplified. Polassar had misliked leaving Allaire to manage things alone. Keeping up the sham that Tristan was still at Crogen would require considerable expertise and a lot of help, even though Tristan's grip on the reins of the state had never been close to firm. Jehan's strong, steady presence would make Allaire's task much easier.

Ways and means had been discussed; plans and contingencies had been settled on. There were no more preparations to be made and no time to make them. The morning set for their departure had dawned.

Tristan, who had slept only a few restive hours, was finishing his packing as the sky grayed.

He poured oil onto a pile of pieces of soft cloth, then stoppered the bottle and put it away while the cloth absorbed the oil. He folded the rags and stowed them inside a leather sack which he'd carefully waterproofed with a coating of wax. He wasn't troubled over the rags staying dry—oil-soaked already, they'd hardly wet easily—but he didn't especially want oil all over the rest of his gear. With that done, he was able to check another item off the list he was rather precariously carrying in his head—oiled rags, to polish and stave off rust—that took care of his sword. Tristan dropped a small whetstone into the waxed bag and tied the thongs that closed the parcel.

Minstrel hopped across the table toward the pack, cheeping insistently.

"Indeed no, I haven't forgotten you. See." Tristan lifted up a small, heavy pouch. It was stuffed full of seeds, so that it rattled only a little as the contents shifted with the bag's motion. "I've also got dried biscuit for you and a bit of apple." He touched other small packets.

Minstrel, appeased, flew to the nearest windowsill and launched into a song.

Tristan continued carefully loading his pack, cushioning more fragile items with spare articles of soft clothing. Earthen jars of herbs and medicines thus went into the middle of the load, along with a couple of wax candles which were probably going to get broken, no matter where he put them. Tristan fitted small sacks of oddments in as best he could—a packet of needles, some thread, and thin leather straps. Gear could easily wear out and need timely repairing. Blais' grimoire he'd leave for last—he wanted that on the top of the pack, where it would be handiest for consulting.

His sword, another thing he'd be wise to keep handy, was scabbarded and ready to be belted on. His box of magic stones was already in its accustomed place in the pouch hanging from the right side of his belt. A peg beside the door held his new cloak, a pleasantly sober plaid of dark green and an even darker blue. It was a gift from Elisena; though it was cut full for warmth, she had draped it so carefully that it hung light as thistledown from his shoulders, warm as sunlight there.

Thomas nosed disdainfully into the top of the pack. Minstrel scolded at him for messing with the bag of seed, then flew away to perch martially on the quillions of Tristan's sword.

If there isn't catnip in here, too, you're going to get a proper scratching the first time you think you're settling down for a good night's sleep.

Tristan touched an especially fat and fragrant pouch. "Got a head cold, so that you can't smell this? It's here. Why not? Catnip makes a fine tea."

Thomas snorted. *Someone's got to look out for my comfort. And it usually has to be me.*

"Shall I pack a couple of mice for you, while I'm about it? Or do you prefer the sport of catching your own?"

I'll let you know. Did you remember to rub a good coat of grease into those boots?

"Thomas! I used a waterproof spell."

And did you rub a good coat of grease in, too?

Tristan rolled his eyes up expressively. "Yes. Of course. Do you think I've taken leave of my senses so totally as to trust *my* magic to keep my feet dry?"

You know, if you ever managed to get that other spell straight, it would make a great parlor trick.

Tristan shuddered, not liking to be reminded of the previous morning's fiasco. He'd been trying to lock sunshine inside some large crystals of clear quartz. It was not inconceivable that such devices would prove valuable in Channadran, particularly if the weather there turned dark and cloudy. And the spell he'd found in the grimoire had seemed promising.

It had even seemed to work. The crystal had lain in the sun while he spoke words over it and tied intricate knots in a bit of scarlet cord to bind the light in magically. Then a cloud had crossed the sky at a less than opportune moment, his tongue had stumbled over a word, and disaster had broken loose. Had the room he'd been working in not been stone-walled and sparsely furnished, he'd have had a worse mess, as sparks came spitting endlessly out of the cracked crystal, oblivious of every quelling Tristan tried on them.

Tristan had followed Thomas in taking refuge under the worktable. After a frantic few minutes, he'd discovered the knot still remaining in the red cord—he'd been sitting on it. Once it was loosed, the fountain of sparks died out after a couple of stray crackles and hisses. Wreckage would have been a flattering description of the room by then.

They could, Tristan had decided, do without the sun-crystals. Now he shrugged off the mishap as best he could, the passing of a few hours having given him some perspective on the matter. But he found he'd lost his place in his mental list.

"Thomas? Have we got everything now?"

One can never pack everything one's going to need on a journey. You ought to leave something out on purpose and get it over with. And you won't need half what you do take. That's a natural law.

"Thanks so much. Let's go—we're going to be late."

Good. Every minute late is another warm minute here.

Thomas pulled his paws neatly up under his thick fur and began to regard the fire on the hearth beside him.

"I'm putting the fire out," Tristan warned.

Not with that spell, you're not, Thomas said helpfully, after a couple of ill-considered passes had sent the flames shooting up to lick at the mantel. Tristan swore and fumbled with the pack's laces, fetching out the grimoire far sooner than he'd expected to need to.

"Toadstools, I haven't done this in ages! The fire's usually gone out by itself long before I'm done with it." Tristan found the spell he wanted and read it, gesturing as the notes in the margin of the page directed. The flames died, the coals ashed, and a tiny whirlwind carried the ashes up the chimney, leaving the grate spotless.

"Say, that's neat! Wonder why Blais never let me use the whole spell?"

Because for you, getting rid of the ashes isn't the problem. It's where they finally drop. Remember the mayor of Dunehollow?

"All too well. Let's hope he didn't get these ashes, too. Now we'd better go."

Valadan was tethered just inside the kitchen gate, where dray horses usually waited with far more patience than he was displaying. Stamps and snorts demonstrated his eagerness to be on the move. Polassar's roan mare was tied well away from him, her gear already loaded. Its weight did nothing to mellow her disposition. She glared about the yard sullenly, yellow teeth bared, splayed hooves as ready as ever to deal kicks. She was as hardy as she was unlovely, however, and any mortal horse that had entered Darkenkeep and left it alive had more than earned the dubious right of assisting on this second quest—however uncertain her temper. Only *this* time, Tristan was resolved that Polassar should tend his own mount. On that point, kingly dignity and self-preservation coincided utterly.

The girths of Valadan's saddle had been left loose while the horse waited, but they'd be riding out soon. Tristan tightened the straps carefully, and tied his pack into place on the saddle's cantle. It would be time to carry it on his own back later. The stallion greeted him cheerfully, blowing warm air down the back of Tristan's neck as he bent over the straps, then pulling playfully at his cloak.

Last chance for a hot meal before we go, Thomas pointed out.

"I'm really not very hungry." Tristan gave the girth a last tug to test it. The buckle held firm. He rescued his cloak from Valadan's teeth. "Had too much for supper last night, I think. I can't imagine what Allaire said to the cooks to make them come up with such a feast."

Thomas regarded him skeptically.

"You can go. I think I'll just walk around a little."

If you want to be alone, just say so. Thomas hoisted his tail and trotted off into the kitchen, well aware that it would be a strange feast indeed that consisted of what Tristan had eaten the evening before. If he'd swallowed more than a crust of bread, then his sleight of hand had improved by better than half!

Tristan watched the cat go, then turned and wandered through an archway and a couple of courtyards. The fruit trees espaliered there were full of green pears. That was a cheering note—spring frosts had not blasted all of the blossoms, nor had the recent storm shaken loose the immature fruit. Elisena encouraged the trees with especial care—but still Tristan wondered whether any of them would manage to bring their burdens the rest of the way to ripeness.

His thoughts puzzled him as he took time to examine them closely. Crogen was not his home, though he'd lived here for the past few months. Yet Tristan found he minded leaving the place—minded very much. He was pestered by a keen sense of having left things undone.

Tristan's fingers brushed the sword that hung by his side. At the touch, his feelings came clear.

He was responsible now—and that fact required an adjustment of thought. Not too long before he'd had only himself to worry about—and had in fact been pretty throughly looked after by Blais—but now, as king, he was directly accountable for the lives and fates of all his subjects, every one of the thousands of them. He'd begun to realize the notion of being a servant to all at his crowning, but it was a thing easy to lose track of, day to day.

Not that he'd ever been all that feckless—he'd had charge of Thomas and Minstrel since he was a child. Then, when he'd been enjoined to take up Blais' quest, there'd been Allaire to look after, as well as the quest itself—and

Polassar and Elisena, to a much lesser degree. At the time, his friends' reliance upon him had seemed a weighty burden, but it was nothing to what he shouldered now. He hadn't known when he was well off. He wondered if anyone ever realized that about themselves.

How greatly the truth of kingship differed from the ordinary person's conception of it! And just what would become of all those ordinary folk if this mission of theirs failed? It wasn't his life alone that Tristan risked.

If this attack on Channadran failed, then none of them had a hope of coming out of the mountains alive. Calandra's troubles would no longer be Tristan's concern— but if they failed, they'd leave their people leaderless and defenseless as well. Tristan shied away from thinking about that, then drove himself resolutely back to it. If they failed, he'd probably die swiftly—and that would be a mercy. But those left behind could hope for no such quick, kind end. And those folk had unexpectedly come to mean a great deal to Tristan.

He leaned on a low wall and looked out across the open ground beyond where Crogen's walls should have been. Close to the castle, a few patches of ground had been scraped with plows and crude harrows, and the peasant folk who'd taken to sheltering within an abandoned Crogen years ago had planted those patches with onions and potatoes. They'd assumed, as they must, that spring would somehow hold, give over to summer, and at last become harvest time.

There were thousands across Calandra like them, dependent on their king, even though they didn't know him and though their king had never seen most of their faces. Tristan stared at the carefully hoed and tended ground, feeling close to all his folk and grateful to the sword for the clarity of the emotion.

"We're just here, and now you're off. That's poor hospitality, Lord."

Tristan found no answer for that as he straightened and turned to Jehan.

"Of course there's no *need* for us to part—I could be more than a little useful—" Jehan was continuing a topic of the evening previous. The smith didn't give in easily, that was sure.

"Jehan, there's no one I'd rather have in this than

you—if any of us has to go at all! But Crewzel and Delmon need you, and I feel a lot better about leaving Allaire here at Crogen, now that someone responsible's in charge."

"What were you planning to do before we showed up?"

"Worry a lot more. That was the part of the plan I liked least—"

Really? I'd have thought the mountain climbing would be right up there.

Tristan nudged Thomas with his boot, hoping to silence the cat. The comments distracted him, even though he knew Jehan couldn't hear them.

Come on. Elisena made Polassar stop eating, and he's grumpy as a just-waked bear. He's looking for you.

Tristan gave the wall coping a last rub, a gesture of farewell to it and all of Crogen. The stone was warm under his fingers.

Everyone had come out of the kitchen. Crewzel's multicolored layers of skirts vied with Polassar's travel garb in rendering the courtyard kaleidoscopic. Happily, the sky was clouded enough to mute the jarring colors a trifle. Delmon was poking about by the horses, longingly fingering saddles but steering prudently clear of Polassar's roan. Beyond him, Kitri had begun a mostly one-sided flirtation with Dickon, who regarded her stoically.

It was not a large group to see a royal party off on even the most hopeless of quests. But no one else inside Crogen had any idea of what they were about. They'd gone to a lot of trouble to ensure that.

Allaire wore scarlet that morning, a bold, brave slash of color against the gray stones, which made her fair hair seem light as silver gilt. She would not be completing their fellowship this time out. The gentle swelling of her belly beneath the red silk hinted at a new partnership entered into. Little else could have kept Allaire from pleading to join them, though none of them had any reason to think she would have been allowed along.

Polassar swept his lady into the vast blue circle of his cloak, his arm about her like a gentle band of iron. To Tristan, it looked as if she'd been swallowed by the sky.

"Guard you our son well, Lady." Polassar rested a broad hand on her belly, as if to take leave of the child within as well as the mother.

"I shall, my lord, as jealously as I will guard our love."

Her voice was steady and proud as bells ringing. Allaire could play a part to the hilt. That was her gift.

"And fear you not—doubtless we'll have returned long ere he's prepared to make his appearance."

Allaire's flower-colored eyes brimmed silver, but her lips never quivered as she answered in agreement with Polassar's impossibility. Whatever shadows of fear hovered about her, few would ever cloud the glory of her face—not while Polassar was there to see. She stood straight, clinging to her lord only with her eyes.

"She has no look of strength, but there's steel in her," Jehan said softly, standing beside Tristan. "Bright as a right-forged blade." His use of craftsman's terms underscored his admiration.

Jehan and Allaire should work well together, Tristan thought. Elisena had arranged for the spreading of certain rumors which would make it seem that Tristan was still at Crogen, though not oft on public view. He might be out a-hunting, or perchance riding borders with Polassar. Allaire's presence at Crogen would be reassuring all by itself, but rumors leaked from less official sources would add credibility to the fiction. Jehan would tend to that, along with most of the actual running of Crogen's affairs, and Crewzel and Dickon—and even Delmon and Kitri— had all been well rehearsed in the parts they each were to play.

Tristan was none too certain such subterfuges would work, but he was becoming fatalistic enough to suppose it didn't matter all that much. And at least Allaire wouldn't be left all alone.

Polassar kissed her, held her briefly at his arms' length, as if to get one last, fixed sight of her, then turned and walked across the yard to his horse, jingling with each step. Persuading the man to give up his armor had been beyond any argument Tristan or Elisena had mustered, even though that armor's weight was certain to prove a cruel burden in the mountains.

Crewzel snorted rudely as she watched the scene. "That's about what I'd expect of that pair, but I vow I've seen more honest feeling expressed in a street playlet! Think you can do any better?"

Tristan raised a brow at her. "Any better?"

"I'll admit, you have learned a bit. At least you aren't sneaking off in the middle of the night this time."

"It might have been wiser."

"Not if I'd caught up with you." Crewzel astonished him by throwing her arms about him and hugging him hard. Tristan could only nod against a faceful of red hair as she admonished him to be careful.

Elisena walked past Polassar, after giving her mare a pat by way of greeting as she added some small item to her saddlebag. She wore a dark gray mantle, clasped at the shoulder with a silver crescent encircled. A heavy shirt, breeches, and low boots completed her gear. But for her long hair, she might have been a stripling boy—she was nearly as slender as Kitri. And Tristan did not suppose the dancer could move with any greater grace. Crewzel saw where he was looking and gave him a clout on the shoulder which could have meant anything at all. Jehan swung her away from Tristan, making small noises which were probably meant to be taken as annoyance.

Allaire had fetched a stirrup cup for Polassar. As he downed it, Elisena drew his lady aside for a last word of instruction.

"If we should fail," she said, very low, taking Allaire's hands in hers, "you will certainly know. I need not detail how—it will be fairly obvious, I should think."

"Do not speak of that, Lady!" Allaire was breathless, trying to forestall ill luck.

"It must be said. If it should be before the child comes, commit yourself to Canfors of Darlith's care. You can trust him in all things, even with Calandra's heir. Jehan will help you, and Tristan says he's asked Dickon to guard you as well. Look to them when there is need."

Allaire nodded mutely, as if speech made no difference. At that, she was right.

Tristan saw that Dickon was still hovering at the edge of the courtyard. It was surprising that he hadn't fled Kitri's advances, but maybe he didn't want to risk missing anything else. Tristan would have gone to speak to the boy, but he didn't feel up to another farewell—or another argument over the boy's wish to join their small party. If he went over or even looked in Dickon's direction too often, the boy might think he'd relented—and Tristan didn't doubt that there was a horse saddled and loaded nearby, just in case. Dickon would be fine, once they actually left; but for the moment, Tristan thought he ought to stay where he was.

So he stood close by Elisena, party to a conversation Polassar was too far from and too busy to attend to.

"Until we return, we rely on you to maintain a front here and to make it look as if we are either still here or intend to come back at any time. After all, what lord could think that we would leave you alone at such a time?"

Allaire nodded bravely, then said, "Polassar says it will be a son."

"Perhaps only because he wouldn't begin to know what to do with a daughter," Elisena laughed. "But as it happens, he's right."

"*You've seen*?" Allaire whispered. "Then the child will at least be born; there's hope for that long—" Her expression altered to one of desperate gladness.

"It wasn't a seeing like that," Elisena cautioned. "Only that all the signs are there. If this babe is a daughter, she'll be a warrior-maid and a great bane to silk dresses and dolls! Take care, Ariana, for the child and for yourself as well."

The use of her true name brought a new brightness to Allaire's eyes, which she suddenly needed to wipe away. Elisena took the cup from her, sipped, and returned it.

Then it was Tristan's turn, with the sound of the horses' hooves and harness loud in his ears. All at once, even the flutter of Minstrel's wings as the canary landed on his shoulder cried of haste. He forgot he'd just laid a hand on Valadan's bridle, and the stallion walked after him as he crossed to meet Allaire. She had always been able to scatter his wits with a word or a look, and it seemed the condition had not passed off yet.

The child growing within had robbed its mother of none of her beauty. Allaire's skin was barely a shade darker than white silk, faintly tinged with rose where it stretched across her sculpted cheeks. Tristan, trying not to drown in her eyes, looked elsewhere and saw that there was a rope of pearls, fine as millet seeds, twined through the single braid that fell over her left shoulder and a silver chain about her throat, glimmering as she drew breath. A thick brass armlet, twin to the one on Polassar's wrist, was shoved far up on her left arm.

She wore no rings, nor ever would wear them again. Tristan took the cup from her soft hand.

The strong wine went from his empty belly to his head almost instantaneously, but at least it was warming on its way. It kept his lips from quivering as he bade farewell to Allaire and kept his hand steady as Tristan passed the cup back to her. Her eyes, once he was able to look at them, brimmed with tears, but held his own courageously.

"You ought to go in," Tristan said. "You'll take a chill."

The business of leave-taking shouldn't be dragged out any longer. The important things, those that could be voiced, had all been said over the past all-too-few days. And there were no bardic witnesses present, for whose ears brave words needed to be uttered. The minstrels would need to invent that part of the tale.

To Allaire, that didn't matter. She shook her head slightly. "If you have the strength to go, I shall have the strength to watch." She brushed a hand across her belly. "It seems to be all I can do now. But had it been otherwise, I would have ridden with you gladly."

Crogen's gates swung shut behind them, and Crogen's farmland fell away as they rode through it unremarked. When all but the castle's highest towers had dipped below the horizon, there suddenly came an insistent tattoo of hoofbeats. Someone was riding hard to overtake them.

Polassar reined in, his roan mare screaming her displeasure as she fought the bit. "What ails those dolts that they must send a message already, when we've not gone half a league?" He was probably concerned for his lady and hiding the feeling under irritation.

Tristan, circling Valadan about slowly, was more concerned that the unknown rider might prove to be Dickon. He'd had a terrible time reconciling the boy to being left behind; perhaps being entrusted with Allaire hadn't been enough to hold him. Tristan was in no mood to cajole or argue now. His nerves were too finely stretched to deal with that on top of all else.

By the time the source of the hoofbeats came into sight, it was already plain that the rider had not come from Crogen. It was a dark figure on a darker horse, with no badges visible at the distance still separating them. No one save a man riding out from Crogen would expect to find them where they were, but the rider went nowhere near the castle. He came for them unswervingly. There was a rasp of steel as Polassar loosened his sword in its scabbard.

Elisena's brown mare neighed loudly as the rider came close, but his mount, also a mare, made no answer to the challenge. Valadan snorted softly and pawed the turf. His nervousness was odd. Tristan leaned forward to pat the stallion's neck, puzzled.

"What is it?" he asked.

Valadan shook his head from side to side, fighting the bit, and shifted his feet, then stood steady. Thomas, crouching on the ornamented leather of the saddlebow, clung tight, but raised his head interestedly. Even Minstrel settled down to watch.

The stranger halted half a bowshot off, then continued his advance more slowly. He seemed to be watching them closely, but the hood pulled up to shadow his face made that difficult to judge. He was dressed all in black, under a black cloak, and the black mare was trapped out in black and silver, unrelieved by any touch of color. He bore no blazonings of any lord Tristan could recognize—and the stranger's dress didn't look like livery.

"If you've a message, deliver it up!" Polassar bellowed, louder than the shrinking distance warranted. They could probably hear him back at Crogen.

"No message." The man's hand came up, and red and gold glinted on the back of his sleeve as he thrust his hood back. "No message," Reynaud repeated. "I'm coming with you."

Coming with us? How did he find out we were going? Tristan wondered that himself.

Polassar swore and curbed the roan so hard that she squealed and reared, kicking out. Reynaud sat his beast calmly, despite the near miss of flying hooves. Likewise, the black mare never stirred at all, but stood firm as iron, her wispy mane curling over her sooty neck and lifted only by the breeze. Her eyes were gray as ashes, the same hue as her dainty hooves.

"I am designating myself Kôvelir's representative in this affair," Reynaud went on imperturbably. "It seems a natural extension of my assignment, if only by extrapolation of my orders. Once all of you go into Channadran, there's nothing of importance left here for me to watch."

Tristan reached for his sword. He'd been right about the danger of leaving Reynaud at his back. Well, he'd give the man something to watch, if that was what he insisted on!

As his fingers closed around the hilt, anticipating its surge of power, the sword *bit* him!

There was no other way to describe what he felt, and Tristan was too throughly occupied to think of searching for one. The pain was as sharp and immediate as if he'd clasped the steel red-hot from the forge. Surprise was all that kept him from crying out. His mouth went instantly dry, incapable of making a sound.

Tristan snatched his fingers back from the sword, not half so fast as he wanted to, expecting to see charred flesh. To his increasing amazement, his fingers were unmarked. The pain remained.

He couldn't close his fingers and couldn't bear to open them, either. A wave of hurt shot clear up to his elbow, then ebbed as its message was made clear. The action he'd been about to undertake—merely to drive Reynaud off, Tristan insisted to himself, not believing he could have gone so far as to try to kill the man—was wrong, and the sword was not disposed to permit it.

"For Kôvelir? Or for Galan? We require no watchdog, sorcerer," Polassar thundered indignantly.

"And you are getting none. My association with Galan is at an end. I doubt if he even still lives, but that makes no difference. I suspect he would not wish to see me again, in any case."

"Meaning you betrayed him as you betrayed others to him!" Polassar reined the plunging mare savagely, but her behavior served to punctuate his own rage, rather than annoying him. "There's no man would trust you now!"

"No man, perhaps. But a woman?" Reynaud looked thoughtfully at Elisena. "You've said little, Lady. Does that mean you agree with my lord Polassar—or only that you're wiser and speak only when you have sense to speak? Do you recognize the need you have for me?"

"Yes," Elisena replied quietly.

Polassar stared at her, even as Tristan did, and read enough on her face to make him drop his dispute—at least until he could discover a fresh one to grind his teeth on.

"Lady, you'll at least make him swear—"

Elisena gave Polassar an unlooked-for smile. "You don't trust him. What can Reynaud swear by that you'd accept? It's in my mind that he has very little harm to offer us beside that which we've already agreed to face. Be welcome, Reynaud."

Fight or Flight

"ANOTHER MOUTH," POLASSAR GRUMBLED. "AND AN empty belly behind it."

"I've brought my own share of provisions," Reynaud said levelly. "And the number we make now is a fair one. We shall stand foursquare, like a table."

"A tripod's as steady." Polassar argued.

"Geometrically. But this is not work for mathematicians, my lord. I doubt you'll regret me." Reynaud smiled and spurred the black mare so that she leaped ahead, her fine gray tail trailing after like a banner of silk.

Tristan exchanged a glance with Polassar, who shrugged.

"The way I look at it, Wizard, he's a deal safer here under our eyes than at our backs—seeing as we're stuck with him anyway." He gave the roan her head finally and sent her after Reynaud.

Elisena hung by Tristan's side, riding knee to knee with him. She kept her mare at a gentle canter, and Valadan held himself to the same gait. It would be time enough to catch the others later; they would have a long day's ride. For now a slow pace permitted speech.

"We are going to need him. You're the one who suggested finding other wizards, and he's the best we'll get."

"If you want another wizard, why *him*?" Tristan tried without the slightest success to wean the jealousy out of his voice. He wondered if he looked as odd as he felt. His hand still hurt. "Is he part of another prophecy?"

"We've outstripped prophecies, long since." Elisena said dryly.

"You trust him, then?" Tristan dared not ask if she preferred a sorcerer of proven reputation in place of one who could—on his all too frequent worst days—barely light a fire by his powers alone. She might have told him the truth.

"Not wholly." Elisena shook her head. "But Reynaud has had the chance to do great harm to us all and he has not done so. Consider his saving Jehan and Crewzel. If not a friend, still Reynaud is not clearly an enemy. I'll need to see a few more moves before I know what game he's playing—if game it is."

"Won't we have enough to worry about in Channadran?" Tristan's tone was sharp. His hand wasn't all that pained him.

"Up there—" Elisena looked ahead as if she could see, even if only with her mind's eye, all the way to Channadran. "Up there, where there's never been a spring, or a warmth that night could not slay with one breath... up there where the seeds of glaciers grow, our sort of magic will be very hard to make. I will take any tool that offers itself to my hand for the task. We'll need Reynaud."

Tristan let the subject drop. He was distracted still by the incident with his sword and the questions it had raised. His fingers ached, deep in the bone, and no amount of shifting eased them. He needed to think and scarcely could. If the blade had the power to prevent its own wrongful use—how then were all of Calandra's ruinous wars to be explained? Or the fatal quarrel between her last king and Esdragon's duke?

Be interesting to know if that last king wore gloves, Thomas said, taking a firmer grip on the saddle as their pace quickened.

They traveled fast, though never approaching the speed Valadan was capable of when running alone. The leagues unraveled past them. Sun-high and their midday meal found them a little way beyond Lassair, though its keep lay out of sight behind hills to their left as they sat eating. Polassar pointed out his home country with pride.

Tristan was not surprised to find that Elisena needed to apprise Reynaud only very slightly of their plans. Of course the man would know all the details in advance, with his usual absolute efficiency. The real question was, how had he spied them out? Tristan chewed morosely at a bit of cooked chicken, then gave it up and let Thomas have the rest. In a little while they were under way again, but he was still lost in thought that had yet to prove productive.

Their rapid rate of progress wore off as the afternoon slipped away. The land turned hilly, broken by long, low ridges whose accompanying valleys ran toward the distant sea and thus slanted across their course with annoying regularity. Such roads as they met often ran in useless directions. In any case, the roads were in poor repair, mere strings of mudholes and scratches in the turf, with weeds moving in to reclaim even those. Tristan wondered if improved roads would revive his realm's commerce, or if greater use would encourage the roads' repair. The question was worth considering, but it would be a good long while before he could do anything beyond thinking about it.

Ahead, the hills were probably forested with beech and aspen, but Nímir's storms had ripped away leaves and many branches, and the view was drab and cheerless. At least, at their present rate, they wouldn't reach those hills till sometime the next day and might with luck skirt them entirely. It didn't look to be a cheerful spot in which to end the day.

Polassar, reckoning by landmarks, announced that they'd reached the outer borders of Westif. Valadan snorted agreement, and Tristan knew they had passed through the country just days before.

Their present course had been calculated to take them far to sunward of Westif Keep. Danac was loyal in theory and by his own swearing of a binding oath, but there was no sense and no time to waste in putting Danac's word or the royal sword's peace-keeping powers to a test now. They rode quietly and as quickly as was possible at the end of a long day's hard travel, hoping to avoid notice. They weren't in farming country, which should have made that easier. After a few more leagues, they might even hope to camp safely.

As it chanced, they needn't have bothered.

It was Minstrel's custom to fly ahead of the horses, returning at intervals when he got lonely or tired or just wished to ride for a while. He came whirring back in a flurry of feathers, too breathless and agitated to make any sense for several moments.

The canary crouched between Valadan's ears, panting, his wings hanging at his sides, and finally squeaked out a tale of "a flock of men wearing metal skins" who were riding along a track which would intercept their own path momentarily. At least, that was what Thomas thought the bird had said. He had stopped looking amused.

Tristan started to shout the news to Polassar, but thought better of it. He urged Valadan forward, and the stallion's hooves dug soundlessly into the heathery turf. Elisena followed him, nearly as quickly.

They caught up to Polassar and Reynaud just at the top of one of the low rises. Tristan cursed himself for having let the group straggle so. Even here, where there was presumably little danger, that wasn't a wise practice and would make for sloppy habits. It would have been no great trouble to keep together.

He passed Minstrel's message on to Polassar, then added sourly, "That's all we need—to be seen here when we're supposedly still at Crogen. We'll have to try to give them the slip."

"I doubt we can, Wizard. Look." Polassar pointed.

Tristan looked and swore again, a little more softly. Half a dozen armored knights were galloping into plain view. Even if the men lacked the keen sight of Danac's falcon symbol, they could hardly miss four horsemen on an otherwise bare hillside. As Tristan watched, the lead rider called out something, and the whole troop wheeled toward them. Tristan sighed, having run out of curses.

"Well, so much for that idea. Now we've got to stand and bluff, I suppose. If they don't recognize us, we'll get dragged back to Danac to explain what we're doing crossing his lands—and if they *do*, we're apt to get dragged back anyway for guesting. Either way, Danac's bound to ask a lot of questions I'd rather not waste time answering."

"If you can get them to come close enough, I can make them forget they saw us," Elisena said.

"You can?" Tristan looked at her happily. "That's handy. And we shouldn't have any trouble getting close to them—"

As he spoke, the group of knights was splitting up.

Three reined in where they were, while their fellows chose to proceed at an angle which effectively blocked the route Polassar had planned to follow—a dip between two steep hillsides. Those riders also stopped and waited.

"That's an odd way for a patrol to behave," Tristan said. Valadan shuffled his feet restively and flexed his neck. They weren't *quite* trapped, but they could be with very little effort.

"Wizard, I can't make out badges on 'em," Polassar said fretfully.

"This is Westif. They'll be Danac's men, surely? I'll just ride down and see what they want." Tristan tapped a heel against Valadan's side, and the stallion trotted smoothly forward. They were past Polassar before the man could protest.

You'll just ride down and see what they want? Thomas asked incredulously.

The action did indeed feel bold and dangerous, but Tristan supposed it couldn't be, or Valadan wouldn't have permitted it. And Tristan was the logical choice to carry out the task—Polassar's tongue would get them into more trouble than it would keep them out of.

This meeting couldn't be random chance, he thought. Those horses looked as if they'd been ridden hard for some time in getting to this precise spot. But how could anyone have expected to intercept them here? There was no way Danac of Westif could expect them. Even had news of their mission leaked from the few at Crogen who'd been trusted with it, it could not have traveled to Danac faster than they themselves had.

Tristan was almost within hailing distance. He slowed Valadan to a walk. Keeping his hands hidden as best he could, he eased a little of his sword out of its scabbard. Drawing it fully would have been more effective, but would certainly have been misinterpreted. The day was overcast, but the old blade shone bright as new steel, seeming to throw back far more light than fell upon it. Tristan opened his mouth to deliver his words of peaceful intent.

As he did, Valadan reared and plunged to one side, nearly unseating him, and Thomas, scrambling, sank his claws into Valadan's neck rather than the leather of the saddle. The stallion leaped again, though not from the pain of the scratches.

The arrow missed by a not especially wide margin, passing before Tristan's face and over the stallion's neck and Thomas' head. It was close enough to show Tristan's wide eyes the stripings of red and ochre on its shaft and its black fletchings. He was so startled that he let the sword go back into its sheath rather than drawing it to ward off the attack, and then Valadan was whirling about, well in advance of Polassar's warning shout, and racing away from the riders. Tristan didn't argue.

Other shafts whistled past. Tristan was fighting for balance, sprawled low on Valadan's neck and trying desperately not to slip any lower or slide any farther out of the saddle, but he knew better than to sit up. There was a muffled impact at the small of his back, but no real pain beyond the hard blow. He rightly guessed that an arrow had hit the saddle's high cantle and stuck there in the wood. One boot slipped out of its stirrup, making Tristan's position even more precarious as they bounded along. He considered kicking free of the other as well, so as not to be dragged if he did fall, but he couldn't manage it.

They reached Polassar, who was riding hard toward them. His longsword was drawn, but it could be of small use against arrows. Polassar hesitated as Tristan sat upright with some relief. Valadan had finally gotten out of the bowmen's range.

Those bowmen were on the move, not loosing more shafts—apparently unwilling to waste arrows in shots from one running horse to another. That couldn't last. Polassar swore and hauled his mare around. He and Tristan both turned tail and fled, anxious to stay out of reach. There was no need for a discussion of strategy. At whatever cost, they had to be rid of the primary threat of those bowmen.

Reynaud streaked past, leaning low from the saddle, his sword in his hand. He let its tip plow the ground, went a hundred paces that way, then straightened, and turned back. He had sheathed the blade, and his hands were making passes as he came. The mare was controlled easily with knees alone.

Tristan heard the final word of the spell being chanted. Then a deep gulley opened up almost under the hooves of the first pursuing horse. The illusion was solid, but not effective enough, even with the handful of dust Reynaud

flung in to make a smoky haze over the scene. One horse
did fall, but the next two were unable to stop and bolted
across unscathed, their iron-shod hooves tearing the illusion. Others quickly followed them across the scratched
turf.

Tristan was still distracted by his sword's failure to
prevent or even warn him of the attack. Had his earlier
mistake damaged it in some way—broken the trust
between him and the weapon? The sword had worked
well in Crogen's Throne Hall, among the contentious lords
of the realm; what could have made it fail now? Such an
unreliability could easily prove fatal to their plans, not to
mention his life. Was he simply too far from Crogen and
the throne the sword was linked to, as it was linked to
him? Tristan had no leisure for such thoughts, but their
fragments plagued him anyway, like nightmares.

The very ground was against them. The slope was too
steep and was forcing them to their left and back toward
the riders. The knights had grouped together briefly, then
fanned out once more, waiting till Elisena and the others
should be forced back down to them.

Tristan's group couldn't run, so they must fight. Of one
accord, all four of them slowed and halted, while they
had the high ground and whatever advantage it might grant
them. Elisena's hands moved in front of her, shaping
something which she then flung down upon their pursuers.
A brightness cracked by, making the horses snort and
plunge. Downslope, it exploded in smoke and fire-flash.

The horses below screamed and tried to bolt, but were
held firm. Arrows were nocked. Bowstrings twanged.
Elisena stretched her arms straight out before her, her
fingers spread wide, her palms flat. The hasty warding
worked. Wooden shafts snapped and steel arrowheads fell
uselessly to the turf. But she could do no more. Danac's
knights wore too much steel armor, leaving her magic
nothing to work upon. If the men chose to fire singly, she
could not deal with each arrow individually.

Reynaud wheeled the black mare and pulled something
from deep inside his sleeve. He hurled it, along with several acid words.

His silver dagger flew toward the knights like a swooping bird, but not to strike at steel. There were snapping
sounds as the blade sliced taut bowstrings. Flying on, it

glanced off steel plate and tumbled to the ground, its magic negated before it could complete its return to its master's hand. Reynaud shrugged grimly and drew his sword again.

The knights had drawn their blades the moment their bows became useless. Such professional efficiency was unsettling. At least the two sides were now matched in weaponry, if not quite in numbers. Polassar spurred his roan down the slope, yelling his war cry and whirling his longsword about his head. That display was impressive and meant to be distracting as well. Polassar leveled the sword like a lance just as he closed with his first foe, and the hapless knight was spitted like a fowl before he could either close his mouth or shift his parry.

By that time, Tristan had reached his own man and saw no more of other action. His sword seemed to chime like a bell as he lifted it and it sang through the air as he aimed his first stroke. As a peacemaker, it might have inexplicably failed him. As a weapon, it did not, he was relieved to discover. Thomas rode the saddlebow like a mad figurehead, his fur bristling impressively.

The charge downslope gifted them with a tremendous momentum. Valadan dodged and then careened past the first knight, leaving him for Reynaud. It was better to engage the second line of knights at once, before they could begin to function as reinforcements. Even with one knight thrown and one dead, that still left them a man apiece and one more who might well slip past and get to Elisena. Tristan sought desperately to prevent that. It meant that he'd have to get rid of one man very quickly, if he was to be in time going after the other.

She can certainly handle one, Valadan informed him coolly. *She had good teachers in Esdragon. A princess must master many skills.*

The knights were heavily armed and even more heavily armored. Even Polassar was having trouble now, and Tristan might have had much more, had Valadan not proceeded to prove his fabled worth as a war horse. Tristan's man could hardly come within striking distance for fear of those flashing hooves and teeth. The horse moved and fought like an intelligent weapon, whisking Tristan into and safely out of attack range.

It was well he did. The knight carried a shield, and

that made a critical difference, especially against a wizard who could bear no armor whatsoever. Tristan must use his blade to parry as well as attack, but the knight could block a blow with his shield, while aiming a cut with his sword at the same time. Holding steel and surrounded by it, Tristan dared try no magic, even had he been more of a wizard than he was. For those moments, his whole life depended upon his right arm and Valadan's legs.

Tristan parried a head cut and caught a second blow— mercifully only the flat of the blade—across his ribs. The high cantle saved him from being swept out of the saddle, but the blow doubled him over, his breath gone. Thomas let out an unearthly yowl. Probably in fright—the sword had gone right over his head.

That howl did what all the magic gone before had not; it sent the knight's horse shying and plunging, so that its master's next stroke went awry. Tristan's counterstroke did not. He went in low, under the knight's arm, and his blade found a joint in the armor as easily as if it had been entering its own sheath. With Valadan's weight behind the blow, it bit deep.

The dead knight stayed in his saddle until Tristan ruined his balance by tugging the sword free. Then the dead man toppled and was dragged, bouncing, as his frightened horse tried to bolt from the smell of his blood. Tristan straightened up in the saddle, catching his balance again as Valadan turned back to the main battle.

He saw Polassar's blade whirl brightly and saw something fly free. Some bit of armor, chopped off—a helm, maybe. Just before it struck him, Tristan realized that there was still a head inside the helm, with blood pouring out of it. It spattered all over him as he flung a hand out, barely in time to bat the gristly missile away. He could see the man's teeth, still bared in a battle grimace. The impact of steel and heavy bone numbed Tristan's bridle hand, and he let the reins drop.

There was, mercifully, no time for him to hold the sight or for him to be ill, though Tristan felt he would be at the first free second he got. There was another sword cutting greedily at him. Tristan ducked it once, then grabbed the reins with his bruised hand and sat tight as Valadan ran full tilt into the other horse. The beast went down screaming, and Valadan somehow stayed on his own feet and scrambled free of the wreckage.

Polassar was just finishing his second man, with a matchless bind that carried his sword point from low to high around the other man's point with blinding speed, then on through an armor joint. He backed the roan mare away, out of the blood. There was a lot of it, all over him and the mare, too.

Tristan sat a now quiet Valadan, thankful that the stallion was standing rock-still. He was shaking with reaction. He didn't know if the man who'd gone down with his horse was dead or not and he didn't care. Even if alive, the man wouldn't give them much trouble for a bit. There were no other sounds of combat, so Reynaud might be presumed to have won his own fight, unless he was dead. Tristan didn't much care about that either. It seemed far more important that he keep his eyes tightly closed for a bit, till he forgot the sight of that severed head hitting the ground at Valadan's feet like a child's bounced ball. His ribs hurt, and so did both of his bruised hands.

"Wizard?" Polassar was wiping his blade hastily clean. "You got a pair of them, too? Good work."

"Was it?" Tristan asked doubtfully. He dismounted, keeping a careful hold on the saddle with one hand, till he was surer of his knees' reliability. His face was on a level with Thomas' as he stood. The cat was slowly retracting his claws, pulling them one by one from the wooden frame under the saddle's leather. His pupils were mere slits, and there seemed to be no tart comments forthcoming.

Tristan saw Reynaud dismounting, too, but the man didn't speak. Elisena was riding down to join them, her dagger still in her hand, though she'd put her sword away. Her mare tossed its head at the blood smell, and Valadan whinnied scoldingly at her.

Tristan bent slowly over the nearest knight and made himself tip the man's visor back. The face beneath the grill of steel was slack in death, the eyes open. They were white as two bits of ice—frost-white and empty. Tristan turned his head away, dizzier than he'd been before. It had not been his failing, then, or that of the sword, that these attackers could not be turned away without this carnage. They'd had no minds left for the sword to call to.

There was blood on the soldier's lips. Even while Tristan watched, crystals of ice formed on the surface of it, as if the man was glacier-cold within. Polassar muttered an oath against witchery.

"A mercy that we had to kill them," Reynaud said, close by. He had reclaimed his silver dagger and now tossed it lightly from hand to hand. "Those taken over by Nímir are better dead."

Tristan stood and cleaned the tainted blood carefully from his own blade, using plucked handfuls of grass. His head still wasn't clear—he felt sicker every time he bent down for more grass. The sword seemed to hum uneasily under his fingers, but he wasn't sure what it was trying to tell him. His stomach churned, and he bit his lip hard, wishing that Reynaud would go talk to someone else before he lost the fight with the sickness.

Reynaud did not oblige him, though. He continued poking at the knights' bodies well after Tristan had finally mounted up once more, though he said nothing of whatever it was that he sought or found.

the Way to the Sea

WITHOUT DISCUSSION, THEY RODE INTO THE GATH-
ering night. Valadan felt there were no other men near
whose minds Nímir might control—the nearest large creatures of any sort were fallow deer grazing several leagues
off. Yet if they were momentarily secure, none of the party
voiced an urge to linger and make camp. Not one of them
could have settled down or refrained from startling at
every shadow their campfire threw. They let the tired
horses make what pace they chose, but kept moving
steadily.

The stars had long since come out. Some had set as
well, and still they rode on.

Are we lost? Thomas, wakening, looked about and saw
nothing save grass-covered hills, dim under the stars, much
the same as when he'd last roused.

Tristan doubted that the cat's suggestion was anything
close to the truth. They had changed course since meeting
the knights—maybe they were skirting some populous
area, or a border fortress of Danac's—but he was sure
Elisena and Polassar knew their precise location as well
as Valadan did. So all of them weren't lost, though Tristan
supposed he himself might be considered so. He hadn't
the least idea where he was and didn't care.

Valadan traveled quietly, for which kindness Tristan
was grateful. It would have taken very little at that point
to send him sliding out of the saddle into oblivion. Only
the thought of the ground's probable hardness kept him
from it. He thought he might have been dozing, too. In

the darkness he couldn't be sure he kept his heavy-lidded eyes open long enough to be considered awake.

They stopped. In the sudden quiet, as the hoofbeats ceased, Tristan heard water splashing.

"I can make this place defensible," Reynaud's voice said firmly. "We're safe enough for what's left of the night."

Tristan swung down from Valadan's back. Though drowsy, he was still in position to help Elisena dismount before Reynaud could get to her. She was fortunately more wide-awake than he was and saved both of them from falling when he stumbled. Tristan grinned at her ruefully and looked around as he let her go.

The place looked safe enough. A rocky outcrop sheltered a spring and some stunted trees. If they laid their fire a little way out from the rock, the stone would both guard their backs and reflect the fire's heat. The water was an added convenience, and there might just be grass to sleep upon.

The night breeze was only cool, but a chill was on them all that had nothing to do with weather. No one spoke much above a whisper. Tristan helped Polassar care for the horses, rubbing them dry before turning them loose to forage under Valadan's care. Elisena gathered dead branches from under the trees, and Thomas promptly curled up almost on top of the fire she built.

Meantime, Reynaud busied himself setting up wards about the camp. He sketched complex signs in the air and on the turf, murmuring steadily the while. The signs glowed briefly, then winked out like wind-flung sparks. Where the sparks fell, a ring of magic sprang up, albeit an invisible one. Reynaud circled only the area about the fire— the horses would be safe enough with Valadan—and stopped abruptly when he was satisfied.

Despite the wards and the smallness of the fire Elisena kindled, its revealing light made them all anxious. Cold food was unpacked and eaten in silence, and they bedded down as soon as hunger was satisfied.

Polassar was soon snoring, and the others were at least quiet; but Tristan, despite having been so weary that he could barely swallow his food, found himself belatedly and contrarily wide awake. The flat patch of grass which had looked so inviting proved to be mostly stone under the thin leaves, each pebble pressing on some bruise he'd gotten during the fight. And he was cold, for all the fire's nearness and the thickness of his cloak over him. Tristan shifted about restlessly, able to find no easement. Just as he was hoping to drift off at last, he was seized with a ferocious cramp in his left leg.

He sat up, trying not to cry out, rubbed at his leg, and bumped Thomas. The cat hissed at him in irritation and was deaf to whispered apologies and explanations.

Go walk it off, Thomas ordered unsympathetically. *That way, one of us can still get some sleep.*

Tristan stood up, tripped over his pack, and nearly pitched onto his face.

And be quiet about it!

Tristan glared at the cat, his expression wasted in the darkness. The pain was like a knot in his calf muscle, getting worse as he used his leg instead of being soothed. He could scarcely move, far less do so quietly enough to suit Thomas. Gritting his teeth, he hobbled a few steps more, then halted.

What would happen if he unluckily blundered through one of Reynaud's wards? It would be just his luck to wake everyone up. Tristan peered about, sure he must be close to the warding, if he were not already outside it. He couldn't see anything magical. But then he wouldn't, necessarily. The cramping seemed better, now that his mind was off it. He only limped slightly as he moved to investigate.

The wards should be set to give alarm only if a stranger crossed them and would ignore all else. That would be the simplest, the least troublesome, and most logical spell for a tired wizard to set up. Surely Reynaud had been as weary as the rest of the company?

But had anyone really watched the man at his work? Treachery would have been an easy matter for one so well versed in it, and Tristan didn't trust Reynaud far enough to sleep now, not before he'd found the threads of magic that shaped the wards and had satisfied himself that the spells used would fend off evil rather than attract it. He should have thought of the matter long before.

His glanced toward the banked fire. No one had stirred, so far as Tristan could tell. That meant nothing—Reynaud could be feigning sleep. If he was, however, and objected to Tristan's examinations—well, where would that leave them? It would be as good as an admission of guilt.

Tristan went stealthily to work. His fingers sketched passes which counterpointed those Reynaud had lately made, and he watched carefully for results. He listened sharply, too, hoping to catch some lingering whisper of spellcraft. The task absorbed him, but he remembered to keep a watch on Reynaud as well.

In the end, though, he was forced to concede that his suspicions were utterly unfounded, though it was many minutes before he was willing to admit so. The wards were the normal ones he'd expected, set to stop humans and dangerous large animals. There was nothing to prevent his going outside the protective circle or crossing it again to return.

Tristan was ashamed that he'd checked, but hardly sorry. Besides, the exercise involved had helped his leg, which only ached dully now.

The dark shapes of the horses blurred together in the night, and a rising mist damped the sound of their movements. Tristan saw Valadan standing apart from the mares, and he stepped carefully through the wards and went to him.

The mares were settling for the remainder of the night, having fed their fill, but Valadan seemed as restless as Tristan was. His eyes scanned the night ceaselessly, though he had nothing to report when Tristan inquired. A coal snapped in the fire, and the stallion started. Tristan rested a hand on the glossy neck and felt the muscles beneath the satin skin taut as a new drumhead.

He had already examined Valadan carefully for any hurts he might have gotten in the fight and salved the scratches Thomas had left on the horse's withers.

"Somehow, I'm not relieved to know that wasn't Danac trying to stop us."

Valadan snorted, right by his ear.

"It's not your fault, you know. It's that sword—it does funny things to my common sense. It makes gallant gestures a little too easy. I suppose I should expect that— it's a king's blade; it wouldn't have the same ideas about practicality that hand-to-mouth wizards have. I must remember that, the next time it suggests I just blindly ride into something."

Valadan tossed his head, refusing to relinquish his guilt, no matter what the absolution offered. Tristan understood well enough—it was a sort of stubbornness they shared.

He stroked Valadan's neck a few more times, watched the dark hills with him for a bit, then walked back to the fire. Maybe he'd sleep at last, though he doubted it. At worst, he could hope to lie still and not bother Thomas.

The cat grumbled again as Tristan settled himself, but it was not Thomas' voice that broke the silence. "Long is the way."

Tristan turned his head, confused. Polassar was still snoring, Reynaud was too far off on the other side of him to have said anything. Anyway, the muffled words were Elisena's.

"Long, longer than any of us has thought, and cold every step of it. And for every one of those steps there is a danger, a promise—and a price."

Tristan shivered. She was dreaming, of course, and her words probably meant no more than the battle cries Polassar was apt to bellow betimes, startling them all out of slumber. There was no reason to take what she said as prophecy—her voice had just sounded like a stranger's for a moment, and he was tired enough to imagine anything—tired enough, almost, to sleep.

The scrape of boots on stone woke Tristan. He began to wish he'd simply stayed wakeful the whole night; as he moved tentatively, half the muscles in his body complained stridently to his brain. The morning mist was heavy, silver where the sun was beginning to break through. From far off, the cry of a swan cut the air. Elisena was crouched by the fire, cooking oatcakes on a small griddle.

Tristan remembered that he wanted to ask her if she remembered what she'd been dreaming.

"Good morrow, colleague."

Reynaud looked annoyingly well rested, Tristan noticed with disgust. One couldn't tell by *his* garments that he had passed the night lying on the ground. Not a twig or a blade of grass clung to the sooty black cloak or to the brightly embroidered clothing beneath. Tristan was not heartened to see by daylight that the spell he'd used the night past to remove bloodstains from his own clothing had only set most of them more firmly. Eventually he'd run into enough other dirt that the dark brown spots would fade into the general homespun gray of the cloth, but just then they were a reminder of the fight that Tristan would rather not have had.

"Did you sleep well? Myself, I found this place one to promote disturbing dreams."

Tristan weighed the need for courtesy and pretense against Reynaud's mocking tone. This might be a very long journey indeed. Certainly it would be better to express himself bluntly at once, rather than let Reynaud bait him for weeks until he ultimately lost his temper anyway. The battle was certain to come—as well now as later. Polassar seemed to be off collecting the horses, so he had no fear of matters getting out of hand that way.

"Go away, Reynaud. I don't want to pass this or any other morning exchanging meaningless pleasantries with you."

Reynaud displayed no anger at the insult, to Tristan's amazement, not even by a raised brow or an elegant flare of his nostrils. For some reason, the man was disposed to be tolerant—or wished to seem so—probably because Elisena was within hearing. His teeth gleamed in his beard as he spoke.

"Your anger at having me here is understandable, but you were overruled for a purpose. I promise you, my lord, the time will come when you won't regret having me at your side. Meantime, I shall seek about for some means of earning your trust."

"Don't bother on my account."

Reynaud's mouth twisted upward, cheerfully acknowledging the battle lines between them. He reached a hand down and, as Tristan watched in consternation, proceeded to stroke Thomas' back. Tristan was even more confused when the cat arched himself and raised his tail under the stroking fingers, unmistakable signs of the cat's pleasure and favor. He might perhaps have expected the cat to tolerate Reynaud's touch, but actually to enjoy it—

Thomas rubbed himself against Reynaud's boot, leaning upon him as the man's fingers found all of his most favored pleasure spots and explored them. Tristan hoped that Reynaud would presume too much and do something unforgivable enough to get himself scratched, but the man never once chucked Thomas under the chin, patted him upon the head like a dog, or touched his feet. The wizard's long fingers made no such errors, and Thomas blatantly encouraged them to continue their good work.

Tristan shut his mouth and fairly glared at the cat, but Thomas only closed his eyes in sleepy delight, the traitor.

Idiot, Thomas rejoined blandly.

Tristan continued to glare.

And jealous besides. A purr of contentment issued from Thomas' chest. *All wizards have good hands. Comes with the trade.*

Disgusted, Tristan got to his feet and walked away. He would have stalked proudly off, but his stiff legs weren't reliable enough for that. At best, he could just manage not to stumble too noticeably. He didn't need to watch while Thomas flaunted his pleasures and he didn't intend to do so. He snugged his cloak tight, both to fend off the chill of the morning air and to cover the stains on his clothes till he had time to tend to them.

He munched at a warm oatcake, feeling distinctly out of sorts and having a hard time meeting Elisena's eye. Eventually she turned back to set more cakes baking, but somehow Tristan didn't feel much more comfortable.

Polassar appeared out of the mist, dragging his roan mare by her bridle and ignoring the considerable fuss she was making. The other horses followed, with Valadan at the rear. Tristan saddled Elisena's mare, then Valadan. His bit of the common work done—and probably done faster since he'd used no magic to help him—Tristan set to work adding to Valadan's gear. He took a leather sack from his pack, stuffing the herb bags it had contained down among other objects now rather jumbled together, and studied it closely for a moment. Then he slit its mouth so that it would open wide. That done, he ran the sack's thongs intricately through his saddle's fastenings, testing, buckling and readjusting.

What's that? Thomas asked. *Planning on feeling sick again today?*

"No." Tristan said curtly. "It's for you—I don't want you falling off, if we have to gallop again. That's if you intend to ride with me today. I suppose you may have made other arrangements."

Thomas yawned.

Your concern for my comfort is truly touching.

Tristan gave the straps a final tug, ignoring the cat.

Thomas rubbed tentatively at his ankles. *I'm sorry. You're so grumpy this morning, I shouldn't have teased you. But even you ought to know that there are several ways of keeping an eye on someone who needs to be watched. Admittedly mine's subtler than yours, but it may yet bear some fruit.*

Tristan felt very ashamed, indeed. He had no time to say much about it, though—camp had been broken and the fire stamped out. Polassar was already a-horse. Elisena stood at his stirrup, conferring on their course.

"We still need to follow the coast—we must follow that to reach Am Islin. But I think we dare not make straight for the sea as we had planned. Danac has garrisons within easy riding. There are sure to be patrols out, and Nímir could well capture himself another set of weak minds to harry us with," she said.

"Better to head for empty country, then?"

"So long as we don't go too far—there's no need to put us in the Winterwaste. It will be safer for us. Nímir has shown us that he still favors one of his oldest tactics, and we will do well to beware of it."

"We accounted ourselves well enough yestereven," Polassar said a little insistently. He had relished the fight; small wonder—of all the dangers they expected, that was the only one he was master of. For most of their perilous journey, Polassar might well be considered a liability, taken along more from friendship and his refusal to be left behind than for the sake of utility. He would want to prove his usefulness while he could, in the way that he knew best.

Elisena knew that, but she still shook her head sadly. "Even did we choose to dare the odds and fight so every day, I was not thinking of our safety alone. We are a danger to all the folk we pass, Polassar. It cannot be pleasant to become Nímir's tool—and remember, he may not always choose soldiers."

Polassar dropped his eyes, nodding. "As you say, Lady."

"Going inland will add time to our journey. The delay does not matter so much as long as we have the horses, but I think we should be moving."

Tristan, agreeing with that, lifted Thomas into his new conveyance.

* * *

The overcast sky seemed to hang just above their heads as they rode. Tristan kept expecting to see Polassar's helmed head disappear into the clouds, leaving him in the semblance of one of the headless horsemen out of legend. They had long since outstripped any pretense of roads, even had they chosen to follow such. There was an occasional deer track, but nothing more, and no sign of human habitation.

The grass underfoot was bleached to various shades of tan and bone, none of them striking to look at. Storms had matted the tussocks together, which made the footing treacherous at times. Luckily they ran into no bogs, though there were occasional brambles. Where rock thrust up through the soggy soil, it could be viewed almost with a sense of relief as a welcome variation. At what passed for sun-high, they ate bread and dried meat, sitting in their saddles because the ground looked inhospitable, no matter whether it was grassy or rocky.

They concentrated on covering as much ground as possible, so there was little chatter as they rode. Evenings were another matter—hard riding and cheerless country could not seem to dampen Reynaud's spirits. He began reminiscing with Elisena about the years they'd both spent at Radak, then slid into regaling her with tales of his student days in Kôvelir. The interest with which she eventually responded seemed to be unfeigned.

By the second night of that, Tristan found he was no longer able to tell himself that she was merely being polite. Bored with a conversation he had neither the desire nor the background to join, Tristan made pretense of inspecting a bramble-scratch Elisena's mare had gotten on her foreleg. He was not altogether surprised that Polassar accompanied him.

"I hazarded 'twouldn't take you long to quit yon gaudy carrion crow's company," he said conspiratorially. The deprecatory reference was to Reynaud's mostly black clothing.

"You'll never lose a copper on that bet," Tristan agreed, with a sour glance back over his shoulder. Elisena was laughing at whatever Reynaud was saying to her. Nothing Tristan had said all day had done more than spark a smile. He turned to bend over the brown mare's leg. The injury was, as he'd known, trifling and all but healed.

"Wizard, I've been craving speech with you ever since we rode out of Crogen," Polassar declared abruptly.

Tristan's startled look was lost in the darkness, since he'd just extinguished his crystal as he finished with the mare's leg. "What's stopped you? You can't say I keep wandering off—there's nowhere for me to wander *to*."

"Nay. A privy conversation."

Polassar's usual booming tone of voice rendered most of his conversations anything put private. But to do him credit, the big man was striving to keep his voice down now. "Go ahead," Tristan suggested.

"Aye, well . . . I'll come straight at it, then. You hid it well enough, but it wouldn't be amiss to say that you've little liking for this business we're about, would it?"

Tristan considered how best to put the truth without showing himself an utter coward. Polassar had no real idea what they were riding to face—he'd never met a trouble that he couldn't settle with fist or blade. Even Darkenkeep itself didn't seem to have made a lasting impression on him, and Tristan wasn't sure he ought to enlighten the man, even if he could find the words. Why should they all be as apprehensive as he was himself?

"We have no other choice," he answered finally. "If we did—I know I'm not brave, Polassar. I'd have been happy enough to stay home."

"So it seems." Polassar seemed to study him a while, though what he could hope to see in the darkness, Tristan couldn't hope to guess. "If you fear something so much, and go against it anyway, 'tis not cowardice to my mind, Wizard. But 'tis not sense, either."

He has a fine grasp of the situation.

Tristan shook his head, determined to rid himself of his gloomy mood, even though Thomas seemed disposed to share it with him for once.

"I think I've been taking fright at shadows, like a child. There'll be time enough to worry when we're in sight of the mountains. I hope I sleep better tonight."

Laughter reached them again, Elisena's silvery, Reynaud's deeper in tone, more like sword-steel ringing.

"Yon's not a shadow, for all he dresses himself to match one." Polassar jerked a thumb in Reynaud's direction. "Doesn't it breed wonder, Wizard, how those knights found us, straight and true, though they'd come half a day's ride and more from their posting?"

"Nímir—" Tristan hated to say it. The very name seemed to give the cool wind the bite of ice, and the mare beside him jerked away, snorting.

"Aye? Or mayhap not, that's my point. Maybe that's just what some would have us think. Having him with us is like bedding down with a viper."

"But as you said, better under our eye than at our backs. And he did fight beside us against those knights."

"Maybe he thought he had to." Polassar fidgeted. "Does the Lady trust him, do you think?"

"I doubt it." He wanted to do so, at least. "If she does, it means we're both very mistaken."

"I'd doubt that first. And I promise you this, Wizard— the first clear sign of any treachery, I'll settle him! Or dost think he'd change me to a toad?"

Tristan grinned. "He might. It would show off his skill to good advantage, and Reynaud always enjoys that."

Nightfall brought neither stars nor moon, but just a claustrophobic darkness and another cheerless camp. Next morning, Tristan was not surprised to find that he and everything else in the camp had been lightly dusted with snow. As if they needed to be told, there was no longer any doubt that they were under Nímir's eye, and on the edge of his Winterwaste.

If summer had ever so much as brushed the fringes of the land, it had left no trace of its passage. Of course, the overcast sky drained the color away, but even the boulder-bedded streams they crossed were narrow and cold and in a great hurry to get on with their journeys and out of the bleak land that had birthed them. Often the horses refused to drink from them, sign enough that they drained from deeper within the Waste itself.

Tristan smelled the sea long before the sound of surf or gulls reached his ears. At first, he didn't realize what it was—he was aware only of a vague unpleasantness, a fleeting memory associated with a salt smell. It teased at him and eluded him for a good while, and they were nearly within sight of the water before he pinned it down.

He was familiar with the sea. Blais had often sent him on errands to Dunehollow-by-the-Sea, once he was big

enough to walk so far alone. Those errands were a proper
part of his apprenticeship. Tristan had delivered love philters and simples to the folk of the coast town, collected
fees and installments on fees, done the marketing, bargained and bartered for flour and fresh fish. Nothing in
Dunehollow was far from the sea, and his tasks had often
taken him to the docks.

His old master could never have suspected how pop-
ular the sport of baiting "the wizard's brat" had become.
Tristan had always avoided what trouble he could and
never further humiliated himself by telling his master that
he'd become an irresistable target for the shipwright's
apprentices' mischief and malice.

Once he was safely back at their cottage, of course,
those troubles no longer mattered. But in Dunehollow,
Tristan was the outsider, butt of every joke or whimsey,
and he could never be quite wary enough—his loneliness
made him too receptive to anything that looked like an
overture of friendship, so he was sometimes not quick
enough to see a trap.

One afternoon the band of boys had managed to lure
him into a small dory, which they promptly loosed from
its moorings. It was well know that wizards crossed
running or moving water with difficulty, and the entertainment promised to be fine that day.

Tristan supposed he hadn't disappointed their expectations by much. His antics as he tried to get back to
shore, without use of pole, oars or even a fish-gaff, must
have been more than amusing. They'd nearly been fatal,
after he'd grabbed for the rope ladder left hanging just
out of his frantic reach and fallen out of the dory. An old
sail-mender had fished him out quick enough—with a
boat hook—but Tristan was sure he'd sunk straight to
the bottom of the harbor before being rescued, and it was
months before he could bear the taste of fish. For a few
days, even the sound of splashing as he drew water from
the well was enough to turn him green.

It was that day, as he'd made his way homeward, sod-
den and shaking, sorrier for himself than he'd ever been
before, and wondering how he'd explain to Blais why they
had no fish for supper, that he had met Thomas.

And the rest, as they say, was history. Thomas popped

his head up from the leather sack and his most recent nap and fanned his whiskers.

"Are you ever sorry?"

Frequently. Thomas peeped out at the bleak country- side they were bouncing over and looked ahead to where the changing color of the clouds presaged the sea. *But someone's got to look after you, and I have a soft heart. And don't pat me on the head like that. This ride is strain- ing my disposition quite enough as it is.*

Valadan snorted offendedly at him.

"I don't think I ever asked you, Thomas. Why *did* you follow me home that day?"

Curiosity. You'd obviously caught cold, and I couldn't bear not to know whether a sneeze through a nose that long would really blow your head off. Of course, I was only a kitten then.

"I remember Blais didn't want me to keep you. He said you'd hunt birds, and I said I would ask you not to. And he let you stay without another word about it. I didn't think at the time, but that must have been the first sign of a genuine wizardly gift that I ever gave him."

Nonsense. I was simply an adorable kitten. Quite irresistible.

By then the muffled roaring of the sea was plain to all ears. The ground rose a little, until the horses stood atop a steep cliff above a narrow beach. The tide was coming in, and the beach was being nibbled away—the little of it that there was.

The horses fretted as if they wished to be moving again, even though the day was nearly at an end and they were surely tired. The wind was still cold, but not so biting as it had been while they rode. Tristan gratefully pulled his gloves off and tucked them through his belt. Like most wizards, he disliked wearing the things even in the coldest weather. A wizard's hands were the most important tools of his trade; they needed to be kept warm and limber. Yet gloves seemed so constricting as to be unbearable. Tristan was never content to wear them long.

They looked upon the sea, and Tristan thought he was not alone in feeling dismay. Sagas might call the seas sapphire or wine-dark, and poets might pen ballads of the ocean's nature, its creatures and colors and moods. But here, on Calandra's farthest coast, the water was the unexciting color of pot metal, not worth a mention, far less a song. The crests of the waves were white as they rolled in, but it was the white of bleaching bones, not of pearls. The waves smashing against the rocks made noise, not music.

Tristan heard a faint purring beside his ear. Not Thomas, but Minstrel, issuing quiet challenge to the sea. As Tristan watched, the canary's body straightened, his stance became more upright, and the tentative, muted notes grew louder and bolder until he was in full song. Tristan grinned, setting his teeth a little at the shrillness, but glad the bird still had the heart to sing. His own hopes rose a trifle, in defiance of all sense.

The clouds were heavier than ever. The sun had become a barely visible red glow, guttering like a candle in a draft.

Elisena shook herself, as if casting away dark thoughts. "We'll camp," she said, over the wind. "Not here, of course. A headland like this is too exposed. We should find shelter that way, before too long." She gestured off to her right.

The cliffs did thrust a good way out into the sea. Perhaps at other spots where the land did not challenge it so, the sea was disposed to be less forbidding. Tristan hoped so. Things seemed bleak enough, without their being forced to ride all the way to Am Islin with this fury at their side. Memory aside, surely all this wild water would be enough to oppress anyone, not merely wizards with their antipathy to moving water. Tristan stole a glance at Reynaud, but could devine nothing of the man's reaction to the coast—Reynaud had put his hood up against the cold.

The horses began to pick a way down from the headland. Low bushes surrounded them, the plants pruned by wind and salt spray. The bushes grew higher as the land offered more shelter and soon were chest-high to the horses. Dog roses and brambles snatched at Tristan's cloak, scratching at his bare hands when he tried to extricate himself. Weary of fighting with it, he finally drew the cloak up and pinned the bottom of it between his leg and the saddle.

They came out of the thickets only when rocks made the growing too difficult for large plants. Elisena began to search for fresh water, supposing that the cliff top must drain into springs among the rocks below. Her rings glowed faintly as she stretched out her hand, seeking.

"Ah, good; it's not very far." She flicked a heel, and her mare moved off daintily into the dusk. Valadan followed her.

The water trickled down between the rocks, forming a small pool; it took Tristan a good while to water the horses, but at least the water was sweet. So near the sea, it might as easily have been brackish, and they could have been forced to seek out puddles of rain water to get a decent drink. Tristan tended the horses while Polassar and Reynaud descended to the beach in search of driftwood for the fire. Storms would have cast up great heaps of wood, though the untangling of suitable lengths from piles higher than Polassar's helmed head could be hazardous if a man tried it unwarily.

A fire could not be lit swiftly enough to please Thomas, who crouched miserably beside the pile of sticks while Reynaud went back for a second load. The wind played with the cat's thick fur capriciously, and Thomas moaned dismally.

Tristan plucked handfuls of dry grass for tinder and laid the fire in the likeliest spot he could find. He considered it carefully. A high fire would be warm, but once the wind left off playing with Thomas and started on the fire instead, they'd be plagued with flying sparks and unexpected flares, not to mention the smoke.

He decided to try a lower arrangement. That big log, there, for a nice solid base. And then perhaps that plank . . .

Stop fussing with those and light that fire before I die of a chill. Thomas had taken what refuge he could behind a tuft of sea-pink.

"It's not *that* cold, Thomas!" Still, his own fingers were numb; the horses had dribbled cold water all over him, and the wind made things worse. Tristan hunched close over the wood and spoke his fire-lighting-charm, making the appropriate passes with the fingers of his free hand.

The wood failed to blaze up, though unhappily the spell worked to perfection. Tristan's clothing had been soaked by rain and then by sea spray, but was still dry enough to smolder. There was an acrid stink of burning wool. At the same time he became aware of a sharp pain on the side of his right thigh. Tristan sprawled backward, slapping at the quickly blossoming flames.

His balance had been none too certain as he squatted over the wood, and his struggles toppled him over sideways. Luckily the tumble finally extinguished the flames. Tristan got to his feet, alternately swearing and sucking at his burned fingers. He found no blisters, but the burns hurt. And Thomas' reaction, as he turned away too late to hide the mirth which he apparently couldn't suppress, hurt even worse.

Elisena looked up from the saddlebag she'd opened, a packet of dried meat in one hand and a rope of onions in the other.

"What's wrong?"

"Nothing." Tristan had already located his firestone—luckily he'd just dropped it, when he might as easily have flung it wide into the bushes. He waited till Elisena had accepted his answer and turned back to her work before he peered closely at the pile of wood. Thousands of times his spells had gone amiss, but never anything remotely like what had just happened.

A sparkle caught his eye, a glint that wood just didn't give off. He reached for it and was astonished and horrified to find an iron nail embedded in the planking. Small wonder he'd been burned—the iron had bounced his own spell back at him, like the reflection from a mirror.

He'd been careless—or maybe he hadn't. The wood had perhaps been a bit of ship's planking, cast up from some wrecked vessel. Suppose its inclusion had been deliberate? Only Reynaud had actually brought any wood back—Polassar was still down on the beach. How like the man to try a little trick like that, just to keep in practice!

Tristan was furious, but unfortunately also short of proof. As he had no intention of humiliating himself by bringing the matter up to Reynaud, there matters would have to rest. He wouldn't even mention the incident to Elisena. Whatever she'd seen was embarrassing enough. He turned grimly back to lighting the fire—this time successfully.

He spent the evening glaring surreptitiously at Reynaud, while they supped on magic-leavened bread and ordinary stew, enriched a bit by some mussels Polassar had found. Maybe the change of diet didn't suit him, or else he should have taken more than one pull at the wineskin as it was passed around. Whatever the reason, Tristan woke cold and shaking some hours later, suspecting that he'd just had an awful dream, but not able to recall even a wisp of it. He shivered, feeling that he couldn't have gotten warm, even if he'd lain right down among the flames of the dying fire.

Careful not to disturb Thomas, he got up and added a fresh bit of wood to the coals, but light and warmth didn't soothe his nerves. Restlessly, he walked past the sleeping horses, patting Valadan before he strolled toward the beach. He stopped before he'd quite reached the sand, not liking the idea of that empty stretch at night and knowing that the wind would be colder out there, too. He had to use some common sense.

Tristan's feeling of unease intensified. The night was dark, and he'd been foolish to venture out alone into it, even the scant hundred yards he'd come. He hadn't seen the place by full light, so how could he possibly guess how it should look or what belonged there and what didn't? And the wind would mask any sounds of danger.

Probably he was only starting at shadows again, and there was no danger out there at all. He'd had a bad dream and he ought to go back to the fire, drop certain herbs into a cup of warm wine, and forget about it. He could recall the sight of the waves crashing in, regular as a heartbeat, silver in the night. That should make him drowsy.

The wind dropped, letting him hear the footsteps behind him. Therefore, Tristan didn't jump when Polassar spoke. He was oddly proud of that.

"Wizard, you ought to try sleeping o' nights. Works wonders for a man's disposition."

"I was just coming," Tristan answered.

Polassar yawned and scratched at the back of his neck. "Good." He didn't sound as if he believed the story.

Tristan had turned to stare back into the night, tense and obviously listening.

"Wizard? What—"

Tristan tossed his head, as if throwing some thought away with the motion. "Nothing. Something. I don't know—" The sound he'd thought he heard was gone, and he was embarrassed to mention it.

"What manner of thing is both nothing and something?" Polassar asked exasperatedly. "Wizard, 'tis awfully late for riddling."

Tristan hadn't meant it as any sort of riddle. So why did a nagging something at the back of his mind keep insisting that he did indeed know of something which was also a nothing? How else might a man describe the wind, felt but never seen? Likewise, what truer way was there to depict the Hounds of Nímir?

the RiveR of Ice

TRISTAN WANDERED DOWN THE BEACH, LEAVING
Thomas feasting with happy abandon upon the trapped
denizens of a tidal pool. He was surprised that he felt
clearheaded enough to do anything beyond staring mood-
ily into space—but maybe he'd finally had his fill of that.
He'd lain most of the night with his eyes wide open while
his thoughts ranged, utterly unable to sleep.

He ought to eat before the day's ride began, but Tristan's stomach rebelled strongly against the idea. With
luck, this little traipse along the waterline would net him
some sort of edible sea creatures, besides the distraction
he'd come in search of. Food would always be welcome,
even if he didn't personally feel up to eating any of it.
There were plenty of pools left by the retreating tide besides
the one Thomas had claimed. There might be fish trapped
in them, as well as the mussels. And if he brought back
something curious enough, perhaps no one would notice
that he didn't eat. Tristan misliked being nagged, and no
amount of arguing would settle either his stomach or his
nerves.

Something looked like a wreck, down the beach past
a couple of great, flat rocks. Tristan felt his curiosity stir
and set off purposefully toward the wreckage. Notice
everything, Blais had always insisted. The oddest things
could be useful to a wizard. Fortunately, the teaching had
meshed neatly with Tristan's own inclinations. Whatever
other traits he'd left behind with his boyhood, he still had
that curiosity, or at least the urge to snoop.

It took him some minutes to reach the wreck, for there

was a lot of sea-wrack cast up on the sand, and whether
he clambered over it or detoured around it, the stuff still
slowed him. He ought, in fact, to have started back, since
Polassar would surely be ready to ride out soon and would
be angry at delay, but Tristan was close by then and decided
he might as well continue.

Unwary, Tristan slipped into the edge of one of the
pools, soaking himself to the knees. He tried a drying-
spell, botched it, and swore abstractedly as he tried to
wring salt water out of the hem of his cloak.

He glanced up in the midst of that, instantly forgetting
his soggy state. What Tristan had taken for a shipwreck
from afar proved, close up, to be the bleached bones of
some vast sea beast. The arches of its cage of ribs, half-
buried in the sand, still rose higher than Tristan's own
head. The sight was awesome.

Wave and wind had scoured the bones as smooth as
polished ivory. Tristan's fingers explored the nearest hesitantly. How could even the vast sea contain a creature
so large? And what power was fell enough to slay it where
it had fallen? He thought it must be larger than even
Darkenkeep's Guardian had been, though he'd never had
a clear sight of that monster and had therefore only guessed
at its total bulk. Tristan found himself hoping that the
waves had brought the beast ashore already dead and that
there were no storms so strong as to capture the behemoth
living and hold it prisoned against a shore, like a fish
trapped in a landlocked pool.

Long green tangles of seaweed trailed from the last of
the bones into the lapping sea. Some were quite fresh,
left by the morning's tide. Little bladders upon the leaves
were popping still as they dried in the air and intermittent
sun. Ghost-crabs vanished into the sand ahead of Tristan
as he prowled about the skeleton. Sandpipers challenged
and then fled the incoming waves.

Light glinted on something in the sand at his feet. Tristan stooped down, discovering a string of clear green
beads—glass or emerald, there was no way for him to
tell. He thought to take them to Elisena; but as he scooped
his fingers under them, their rotted string dissolved at the
touch, and the beads gave up the illusion of being strung.
Most of them vanished back into the white sand. One
remained between Tristan's thumb and forefinger. He made

to toss it out into the waves, then shrugged and dropped it into the pouch at his belt.

He turned to go back, but he had not retraced many of his steps before he could make out another figure far down the beach, apparently watching for him. Tristan scowled, as shortening the distance between them failed to add color to the figure's dark garments. What right had Reynaud to hang about spying on him?

Tristan half hoped that the man would content himself with watching and not wait for Tristan to approach. The hope was futile, though, for Thomas was standing at Reynaud's side, a speck at first, but swiftly grown to his true size as Tristan came close.

"It's always prudent to scout the way before commencing a journey," Reynaud said pleasantly. "Of course, we'll be riding in the other direction—"

Tristan returned such suspect amiability with a cold stare. His tongue itched with studied, scathing rudenesses, but it would be pointless for him to utter them. Obviously, no mere words of his could run Reynaud off at this point. Words had failed, and the man had given him no clear excuse for other action—assuming there was an action that both Elisena and his sword would let Tristan consider. Like two wary chessmen, he and Reynaud must circle on a while, seeking victory or advantage within the rules of the game. Tristan kept his fingers very carefully away from his sword hilt, taking no chances.

"I don't mind looking back," Tristan said with a smile so false that his cheeks were ashamed of it. "If you don't know where you've been, it can be difficult to discover when you've got where you're going."

"And now you know where you are, my lord?"

"Oh, yes," Tristan assured him. He bent down and scooped up Thomas, who seemed a trifle heavy. The cat must be positively stuffed with hapless crustaceans. "And if we're going to start early enough to satisfy Polassar, we'd better be about it." He started off up the beach, not waiting for Reynaud to follow.

Well played, Thomas commented. *This sea air is going to make a philosopher out of you, if not a diplomat.*

If nothing else, his early morning walk enabled Tristan to lend weight to Polassar's recommendation that they not try to ride along the beach. The sandy strip was simply too narrow and too clogged with storm-wrack; they'd make precious little progress. Riding a little way inland seemed much more sensible, so they climbed back to the top of the cliffs and set off.

It was still miserable going. Rain draining from the heartland had cut gullies great and small as it ran over the cliffs to the sea. The large ravines were a continual nuisance, but the small ones were a greater danger, since they were thickly overgrown and frequently hidden by scrubby bushes, impossible to see until a horse was hard upon them. Making any sort of speed was to risk a bad fall. Valadan led and made a good job of it; but by day's end, Tristan was as exhausted as if he'd been jumping the gullies with his own legs.

That night they camped by the sea again, hoping to take advantage of the food to be gathered there. In that, they were disappointed—the coast was rougher and more barren by then. They found no shellfish on the rocks. The sea, an opaque green that looked as solid as soapstone, showed no sign of any fish that they could hope to catch from the shore, either.

Their provisions were nonetheless holding out well, and surely they could expect to collect more from Royston Ambere when they begged his aid. The horses could carry a great deal, and they were certain of reaching Am Islin without having had to touch the separate packs Elisena had carefully made of food for the journey into the mountains themselves. Tristan had seen a little of what she put into those bundles. Most of the stuff was dried for lightness and convenience, and some of the foods were marvelous and ingenious.

They had plenty of food, but Tristan had little appetite for it. He sat staring into the weirdly colored flames of the driftwood fire, listening to the wind and letting his supper sit forgotten beside him. Thomas got as much as he wanted of it without bothering to ask or scheming to steal. Elisena's scoldings about it went unheeded.

There was no reason for Tristan to feel such disquiet, and he knew that. They had spent two days riding along the coast without trouble. No men or monsters appeared from the sea. Valadan sensed no pursuit—and the horse had been specially bidden to watch for the Hounds, as if he needed to be so instructed. Reynaud had played no discernible pranks and had even mostly kept his own council.

Tristan thought he would almost have welcomed some incident or any distraction. He felt as if a month had passed since he'd left Crogen—as if this journey was as outside of time as a trek into Darkenkeep would have been. His sense of forboding grew stronger by the hour.

Elisena, sensing that—it couldn't have been difficult— stayed close to him and smothered all evidence of whatever fears and misgivings she had of her own. Tristan didn't think she'd attempted any Seeings. Either they weren't necessary or she'd been unable to find a receptive spot near their camps. Tristan could well understand that she might prefer not to search out the future again, especially if her sight let her see only part of the way ahead, but not its conclusion.

Finally the cliff tops were furred with wind-brushed salt grass and they were too high for gullies. The companions could make some speed again and let the horses gallop. They were strung out in single file when Polassar, who was leading, crested a low hill and reined in hard enough to jostle all the rest of them, as the horses strove to avoid colliding with each other.

Tristan, expecting another ravine or maybe a steeply eroded slope on the hill's far side to be the cause of the halt, was utterly unprepared for the view to be had from Polassar's side. The broad valley below them was filled from one slope to the other by a river of ice extending from the distant horizon—and the mountains—to the sea.

Even Polassar was silent, at least for a while. At a glance, the ice could have been taken for a fog bank lying over a channel of the sea. Indeed, there was some mist hanging about it, for the sun had begun to shine brightly, giving them a fine view of the glacier and making steam rise from the ice. From hill to hill, the width of the ice was at least a league. It filled the valley far more completely than the river that had originally cut the channel had ever done, though the ice must have pushed down the very same course to find the sea. A puff of cold wafted off the glacier, to chill them where they stood.

The ice was dirty in places, as if silted rivers had drained onto it, sullying its surface. It was like a filthy, pale tongue thrust out of the mountains to lap at the sea. Tristan shivered, his fingers tightening on the wide leather reins they held. As far as his eyes could see, the ice lay across their path.

They rode hesitantly forward, reconnoitering. The worst was all too soon obvious—there was no way they might hope to ride on across the glacier's top. Surface melt had cut twisting channels across it; those no worse than the ravines, they might have managed easily enough, but everywhere blue fissures gleamed, where the skin of the ice had cracked as it forced its inexorable way downhill, shoved from behind by more ice. The top layer was a chaotic waste of cracks and great blocks and pinnacles of ice. Tristan couldn't see ten yards of ground upon which a man might safely walk, far less four horses.

The wind whistled cheerfully among the towers of ice. It played delicately with Polassar's blue cloak as he dismounted and strode to Elisena's side.

"There'll be no passage this way, Lady. Have we much farther to go?"

"Some miles. Another day at least with the horses." Minstrel had been in communication with seagulls all morning, and they had spoken of the tower, though it was still too far off for sight, even given clearer skies.

Their course was clear enough. Reynaud had already let his mare begin to pick her way down to the beach. Perhaps the ice did not quite reach the sea, and they might get around its leading edge when the tide went out. Tristan, who'd seen the chunks of ice floating in the waves, some of them very far off from shore, did not think the hope a likely one. The ice smelled like Darkenkeep to him. He shivered with more than the chill of the wind as Valadan followed the other horses toward the beach.

From the narrow spit of gravel that the high tide left dry, the view was worse than hopeless. The ice rose to ten times the height of a man on horseback, coming up sheer from the water, except for the spot at the edge where they stood. Tristan dismounted and joined Polassar at the water's edge, scanning the ice cliff.

"Wizard, you grew up near the sea—does yon look as if the tide's full in?"

Tristan looked hard. He could see no sign that the waves ever reached higher than they presently did. However, wizards were hardly noted for taking a consuming interest in the ways of the sea. Tristan could observe that the tide was high. How long it had been that way, he had not the least idea. Nor could he guess when the low tide would come. Polassar, hailing from landlocked Lassair, could have made just as good a judgment himself.

As they stood debating it, Valadan let out a shrill whinny of warning. Reynaud shouted something incomprehensible and started dragging Elisena up the slope from the beach most unceremoniously. She only resisted him for an instant.

Tristan stepped toward them indignantly. A great cracking sound from the ice sheet arrested him, and he forgot his alarm—at least the one connected with Reynaud's rude behavior. As he stared, a block the size of a castle's watchtower broke free of the ice face and toppled slowly into the waiting waves. He and Polassar recognized the danger of the resulting surge of water at the same moment and turned to run, but Tristan had taken only half a dozen steps when the wave hit him, knocking his feet out from under him.

Blinded by the salt water and the shock of cold so great that he couldn't breathe and didn't know whether his head was above water or not, Tristan felt rocks and gravel under his fingers one moment—then nothing, as the wave started to drag him back to the sea with it. He tried to stand up, slipped, and went under again. Just for one instant, the awful fear he'd known that day in Dunehollow returned.

Something caught at his belt. Whatever it was snagged fast, and Tristan's unicorn buckle was pulled hard into his stomach. Then he was hauled abruptly to his feet and swung about.

"Keep forgetting you don't swim, Wizard," Polassar said convivially. Foam dripped from his red moustaches, and he was nearly as soaked as Tristan was, but his eyes gleamed with pleasure. "All right now. Got your legs under you? Good. Best get dried off before my armor rusts and you sprout mold—or whatever it is happens to wet wizards."

Actually, wet wizards steamed—or at least they did if put close beside a very large fire until their clothes dried

out. Tristan shivered in spite of the warmth. The calamity
had happened too fast—it had taken him some minutes
to realize that he'd nearly drowned, and he hadn't had
time yet to assimilate the fact that he hadn't. He'd dried
his sword off and was trying to wipe the blade down with
oiled rags, but his hands had started shaking, and he kept
cutting himself. Tristan sneezed violently; with all the
shaking, it was a painful experience.

"All right," Elisena said sharply. "Now do you believe
that your clothes will *not* dry while you've got them on?
Off with them."

Tristan glared at her from under his still dripping hair.
The wind was bitter, doubly so for him. He'd rather not
be left naked to it. He said so, but his teeth chattered,
robbing him of any hope of dignity.

"*Off*, I said."

"Here." Reynaud flicked the silver throat-clasp of his
cloak open and tossed the garment to Tristan. "I can easily
keep moving." He strolled away and joined Polassar, who'd
wrung the seawater from his cloak and gone back to keep
a wary eye on the tide. Polassar, after tending to his armor,
felt no need to dry off, since he'd been more wetted than
soaked and at least hadn't fallen into the sea.

Tristan was more discomfited than ever, swaddled in
Reynaud's black cloak while he glumly watched Elisena
arranging his own clothes about the fire. The sleek fabric
seemed to crawl against his skin, and he didn't trust the
cloak any farther than he did its owner. He'd been happier
wet to the skin and shivering. He jerked suddenly, convinced that something definitely *had* moved against him.

It's only me, Thomas said disgustedly. *And don't touch
me. Your hands are cold. By the way, that waterproof-
spell on your boots held up very well. Pity the water came
right in over the tops like that.*

Tristan ignored the cat, accepting a cup of tea from
Elisena. He took a swallow and nearly choked. The mug
didn't hold tea, but mulled brandy.

"Go easy with that," Elisena said. "If Polassar finds
out I gave it to you and not to him, he'll have your hide.
Not that he needs brandy. The man's blood's up enough
to keep him boiling a good while."

Tristan knew precisely what Elisena meant. Polassar
relished nothing more than a good fight, and the glacier

probably struck him as an even match in an adversary. Tristan took a second, more careful sip from the mug. Much better! The first swallow had stopped burning his lungs away and dropped down to his stomach, where its warmth was more welcome.

"Do you think he's right?" he asked. "That we can cross, once the tide goes out?"

Elisena poked at the fire. "That depends on how far it goes out. Valadan's nervous about it."

"I can understand that. I don't feel so steady myself. Are those things dry yet?" He reached out hopefully.

"No. Stop fussing. The gulls told Minstrel the tide won't even turn for an hour. You don't need to get dressed yet, unless you enjoy being cold."

"I'm cold *now*." Tristan touched a finger to the warm back of Elisena's unguarded neck to prove the point. "See?" She exclaimed with surprise and slapped his hand. "In an hour, then? By the time it's all the way out, it will be getting dark. Those hills will block the sun early."

"I know." Elisena sat down beside him.

"What if we went farther inland?" Tristan pressed. "Maybe the ice only breaks up like that when it starts to drop into the sea?"

Elisena sighed. "No. Valadan went to look. He says this ice is moving very quickly, for ice. That's what makes it crack like that, and it's just as bad leagues inland. He couldn't find a spot he thought even he could cross."

"Then we'd better hope the tide goes out a long way tonight."

In his heart, Tristan knew the tide wouldn't oblige. The cycles of the tide attended those of the moon. A full moon generally meant high tides and a great variation between the high and low points of the day. And the moon above them now, faintly visible, was new, a bare sliver of silver.

Single file, they rode out into the shallow water. To Tristan, in the lead, the action felt worse than foolhardy. The water had receded as far as it was going to, and still the sand and rock before the glacier's face were covered by the sea. They hoped it was only to fetlock depth or at worst to the horses' knees, but Valadan must go first to test the ground for danger. Riding forward alone with nothing before him but Valadan's pricked ears and the

swirling sea was hard for Tristan. He'd rather have let
Polassar lead, since, after all, this was *his* plan, but he
had no choice.

It was not, Tristan insisted to himself, as bad as crossing the Est that first time had been, when they'd had no
boat and had been forced to swim the horses across that
savage river. The water here did not run beneath Valadan's hooves; indeed it barely lapped at them. Running
water troubled wizards. This was only very wet ground.
Tristan's stomach fluttered, insisting otherwise. And the
ice, rising sheer on his right hand, so close that he could
touch it if he wanted to, made its own contribution to his
nervousness.

The ride was far from silent. The creaking of the ice
was constant, like the hissing and sucking of the waves
upon the sand. The horses' footfalls were dull and muffled. Tristan thought the sound of his own heart beating
was louder, certainly more rapid.

This was a bay, Valadan stated casually, *before the ice
came. There may be a channel where the river was, and
deep water. Do not be alarmed if I must swim.*

Tristan nodded, dry-mouthed. He looked back at the
others. Elisena came just behind him, Polassar after her,
and Reynaud farther back still, having chosen for some
reason to lead his mare. The light was failing fast; already
the black mare was hardly more than a shadow, though
Tristan saw all the nearer horses and Reynaud well enough.
It seemed surprising that Reynaud should keep a horse
so unreliable.

Tristan wished they might go faster, though they dared
not. They were a bare quarter of the way across, and the
groaning of the ice seemed louder. Somewhere far ahead
there was a great cracking, then a brief silence as ice fell.
Valadan halted, knowing what to expect.

"Stand fast," Tristan called. Dark water surged around
Valadan's legs, and receded. The ice had fallen a good
way ahead. They could only hope that the bits would float
off before they reached them and had to try to get round
or over. This is madness, Tristan insisted unhappily to
himself, though he'd readily agreed to the attempt as being
their only choice. Agreement had been easier on land.
Now matters stood otherwise, and regrets came.

Plainly, a calving glacier was not safe to approach so

closely. All the ice had been deeply undercut by the waves at high tide. Now the ice edge lacked the water's support, and its own weight might bring it crashing down at any point and at any moment. They moved on, in spite of that. Polassar was muttering something about kelpies, but Tristan knew they'd need no such unnatural help to bring them to disaster. He made a check of their progress.

They seemed to have come a long way and, so far, safely. Tristan kept holding his breath and had to force his lungs to let it out. His fingers were cramping on the reins, because he was gripping the leather so tightly.

Meltwater, trickling unseen through the ice to spout out unexpectedly, drenched him like a flung bucket of water. Tristan, who'd barely been dry by the time they started out, swore briefly, but he had little leisure to spare for cursings. Something else was hitting him. It felt like pebbles or a spatter of fine gravel. He ducked his head, flinging an arm up to shield his face.

One of the bits lodged against his neck inside his hood, and it was burning cold. *Ice*! Chips of ice!

Tristan twisted in his saddle, putting a hand on Valadan's rump to maintain his balance. Elisena was some dozen feet behind him, as if she'd sensibly halted to let the spouting water pass before coming on. Before her, behind Tristan, the whole face of the ice was quivering. She'd never get past it before it fell, Tristan saw.

"*Get back*!" Tristan shouted, waving his hands to shoo the mare back the way she'd come. Wind blasted at the ice cliff, as if to steal his words, even as it wrenched the ice above free more swiftly. Valadan slipped and splashed about in search of footing. Tristan nearly lost his seat and only saved himself by a cruel dragging on the reins. He had no chance for further warnings.

Yet Elisena either heard or saw the danger for herself. Her mare spun neatly about, its hooves churning the surf to foam and throwing gouts of wet sand.

She would be expecting him to follow her, but Tristan knew he'd never make it and didn't need to ask Valadan if the horse agreed. Tristan shoved his boots as deep into the stirrups as they'd go, bent low, and flung his arms about the stallion's neck. Valadan planted his hooves wide apart and stayed where he was.

The ice toppled—gracefully, leisurely. It seemed to

hang above them endlessly, before it smashed into the gravel and the shallow sea. Tristan buried his face in Valadan's mane as it hit. Cold seawater drenched him.

As the ice grounded, Valadan leaped forward. Tristan saw the swirl of water beneath him and the glint of the riven ice. Valadan's hooves found some miniscule purchase upon it. The horse scrambled up and over the fallen ice and landed running in the boiling sea with a splash that soaked Tristan again to his eyebrows. More ice pelted them, as if hurled purposefully from above.

Tristan ducked, then was knocked halfway out of the saddle when a small chunk hit his shoulder. Another, larger block toppled before them and Valadan scrambled over once again, urged on by the waves from more ice falling behind his tail.

It was plain by then that the ice would never let them gain the shore. For every block that they scaled before it began to float, two more fell in their way. It would be a matter of moments at most before one fell on them as they struggled. Valadan snorted and turned straight out to sea, the only direction that promised him free movement.

The water deepened rapidly, and the waves were choppy, but the stallion neither hesitated nor faltered. The sea was thick with floating, broken ice, but the bits were small enough to bob away from them and let them pass through unhurt, if not unbruised. Valadan's churning hooves struck many aside. He swam strongly, letting his breath out in snorts that cleared the wavelets from his nostrils.

It seemed Polassar had mistaken the tide badly. The water was still going out, and the drag of it, in the deep water, was terrible. Against such an undertow, Tristan was afraid even Valadan might not be able to regain the shore. He could tell that they were being carried steadily out to sea, even after the stallion had skirted the last of the ice and turned back toward the beach. Tristan, fighting the sickness in the pit of his stomach, was growing more apprehensive about that with each moment.

The stinging waves, the wind whose ferocity was increasing, and the gathering darkness were all seemingly fatal handicaps. Already they were almost carried out of sight of shore, and Tristan could hear Polassar shouting his name, as those on shore realized what was happening. Valadan struggled mightily for little gain, and Tristan's answering shouts were carried back to his own ears by the wind.

He realized that his weight was hampering the laboring horse. Water was not Valadan's proper element; no matter how strongly he swam, they were low enough in the water that waves continually broke over the stallion's head. That couldn't continue, or Valadan would slowly be drowned. Tristan knew he had to lighten the load, but he had no baggage he could easily cast off, and none of it weighed enough to matter—except himself. If he could let Valadan drag him, instead of continuing to carry him above the waves—

Tristan kicked loose from both stirrups and slid out of the wet saddle into the cold water. He almost sank—would have sunk if he hadn't caught hold of one stirrup. His soaked clothes were heavy; even if he'd known how to swim, he couldn't have managed to do so. Valadan snorted back at him. Minstrel bobbed worriedly about in the air over his head, hardly safe from the waves himself. "It's all right. I won't let go." Pulling the right stirrup up over the saddle to gain a secure hold for his right hand and clinging to the saddle's pommel with his left, Tristan tried to float alongside the stallion. He had to try to keep himself free of Valadan's hooves; he didn't want the horse's swimming hampered by worries about kicking him.

He hadn't thought that water could get so cold and still stay unfrozen. It was enough to make his heart shrivel up within him. Now, low in the water, with salt burning his eyes, Tristan could see nothing but the black water and Valadan's black side above him. He couldn't tell if they made any progress at all. His teeth started chattering. Thomas was watching him from the saddlebag, mute with fright, but there was no sign of Minstrel. Tristan hoped the bird had had sense enough to fly to shore before his feathers got wetted by the waves.

Maybe Thomas could see the beach. His eyes were better suited to the lack of light, and he was higher above the water. Tristan tried to ask, but his teeth hit together so that the words wouldn't come. He felt as if he'd been in the water for hours, hanging onto the stirrup with frozen fingers. Wherever the wind touched him, he grew colder still, and his face went stiff.

After an eternity, Tristan became aware of another discomfort. His right arm ached as if something were dragging it out of its socket, and something else kept bumping at his knees. It felt like rocks, but Tristan had so little sensation left by then that it could have been anything. Gradually he realized that he was still being dragged, but that the process had become painful because he wasn't floating any longer. He was still cold, but the water no longer supported or cushioned him.

Valadan turned his head toward him. *I could have swum much farther. You need not have worried.* He staggered up onto the gravel of a beach, his sides heaving, and Tristan tried to get his feet under him as the horse pulled him up. He couldn't. He stumbled, his knees buckling and his feet sliding helplessly.

Finally, infinitely weary of being dragged, Tristan simply let go of the stirrup and fell face down onto the wet stones as Polassar ran toward him.

the Berg Ship

"No need to drown yourself for the sake of another brandy," Elisena said. She held the cup to Tristan's lips and tilted it for him, while Minstrel watched from his perch on her shoulder.

"Twice in one day," Tristan whispered mournfully. The cup's metal felt hot enough to burn the skin from his lips, though Elisena was holding the silver comfortably with her bare fingers. "You'd think I'd learn, wouldn't you? Valadan—"

"Is fine. He's been rubbed down, and Reynaud magicked him a blanket out of some seaweed. He's warm as toast and in better shape than you are. Drink the rest of this now."

The brandy burned a bright trail from his throat to his stomach. Its warmth was welcome, even if the news of Reynaud's helpfulness wasn't. Tristan didn't want the man touching Valadan, but he was unable to offer even a token protest. It was all he could do to keep his eyelids apart, and soon he couldn't manage even that.

Tristan spent the whole of the next day with the others, watching Reynaud's numerous attempts to craft a boat out of driftwood and sorcery. The exquisitely laid spells were foredoomed, of course. No magic could exist upon running water. Each boat dissolved as fast as Reynaud could launch it, the moment a wave touched it.

Tristan privately questioned the man's motive. If Reynaud was trying to delay them, he was doing it superbly, only Tristan couldn't fathom why he should want to or

what the wasted time could gain him. Tristan kept remembering how Reynaud had hung back as they'd tried to
pass in front of the ice. Who could tell what mischief he
might have worked, back there out of sight? It would not
have taken much to make that unsteady ice start falling.
But once again, Tristan had no proof to offer with his
suspicions, nor any plausible motive for the treachery,
and so was forced to hold his tongue.

Reynaud never did achieve a workable boat. Still, it
probably needed to be tried. They had neither the skills
nor the wherewithall to construct a proper boat, and no
one was ready yet to chance a raft in that turbulent stretch
of water and tossing chunks of ice. Tristan could not quite
rejoice in Reynaud's failure.

What else, then? They had not yet tried the surface of
the glacier, since that was too obviously madness. Tristan
wondered if there might not be some magical way of bridg-
ing the crevasses, but there were simply too many of the
deep chasms. Even if they proceeded on foot, the attempt
would be impossible.

Perhaps, Polassar suggested, they could make some
sort of ladders out of the driftwood, light enough to be
easily carried, long enough to lay across the rifts so that
they could be crawled across. So mountaineers dealt with
crevasses. That sort of passage would mean the aban-
donment of all the horses and most of their gear, though,
an unwelcome idea.

"The horses we might leave," Elisena said thoughtfully. "Valadan will see them back to Crogen, and beyond
Am Islin we could not have taken them in any case. But
to go out on that ice—that I do not like. Nímir could
strand us there too easily with a storm such that we dared
not move. Despite that, I find much in our plight that
should give us hope."

Tristan's eyebrows lifted. Elisena smiled at his obvious
surprise.

"He's keeping us from reaching his mountains, rather
than letting us in. That is significant. It means Nímir fears
us too much to let us come close."

"That's a funny kind of hope," Tristan protested.

"A frail one, true. So are flowers frail, but it has been
written that each bud blossoming in Calandra is as an
arrow into Nímir's heart."

"*Flowers*?" Polassar grumbled. "Trust wizard folk to be always off at tangents. Slippery as snakes when you try to pin 'em to a subject."

"A flower would be safer not to try to bloom," Reynaud said, joining in smoothly. "Yet it has no choice, if it is to live. No more do we. We must cross the ice, if we're to reach Ambere. We must play this game as we find it. We will see a storm coming, at least, and be able to make ready for it."

Tristan wondered darkly if the man had some deeper reason for wanting them out on the perilous ice. If Reynaud had prevented them from going by sea, leaving them no choice but the land—

Keep quiet, Thomas cautioned. *He's not the only one who can play games. Do what he suggests—play the game as you find it.*

It was agreed, after much discussion that in the morning they would make the ladders and such climbing tools as they could. Then the glacier would be scouted from atop a near hill and the best route mapped. The less time they spent actually upon the ice, the better their chances would be. Glaciers were too near to living things in Nímir's cold hands.

The dawn sky was red as new-spilled blood when Tristan woke. That sort of color could be, he knew, the first hint of a brewing storm, the kind Elisena most dreaded. Tristan got up, stepping carefully over cloak-wrapped sleepers and, snatching up a crust of bread left from the night before, headed for the beach. Thomas stretched and trotted after him.

The trail down was steep—they must have brought the horses up a different way the night before, Tristan thought, not remembering anything about the journey except that he'd been terribly cold, even muffled in Polassar's fur-lined cloak. It was steep, but for a man afoot it was negotiable. Tristan only fell twice, with no worse harm done than scraped knuckles and muddied clothes. Small stones—and some not so small—bounded downslope in front of him. Thomas followed with more agility and less recklessness.

Most of the fallen ice had floated off, so the ice cliff presented much the same aspect that it had when first Tristan had seen it. He took his eyes away from it and

began to search the beach instead, letting his mind roam
freely. Games had rules. You played better if you knew
them.

Under ideal conditions, crossing over the top of the
ice would take them more than one day, whereas to use
the sea would be a matter of hours, however unpleasant
those hours might be. The troubled sky suggested that
they ought to value speed.

However, to make use of the sea, they required a boat,
and they had none. A magical boat, except as an artifice,
was not only useless but impossible. A boat that could
not bear the touch of water was limited in its usefulness.

I told you you were turning into a philosopher.

Tristan tossed a twig into the water and watched it
float off, thinking busily. Wood—even wood that had once
been a ship—was of the land. He'd need something of
the sea, to work a suitable magic—magic that could stand
up to running water, if such a thing were even remotely
possible. But what could he use? He wondered if the sea
had stolen his wits, letting him now consider a sorcery
even Reynaud had failed at.

Shellfish would not float. Seaweed seemed an unlikely
choice, unless one used the bladders as floats—but his
own experience of the previous night proved that the water
was too cold to float across thus, even aided by magic.
They would freeze to death before they could reach the
other shore. In a storm, the cold would be worse. However they crossed, they must stay as dry as they could.

Was there a beast to bear them through the sea as the
horses did upon land? Tristan paged through Blais' bes-
tiaries, in his mind. There were whales and monsters in
all the seas, by the mariners' reports. And there were
perhaps spells to control such beasts. Reynaud might know
one. But mariners tended to exaggerate—

*And if I were a sea-beast, I wouldn't come to this coast
unless I were as dead as the one whose bones you found,*
Thomas said. *There aren't even any gulls here.*

So there weren't. Tristan had not noticed in his preoc-
cupation, but it was so. Minstrel, flitting about him now,
was the only bird in sight. That was another sign of the
coming storm. And he hadn't seen a single fish. The rocks
were bare of mussels. This was not a pleasant strip of
coast. It looked like exactly what it was—a battered,

ravaged edge of land, continually torn by the sea, hostile to all life.

As he was making that discovery, Tristan noticed something else. The landscape was *not* precisely the same as it had been the day before. At the near edge of the ice wall, a pinnacle of ice had broken partly away but failed to fall, as if it were a mightly weapon readied but held in reserve in case they should try to cross in front of the ice again. The morning's flood tide had crept in behind the pinnacle, eating a channel between it and the wall. The waters were lower now, leaving a bridge of slippery ice between the wall and the fledgling iceberg.

Tristan stuffed the rest of the bread he'd been chewing into the front of his jerkin, squinting at the ice bridge. Thomas spotted the look, and mewed apprehensively.

You're not getting curious again, are you? I should think you'd have learned better by now.

Tristan barely heard. Crossing the dirty sand, he started peering at the ice. Before he knew it, he was out among the tumbled blocks and chunks of the bridge.

Snooping, Thomas said, joining him hesitantly.

"Something you can't resist either," Tristan reminded him, but absently.

Close to, the ice was not white at all. The shadowed spots were a deep, incredible blue, bluer than any sky Calandra had ever seen in Tristan's lifetime, shading away sometimes to emerald and peridot green. The effect was most noticeable a few yards ahead, where meltwater had cut what looked like a deep pothole between heaved-up blocks. Huge crystals of hoarfrost rimmed it round. Tristan had never seen such a color, not even in the gems in Darkenkeep or an alchemical fire. It was incredible. He had to get closer. He clambered nearer, steadying himself with one hand against the ice wall.

Come on, be careful! Something might live in there.

That seemed unlikely. The sides of the blue hole were smooth and twisted as if licked out by a dragon's tongue. Nothing living could—

Watch out!

It was too late for that. Tristan trod on a spot where meltwater still flowed over the slick ice, and both his boots shot out from under him at once. He went down hard, banging the back of his head on the ice, saw stars, and felt as if he hadn't stopped falling.

When the lights in his head vanished and the dizzying sensation of motion ceased, Tristan tried to sit up. Everything around and above him was blue—and not the familiar gray-blue of the sky, either. He was rather startled at that, though he wasn't hurt beyond bruises, only surprised. He realized that he must have slid right down the hole after he fell, going the same way as the water which cut it.

"Thomas?" There was a slight echo. Far off, he thought he heard Minstrel give a questioning call.

Hang on. This isn't as easy as you made it look. The cat was creeping down the hole backwards, all his claws out for traction, though Thomas didn't look any too confident of them. In a few seconds he was safely down and jumped to the ice beside Tristan.

Tristan, discovering that he had room to stand, did so. He rubbed at the back of his head, then bit his lip till the pain ebbed.

Someday you're going to listen to me, and I shall expire of shock. I take it you aren't hurt?

Tristan paid the cat no attention. "These colors—it's—I've never seen anything like this." He turned about slowly, taking them in.

How nice. A pocket Darkenkeep. You're not going farther in? Look, it probably drops straight into the sea.

"Just a step."

A step was all it took to get you in here.

"And it's given me a chance to see something I may never see again."

Thomas winced at the soft wonder in Tristan's voice. *Out on that glacier, you'll see all the ice you like—and then a bit. You know, there's nothing to stop this bit breaking off from the rest. And you've already seen the sea. Repeatedly.* Thomas flattened his ears, looking uncomfortable.

The daylight filtered eerily through the ice. Nowhere were the walls thin enough or clear enough to be seen through, yet the light soaked in like milk into bread. Tristan didn't even need to light his crystal to see where he was wandering. The light had a dramatic quality that lured him on, though he knew it was unwise. He was even bold enough to climb, when the jumbled floor made that necessary. The going was slippery, but passable.

The light was brighter ahead, promising and inviting. At his side, Tristan's sword hummed and tingled.

Thomas shivered and mewed more misgivings. The sea could be heard plainly, lapping and chewing at the ice. At least Thomas could hear it. Tristan pressed on, his face rapt with the delight of exploration, squirming unhesitatingly through a narrow spot Thomas could have sworn should have stopped him.

He halted, finally, and Thomas was torn between relief at that and concern over how he might get Tristan to turn back as rapidly as seemed vital. The space here was vast—considering that water alone had hewn it out of the ice. Its wavy ceiling was a good span above Tristan's reach, and it was wide enough that he could not touch both sides of it at once, even stretching. Such a cavity greatly undermined the berg's stability. Thomas twitched his whiskers, calculating stress and ice's inability to stand much of it.

Still, the ice was thinner here. Thomas wondered if there might not be an opening to the outside, relieving them of the awful necessity of retracing their way. He saw none, but he continued to fan his whiskers. He might locate an opening by the air passing through it when a breeze blew.

Tristan was still poking happily about. He'd gone down on one knee and was examining the frost crystals which had formed on the floor. He'd trampled some, but was being careful of the rest. Some of them were dark—not ice crystals then, Thomas realized, but stones carried along by the ice.

The sound of the sea was louder now, as if the tide had turned, but Tristan was still oblivious to it. And he was likely to be so for a while, once he got this caught up in investigating something that had piqued his curiosity.

One teaching of Blais' sticks with you and it has to be this one! There are times for studying, you know. Just as there are also times for getting a healthy distance away from places like this.

"Why do they say cats are so curious, I wonder?" Tristan asked absently. He still retained one other of Blais' earliest teachings, he thought. He could still recognize a stone with magical properties.

Come on, won't you? I'm cold.

Tristan wasn't the least bit cold, though he was shivering with excitement. He picked up one of the pebbles from the floor, cradling it in his palm. Frost crystals filled the hole it had left behind in the ice and grit. He realized then that he could see his breath and that more crystals of frost were falling out of the cloud it made.

Couldn't you play with that outside? The cat would have been warmer if he'd tucked his paws under his fur, but he was too tense to lie down, so Thomas shifted about, keeping his feet off the ice singly as often as he could.

The stone almost looked hewn; its edges were sharp and regular. Yet there was no feel of man about it, so its formation had to be natural, against all appearances. It was a little pyramid of dirty gray, tipped with white. What sort of magic it could be used to make, Tristan didn't know. Maybe Elisena could help him discover it. It was a find, right enough. It had been a long while since he'd felt magic this strong in a stone.

Tristan blinked. His knees were stiff, when he got back to his feet. So was his backside. He must have bruised it when he fell. He turned back to Thomas, still blinking.

"Well, come on. Don't dawdle."

Thomas hissed at him and spun about.

Seawater had begun to trickle across the ice bridge. Tristan stepped over it carefully, carrying Thomas slung over one arm. He slipped once or twice, but gained the shore with all save his feet still dry. He was breathing hard from his scramble up the ice hole, since he'd carried Thomas, too, so he paused to get his wind back and straighten his clothing. His cloak in particular was twisted most uncomfortably, its clasp pressing on his throat.

He hadn't crossed a moment too soon. The bridge was submerging. One bold wave slapped at his right boot. A wind was picking up as the gray clouds came in, whipping the sea this way and that. He'd better get back to camp and find out whether plans had been changed by the weather or merely accelerated.

The pebble, still in his hand, pressed against his palm. Tristan opened his fingers and looked down at the stone. He was struck immediately by the likeness it bore to the nearly severed pinnacle of ice from this angle. The shape was precisely the same, as if the stone were a model or the seed of the berg. The angles of the sides weren't just similar—they were exact matches.

Tristan's thoughts tumbled over each other, eager as leaves before the wind. Gray pebbles and black ones made rainclouds, and rain-clear crystals made light. White stones made snow, all at a wizard's behest, like being compelled by art to respond to like. So why not—

The waves had cut the berg nearly free of the glacier. It groaned and trembled already, eager to go. Tristan knew he ought to head for high ground at once; the spot where he stood would be flooded when all that ice hit the sea, and it was dangerous to remain. Yet remain he did, his fingers sketching a binding in the air above the pebble, wondering if it could—would—hold. He drew the forgotten green glass bead out of his pouch, made passes with it, and put it away once more. Linked to its fellows, it represented the power they had, buried at the interface of sea and land. Tristan performed the delicate juggling act with a skill he never even noticed.

With the spell finished, he held his breath as if not to disturb it. The waves hissed in quietly, as if bound to silence also. The ice did not break up further. It seemed as solid as a pinnacle of rock, steady as the pebble resting on Tristan's flat palm. That could have been an illusion, though, a deadly one. He'd have to test it.

Tristan prodded the stone gently, with a fingertip, and spoke a throat-torturing word. The block of ice quivered, and chips rattled down through the crevices in it. Tristan stepped back hastily, in case the testing had been too much for the fragile hold the berg still had upon the glacier, but once he ceased to touch the pebble, the shaking also ceased. *Had* the binding worked, then?

Tristan's face split into a broad grin. It was just barely possible. And if that was possible then so was much else.

"Thomas, I think I've got that idea I came down here looking for."

Am I supposed to be glad?

Tristan set off briskly to lay his plan before the others—or at least Elisena. The pebble was tucked away safely in his belt pouch, with the strings double-knotted behind it. Thomas stared a moment, then followed, one jump ahead of the tide.

The sky was oppressively dark. Polassar, his bright

clothing especially vivid in the failing light, stood with his head flung back, trying to read weather signs from it. He scarcely needed to peer so; the wind carried a tang of snow, sharp and unmistakable as ammonia. Polassar spotted Tristan the moment he reached the top of the trail leading up from the beach.

"Wizard, I was on my way after you! What do you make of this?" He jerked his chin in the direction of the lowering clouds.

Tristan looked at the sky dutifully, if unnecessarily.

"It's a storm. There were signs of it earlier. Come on. I've got something to talk to you all about."

"We've no time for parley, Wizard." Polassar frowned. "If yon storm catches us on the ice—"

"It will, anyhow," Tristan said, trying to make an end so he could get to Elisena. "Nímir will see to it. We can't outrun a storm on foot. That's what I want to talk about."

His urgency carried weight at last. Polassar paid heed and gave in.

"Ho, mysteries!" He swept out an arm. "Lead on, then, but with all speed."

Elisena had adjusted the straps of the saddlebags so that they could be worn as backpacks. "These will be heavy," she warned Reynaud. "At least till some of the food's eaten. We'll be several days from Am Islin, even after we cross the ice. Afoot, it will take us longer."

"Can we drag a sledge?" Reynaud asked her. "If we can get it across the ice, we could carry much on it. I'll find some wood—"

"Not yet." Tristan said.

Reynaud stopped in his tracks, his cloak flapping about him. "We haven't a moment to waste," he said with asperity. "As it is, I'll barely have it done by the time we need to set off."

"We aren't going over the ice," Tristan said flatly.

Elisena's eyes flicked at him, startled. "That wind won't push the tide out any farther than it did last night, if that's what you're thinking of. We still won't have enough room to ride by."

"Not on the horses, no. I agree we'll have to leave them." Tristan sat down beside Elisena and winced. His seat was still sore; he'd be happy to stop riding. He opened up his pouch, took out the carved wood box inside and held it between both his hands as he spoke. "I don't need to tell you what will happen to us if that storm hits us up there on the glacier. We'd be beyond lucky to get across alive, even in good weather. In one of Nímir's storms, unable to see our fingers in front of our faces, there's no gambler would even give you odds on it. It will be impossible to go over the ice. We can still go around it, though. It will be faster—fast enough, if we use something that will make this storm our partner, even an unwilling one, instead of an enemy. In a ship we could do just that, using the storm's winds."

He opened the box with all of them watching and took out the sharp-sided pebble. He held it up, then pointed at the berg hovering at the shore. "That's our ship."

There was general consternation, most generally from Polassar, who suspected—and suggested—that seawater had rusted Tristan's wits.

"I have a binding spell on it now," Tristan went on, mostly to Elisena, since she was the only one he cared to convince. "I don't say I'll have a great deal of control over it, but it won't leave the shore until I release it. If you can witch the winds just a little while we're out there, it will be enough to push that ice along. It won't need to be much—a thing that big *can't* sink."

"It can, if bindings don't hold over running water," Reynaud said.

"It's over running water *now*, and the binding is holding very nicely," Tristan pointed out. He had no time to waste quarreling with Reynaud over technique and little inclination for it at that moment. "I can release that berg once we're on it and I can beach it when we get across the water. More than that I can't promise, but more than that we won't need."

"Magic doesn't function over running water," Reynaud said sternly. "I doubt you'll have the control you expect. Unfortunately, by the time that's proved to you, it will be too late to try anything else."

"You don't have to come," Tristan pointed out. "You're a free man."

Reynaud smiled. "And one you'll not be so easily rid of. That's rather transparent of you, my lord. I expected more guile. What I begin, I finish. At least this day does not offer ennui."

How nice for us.

"You plan to master that ice with a *rock*?" Polassar queried incredulously, as if the wizardly exchange and Reynaud's capitulation had gone unheard.

"It's just part of the spell," Tristan answered, knowing the big man knew, and preferred to know, nothing of magical procedures. "I found the stone in a hole under the berg. It has power, and like masters like. It—"

"It tastes like a trap," Elisena said. "I don't like it. It turned up too conveniently."

"You won't like that storm any better," Tristan insisted. "We can get across the water before it hits. We can't get across the ice that fast."

"Wizard, none of us be mariners," Polassar protested.

"We don't need to be. That berg is bigger than any ship, and we'll only be passengers. We haven't got much time, even this way. We've got to move fast."

"*A danger, a promise, and a price*," Elisena whispered beside him. "You are trying to bend a tool of Nímir's to your will, and the price for such is high indeed. Even if this is not a deliberate trap, still it is not safe."

Tristan took her hands and felt the rings cool against his fingers. "Neither is the ice, nor this spot, in a storm like that. We have to go on any way we can. If we'd chosen false safety, we wouldn't be here. We'd still be back at Crogen, waiting to die."

"I know." Elisena's eyes glistened, then a tear tracked her cheek. "I know."

They'd been prepared for a hasty departure, and an hourglass could not have poured out half its sands before the camp was broken, but even by then the weather had deteriorated. Whatever means Nímir used to spur his winds, they were effective, and those winds bore the foul weather on their backs.

Tristan finished tying the cords that held his sword securely in its scabbard and looked up at Valadan, who stood pawing at the sand restlessly. The stallion's starshot eyes met his, sharp as a crossbow bolt.

It is not meet that you should face this peril without me, King of Calandra.

Tristan stroked Valadan's neck. "I know. I want you there, but it may not be. This may be your fight, too, but

there's just no way to get you to it." He unfastened the
girths, let Valadan's saddle drop to the sand, and tossed
the blanket beneath after it. Valadan responded by twitching his skin, happy to be free of the harness, even if he
was far from easy in his mind. Just behind his withers,
the hair grew in a circular pattern, a spot the size of
Tristan's palm. Tristan, who knew why that was so, shivered at the tangible reminder of Valadan's struggles with
Nímir's power. He traced the spot shyly with one finger.

"See the other horses safely back to Crogen. And be
ready when I send for you."

The stallion's head dipped in consent. *Shall we then
meet again?*

"I'm not the prophet here. But I hope so—I'd hate to
have to walk all the way back to Crogen." Tristan tried
to smile at the jest he'd made; but with stiff lips and an
aching throat, it was a vain attempt.

Elisena was by his elbow. One of her ringed hands
reached out to rest upon Valadan's forehead. The horse
closed his eyes, happy at her touch. "You are the last of
the Old Magic left to Calandra, Warhorse. Guard it well
for us." Tristan trembled at the grace and the sadness in
her voice.

Again Valadan's head dipped and rose, his mane tossing upon his neck. He reared high, shrilling a challenge
to the storm, to Nímir's winter, and to death. Wheeling
then, he galloped toward the three mares, unsaddled even
as he was. He circled them once, to satisfy himself that
he commanded their attention.

Reynaud, shrugging into his pack, took in the scene.
The black mare stood watching him, her smoke-colored
mane drifting fine as ash about her face. "Ah. No need
to send *you* back to Crogen, I suppose." His left hand
chopped down, twisting as it went in a gesture of dismissal.

A crackle, a pop like a coal bursting in the fire, and
the mare was gone. A wisp of smoke hung in the air,
faintly, and a handful of soot sullied the grass.

Tristan's mouth fell open. A conjuration! All this while,
the man had been riding a conjuration of smoke, and none
of them had suspected, not even when Reynaud lagged
behind to ford streams or made as though he led his mare
through wet spots to spare her, when the mare's eyes

flashed red as coals in excitement, or when she moved without the sound of a hoofbeat, silent as smoke. Tristan was grudgingly impressed and instantly determined not to show it. How Valadan had been likewise fooled, he could not guess. The stallion, snorting now at the soot, offered him no clue, but perhaps there had been greater matters on his mind.

Polassar was first out on the ice, steadying himself with a staff he'd rigged from a driftwood spar and a bronze spearhead. Reynaud handed Elisena across to him next, swinging her over the curling fingers of the sea before Tristan could come close enough to help.

Valadan stood upon the cliff top looking down, watching over their departure. Minstrel sat on Tristan's shoulder, feathers fluffed till he was as big as a fist, and chirped a plaintive farewell to his friend. Tristan touched his soft feathers gently with one finger.

"I wish you'd go back with them, little one."

Minstrel gave a bright chirp and bit his finger. *That* for a wizard's wishes, the gesture said. He lifted one foot, clasped it around Tristan's finger briefly, then followed Elisena with a resolute whir of his wings.

It was Tristan's own turn then. He jumped, instead of waiting for Polassar's guiding hand, slipped, and had to be grabbed by the neck of his cloak. Thomas, inside his sweater, complained loudly.

Save the heroics till you're on your own, if you please!

Tristan dutifully made sure of his footing. He then inspected the ice carefully.

"Get as high up as you can," he instructed. "Keep to this side. The water will break over the far side of the peak when we launch. This side has a better chance of staying dry." The berg sloped upward gently before rearing itself to its highest peak. That slope was still steeper than Tristan liked, but there were plenty of crevices that would offer some shelter and footholds. He was glad of that. They'd need them.

The other bergs had toppled into the water as they broke off, falling and submerging almost totally before they bobbed back to the surface. That must not happen now. *This* berg must float free gently on the waves. Luckily the water was high on the sea side already. Tristan moved cautiously to a point where he could make sure of that. Yes. The tide had turned; already the waves came in far enough.

A lateral ridge of snow cut across the side of the berg, perhaps a third of the way up. Polassar and Reynaud had dug in behind it, and Elisena stood beside them, a little distance away. Minstrel perched on a driftwood log wedged in the ice. The location was not ideal—when the berg was afloat they'd be but a few feet above the waterline—but it was the best hold the berg offered.

Tristan made his way to Elisena. "Ready?"

Her chin came up—better affirmation than a nod.

Tristan took the pebble in his left hand and folded his fingers around it. He didn't need to see it any longer and he didn't want to risk dropping it when the berg moved. He checked his finger position on his right hand, braced his feet, took a deep breath, and made the first pass over his closed fist. He didn't have long to wait for the results. With a shudder, the berg tore free of its tethering ice and dropped into the hungry waves.

It didn't fall far, but the water it splashed up rose above all their heads, even Polassar's. The berg came up, the water fell back. The wind swept some of it over them as spray, but mainly they were untouched. And they floated. That information was transmitted to them instantly as the berg rocked with the first wave it took, wallowing heavily.

They were crossing running water. That reality hit Tristan like an axe blow between the eyes. He went as white as milk and staggered. His knees had turned to jelly, and his eyes were rolling back in his head. It struck him, just for a moment, while he could still think, that Reynaud might have been serious in his objections—and right.

Elisena took one look at his face and cried out in alarm, relinquishing the slight control her rings had been achieving over the wind. Already they had come too far to think of turning back in safety, and the gusts of wind were whipping the waves high. The sea crashed against the berg, driving it farther from the shore and spinning it about so that she could not move to Tristan's side to give him aid. At any instant, they would surely all be hurled into the sea.

Tristan, as the world seemed to close in around him and his senses fail one by one, fought the dizziness with all his strength, against all reason and the laws of wizardry. Half the trouble with running water for a wizard was the fear it engendered—the sense of utter helplessness. Wizards were not used to such. For Tristan, though, with years of failed spells behind him, the sensation was less unfamiliar. He was in acute distress, but his thoughts still ran, if sluggishly.

He could fight back. He wasn't helpless, as he tried to remind himself. The binding he'd laid had held, even over water. If that had worked, other magic presumably could, if only in the most minor way. He could lift his head. He could open his eyes. He could look upon the sea as he had looked upon the Est. He could cross it and he could survive.

Tristan fought the panic in his mind and the sickness in his belly. He fought his worst fear of all, that he was going to be responsible for drowning them all with his mad scheme. He confronted his doubts. *Was* this all a trap, with the others hopelessly enmeshed, thanks to him? He faced it and finally threw the question aside as irrelevant to the moment.

He became aware of the stone in his hand, a stone like that Crogen's throne was cut from, whence came the power of his sword and his right and necessity to be where he was at that moment. Tristan's fingers closed on the pebble till its edges cut into his palm. He found the pain helpful. Gradually, he could breathe again, could see, and could hear. He liked neither the sights nor the sounds that confronted him, but he had them at his command.

The berg was plunging like a terrified horse. It had settled to its level in the water at once, but the waves threatened to swamp it still further. Behind the low ridge of ice, Reynaud and Polassar clung desperately to the ice and to their gear. Elisena could not stand upright and keep her footing—she half crouched, her left hand struggling with the winds, her right ever ready to grab for support. That hampered her weather-witching greatly, and the winds came at them fitfully, from all quarters. They screamed over the berg, mad with delight.

A virtual wall of water broke over the berg, cold and nearly as solid as ice. Tristan, choking, swallowed salt water, slipped, and struggled upright, pulling Elisena back to her feet again.

The movement brought success as well as safety. It

seemed to free his tongue, and Tristan began to drone words that supported the binding-spell. His fingers shaped the appropriate gestures once more without faltering. The berg, quivering, steadied. The next wave took it lower and rocked it less. As Elisena caught the winds again in her net of silver, they began at last to make headway.

It was a heaving, rolling progress, but at least they moved toward the far shore. It looked to be much like the one they'd just left behind, with cliffs rising sheerly from the beach. But might those dark shapes be shoals of rock in the water? That was a hazard Tristan had never considered. He was not master of the berg completely enough to hope to navigate narrow passages. He must be careful about where he brought them to shore and choose a safe spot.

Tristan peered ahead, hindered by snow blowing across the water. Between that and the berg's rise and fall in the waves, he couldn't see clearly, but he soon knew that they dared not make landfall at the closest point past the glacier. They'd have to voyage farther. He shouted as much to Elisena, pointing at the rocks over which the running sea broke.

She agreed with his judgment. Indeed, once past the headland, they might well have an easier passage. Those cliffs would blunt much of the force of the wind, making their eventual landfall easier to accomplish. Their only safe means of dismounting the berg was to run it up upon a broad beach, Elisena thought, and it made good sense to seek such. Her hands moved, the winds shifted, and the berg veered away from the perilous shore.

Reynaud moaned softly to himself. By then the sky was as dark as the sea had been, and the sea was as black as ink. The two steering the berg ignored that, but Reynaud, occupied by nothing more than keeping hold of his senses, could not. He'd already bitten through his lips trying to still sickness and fear, and the metallic taste of his own blood in his mouth made the seasickness worse. He didn't need to see the storm as well.

The leading edge of it was upon them, fierce as a wildcat. Sleet lashed down, and hail fell or was blown upon the wind with lethal force. Polassar tried to get to his feet for a better sight of their progress and was forced to rethink and then retreat from the action when he was nearly pitched headfirst off of the ice. He stabbed the berg fiercely with the tip of his staff.

What was the wizard about now, grabbing at the lady's shoulder and turning her to see something he was pointing at with his other, fisted hand? Polassar strained his eyes through the false night of the storm to catch sight of whatever they'd seen.

At first all he could make out—and that barely—was the darker line of the land above the black water. They were farther out from it than he'd expected, a lot farther out than he felt was safe. They'd been skirting rocks, he knew, but this was deep water they were in now, safe from such. They need not have come out so far.

There, though. Was that a finger of white, poking up at the storm-rent sky—a tower, or a trick of what light there was? Beside him, the other wizard moaned sickly, offering no help at all.

There had been no mistaking it, Tristan thought, though he'd gotten Elisena's confirmation anyway. What he'd seen could be nothing other than Am Islin, on this lonely coast. There were no lights in whatever windows it might boast, but the tower seemed to shine against the darkness all around it. It was far off—days of walking, in this weather. But if he could bring the berg to it . . .

They had come a long way and much faster than Tristan had anticipated or dared to hope. At this point, they could reach the tower almost as swiftly as they could reach the shore. Adjusting his plans hastily, Tristan decided to try for it.

Vast swells lifted them and dropped the berg sickeningly into troughs between the waves. Tristan almost reconsidered, but decided it was too late for second thoughts. He no longer had any bearing on the land, anyway. All that was tall enough to be seen in the heavy sea was the tower. They headed for it, as best they could.

Tristan's knees were aching with the strain of riding the berg, of adapting himself to the continual rise and fall, and of keeping his balance when waves washed over his feet. Sleet raked his face and tried for his eyes. There were voices in the wind, promising his imminent destruction. The magic was as hard to hold to as his footing. The tension was fearful, and he was afraid that soon he'd be unable to control his own hands, when the cold, cramped muscles began to twitch.

Beside him, Elisena looked worn out, sea-soaked, and barely able to stay on her feet. Tristan longed to hold her, but he had no support to give, no strength beyond what held the berg together under the waves' punishment. The most he could do was get her and the rest of them to land as quickly as the waves could hurl their ship. Get them to the tower! His concentration narrowed in on that gratefully.

They almost lost Reynaud on their way in. The man began sliding toward the edge of the ice, making little effort to stop himself, and Polassar was barely able to fling an arm around him in time to stop his going into the black water. Reynaud smiled wan thanks, but he looked likely to repeat the action as soon as he was released. He had scarcely the strength to sit up, and his cold hands could not grip the slick surface of the ice.

Polassar cast about him frantically. He had no hand free to support the man long, not unless the major portion of their gear was to be sacrificed. He did not think the exchange a fair one—howbeit, no one else was free to hold the sorcerer either. Finally he drew his dagger and pinned Reynaud's cloak to the ice with it, shoving the blade hilt-deep into the berg, pegging the man down like a tent. Polassar chuckled.

The measure wouldn't hold Reynaud long, but it would buy a few seconds for a rescue if he started to slip again, probably long enough. And if not, what did it matter? Polassar was beginning to doubt that any of them would set foot on solid land again in this life. Well, so glorious an undertaking deserved so grand a defeat. It was meet. Polassar fingered the ring of brass upon his arm briefly—all the regret he allowed himself—and lifted his face defiantly to the storm.

Lightning had begun to play between the clouds. Now and then a bolt flashed down to strike the sea, revealing waterspouts prowling about them like hunting wolves. Minstrel went to Elisena, daring the one flap of his wings it took to reach her. Thomas poked his head up out of the neck of Tristan's sweater, then ducked back as thunder boomed almost directly above them. His claws shot out reflexively, but Tristan gave no sign of feeling them against his skin.

The tower was nearer. Slender as a needle, it sprang from the waves as if it grew out of the white foam. Perhaps the storm's flood tide had surrounded it and cut it off entirely from the land. Tristan couldn't tell. He was hard put to remember that the night could not have fallen and that the hour was not past sun-high. This deep darkness was only a storm—

Lightning flashed off the black cliffs behind and beside the tower. Tristan had taken the rock for the cloudy sky, in the gloom. Now they were closer than he'd guessed, and a following wind was pushing them in hard. They were close enough that he must give full attention to their course.

Tristan signaled to Elisena to release the winds to slow their speed. With dread like a coldness squeezing his heart, he saw that there were rocks before them still—great ones. A sizable section of the cliff had dropped into the sea once, and the surf broke wildly over its remains. Thunder crashed in Tristan's ears, but not much louder than the sounds of the sea, as waves fell on stone. He couldn't see a single clear spot, and they'd have to make landfall whether he found one or not. They were too far in to turn back.

The sky was torn open as a bolt hit the topmost peak of the berg. Flash and thunder came together, and the peak was gone. Chips of ice flew everywhere, and Polassar shouted something Tristan couldn't make out. The berg hit one of the rocks and rebounded from it, grinding and spinning. Tristan grabbed Elisena as she staggered, shoving her down beside Reynaud. Minstrel tangled his claws in her hair.

"Get down and hold on! I'm taking us in!" He had to scream the words in her ear; he couldn't hear them with his own. Tristan didn't think that the thunder alone had deafened him, for the ravening wind was terribly loud, and the sound of the surf was worse. Another bolt struck the water, quite near. When its light faded, the sea was darker than before, and Tristan could scarcely see.

If there *was* a passage between those rocks, it was neither wide nor safe. Tristan guided the berg toward it as best he could, trusting to the force of the waves behind him to carry them in. He had to keep away from the cliffs, or at least keep the bulk of the berg turned that way as a cushion, lest they all be crushed between ice and rock. A skilled steersman with a responsive boat would have been hard put to do it by day. For a seasick wizard aboard a floating, tossing, rudderless chunk of ice in a storm, the task seemed hopeless.

A wave slammed the berg against rock and held it there. As the surge passed, they slipped free, shoved on by the next wave. It worked. It worked so well indeed that Tristan used the same tactic deliberately twice more, but he found it hard to stay on his feet while he accomplished it. He was thrown to his knees, which hurt as if bones had been smashed. He struggled up with difficulty, only to be knocked down once again. Reynaud flopped helplessly on the ice, limp as a doll. Polassar kept as much of a hold on him as he dared.

Thomas was crying piteously over the share of battering he was getting through no fault of his own. The cat stopped whimpering abruptly, half because it was useless and half because he was briefly too frightened to utter another sound. That silence ended quickly enough.

Look out!

The cliffs rose directly in front of them, not a dozen yards ahead. Even close, their height could not be gauged—they disappeared into the dark of the storm at a point at least three times the height the berg had been before the lightning had blasted its pinnacle away. Tristan's mouth was still dropping with amazement as he swung the berg about desperately. They somehow brushed by, grating hard on rock, then on what he hoped was sand.

They were as close in as they could get. They probably would have to scramble a bit getting off, but it would do, if they went quickly. The berg wasn't firmly grounded, and the sea was tugging at it with ever greater insistence, as if it sensed it was about to be cheated.

Tristan turned to Elisena, helped her to her feet, and held onto her until she was steady. Her face was blank and lifeless, as if she were about to faint. Minstrel hopped onto his shoulder, but Tristan transferred the bird carefully back to a sheltered spot inside Elisena's hood.

"I'm going to try a delayed dismissal," he told her,

hoping she could understand him. He smiled tensely in the dark. "I've been in the water twice in the last day, I don't want to go in again." It was a jest even he couldn't laugh at. "I'll be right behind you. Get ashore now."

He gave her tenderly into Polassar's care. Elisena went unresisting, like a dreamwalker. Then, at the last moment, she turned back, her lips parting. Tristan didn't see, and Polassar pulled her on, urgently. There was need for haste.

Polassar had his hands full, literally. There was all the gear to be managed, and Reynaud showed no sign of being able to stand unsupported. Elisena helped with the wizard, while Polassar shifted the rest. Tristan watched the slow-seeming process of disembarking, striving to hold his binding just a bit longer. The storm worsened, the waves were higher, and bits of the berg were falling into them and being dashed into smaller bits upon the rocks. Tristan held on, remembering nothing but the need for that.

A blackness was descending on his mind, overlaying all like a veil of sable silk. Tristan could no longer see, so he shut his aching eyes wearily, concentrating other senses to take their place. They seemed to be sharper than he remembered. He could feel every ridge and crevice upon the pebble in his hand. He could even discern a change in texture between the white crown of it and the darker bottom and tell one from the other as easily as if he could see the stone. His hearing was acute once more; the waves made a perceivably different sound upon the berg than upon the rocks. He could anticipate the rocking of the ice under their onslaught and maintain his footing, more or less.

The berg must hold steady for just a bit more while he left it. The others would be clear now, surely. There had been time enough. Tristan wished he'd thought to count heartbeats, but he was sure he'd allowed them the time they needed. He opened his eyes.

The berg had shifted and was drifting now. He'd waited too long. Two yards of swirling water lay between him and the shore. That was unfortunate. He'd have to jump for it, and the gap widened each instant. Tristan made the passes for the dismissal as rapidly as his numb fingers could manage. He suspected that the berg wouldn't last one heartbeat after his feet left it. That was fine. It wouldn't have to.

The gap was wider still, and the sea was running fast between the cliffs of rock and the cliff of ice. Tristan ordered himself to jump, but he might as well have tried to fly. He couldn't move. He had, never realizing it until then, bound himself to the iceberg as thoroughly as he had bound the berg to his will, and he was trapped by that, wavering on the edge and unable to leave the ice, even as it broke up around him. The binding was dissolving by stages as he'd meant it to, but he hadn't expected that it would bind him, too! It would not let him go—not in time. He saw his mistake and the steps he could have taken to prevent it, but again too late.

The waves pounded the berg against the cliff once more, but Tristan still could not release it. He fingered the pebble in his hand vainly. He was so cold that he couldn't feel its edges digging into his already wounded hand. The berg rocked. He fell, sliding across the ice, and went down twice more before he got to his feet again and staggered back to the berg's edge.

Broken-off bits of berg choked the water. He was too far off to jump, Tristan saw, even if he'd been able to try. The ice shuddered beneath his boots as it grated against a shoal. It sounded as if the rock had cut deep that time. It wouldn't be long then, Tristan thought. He tried to remember which way the shore lay, so he could strike out for it when he was thrown into the water. The binding would surely release him then. He couldn't see anything in the blackness all around to give him the least clue.

He doubted it would have been much use, anyway. Probably he'd never even surface. Wizards didn't risk drowning and escape more than twice. He'd long since used up all his luck, plus a lot more that was probably due to someone else.

All in all, it was a stupid, futile way to die, but by then Tristan barely cared. He was soaking wet, and the wind was loud and cold.

Tristan dimly heard shouting and made out his own name, but the berg pitched, and he was too dizzy to answer. A backlash of fear and pain hit him. Why try to hold on and stay on his feet to the end? It was impossible, anyway. It was easier to let go. The ice tilted under him obligingly.

He felt himself going, slipping away at last as the pointed pebble slid from his bleeding fingers into the tossing sea.

Ambere's Welcome

POLASSAR'S LONG DIVE CUT THROUGH THE FIRST rushing wave before Elisena's frightened scream could possibly have reached him, so he must have been as watchful as she was. By that sign only did Elisena know of his alertness—the whole of her world had been totally centered on Tristan's white face as he wavered and swayed and finally crumpled, dropping like a storm-torn leaf among the remains of the foundering berg, to vanish from her sight. Elisena paid no heed to Reynaud, sprawling on the sand beside her, or to the waves that plucked at him and at her own legs. Her mind emptied as the sea had.

She saw Polassar's head once as the waves momentarily dissolved to quiet foam and saw the heavy helm that he had not bothered to remove gleaming in answer to the lightning that still played. Then even that disappeared, and the sea was again an empty expanse of darkest gray, broken only by whitecaps and ice.

Tears blinded her. The wind snickered in her ear, mocking her grief, mimicking the farewells that fate had cheated her of offering. The wind might well have frozen her heart within her, but Elisena would scarcely have noticed that change. She had no time to know grief or recognize loss. The sand around her ran with so much water that it hardly seemed solid land, and she thought her reeling senses would never answer to her commands again. She was not recovered enough to remember safety. She stared at the sea with aching eyes, forgetting even why she did.

She clasped her hands together to stop her fingers shak-

ing and swallowed down the sickness in her mouth. Her
ten rings meshed tight together, bruising her fingers and
prodding her with memory of their purpose.

Could she snatch control of the winds back again, having relinquished what little she'd gained? She must; the
waves must not be whipped any higher than they already
were, not if Polassar were to find what he sought, or ever
to regain the shore again. Elisena's fingers wove, and her
lips spoke commands.

The wind shrieked disdain and did as it pleased. Elisena
wept with despair, but did not cease her effort, though
salt tears mingled with the cold sea spray on her cheeks.

Reynaud staggered to his feet beside her, confused and
surprised to see her rings glowing upon her hands. He
too turned to look at the sea, his head ringing with the
wash of spells.

The globe of light might prove a beacon in the darkness,
if a man did not drown before he saw it. Elisena's lips
were moving with the spell, but all she heard was the
whirl in her mind, over and over to the point of madness:
He won't find him. He won't find him. He won't find him.
The darkness around her deepened, and she knew what
that meant. *Too late, too late*, her thoughts whispered.
Or was that the gossip of the winds?

Someone tugged at her shoulder—frantically, when she
dazedly ignored him. Reynaud was pointing at the sea
wildly. Reluctantly, Elisena let herself be turned and
blinked her eyes free of tears.

Polassar had surfaced and was making his way shore-
ward, struggling to stand before the water was quite shallow enough to let him, losing and finding his footing.
There was something dark in the water beside him, being
dragged in with what seemed to be great care.

Elisena was knee-deep in the boiling surf by the time
Polassar finally reached water shallow enough to stand
easily. Her soaked mantle dragged at her unbearably, so
that she would have cast it away, had that not meant the
loss of a precious instant. She fought her way through
the wavelets and soft sand to Polassar's side and there
dropped or was thrown to her knees, as he laid Tristan
down. She gave Polassar no chance to drag him farther
ashore, though he was barely out of the grip of the waves.
Cradling his face in her silvery fingers, Elisena called to

Tristan desperately, some entreatment too muffled for Reynaud to catch as he struggled close. There was no response. The surge of the sea shifted them all a little, Tristan most of all, since he did not fight it. Elisena clutched him to her, then sat back with a despairing moan.

"Lady, he's not—" Reynaud knelt hastily and touched Tristan's throat and his chest. He looked up, surprised, his concern switching from Tristan to Elisena.

"It's faint, but his heart's still beating," he said. Then he added, as if she might not have understood, "He's alive."

"Not for long. He's gone too far, I can't reach him—" Elisena bit her lip, fighting for calm, thrusting back the dark that panicked her. Her hair and clothes streamed water, and her lashes were beaded with rain and tears. The sea and sand around her were as cold as Darkenkeep—cold as the prophecy she'd made, and as empty—but she must find the strength to ignore that.

"A price," she whispered, then lifted her head and voice to Polassar. "Now we shall learn if Royston Ambere will help us or no. And if he will not—"

Polassar bent over Tristan, lifting him out of her arms. "I think he'll be right enough, once we get him out of this weather, Lady." A few steps brought them all to drier sand. "Likely he struck his head—there are rocks enough out there just under the surf to build a wall from here to Radak! Plague take 'em, I'm bruised black myself." He rubbed at his left shoulder as he knelt down with Tristan.

"It's more than a bump on the head." Elisena's fingers probed and quickly found a lump hidden under Tristan's hair, but the bone beneath was whole; the injury was not serious or severe enough to have caused his condition. Even a cracked skull would hardly have caused the sea spray to freeze so quickly on Tristan's white face.

"Well, and he's surely swallowed half the sea," Polassar insisted. "He'd gone under by the time I got to him. Didn't swim a stroke, fool that he is." He rolled Tristan carefully over and slapped him twice, hard, across the back. He was rewarded by a feeble cough and a trickle of water out the corner of Tristan's mouth. Not satisfied, Polassar repeated the treatment.

Tristan's chest heaved convulsively, and Polassar started to lift him to sit up, smiling with relief. The smile slid away into an incredulous stare as Thomas wriggled free of Tristan's soaked clothing and staggered onto the sand.

"If yon cat didn't drown, the Wizard won't have either, surely? No matter what he's swallowed..." Polassar's brows knotted as he watched Thomas wobble about. Tristan still slumped against his chest, breathing shallowly, but unresponsive to further attempts at reviving him. "What ails him, then? 'Tis more than a fainting fit."

"It's not the water." Tristan had, Elisena suspected, been unconscious before ever he got among the rocks or into the water, thrown right out of his senses by the power he'd called down. He was burned out like a candlewick. The same thing had happened when he fought Darkenkeep's dragon, only now he was schooled by the earlier practice. He'd thus held on far longer and been hurt far worse. Elisena's fingers brushed Tristan's cold cheek with a tenderness he couldn't feel. He must have know what he'd risked. It could hardly have escaped his notice. He'd known and done it anyway. Fool indeed!

Polassar was softly cursing wizards who would not learn to swim, nor have sense enough to jump clear of sinking ships. Elisena shook her head, aware that her calm was paid for in wasted moments.

"It wouldn't have mattered, I tell you. Come. We'll seek shelter in the tower."

"We can carry him on our cloaks," Reynaud suggested, reaching to unfasten his.

"Nay, 'tis faster that I take him so. He's not much of a load, for all he's tall." Polassar lifted Tristan easily in his arms. True enough, Tristan didn't look to be much of a weight with his head drooping against Polassar's chest. Water began to drip from his boots. "Lead on, Lady."

They crossed the sand. The storm winds assailed them once again when they were within paces of the tower's base, fierce as starvling wolves. As they shouted for entrance, hail the size of cat's eyes pelted them, and they could not make themselves heard over the thunder which rolled ceaselessly. Lightning made the curving walls of the tower leap into view before them like a conjuration endlessly repeated.

Yet the lightning showed them no door. Elisena made out one small window, unshuttered and quite high up, but it was dark, and there seemed to be no other, lower openings. The tower's white walls were as featureless as the cliffs behind them. Polassar searched furiously, beginning to growl low in his throat.

"Here, take him." He shoved Tristan into Reynaud's arms; together they laid him on the ground as gently as was possible. Such care hardly seemed needful—it was plain that Tristan felt nothing of what was done to him. Thomas mewed dolefully and huddled against him.

Elisena knelt down and spread her mantle over them both to keep the storm out. There was a loud rasp of steel as Polassar drew his longsword. Reynaud said something in a questioning tone. He had been searching for a word of opening, but had given up. The lightning and his continued weakness made the pages of his spell-book waver unreadably, and memory did not suffice.

"I've done with words, sorcerer," Polassar stated angrily. "There's a door here, though the tower's master hides it from us. I'll make him open or I'll hew his tower down!"

"Through solid stone?" Reynaud asked acidly, not too ill for temper.

"If there's one thing I've learned from truckling with your kind, it's that a man's eyes aren't to be trusted where you're concerned, sorcerer. My arm I trust. And do I mistake, or does not iron break your magic?"

"Not as you think—" Reynaud cried out, and ducked frantically as Polassar's first two-handed blow swept over his head without warning and sent a shower of stone chips over both of them. "Have a care with that, you great fool! At least let me *find* the door, and show you what spot to strike—"

Unnoticed, Minstrel flapped his wet wings and flew toward the high window. The wind beat at him, trying to turn him from his course, and the window was a long way above, but he persisted.

Polassar, ignoring Reynaud's increasingly angry protests, continued to chop at the wall, choosing a different spot for his attack each time. His blade was acquiring notches, a fact which he also ignored.

In the midst of his hacking, the stones of the tower suddenly vanished in front of him. A tall, narrow door replaced them, its panels crafted of weather-bleached driftwood closely bound together, framed with an arch made from the great ribs of a whale. The portal swung open, and Polassar's long blade clove the dirt at his feet in place of the wood. Yellow light seeped out of the portal and puddled about him while he struggled to free his sword from the ground.

"Importunate man, put up your weapon before you break it. Am Islin is not open to brigands. There is no treasure here for you to seek. Begone." It was only a voice out of the light.

"We seek naught but shelter, porter." Polassar rammed his sword home into its sheath with a great clash of metal, content that he'd made the door open. He flung an arm toward the spot where Elisena huddled over Tristan. "I have a man dying there. He must be got out of the storm."

"No." the voice said, cooly. The door began to close.

Polassar shoved his shoulder in, blocking the door open. "Is it your custom to turn pilgrims from your master's door, fellow? You'll think twice before you—"

Polassar leaped back, nearly falling, with an astonishing squawk of alarm. The portal flung wide open before a tall man who held a blazing lantern high. A sea-eagle perched upon his right shoulder, its wings still flapping.

Something white and blue fluttered wildly through the door and into the lantern light, chirping furiously. Minstrel alighted upon the strange man's right shoulder, glaring across at the osprey, and chirped several more times, jerking his tail up and down for emphasis.

Elisena laid her mantle over Tristan; she straightened and walked, clad only in shirt and breeches, toward the man and the birds.

"My lord Ambere."

"Greetings, Lady. I noted your approach from afar. I did not think you would be such a fool as to come here." The osprey's eyes burned upon her. Elisena lifted her chin.

"Need cancels folly. We beg shelter of you."

"So said this little one." Ambere offered a finger to Minstrel, who warily forbore to perch upon it. Black as drops of obsidian, the bird's eyes glittered. Ambere chuckled. "For his sake, then, I bid you welcome. Enter."

Ambere stepped back, still holding the lantern high, to let them pass through the doorway. The osprey folded its wings, but its yellow eyes continued to cast maledictions upon them. Polassar lifted Tristan up once more and passed carefully by the bird.

Inside the tower, the lantern light seemed to reach no farther than it had outside, where there was a storm to swallow it. Above their heads, it touched no ceiling, but only failed against a velvety blackness. Ambere was better lighted by the lantern, so brightly that the man was encased in a nimbus of light, and no details could be discerned of his white garments. Behind him, and all about them, that light picked up the glitter of eyes, and there came a vast, soft stirring of wings and a rustling of feathers.

Polassar stared. The tower's walls were covered with rank upon rank of nesting birds, so far as he could see, as high up as the light reached—and beyond it, too, he suspected. Niches and ledges ringed the walls. Every space upon them was filled, and every bird was wakeful, each revealed as its eyes opened and took the light. Every one of them was watching him in a most unfriendly fashion.

There were gulls of all kinds, and ducks—eiders and scoters and royal golden-eyes, crouching on their nests. Petrels, terns, great fulmars and cormorants with beaks like dark daggers lurked above them. There were wading birds, divers, ungainly auks, and comical puffins—whose looks were not such a joke at present, judged by the hating expression their eyes shared with the tower's other inhabitants.

Higher than the sea birds were the hawks, merlins, and falcons, the raptors of all descriptions, the fierce, deadly birds of prey. Outside, they would have been feared by the lesser birds they normally preyed upon, but something within the tower bound all the birds to a higher law, a common cause. Small wonder the company had seen no gulls or shore birds during the last day of their traveling. Every bird in the world must have sought shelter at Am Islin, under Ambere's command and peace.

Polassar was loath to set his charge down and to let the wizard lie helpless in the midst of so many hostile creatures, but Elisena silently directed so, and he obeyed. The floor was stone, smooth but cold. Polassar hesitated again, but could think of no remedy for it. He wished he could see some sign that Tristan was still breathing. The

wizard was as still as death and had been freezing cold
ever since he'd been pulled from the water. The cat, who'd
been skulking in the shadow of the lady's boots, crept to
his master and wormed in by his side. The beast was
properly terrified, but faithful.

Elisena gathered her wits and marshaled her words.
She would rather that this first, crucial encounter with
Royston Ambere had come at some less desperate moment,
when they were not all of them exhausted and half-
drowned. Then she could concern herself only with the
words she must say and not speak hurriedly, forgetting
proprieties in her haste, flogged on by the knowledge that
Tristan's life hung in a balance that was rapidly tipping
against him.

Ambere was waiting for her to speak. Elisena looked
at him long, trying to gauge the man beneath the legend
he had become. He was tall enough to have been a hero
in his younger days, if indeed he had not somehow been
birthed at his present, indeterminate age. Ambere's bearing was as stately as any king's, but his face was unread-
able, as alien as the osprey's beside it. Where the bird's
eyes were golden, Ambere's were blue, a blue as cold as
the winter sea.

Elisena wet her lips, tasting the salt of the sea and of
her tears, and began.

"My lord Ambere, we are not chance-come to your
doorstep. We have journeyed long and far to have speech
with you and to ask of you advice and aid in matters of
great import to Calandra and to you." She paused. There
was no least flicker of human interest in Ambere's eyes
nor any encouragement. Elisena refused to falter.

"You know me, it would seem, though we have not
met before this day. Permit me to make known to you the
others of our fellowship. This is Reynaud of Kôvelir.
Polassar of Lassair. And Tristan of Calandra, who has
been most grievously hurt in coming here. My lord, I must
beg your leave to tend him now and your indulgence that
we may talk at another time, when he is out of danger."

Somewhere above, a bird screamed accusingly.
Ambere's eyes narrowed, and their color shifted from blue
to green. Otherwise, his expression never altered, but it
was as if a chill wind wound its way through the room,
brushing them all.

"It was he who grounded that berg almost upon my kittiwakes' nesting cliff? Another ten yards and thousands of them would have been slain!"

Elisena's eyes went wide with shock at the rage in his voice, and her rings flamed upon her hands by reflex. The osprey screamed and beat its wings, but by then she had mastered her emotion and was able to speak calmly and placatingly.

"Magister, we didn't know about the birds. And we were storm-tossed, helpless. We landed where we might."

"You came here of your own will and desire," Ambere answered icily. "There was help for that. A journey's intent is complete in its beginning."

Elisena's humility dropped away from her like a soggy cloak, and her chin came up again.

"I will not argue philosophy with you while Tristan dies! I am not responsible for your kittiwakes' choice of a nesting site, nor for the place Nímir's storm chose to throw us. I *am* responsible for this man's life and I will not bandy words with you while it slips away. Give us help, or let us be to help ourselves!"

"Ah." Ambere's eyes flicked at Tristan, lying limp upon the stone floor, a puddle of water growing steadily about him. The look held little sympathy. "Let him go, Lady. He's dead already."

"No," Elisena said, so calm that she had no need to confirm her words, and made no attempt to. "Not quite, nor will he die. Not if I am granted what little I ask—a warm place to lay him down and a fire to heat my medicines. Surely you can allow me that."

Minstrel had been darting to and fro, in great agitation, throughout their speech. He had sought a perching place and found none that was not filled by a strange, hostile bird. He dove down, finally, and settled himself like a hen upon a nest, in the hollow of Tristan's throat. He fluffed his feathers and spread his wings to shed more warmth onto his master. From under his still-soaked head feathers, his black eyes glared reproach at Ambere.

Ambere traded stares with the canary, stroking his beard with one strong hand. "Oh, very well. For your sake again, then, little one, or I suppose you will take his chill and die with him. Come. There is a chamber, and a fire . . ."

The chamber held precisely what Elisena had asked—

a hearth and a bed, the latter set into the wall and curtained against dangerous drafts. The bed was already filled with soft furs of all sorts, but two snow white owls brought more pelts as Elisena watched, entering upon their soundless wings. The room did not look to be hastily prepared. Reynaud raised his brows at it and what it meant.

Polassar stripped Tristan's salt-soaked, ruined clothing from him and laid him naked among the furs, so that he might take their warmth the sooner. He kept one wary eye upon the owls as he performed the task, narrowly avoiding collisions, more through the owls' watchfulness than his own, however.

Well, the waves and rocks had done a fair job of battering the wizard, that was sure. There were dark bruises everywhere on him, and some cuts. Polassar was careful of the hurts as he stripped him—not that the wizard seemed to notice the consideration. He lay so still! Polassar looked doubtfully at Elisena.

"You should go and rest now," she said dully, tucking furs close in at Tristan's sides, her hands moving automatically though precisely. Tristan was at the center of a small mountain of pelts by then, propped nearly to a sitting position for the easier administering of medicines. Polassar reluctantly yielded his place to Reynaud, who'd filled a brass warming pan with coals.

"Yes, that's good." Elisena put the pan by Tristan's feet, careful that it did not touch him. There was no fear he'd accidentally roll against it, she thought sickly. The enormity of the fight she faced staggered her, and she closed her eyes. Her boldness before Ambere had been as false as Minstrel's and left her as quickly.

Reynaud lifted a few of the furs back, and his fingers began to probe deftly, gently. "I think Polassar was right. He *has* been hit on the head, more than once by the feel of it." His fingers moved on as he spoke, flexing Tristan's arms, feeling his legs. "At least he's broken no bones, unless those ribs are cracked as well as bruised. Most of this is superficial, easily dealt with."

He became busy for the next few minutes with salve, bandages, and words of healing. Elisena barely attended to him. She was no longer concerned with physical injuries.

She reached out through the dark again, trying to find

some trace of the path Tristan had taken. How could he have strayed so far so quickly? She was unable to touch him at all, search wildly as she might, careless of losing herself in a dark tangle worse than any forest. He simply had too long a start, since the berg had foundered, as she had known the moment Polassar dragged him from the water.

"There, that's done. A few cuts and some scrapes. His clothes took a real beating, but they saved his skin, mostly. No reason he shouldn't start coming around now," Reynaud added reassuringly.

Elisena opened her eyes, and Reynaud stopped in midsentence, shocked at the expression he saw in them. Her face was nearly as white as Tristan's as she lifted his head to slip a poultice of healing herbs beneath it. After a minute of weighing other encouraging words he doubted she'd hear, Reynaud slipped back between the bed curtains and went to stir up the fire.

Polassar had thrown a quantity of wood on it, probably more than was needed, and already the chamber was warming. Reynaud found a bronze cauldron by the door, full of water. He was too weary to lift it, with arms or with a spell. Polassar was an obviously slumbering heap under his still-soggy cloak, drugged by exhaustion and beyond hearing requests for aid, but that didn't greatly matter. Reynaud began to drag the pot. He'd strength enough for that.

Once he got to the fire, he intended one trifling bit of magic, also just within his capabilities at the moment. A neat little gesture which, if its range was strictly limited, was at least economical. With it, he could waft the weighty cauldron onto the firecrane and thence over the flames. He hadn't counted on surprising Thomas, though. The cat was turned broadside to the fire, close enough to scorch his fur, baking himself almost among the ashes.

Reynaud tried unsuccessfully to nudge him out of the way with one toe, while he still heaved at getting the cauldron the last foot or so that he needed to move it. Water slopped out onto the floor and over his legs.

"*Please*—" Reynaud suggested, the irritation in his tone negating the politeness of the word.

Thomas hissed at him in vexation, then sprang from the hearth to the bed in two long bounds. Truth to tell,

Reynaud had made him move none too soon. Panting, the cat pressed his superheated fur close to Tristan, ignoring his own discomfort and wish for cool air. He'd been a trifle too close to the fire, perhaps; his sense of that had increased steadily over those last few uncomfortable minutes. He seemed to be cooling off rapidly, though, even among the other furs stuffing the bed space. In spite of them, the warming pan, and his own heroic efforts, there seemed to be no warmth to Tristan at all.

By the flicker of the flames licking the pot, Reynaud set out medicines, both Elisena's and those he had brought for his own use. Behind the curtains, Elisena felt carefully at Tristan's side, deciding that, even if a few of his ribs were staved in, it didn't matter much so long as he stayed still. She could bind them later. Probably Reynaud was right, and the bones were only bruised anyway. None of Tristan's hurts were so serious as they had looked at first glance—his pallor made the least bruise stand out as sharply as if it had been painted with ink. If he were suffering from the near-drowning and the wave-pounding alone, he would indeed wake very soon, as Reynaud had predicted; but Elisena did not expect him to, and she was not surprised that Tristan's condition did not change, even after many minutes in the warmth of bed and room. His less visible hurts were as deep as she'd feared, maybe deeper than her healing could reach.

Reynaud was back, this time with a selection of herbs. "There's water boiling. Show me what you want brewed, then you needn't leave him."

His concern would have surprised Tristan very much indeed, Elisena thought. It rather surprised her. She touched a bag, sniffed to be sure what it held, then fingered a pot of finely ground leaves. "This. And these. Three parts of the first, two of the others. And some shepherd's purse, if you have any, in case there's bleeding around those ribs."

"I have a bloodstone."

"I'd rather the herb. Bring the brew as soon as you can, but it should steep at least a quarter-hour." He would know that, of course.

"The Arts Magical ought more properly to be called the Arts Perilous," Reynaud said soberly. "Do you think he knew what he was risking?"

Elisena looked down at Tristan's still face before she answered, and then her voice came only as a whisper. "I'm certain he did."

Presently Reynaud brought a steaming cup and a horn spoon. The quarter-hour had passed swiftly. Elisena tasted the brew, nodded approvingly, and sent Reynaud back to the fire's warmth.

He went without protest. The man looked sick with exhaustion, a greenish tinge underlying the white of the skin that showed above his neat, dark beard. Their voyage had been hard on Reynaud, without mistake. He'd gathered his strength remarkably, but it was a borrowed vigor, and he looked as if his legs wouldn't hold him up much longer. At least he could sit, tending the fire. And the man was probably skilled enough to brew medicines in his sleep, if she asked him to.

Those medicines might have been of more use, Elisena reflected, if her patient had been well enough to swallow them, but in that case they'd scarcely have been so desperately needed. She fed the herb tea and other, stronger potions to Tristan drop by drop, using a feather Minstrel obligingly shed for her, but nothing she tried produced even a slight change. Tristan's face remained as pale and cold as candle wax, and his fingers were still chilly to her touch, despite the warm furs about them. His breathing was so shallow that Elisena was often uncertain of it and anxiously put her ear to his lips, not once but many times. She cleaned his face with warm water and replenished the coals in the warming pan. Thomas made two more trips to the fire and came back weaving on his paws the last time dizzy with heat that worked no change on Tristan.

Reynaud dozed beside the cauldron, refusing to ask Polassar to spell him at the task. It didn't matter, Elisena thought. Tisanes and simples had failed, as she had expected them to do, and there was no need for Reynaud to brew more of them. She kept her vigil alone, dazedly waiting for it to turn into a deathwatch.

Weary as he was, Reynaud slept the light sleep of the healer on call. Some noise, or mayhap only the sense of time passing, waked him; then he was at her side once again. Elisena lifted her head. There was no more help

Reynaud could give her, and she ought to send him off
to rest as best he could. She turned to tell him so.

"He's dying, woman." It was not Reynaud, but Ambere,
with one of the white owls on his shoulder. "He's driven
his spirit right out of his body, and it's afraid to come
back. Considering the cause that brought you here, I do
not marvel at that. It would be a mercy to let him go."

"If you believe that, why are you here?" Elisena asked
dully, not expecting an answer. There was little Ambere
could accuse her of that would add to her torment. There
was nothing he could give her that she must beg for politely.
There was no need for speech at all, and it only distracted
her from the watch she was keeping.

Of necessity, she was good at waiting, but when this
black night was over, there would be little left to require
her skill again, Elisena knew. She thought of broken plans
and blighted hopes crueler than any she had known before,
and shivered to number the decisions she must make come
morning, not doubting that she would make them. No
catastrophe had ever lifted the burden she had been chosen to bear or rendered her rings quite useless enough to
let her give up her quest. If they lost Tristan, they lost
his sword as well and its power that they so desperately
required, but they did not lose the job they'd set out to
do.

"Oh, yes, you are strong, Lady. But at what cost came
that strength? Did you deny yourself all human feeling,
armoring yourself until now you do not notice its lack,
or recognize its finding?"

Elisena lifted her head sharply and wished that she had
not, for the movement locked her eyes with Ambere's,
and she could not break that binding quickly enough to
protect herself. She had never beheld a green so cold and
so impersonal as that in Ambere's eyes. If she could not
break his gaze, those eyes would strip her skin away until
the shameful emptiness within was revealed to Ambere's
eyes and to her own, in a mirror she could not avoid.

It's not true! she pleaded, and tasted the lie in her
mind, bitter past bearing. *How could I live, if such a thing
were so?*

When Ambere released her, she slumped brokenly.
After a few moments, she realized that she was staring
at her hands. The rings on them seemed as binding as

steel, yet as insubstantial as cobwebs—most paradoxical. What use was the strength to bear Tristan's dying, if she had not the strength to risk keeping him alive? Her ears rang, and her heart pounded.

"So," Ambere said, his voice deep as sleep. "There is hope yet, if you can still recognize a strength as a weakness. That is well and more than I expected. Hoard that strength a little longer, woman. You will need it a while yet."

Ambere smiled as Elisena sought to meet, then flinched from, his eyes. "Recollect the power of the sword he carries. Cold iron may poison wizard folk, but some poisons make excellent remedies, if administered with skill. That sword could save him..."

Elisena again lifted her face quickly, hope flaring, a question or a thousand of them on her dry lips, but the man had gone as silently as one of his owls or as a dream. The chamber door was shut firmly, and the room was empty, save for the two men sleeping by the hearth and the piles of wet gear tumbled about.

The sense of dream was so strong that Elisena wondered if she had slept as well, and she looked hastily at Tristan, dreading what she might see after such a lapse, but his condition was unchanged.

Ambere's parting words chased about in her head like mice. How did one magick a sword into a medicine? It was a royal sword and enchanted, no common blade at all, yet still it was only dead metal and, as Ambere had admitted, a deadly metal as well. Was there a magical paradox there, a principle that what would kill a healthy man would save one dying?

She was not even sure where to find the blade and grudged the time a search would take. For all she knew, their weapons might be in the outer hall, left behind or carried there by the owls. They had all of them been distracted, throwing their gear down wherever it happened to fall. Yet Ambere would surely not have offered a remedy which was not ready to hand. Elisena slipped from the bed.

She found the sword in the first place she sought it. Polassar had propped it in a corner, beside the rest of the wreckage of Tristan's gear. There were white crusts of salt on the drying leather of the scabbard, and the blade was dull when she drew it out, filmed with seawater. It balanced easily in her hand, but seemed as lifeless as its master.

Was *that* some sort of key? There would seem to be little that dead metal could do for Tristan. Elisena's mind felt as dim as the sword. What could Ambere have meant for her to do with it? What power the sword possessed, it had only in Tristan's hands, since his crowning. Perhaps if she put it by him, something might be done, but Elisena was expecting no miracles.

She carried the sword back to the bed, anyway, and sat with it across her knees. She stared at the cool blade, wondering.

A sword was a weapon, taken up and used for defense; and such this sword was, Calandra's last defense. But hers was not the hand it was meant for, and it was not the weapon that had been laid out for her use. She bore the rings, and they filled her hands.

She did not think she wanted a weapon—certainly not one which was not hers to use, and therefore she could not take it up and follow Tristan through the dark forest he had entangled himself in. He had gone too far to be followed, in any case. She had known that from the first. Pursuit might only frighten him farther off; in the darkness, he might not recognize her and might misunderstand.

She dared not follow him, but there was still a chance that Tristan might return if he could find his way back. He had left the sword behind, the weapon bonded to him closer than bone. It would draw him, or could be made to.

It might work. Elisena sensed that Tristan was wandering still, lost and confused and far yet from any final destination. If he'd kept on at his early pace with any determination, he'd have gone too far from the light long since—gone so deep into the shadows that nothing could ever reach him. And if he had done so, he would no longer be breathing, even so faintly as he was. She fingered the barely palpable pulse at Tristan's throat, and it was some time before one of his heartbeats answered Elisena's own.

Now, as to form . . . Elisena looked at the sword again, considering. Not a voice, certainly not the ring of steel. Tristan would not answer to the sound of battle. He was frightened already. Scent and touch were powerful senses, able to command much, but neither could reach far enough. It must be sight, then, the longest sense and the best choice of any.

And in the dark, what could be better than light, a light to help Tristan see his way home, a light such as Blais would once have left for him, when some errand kept him out late, past sun-fall? A light desperately needed now, when Tristan wandered in a deeper, darker night, beyond reach of moon or stars.

The small candle Elisena lit flickered and wavered in otherwise imperceptible drafts, so she drew the bed curtains shut to keep the air out. She set the taper carefully at the head of the bed, in the tiny niche she found there. Already the warm-honey scent of it filled the small, enclosed space. The light the candle gave was equally warm and comforting, but was not quite yet the light she required.

The tiny flame was vital to her purpose. A larger blaze would terrify, not lure with a promise of home and safety, and would speak of burning rather than warmth. One single candle shone brighter in the night than dozens of lamps filled with perfumed oil. Elisena's task now was to make that small flame burn brighter, purer still, so that its guiding, welcoming light might be seen from the greatest distance.

Once her rings would have been bright enough, their fair and steady light all the direction Tristan would have needed. Now their light did not reach him. She had tried them, despite her exhaustion after the fearful sea passage, and did not reckon mere weariness to be the cause of her failure than. The rings' power was simply not great enough. The darkness between was too thick, and Tristan's back seemed to be turned to her.

She lifted the sword slowly, turning the blade so that it caught the candle's flame, mirroring it, as might any sword, and with as little effect. Elisena looked at the candle, to let her eyes reflect it as well, and knew that she was failing once more.

Even tripled, the light was a mere gleam in the night, not reaching past the thick curtains about the bed where Tristan lay. The light she needed would not kindle. Loving Tristan, wanting him with her, was not enough. Or did

she not want it enough? Elisena's spirit writhed, as
Ambere's vision was proved to her.

Nímir had destroyed with precision each thing she had
cared for. The lesson had sunk in early and put down deep
roots. If she did not heed it now, she would know once
more a pain she had learned not to feel, had sworn never
to feel again, and spent lives learning to avoid. *A mercy
to let him go*, Ambere had said, and she knew he was
right. Kinder, it would be, and easier, too. Easier than
what she had just been trying to do, until she had remembered herself.

Why then the tears, falling onto her hands, so that
the sword trembled in her fingers? The Kingstone on her
right hand brushed against the blade, with a flicker and
a useless flash. Bright, but not enough so, of course.
Irrelevantly, it reminded Elisena of Tristan's continued
embarrassment about the King-mark on his palm. Small
good that mark of royal heritage had done him, she thought.
He'd had little but pain, hurt, and responsibilities he didn't
want in all the time since she'd met him at Radak.

Elisena shut her eyes on the regret, squeezing back
the tears. There had been so many times when she might
have smoothed Tristan's way and had instead let preoc-
cupations sweep her away from him, leaving him to be
bounced from one hurt to another, recovering as best he
could on his own, thinking himself alone . . . It had been
crueler than she'd realized. He'd never been sure of anything, himself or her love, and had been brave enough to
let her see that. And he'd done this thing, brought them
across the sea, knowing what the cost would be, the
passage-price he'd pay. Tears squeezed out between her
lashes. This foolish, impossible, gallant gesture—

Thomas gave a low moan, and Elisena's eyes snapped
open in alarm. She tried to look at Tristan and couldn't
even see him for the glow of the sword she held, the light
beating up from it warm as a hearth-fire. Somewhere, high
among the bed curtains, a wakened Minstrel chirped
sleepily and began to sing.

Made of the mingled glows of the sword, the candle,
and her rings, the light was odd indeed. Far from hurting
the eyes or dazzling with its radiance, it seemed to bring
a comfort beyond all measure to mind and body, a hope
brighter than any dawn could spark. It spoke of home,

and of welcome. It was warm as the sun in summer flowers. Elisena could almost smell a breeze scented gently with clover and daisies. She could have gazed at the light forever, she thought, drawing from it a nourishment better than food or wine.

At length she forced her eyes away, lest she become too rapt. It was a danger, that. And she wanted to watch Tristan come home.

Tristan's eyes began to open just when Elisena had begun expecting them to, soon after the first, faint color had returned to his face. He didn't focus on her when she reached down to smooth his hair; but in a little while Elisena felt the furs stir as he moved, and Tristan rubbed a hand over his eyes—slowly, as if the effort involved in the movement was beyond all measure.

"Delayed dismissals don't work," he said faintly.

"I tried to tell you." Elisena put a cup of cool water against his lips and held his head up while he drank. His thirst would be great, after swallowing all that salt water, and the aftertastes of the medicines would hardly be pleasant. Tristan drained the cup.

"We're in Ambere's tower, then?" He yawned hugely, helplessly.

No thanks to your nearly drowning us all. Thomas walked across the furs to them, weaving and rocking like a ship upon the sea. *My mother told me to shun the sea. Better she'd told me to shun wizards.* The cat licked tentatively at Tristan's fingers, until his tongue informed him that they were safely entwined with Elisena's among the furs.

An Islin

THE WHITE OWLS BROUGHT CRUSTY BREAD SO FRESH
that it was still smoking-hot and a little pannikin of porridge laced through with honey. Tristan sat propped up
among the furs, trying, as Thomas insisted unkindly and
he didn't bother to deny, to eat all the honey without
touching the porridge. He was still busy at the task when
Polassar thrust the bed curtains apart.

Sleep was a marvelous restorative, at least for Polassar. The man looked hale as an oak tree, positively bristling with life. Polassar's notion of proper sickroom
behavior ran more toward heartiness than consideration
for the patient's eardrums, and his vigor was somewhat
daunting.

"Wizard, I've never seen anything that intended to live
look half so bad as you do! Are you really better?"

Tristan, who'd been hoping that he at least *looked* a
bit better than he felt, still managed a smile. "I'll let you
know when I remember what being better feels like. You
must be getting awfully bored with fishing me out of the
sea by now."

"Aye, well, you're not much of a catch. You might
consider learning to swim. Be easier on all concerned."

"Maybe at another time. I don't expect I'll be doing
any more boating for a while—the water's a bit wild around
these parts." Tristan set the porridge aside. Even empty,
the bowl seemed heavy to him.

"Aye, 'tis that. Rocks thick as daisies in a field. And
of course you had to drop right in among 'em! Did a proper
job of knocking yourself out—I was worried for a while."

Polassar gave Tristan's shoulder a rough squeeze, catching a bruise so that Tristan had to swallow a gasp of pain, and made to withdraw before he could show further unmanly concern. His hand brushed something hard among the furs—hard, sharp, and unusual enough to coax a tuneless whistle out of him.

"What's this, Wizard? 'Tis very martial, sleeping with your sword by you, but 'tis bound to cut you."

"What? Oh, that's all right, you can leave it—"

Tristan, to his utter if brief dismay, found he hadn't strength enough to fight off sleep for even a moment. One minute he was wide awake, the next he could scarcely hold his head up. He lost the sticky porridge-spoon somewhere in the furs—it seemed, impossibly, even heavier than the bowl as it slid out of his fingers. "Please," he managed to finish, and then knew nothing more of whatever Polassar said or did.

Tristan slept peacefully through the whole day, rousing only slightly when Elisena sank down among the furs beside him, taking the sword's place by his side. Half-asleep still, he heard Minstrel singing lustily and recognized the sound for the silvery thread that had pleasantly underlain his dreams and kept them from becoming nightmares.

At evening, two eagles appeared, bearing bundles of cloth but no dinner, much to Polassar's rather vocal disgust. The birds, equally displeased at him, hissed back.

Wakened by the commotion, Tristan sat on the edge of the bed, blinking drowsily as Elisena examined the bundles.

"Well, if we're to have nothing more of Magister Ambere, at least we've got clean clothes," she said brightly. She lifted up a long shirt of cream-colored wool, its bottom and sleeve ends intricately bordered with stitchings of dark blue. "This should fit you; someone here is observant. A good thing, because your own clothes were so full of salt that Polassar burned them this morning."

Tristan gave her a surprised look as the news penetrated. He glanced at Polassar then, but the man seemed unwilling to meet his eye.

"I'm surprised the smoke didn't wake you," Elisena

added wickedly. "Reynaud must have cleared it out in time after all."

"*You burned my clothes*?" Tristan groaned. Just when he'd finally gotten himself a sweater that didn't leave his wrists hanging out in the cold—and those breeches had only been patched *once*—

Polassar shifted uncomfortably in his seat by the fire. "They were ruined anyway, Wizard. Naught but tatters. And look, I've got the sea-black off your buckle." He held up Tristan's belt, with the silver unicorn buckle polished so that it flashed in the firelight like a flint-struck spark.

"Better than new," Polassar said hopefully. "Nothing like seawater to add polish."

Tristan thanked him most politely, hiding his smiles as best he could.

Don't be too bothered. He needed something to fidget with, Thomas said scornfully. *Helps his nerves, with all the waiting.*

Tristan dressed himself slowly. He had to be careful. He still felt wobbly and, after one one near-disaster, he didn't stoop over too quickly. His head and his side both ached, despite Elisena's work. He knew he was lucky that he didn't feel worse, but he hoped his sense of balance would be steadier by the time he'd put on the rest of his new clothes.

There were breeches to match the blue in the shirt, and they were well fitted. Likewise the sleeve-length of the shirt was precise. Someone about was indeed observant, but Tristan was too nervous to be purely grateful.

"Has Ambere refused to help us, then?" he asked Elisena quietly, recalling the question he'd begun forming earlier, and also remembering Polassar's obvious unease.

Elisena slipped into the mantle that had made up the second bundle and fingered the soft fabric appreciatively. The color, a silvery green, suited her well.

"No. I'm certain he knows why we came and he disapproves of it very much, but he hasn't refused us outright." She sighed. "Not yet, anyway. There wasn't time for lengthy discussions last night, and I haven't seen Ambere since then. I did seek him, but he's nowhere to be found."

"My apologies for that, Lady, but my duties are many

and do not permit me to play the proper host. I thought you to be resting still."

The chamber door had opened silently, as if it were made of feathers, and Royston Ambere stood framed by its posts and lintel. The travelers froze in their places, like children caught at gossip. Ambere brought a tang of the sea with him into the room, sharp over the hot scent of the oil in the lantern he held, and grains of sand clung damply to the skirts of his long robe. Magister Ambere had been outside his tower, then, probably for a good while, perhaps all that day. Tristan stared quite unashamedly. This was, after all, the first sight he'd had of his host. He wanted to observe more than grains of sand.

"I hope you have all recovered sufficiently from the rigors of your journey and that you may sup with me now and let me make amends for my neglect of you."

The words were directed at them all, but the greenblue eyes rested upon Tristan alone as he stood beside the bed, his fingers on the catch of the unicorn buckle that he'd only just fastened when Ambere surprised them. He might, Tristan thought, have been alone in the room, or the world. Ambere's eyes measured him and searched him, finding answers to questions that Tristan himself barely understood. The hissing of the flames in the grate seemed suddenly loud enough to drown out his own heartbeat. There was an osprey perched upon Ambere's broad shoulder, its wings half-spread, its great yellow eyes full of a shriveling hate. Tristan wanted to flinch from the combined scrutiny and wondered if he dared to.

With one neat, economical beat of his wings, Minstrel left his perch atop the rod that supported the bed curtains, dove to Tristan's shoulder, and took up a stance there as bold as a sea-eagle's, his tiny wings spread wide. At the sight, the green left Ambere's eyes, and some of the hairs of his beard twitched, as if a corner of his mouth lifted, unseen. The fell mood was broken by a whir of canary feathers. Ambere's right hand swept out, indicating the doorway behind him.

"Come."

The meal was served by ravens, bright-eyed and attentive as any manservant could have been expected to be, dressed in impeccable, inconspicuous black. A course of oysters came first, then fish steamed in wrappings of hot seaweed, which tasted even better than the fish, once Tristan made bold enough to follow Elisena's example and sample some. There was roasted saddle of venison, and little, sweet cakes served with pots of beach-plum jam. All was partaken of in silence, save for the slight noise that bone knives could make upon wooden platters and the efficient rustle of the ravens' wings.

Elisena made to speak once, at the meal's beginning, and was motioned peremptorily to continued silence by Ambere. Polassar looked vastly discomfited the whole while, hardly able to do his usual justice to food, and Reynaud touched little of anything, though he watched the ravens flying to and fro with keen appreciation.

Tristan was hungry enough at first; but as the edge came off his appetite, the mood took him, too. He only played with the cakes, feeding bits to an appreciative Minstrel, and quite ignored the tangy jam. On his lap, Thomas nibbled warily at an oyster, too tense to enjoy the rare taste.

Wine went round at last, an ancient vintage that slipped down the throat like honey and left behind a taste of smoke on the tongue and a flame in the heart. Tristan took one sip and then carefully put his goblet aside. His head was still light, even without the wine, and he wanted to keep his wits about him. He might need to have them handy. He wished he knew what had passed between Elisena and Ambere the night before. There'd been no point at which he could ask, but the air was heavy with the dregs of it still.

Ambere was watching him again. Tristan felt the weird eyes upon him, looked up, and saw them through the white flame-points of the candles stuck in the twisting driftwood holders at the table's center. He found, as his perspective shifted, that he was on his feet, his high-backed chair pushed carefully away from him. Then he was walking, ever so slowly, toward the head of the table. Once there, he knelt on one knee. Thomas, plainly torn over whether or not he ought to follow, stayed crouching by the chair Tristan had left.

"My lord Ambere—" No least flicker of welcome shone in those eyes, Tristan saw with a stab of confusion. The colors came and went in them like colors on the surface of the sea. "My lord, I was not able to thank you last night for the shelter you gave us, or for your help. Let me do so now."

"By that, may I take it that you intend to content yourself with that help?" Ambere said as Tristan got awkwardly to his feet. "And that you will turn back now?"

Tristan blinked, surprised. He hadn't seen that coming at all. Had what he'd said sounded that way? He certainly hadn't intended for it to. "Oh, no, my lord. We must go on."

He knew then why Elisena had felt that Ambere knew perfectly well what their quest was, however he otherwise pretended. Tristan had no doubt that the man knew exactly where they were going and why they had come to him first, though it might suit Ambere to pretend ignorance of both.

"He's as stubborn as you are, Lady," Ambere said. "It cannot have been easy to find such a fool."

There came an angry rumble from Polassar, a habit stronger than manners, hastily but not easily quelled. The osprey had left Ambere's shoulder, sent upon some errand, but the two great eagles that Tristan had thought to be carved upon the wood of his chair-back shifted their feathers menacingly, and their dark eyes blazed like old rubies.

Elisena answered softly, imperturbably. "I did not seek him out, my lord. Nor did Tristan seek this destiny. What shall be, must be. And if folly is our only course, then 'tis all the more vital that we be well guided in it."

"Aha, so now we come to it, Lady—what you want of me." Ambere's gaze was as hard as a cast dagger.

"I had taken you for a man who valued plain speaking, my lord," Elisena said challengingly.

Tristan found he'd stumbled back to his seat somehow, as the exchange began in earnest. The edge of his chair bumped at the backs of his knees, and he sat down bonelessly. Minstrel hopped onto his shoulder, standing at attention by his left ear.

"That very much depends upon the words that are spoken, my lady."

"Must I then pretend that you do not know why we have come here, despite all the evidence to the contrary you've given us?" Elisena asked, raising her brows. "Such games are for children. But very well, it shall be as you like."

"I would have what passes here stated before all, so that there are no misunderstandings, Lady." Tristan was surprised that Ambere offered so much of an explanation. He probably was not used to such. "Yes, I know why you have come. But let me have it from your own lips, if only because it may serve to clarify your purpose in your companions' minds."

"We're of a mind," Polassar interrupted hotly. "And one you'll not change, master, however you dress it up with your clever words." Polassar's own words, though begun boldly enough, faltered under Ambere's stare.

Ambere smiled coldly upon his silence. "You will need your determination, Lord of Lassair." He turned back to Elisena. "This one is a good follower, Lady. See you use him well—such followers are a weighty responsibility to those who would lead them."

Elisena's chair shot back as she stood, without any hand upon it. Her own hands were both revealed and hidden by the white light of her rings, kindled to their full glory now. She stood straight as a sword blade in the mantle Ambere had gifted her with, her head high.

"Magister Ambere, let me speak now as I would have spoken last night, if other matters had not pressed us both. We are come as pilgrims to you, but not as beggars. The task we undertake, the risks we run, are not for our own sake or hope of glory alone, but for all this land; and the help we ask of you is no more than your rightful share of the task, a share we ask of you as the right of one friendly power to another."

"I thought you said you'd come to ask something, Lady. This seems curiously similar to a demand."

"The time for careful words is long gone, my lord. The hour is late, and Nímir's power is strong. If we turn back as you counsel us, his strength will grow while ours fades. Nímir will hardly be unaware of such a salient point, and there is no hope that he will risk a final battle upon our lands, where he has been defeated in the past. Therefore we must go to *him*, and we are doing so."

"And it is to this end you go, the four of you alone, into Channadran? There is none among you trained to climb anything higher than a flight of stairs. How do you hope to scale the sheer peaks you will find ahead of you?"

"One step at a time," Tristan said firmly, before Elisena

could answer. He should have held his tongue, he knew, but he couldn't bear to let her fight on alone.

"I hope, King of Calandra, that none of those 'steps' is such as to make you regret those words. Have you ever been among mountains?"

Tristan began to wish he'd kept silent. Being singled out by Ambere was as comfortable as being speared through the chest. But he gathered his wits and recalled the riddling games Blais had both taxed and trained him with.

"No, my lord. But surely we intend to go *through* the mountains, not over them as you suggest." His mind was working again. He just hoped it wasn't working him into trouble. "That's why we've come to you, after all, to learn where the passes are between the peaks."

Ambere answered with a dismissing shake of his head, then looked back at Elisena. "And such a fellowship you have here, Lady: one half-drowned, one with no magic at all to shield him, one trusted by no one other than you." Reynaud smiled in salute to that. "You say you are all of one mind, but you show me the oddest proof of it."

Polassar was plainly angry that Ambere should number him among their liabilities, though the man had objected to each of them in some way, most impartially. Battle-trained as he was, Polassar considered still that magic was the height of frivolity, though he might grudgingly admit that it could be useful betimes. He played with his dagger, bristling at the insult, but apparently not willing to risk Ambere's tongue again. Tristan was slightly relieved at his restraint.

"For our fellowship, I will answer," Elisena said. "There is not a member of it I would exchange for any other on this earth. And even if I would, it is our affair only."

"Not if I'm expected to help you, Lady," Ambere replied severely. "You need more than you've got to weight the scales toward your success. So you will tell me, now, what other reckoning brings you here. Why should you not simply go home, and take your people to warmer lands where you may live in peace? Nímir moves slowly. You would have your lives and your children's children's. What more do you require?"

Elisena held her hands before her, cupped, full of light as if they held a star between them. Inside the soft, warm glow, little images of Calandra flickered. Tristan saw spring lambs, white roses, children, and butterflies. He could have watched all the night, though those sights and the others that followed them made his throat ache with longings he had thought he'd left behind. When Elisena dropped her hands, he was surprised to discover just how far he'd been leaning over the table toward them, and he barely recovered his balance in time to stop himself tumbling over.

"My lord, it is my rings' purpose to fight Nímir," Elisena said softly. "And my sworn duty to use them, by whatever means I may or must. I will not set this burden down."

"Ah. And do we now come to prophecies, Lady?"

"It is time to dispense with prophecies, my lord." Elisena's countering stroke was sure and swift, ignoring the hint of insult in Ambere's question. "We have long since outstripped such things. Those foretellings were spoken long ago, and plans that were once deemed expedient are so no longer. And expectations can be mocked." She looked meaningfully into Tristan's eyes and smiled. "Can they not, my lord?"

Tristan took thought of his own most unlikely coming to the long-prophesied kingship and returned the smile sheepishly, remembering also how he'd fought the somewhat dubious honor.

Elisena turned back to Ambere.

"There are no more foretellings. But I assure you, Lord, that these rings and that sword Tristan carries do not exist without a purpose."

"Perhaps not. But I can also make pretty pictures in the fire, Lady. Let me show you."

At Ambere's words, the candles on the table flared so high that wax and driftwood were alike consumed. The flames did not then die, but remained crackling in a rough sphere the size of a warrior's shield, green-white as fox fire, where the candles had been. There came a great rustling from far up in the tower, as birds awoke there. Tristan looked up at the sound, to be startled at his first clear glimpse of Am Islin's central shaft. The candles had given him no hint before then of its height, and he had overlooked the quiet birds outside the ring of light about the table. Paired eyes reflected the light back down, numerous as stars on a clear winter's night. Tristan was as awestruck by that as by anything Ambere could propose to show him.

"You do not know mountains, so you will not be able to judge the scale of Channadran against others, but this view should still be sufficient to chill your hot blood," Ambere said.

There were pictures in the fire, and Tristan knew then that the flames did not harm the table because they were not hot but ice cold, mirroring what they magically pictured for Ambere. He saw great fangs of rock thrusting up out of snowfields miles deep, surrounded by slopes so sheer that no snow could cling. Indeed, the rock itself could not support the angle for long—as they stared, the whole side of a mountain broke away, slipping down to shatter the glacier that had formed at its base.

The picture changed, shifted. Across a glacier, eddies of snow drifted on the wind, moving too quickly to drop into the crevasses they passed over. The landscape was empty, with nothing visible but continuously moving snow. No blade of vegetation broke its surface, nor was there sign of animals, however hardy. Where the snow halted, it piled up, grain by grain, more and more weight upon the flakes beneath, which were gradually compacted to ice. As the load increased, the ice began to flow in the only direction that it could, downslope. All that it met, snow or sand or rock, it carried with it, before it, and under it.

A full moon shone down, and the night air was so cold that the very rocks shattered into powder . . . Tristan shut his eyes, dizzied. He was afraid, but sleepy as well, Exhaustion could still claim him in an eye-blink, as it threatened to. He fought it, shamed, forgetting ice and cold.

"This, then, is the fate you choose of your own will. To wander in a mapless land where the greatest shelter you will find may be a rock to break the wind a trifle, seeking to slay a thing which may not even be alive as you understand it, searching among a thousand fearful peaks for your own deaths. And for this, you ask my help?"

"Yes," Elisena whispered. "Yes, for if we perish so, Calandra's fate is little different than it has ever been.

While we have weapons, we will fight. Yes, we ask your help, Magister Ambere. I think you are our only hope."

"And if I refuse you? What then?"

None of them, really, had considered that he finally might. They'd been certain that all life must oppose Nímir, surer of that than of their power to convince. It took a moment for disaster to sink in.

But to Tristan, the refusal didn't matter. He was remembering an orchard he'd ridden through, its apples frozen solid on ice-coated boughs. He thought of the fields that ringed Crogen and the trusting way the grain had sprung up there, planted by folk who barely dared hope for a harvest and yet went on living as best they might—living for a chance of a better day, seeing that day in a single sunbeam escaping a cloud at a wizard's behest, content with so trifling a miracle.

"We'll go on," Tristan said, tired of the argument, weary of talking, and of listening. Fighting sleep had made his head ache again, and the seat of his chair had come to seem unbearably hard. He couldn't hope to get comfortable without a great deal of unseemly shifting about, and his back hurt, as well as all his bruises. He wanted to go to bed quite desperately and to lie quiet with no quarreling voices to claim his attention, no sudden lights to make his eyes burn, and no doleful sights to bring him nightmares. He suspected that Ambere had made up his mind about their request a long while before, perhaps even before they'd left Calandra. What that decision was, Tristan couldn't quite guess, but he was certain that nothing any of them said or did would alter it. The dinner and the pretense of discussion, were nothing but a cruel sham of hours and words stretched out like iron-shod tips of a scourge. It was past time someone put an end to the evening.

"And no word of mine shall turn you back?"

Tristan shook his head. He was drained, able to form no more words, polite or otherwise.

"Then, Tristan of Calandra, you prove yourself worthy of the sword you carry. I would not have guessed that to be possible. I mean you no insult, but few such men have I met. Fools, maybe, but such fools are rarer than heroes, and needed more often than they come. What help I can give, you shall have."

the White Lady

TRISTAN STOOD, PUSHING HIS CHAIR BACK, THEN gripped it tightly while he waited for the tower to cease its swaying. *Must be the wind*, he thought. Ambere's voice was only a dim echo in his head. Funny, he would have thought Am Islin more solidly founded, less subject to influence of storms.

The motion hadn't stopped yet when he felt a hand on his elbow. Reynaud had been closest to him on that side; it followed that the hand must be his. Irritated that he couldn't even be ill in peace, Tristan made to shake the grip off. "I'm all right," he insisted crossly, tugging to free his sleeve.

"You will be," Elisena answered. "It was poor judgment to let you up so soon and for so long. I'm sorry."

Tristan felt woven fabric against his jaw and temple, then the softness of a pillow under his head as he sank downward into it. After that, softest of all, so that his senses barely caught it, Elisena's lips brushed against his other cheek. He might have felt her tears as well, but he was too close to sleep by then.

Tristan woke eventually, sweating from being snuggled down in the middle of the heap of furs, with his nose stuffy and his mouth dry. He was far too uncomfortable to think of sleeping longer, whatever he should have done. He sat up, rubbing with his fingers first at his eyes and then at the back of his neck. Thomas rolled against him, stretching and purring.

Elisena said it would be a shame to wake you just to

look at some old maps, and Ambere agreed with her for once. You're supposed to get all the rest you can. We're leaving soon.

Tristan pushed back the bed curtains, and stared around the deserted room in front of him. "Thomas, where is everybody? Oh—reading maps, you said?"

Very good. You certainly picked that up quickly enough. Twisting his head about, Thomas licked vigorously at the fur on his back.

There was a basin set handily by and a razor. The ensorcelled water in the basin was still warm. Tristan washed the sleep from his face and shaved, then dressed. He felt better, at least more awake and likely to stay so for a while. Just when he'd begun to feel hungry as well, he spied a bowl of fruit and some loaves of bread. He fell to on them and some nuts and bits of cheese which had been out of sight behind the bread.

Once he began thinking actively about it, Tristan found he was somewhat confused as to the exact time of day, and the meal offered him no clues. Nor was there a window anywhere in the chamber. By the way he felt, Tristan supposed he might easily have slept both the night and the day away. Bothering himself about it seemed irrational, but he wished rather strongly that he knew whether that was true.

After all, there were those legends about the hollow hills, and sleepers spending a thousand years there in what seemed a single night. There was nothing to connect such tales with Ambere or even with truth, but Tristan's nerves were not so steady as they might have been, and the thoughts troubled him. Surely someone ought to have come to fetch him by the time he'd done eating. How long did Elisena expect him to sleep? But none of his friends appeared.

Tristan washed his hands again and dusted breadcrumbs from his clothes. Ordinarily, Minstrel would have stooped upon them, falconlike, but the bird was missing also. Looking at maps? Tristan wondered. He rolled a fat orange across the floor and watched Thomas chase it. As a diversion, it was rather paltry, though Thomas seemed to enjoy it well enough.

Still no one came. Tristan would have been glad to see even Reynaud. He wondered what he was expected to do—sleep, probably. But he didn't feel the least need of more rest and he didn't think he could concentrate on Blais' grimoire either. He didn't feel like sitting still.

"Thomas, do you have any idea what time it is?"

No. Thomas had caught the orange at last and gave it a killing bite, drawing his lips back and sneezing at the bitter oils his teeth released from the rind.

"Well, how long ago did Elisena leave?"

A while. I really didn't notice. I was asleep, too. Had a rough night, you know.

Tristan shook his head. "I think I ought to see if I can find her. Any idea where she is?"

No. This tower has many rooms, and I have only seen this one and the place we were last night. There are a lot of rooms above us. Thomas licked at his paws.

"Well, I suppose we could look."

They're just poking at a lot of old maps and charts, and you know how that sort of thing bores you. If they needed you, they'd have waked you. Why don't you just settle down and do some finger exercises? Elisena should be back soon. That candle makes lovely shadows; it would do you a world of good to get some practice in.

Tristan looked at the cat suspiciously. "Is there some reason you don't want me to go out there, Thomas?"

No. Why should there be? It's just not polite to go wandering around a strange house—or tower.

Tristan raised an eyebrow. "It wouldn't by any chance be those birds, would it, Thomas?"

The cat began to wash himself, in an almost frantic display of unconcern.

"I don't think they'd hurt you, Thomas. Especially now, when we have Ambere's promise—"

I don't care what you *think. I'm worried about what they* think.

Considering that, Tristan was constrained to admit that the numberless birds lining the tower's walls had made him uneasy, too and he was not inclined to mock Thomas. The birds were only protecting nests and mates, of course, but still their hostile glares were disconcerting. He remembered that feeling clearly from the previous night; by day—if it *was* day—he'd only be able to see more of the birds and their eyes. And they'd be more active.

However, he was restless, and his bruises were healed

enough that he could move about easily. He ought to
move, if only to be sure he didn't stiffen up. He had slept
himself out, and the prospect of spending several bored
hours waiting for someone to remember him was not particularly attractive.

"We may not get another chance to explore, not if
we're leaving soon, Thomas. Coming? I promise I'll see
to it that nothing with feathers takes a bite out of you."

*Considering the scrapes you usually manage to get
yourself into, I'm sure I'll only regret it. I'll just stay here
by the fire.* Thomas jumped onto the bed and settled himself.

"Considering the scrapes I usually manage to get myself
into, don't you think it's your sworn duty to come along
and keep me out of them? Besides, I might do something
amusing. You never know." Tristan crouched down beside
the bed, putting himself at eye level with Thomas.
"Hmmmmm?"

There was a gap in the masonry above the chamber's
wooden door, a sort of open transom by which the servant
birds came and went. Minstrel entered through it and
made a haphazard landing on Tristan's left shoulder,
clutching at his collar. The bird's flower-soft head brushed
once against his neck, in greeting.

Tristan gently stroked Minstrel's white breast feathers.

"Well, and where have you been? You should like it
here, if any of us does. The Kingdom of the Birds, and
you the only one of us a citizen."

Minstrel balanced himself casually on one foot, freeing
the other for the grooming of his wing, which he did twice
before beginning an earnest chirping.

"The *who* wants to see me?" Tristan asked, alternating
frowns of confusion with winces at the shrillness of Minstrel's notes, so close to his ear. "The white lady? If you
mean Elisena, why do you call her that?"

Thomas had been listening too. *I don't think he means
Elisena at all, but he wants you to follow him.*

"Yes. I got that part. Looks like we go exploring after
all, Thomas."

Snooping. Meddling.

"*Someone's* waiting for me. And it's not likely that
we'd come to any harm inside Am Islin, is it?" Tristan

straightened. "Come on. Try and work up some sort of spirit of adventure."

Must I? Thomas dropped resignedly to the floor, his ears lowered.

Stairs spiraled up and around the tower's walls, like a unicorn's horn turned inside out. Tristan had thought that he needed some exercise, but he got a good deal more than he'd bargained for. Minstrel seemed bent on leading him to the tower's very top, up definitely thousands of leg-wearying steps.

Am Islin was very tall, higher than Tristan had guessed, even knowing how it had been visible so far across the sea. He looked up once, down a bit later, and repeated neither action because they both made him dangerously dizzy. The white treads of the stairs were wide enough, but birds had nested upon them as well as the walls, and he had to go carefully, lest he trample a nest or disturb a brooding and defensive mother. Nor was there any rail to grasp for safety, not even a length of rope.

At first, it was only ducks that he climbed past; but as Tristan went higher, there were gulls, a few kittiwakes, and fulmars, which looked like the gulls but were larger. Minstrel cheerfully informed him of those types he did not recognize. They passed many doors, but the canary never paused at any of them. Tristan was longing to. He would have paused for anything.

There were no windows. Tristan was surprised to notice that, for the whole inside of the tower was suffused with a clear, white light, bright as could be wished. Could it come through the supposedly solid walls themselves? Tristan touched the nearest spot not nest-filled and found the stone reassuringly solid. Just for a second, he'd harbored the unsettling thought that Am Islin might not really exist at all, save as a construction of magic. They were up too high for him to like that sort of speculation.

If the light did not come from the walls, then it must fall from somewhere still above. But to learn if that were so, Tristan knew he'd have to look up again and he preferred not to do that. It made his head swim. He accepted the light without further question. At least it told him he'd awakened in daytime, not night.

Now the nests were built of tidily arranged sticks, in place of the bare ledges or bowl-shapes filled with eider down. Most of the nests were empty, but on one a kestrel sat, watching with noble, troubled eyes. Higher still they went, till the nests were those of bigger hawks, perhaps even of eagles. Tristan's ankles ached, and he thought his knees were swelling. He could scarcely lift his feet to clear the steps. He might, he thought, manage one more turn of the stair, but then he would have to rest and maybe turn back, once he had his breath again. Minstrel had been known to get his messages muddled, and this trek could well be fruitless. His side hurt, too, dully but insistently, promising to worsen.

Around the twist of the stair, the steps abruptly gave out, and where they stopped was one last door, slightly ajar.

He was, Tristan supposed, as high up as the clouds, and he could hear a wind sighing softly all about. The sound was lighter than a breath, but there was a clacking noise, too; though it was likewise soft, it puzzled him. Familiar it was, somehow, but he couldn't place it. At least, it was nothing he expected to hear at the top of a tower. Nor was what he saw anything he might have anticipated.

Entering through the door was like walking into a bank of heavy fog, thick as cream and no less white. The door he passed through was the last solid thing that Tristan beheld. There was no ceiling over his head, nor any walls that he could see, not even a floor. Only a shining whiteness upon all sides, like mist where the sun begins to burn through. Muffled, so that they sounded further off than they could have been, came the mewing cries of seabirds.

Tristan ventured through the door hesitantly, without knocking, since he'd found it open. After a single step inside the room, he halted and watched the scene change as the fog lifted. The chamber's walls remained indistinct, and most of its furnishings were the same, but in the center stood a great loom, and a woman weaving at it. *Magic*, Tristan's trained nose told him, and he ceased worrying about his senses' conflicting reports. He tossed logic away and felt more comfortable at once.

He had seen weavers at work before—now he recognized the sound of the shuttle for what it was—but never one such as the woman. Her shuttle darted across the face of the loom like a fish through falling water, and a picture rapidly took shape below it.

His eyes could make out no color at all to the thread on the shuttle. It seemed to have none until it had been woven into the tapestry, where the hues were suddenly brilliant as jewels, brighter and truer than any dyes Tristan had ever seen. The swiftly growing tapestry pictured a castle among fertile fields, with the sun rising through a copse of apple trees behind it. The grass before the castle's walls shone with dew, as if the woman had woven with light itself for thread. Clouds, gold and rose, filled the sky, and a banner flaunted across them, above the ancient stone walls—a banner that bore a leaping silver unicorn for its device. Peace filled the scene like wine in a jug.

The shuttle reached the top of the loom and ceased to move. Doves and white sparrows flocked to the frame, snipping warp threads with their beaks and knotting them, then all together lifting the whole great tapestry free of the loom. What they did with it then, Tristan did not see, for just at that moment the weaver turned, and her eyes fastened on him.

Her eyes were green, and they and her red hair were the only points of color in the chamber, once the tapestry was gone from it. Her robe was white silk, falling from a high waist a long way before it reached the floor, for she was nearly of a height with Tristan. Her skin was slightly darker than cream. She wore a torque of silver about her neck and a circlet of the same in her high-piled hair.

Amid that glorious color, which was like red oak leaves newly turned, ornaments were woven and twined. Things of the sea, but not only the expected pearls and white shells. Tristan saw purest white sand-coins, bits of driftwood, the snowy gossamer down of egrets, fragments of glass smoothed by sea and sand till they were as misty white as the dawn sky over Lake Istel. She might have risen from the sea, not drowned but glorified. Tristan couldn't see her feet and wasn't moved to look, since he couldn't remember having seen any floor either. She was—though he didn't necessarily want to confirm his suspicion—suspended in the bright white light as he himself seemed to be.

"You have come," the woman said. "At last."

Tristan expected that by then his face had taken on a permanent expression of surprise. He was confused as well as dazzled by the brightness and half-dizzy from the stairs. He'd come at once to her summons, hadn't he? Why the 'at last'? Who was she, and why had she called him to her?

Minstrel left his shoulder and flew to the woman, performing a sort of aerial curtsy in the manner of a courtier who had successfully completed a duty.

"You are nearly as white as one of my own birds," the woman told Minstrel. She reached out a hand to Tristan as the bird returned to him. "Come. Sit with me."

She drew him, resistless, to a cushioned seat before what might have been taken for a window. Yes, surely it was a window, though Tristan could make out neither sill nor frame. He had an odd fancy that the one window looked out upon both the sea and the land, though the land lay behind the tower and only the broad sea lay before it. Somehow he knew that the conflicting views were nonetheless both utterly true.

Tristan rubbed at his eyes, then his forehead. All those stairs! Toadstools, he must be in worse shape than he'd thought. He was surely hallucinating. He wondered where he really was.

"The view from my window is wide indeed," the woman said, as if all his thoughts were as her own. Perhaps she'd plucked their meaning from his face. "The ends of the world may be seen by those who have the way of looking." Her tone soothed. Tristan found he accepted whatever she said without question or thought of one.

Her birds settled like a snowfall about her feet, jostling for place. Thomas' tail twitched spasmodically, and he hid behind Tristan's boots, though the doves hardly seemed aggressive and the sparrows were tiny.

"One day I looked down from this my window, and my heart beheld you."

She put both her long white hands on his arms, holding him still before her, and looked at Tristan, long and slow, as if she would drink his soul. Tristan met her gaze, feeling as if time, or at least his heart, stopped.

"Yes. It was you. I would know even did I not see your face. My heart is quiet, satisfied at being near you."

Tristan, looking not at her but past her, out the window

since that seemed safest in his utter confusion, saw only the white sky above a silver, fog-shrouded sea and the white gulls flying in the white air, thick as the fish in the sparkling waves far below. He was still breathless—from the long climb, he told himself.

"I am Welslin Amberesdaughter," the silver voice said, in his ear. "And you are my heart's desire."

Tristan thought he must have jumped, startled, blushed, or paled. Surely he had not sat there dumb, stonelike, unmoved by her words. He still wasn't certain that his own heart was beating. The surge of his blood in his ears might just as well have been the sea upon the shore below, rising up the tower.

"Lady—" his voice was a cracked whisper, and he didn't think she heard. He needed a moment before he could try again.

He couldn't seem to see her face, now that he wanted to. No matter how Tristan turned, the light was always behind the woman, sourceless and filtered, but bright enough to melt the edges of objects and hide her features from him. It was the white light of fog, untouched by the sun's gold, yet bright for all of that. He was left with nothing but an impression of whiteness, as different from Allaire's ivory beauty as the sun might differ from a firefly. And he had thought once that Allaire was the end of all possible loveliness, beyond surpassing.

She was watching him again—or still. He knew, though he couldn't see her eyes.

All the while, birds came and went at the window, their wings whistling and beating softly. A pile of something grew upon the floor at Welslin's feet, and breezes stirred it with gentle fingers. Tristan found he could see the pile plainly enough—tufts of wool, he realized, and was surer as Welslin reached down to pick up a spindle and set it whirling. Her movement broke the physical contact between them, but not the conversation—if such it was. Tristan could remember speaking only the one word, before his throat had seemed to seal shut.

"I sent for you," Welslin said, "to offer you a gift. Not offer, in truth, for you cannot refuse me." She looked full at Tristan once more, paying no attention to the thread she flawlessly spun out.

"My heart."

Tristan was very sure that the room was whirling round like the spindle, that the tower was rocking in the sea. He wondered if he were really still lying in his bed, fevered and dreaming and whether, in such a case, he'd be able to wonder such a thing. The circular question was too much for his reeling senses, and he abandoned it with little regret. Yet even accepting the situation as real and no hallucination did not resolve his puzzlement. Welslin behaved as if he had spoken volumes of words, love words at that. And all he'd said since he came into the room— had he said anything at all? How and when had she seen him, as she claimed, when he'd come to this land but the day previous, never before having come so far from his home?

The bright light was behind her; but for all that, she cast no shadow. Yet the image of her twirling spindle flickered on the tower's rounded walls and across the empty posts of the great loom. The shadow brushed Tristan's face lightly, and he flinched back as at a sudden touch of ice.

Softly, as if she spoke a spell, Welslin went on, paying no heed to the movement or the panic that Tristan felt sure must be huge in his eyes. "My heart has belonged to you since time came to be. It is only right that you should take it into your keeping, now that you have come to me."

Reaching into the neck of her gown, Welslin drew forth a small, white bag. From it she removed a tiny object and pressed that against Tristan's palm. He couldn't remember when she'd taken his hand again, but her fingers held his own, prisoners.

He looked down at his hand, wondering what he'd find. He saw only a rose-and-honey colored stone lying upon his palm, warm as sunlight in his fingers. It was smaller than his littlest fingernail, veined faintly with red-brown. He had never seen a gem like it, but its magic communicated itself to him clearly.

Tristan knew he must grope, somehow, for proper words, though his mind was as close to blank as it might be. He felt as if he'd gone to sleep with both his eyes wide open, able to understand but not to react. Again he wondered about dreams; but surely in a dream he'd have known what to say to her.

"Lady, such . . . such a gift demands recompense, and you must know I can make you none." He felt as if he ought to kneel to her, but Tristan couldn't stir an inch; his legs refused his commands. "It's not . . . you're beautiful beyond all imagining. Your love would be an honor, but it's one I can't possibly take. I'm wed to Elisena."

Somehow, he'd thought she would have known that, though he couldn't have said precisely why. He tried to pass the stone back to her, with stiff fingers, but the pebble clung to them, and Welslin's hands were busy with her spindle once again.

"*I love her*," Tristan said, desperately.

"This I know. Be easy. I do not ask you to forsake that pledge." Welslin's eyes were like her voice. Serene, emotionless.

"Then you must take this back again." He tried once more to press the stone upon her. Why couldn't he seem to let go of it or at least drop it in her lap? He was beginning to weep with frustration and felt shamed by the weakness.

"No. Fate decreed that I must have a woman's heart. It did not ordain that I must keep that heart by me, to torment me forever. No."

Upon the gentle denial, Welslin stood and walked shimmering to her loom, which the birds began to string with fresh warp threads as she gathered what she had spun onto the shuttle. "I shall stay here alone by my loom in my misty tower until time ceases to be and I shall be well content. Such is my destiny, my glory, and my duty. But my heart has a longing for the world and for you. Let it therefore follow that yearning and go with you. Its powers will serve you at need. And better it should go with you now than wither here."

Her eyes, as she raised them from the room and to him, were alight with some emotion Tristan did not quite grasp. Joy, or was it relief? Tears of pain as well? His throat hurt from holding his own tears back.

"I shall no longer keep watch from my tower, feeling a sorrow I cannot put a name to, longing for a stranger's face, a face I see now before me but knew too well before ever you came. I shall have peace, at last! You shall go forth and fight your battles with the world, and my wayward heart shall accompany you. Each of us shall then be content. There can be no fairer bargain."

Still he would have protested, on his feet by then, but Tristan began to sense that Welslin was reaching out to him on a level beneath her words, pleading in a way he could barely sense, but must yield to.

"Take it. I have no need of it, no use for it, but you shall have both. And when you look upon it, remember that one thing in this world will never change—this tower will stand forever between air and land and sea, and I will always be at its window, looking out."

Welslin watched Tristan's slowly retreating back. He was gone into the mist before he reached what he thought of as the chamber door. Her expression was wistful, as was the smile her lips shaped.

"Birds must fly," Welslin said in dismissal. She lifted her shuttle once more.

Ambere's Help

TRISTAN WAS SEATED ONCE AGAIN ON THE EDGE OF the curtained bed, watching the fire burning in its grate, gold and apricot with an odd flicker of sapphire now and again, gift of the driftwood it was built from. He didn't quite know how he'd gotten to be there. He must have walked, he supposed, but he had no memory of having been led down the twisting stair, and he had remarked nothing along the way. He was just relievedly passing the whole thing off as a strange and rather lovely dream when he chanced to open his right hand from the fist he found it clenched into. There, lying against the King-mark on his palm, was the stone that was Welslin's heart.

Tristan looked up from the stone into the twin enigmas of Thomas' green eyes.

"Thomas? What do you suppose she is?"

Whatever Thomas might have supposed of Welslin, he had no chance to say. The door opened, and Elisena came in, seeming pleased to find Tristan up and about and apparently likely to remain so. She seemed to find nothing odd in his hastily arranged expression.

"Had your sleep out?" she asked brightly, kissing his cheek. "You look much better. Come along, then. Polassar keeps insisting that you don't understand maps in the least, but I've told him that no wizard's sense of direction can be as bad as all that. Come see what we've been doing this morning."

Tristan privately wished that he might know what *he'd* been doing all morning.

* * *

On the table in the hall where they'd dined the night before, there was set a wide, shallow box, filled with dampened white beach sand. The sand was much grooved, scooped out, heaped, and mounded up, until its intent would have been plain to a simpleton. A map had been made of it, a map of the mountain chain named Channadran. Tristan found it impressive.

At one edge, by Ambere's right hand, a half-burned white candle was thrust into the sand, obviously as a point of reference. It wasn't lit. Ambere glanced up as they came to the table, nodded absently to welcome Tristan, then looked back to his work.

An eagle perched upon his fist, its unhooded eyes as yellow as fine gold. Its great hooked beak was opened slightly and it made odd, crooning replies to the questions Ambere put to it. In response to the bird, his fingers made fine adjustments to the sand in the center section of the map, adding a sprinkle here to deepen a snowfield, cutting away part of the side of a peak to mark a recent snowslide. He worked steadily for a bit, then ceased and released the bird.

"Well, that is all that he can tell us. My birds do not willingly penetrate past a certain point in Channadran, and a little beyond that, even I cannot compel them to venture. Draw near now, let us see what we may descry from this." Ambere thrust his sleeves back, so as not to risk disturbing the carefully arranged sand.

Polassar leaned close, too, one hand on his sword hilt to keep it out of his way. Tristan smiled ruefully at that. One didn't go armed in the house of a friend, so it was plain that Polassar still had little trust for Ambere. Well, the man could hardly be blamed for that, Tristan supposed. Thomas had told him of the troubles there had been in getting into Am Islin.

"Now. As you see, your way into Channadran is plain enough. You must cross this tongue of the Winterwaste to reach this upland which is scarcely more hospitable. This is far from the straightest way, but it will prove the swiftest. You will reach these mountains—Channadran's postern gate, one might say. The peaks are not particularly high, compared to the main upthrusts. They will teach you to climb, so study them well and neglect not their lessons.

"There are three passes between them. I recommend the second of these, as it is somewhat the shorter, but you may find it choked with this glacier before you can reach it." Ambere's fingers indicated the ice mass, but did not quite touch the sand. His reticence looked deliberate. "I should not care to venture upon that ice."

Reynaud held a horn of ink and a delicate pen, making notations in a little volume bound in black sharkskin. The pen leaped rapidly about—either Reynaud wrote an extremely flowing hand or he was sketching the topography as Ambere explained it. Tristan was chagrined that he hadn't thought of the idea first.

"You will find the mountains wilder as you penetrate them more deeply," Ambere continued. "What those parts even my eagles cannot reach are like, you may well imagine. Those peaks are like the Winterwaste turned on end and broken to bits. You must steer always into the worst terrain or you will risk being led into a trap. Only so may you be sure that you are coming closer to Nímir. Though I suspect, Lady, that you will have your own ways of searching him out."

Elisena nodded gravely, but did not speak. Ambere did not seem to have expected her to.

"You cannot, of course, expect to live from the land itself. To say Channadran is barren would be to understate. Only snow grows there. The matter of supplies has, however, been arranged, and you need not fret about it."

"He means to send his eagles to us with food, as was done for Lord Barrick of Comten, when he wandered on quest in the wilderness of Assid Hist for a year and a day," Polassar said in what Tristan supposed was meant to be a conspiratorial whisper.

Ambere looked pained. "I have birds other than eagles, Lord Polassar, and you will have need of them. And pray remember that Barrick of Comten barely lived to tell his tale to the bards who made it famous. You are not the first to come here begging aid of me, though you are the first in long years. Most I have turned away—the time was not propitious for this sort of undertaking. Indeed, I am not sure that matters stand better now, or that the time is any more right for this venture. You may have a destiny written on you which will not be denied, you may have my help, you may have those rings and that sword, but do not take this venturing lightly."

Tristan continued his careful scrutiny of the map, steering clear of the quarrel. Ambere had applied a rare skill to his birds' reports—though the scale of the map was small, a great cold seemed to breathe out of the wooden box. Those mountains, no bigger than Tristan's hand, looked miles high. There was no way he might judge between his contrary senses, but he was not afraid to follow his feelings and appreciate the sorcery's quality.

The next morning, as preparations went on, Tristan managed a few moments alone and went climbing up the stairs into the tower, seeking again that topmost door. He reached it sooner than he had expected, surely much sooner than he had on the day previous. Had he been that weak, then? He was glad to have recovered so quickly. The door opened to his tentative knocking; it had not been latched.

The portal gave onto a high parapet, bare to the sea winds and deserted. There was no sign that it had ever been otherwise. Baffled, Tristan made his way back down the stair, ignoring the sea birds that he disturbed at every step.

Unable to find Welslin, realizing that for some reason she might want that so, Tristan sought Ambere instead. What he'd wanted to ask of Welslin, he could as well ask from her father—some of it, anyway. He found Ambere engaged in mending a falcon's wing and watched silently as Am Islin's master cut the broken flight feathers away and fitted the hollow shafts of some hawk's feathers over the stumps of the quills, tying them in place with thread which he sealed against water with beeswax. The falcon watched nervously the while, but made never the slightest resistance to the sure touch.

"There, pretty." Ambere smoothed the feathers of the other, whole wing back into place. "The air is yours again. You'll not fly your best till after next moult, but you'll fly. Tell your tiercel that he must do your hunting as well as his own, till then."

The falcon cried softly once and beat her wings to try them against the air. Ambere gathered up the stray snippets of thread and quills and made them vanish with a complicated-looking snap of his fingers. By then the falcon had taken wing and disappeared.

"Well, Tristan of Calandra. Have you come to learn the craft of falconry from me?"

"No, my lord." Tristan smiled. He had covertly searched Ambere's face for some trace of Welslin and had seen no resemblance. "I don't think a bird like that would trust me as it trusts you and I need all my fingers for my magic. Thank you for letting me watch—but I've come to beg another sort of favor of you."

Tristan glanced across the table to the spot where Minstrel had discovered a cuttlefish skeleton. The canary danced about, whetting his beak furiously upon the white shell. It was easier not to look Ambere in the face as he spoke, though it would have been even easier not to have to look at Minstrel, either.

"I can't take him with me into the mountains, my lord. It's not right. He isn't made for that kind of cold and he's too small. He'll die."

"Isn't there that danger for all of you?"

Tristan shook his head. "I'd like to think there's something left behind and safe. It would make going a little easier."

"Nothing will do that for you," Ambere cautioned.

That thought was hardly new. "No. Knowing that it's highly unlikely any of us will be coming back and going anyway is hard." It was harder still to speak of it openly and it was not germain to the business at hand. "You could make him stay, I think. He'd be safe here with you."

Minstrel abandoned the cuttlebone and winged to Tristan's shoulder, nearly as fast as thought. The first that Tristan, who had his attention directed elsewhere, knew of it was when Minstrel dealt him a sharp nip upon his earlobe.

"He'd follow you, I think," Ambere said, smiling.

Minstrel gave a loud chirp of agreement, then several other notes both angry and pleading. Ambere smiled once more.

"How much of that did you get?" he asked Tristan.

"Only a little. He wants to go with me. I knew that." Tristan offered his finger to the canary, hoping to distract Minstrel's attacks, if not his protests. Minstrel struck sharply at his nail, then nibbled about underneath it, with great affection.

"He's angry," Ambere interpreted, "because there is never any question but that the cat goes along, yet you continually conspire to leave *him* behind. He says it's not fair. He says he will follow you if you try to make him stay."

Tristan was surprised at the bird's perception. "My lord, he's very brave. I don't question that." A picture flashed across Tristan's mind, a memory of how Minstrel's fearless singing had once held a dragon at bay in Darkenkeep. "He saved my life, once. I should try to do as much for him."

His throat hurt. He was choking on the words. Minstrel began to rub his head against Tristan's chin, making further speech impossible, and Tristan had to turn his face away. Minstrel made squawking noises and stretched to reach him again. Failing, he ripped a thread out of Tristan's collar.

"Shouldn't you consider his wishes?"

Tristan couldn't speak. He couldn't even shake his head without sending the canary tumbling. Picking at his collar, and rubbing against his neck, digging tiny claws in teasingly . . . Those were little things the bird did every day and which Tristan must now learn not to miss. Not to mention the songs . . .

"Make him forget me," he finally gasped out, his voice harsh. He wished he dared claim such a boon for his own sake as well. Minstrel's feathers were tear-wetted. The bird shook himself to fluff them and began unconcernedly to preen.

"You have the power to do that," Tristan went on when he could. "If that's the only way, just make him forget me." He lifted Minstrel from his shoulder and transferred him to Ambere's finger. Minstrel cocked his head questioningly, but stayed put.

Ambere failed to mask a troubled look.

"My son, are you certain—"

"*Yes!*" But if he listened to arguments, he wouldn't be, Tristan knew. "I'd go this instant, alone, if I thought I could do it. I can't make the others stay, but Minstrel—" Tristan thought the barely contained sobs would tear him in half. "I want him safe. Cage him if you have to. He's used to it—he was hatched in a cage. But he must not follow after me!"

"My lord Polassar, iron weighs heavy in the mountains. Your sword may be a necessary weight, but you will find armor unhelpful. You would be well advised to leave behind even your helm."

Polassar regarded Ambere doubtfully, if not scornfully. It was bad enough to be the only normal, unmagical member of the expedition, but being stripped of his armor was worse to Polassar's mind than being stripped of his lands, for Lassair had often been in peril and danger of loss, but Polassar had borne arms since early in his childhood.

"Polassar, he's right," Tristan put in gently. "It won't be any use to you. You'll get it back—we can go home this way and stop for it." They were keeping up the fiction that they might make it into and then out of Channadran alive by unspoken but unanimous agreement.

"Just the mail shirt?" Polassar half begged, his big fingers all but crushing the steel rings as he kept hold of them.

It seemed only decent to yield on that. No purpose would be served in stripping the man of his dignity while saving him a few pounds of weight. Tristan relented, and Ambere gave up. Those few extra pounds wouldn't matter to someone of Polassar's size, anyway.

Tristan looked over the other clothing Ambere had presented to them. All the garments were made of double layers of wool with downy feathers stuffed between. Shaped for utility, there was no style to them, but they were surprisingly light in the hands for their apparent bulk. There were pairs of heavy mittens and high boots, both with laces which mated with loops on sleeve-ends and breeches so that they could be laced on tightly to keep out snow and cold air. There were liners for the boots as well, promising soft warmth and some protection from sharp rocks underfoot.

All the cloth was a dark gray wool, spun and woven just the way it came off the wild sheep, with the grease left in it to shed water as easily as the sheep had. Ambere said that the color served a purpose as well, aside from making them inconspicuous against the mountain rocks. Its darkness would help to catch the sun's heat, soaking up its warmth like a dry rag. They'd have reason to be glad of that, he continued, for the mountain air was thin and did not hold heat well, even when the sun managed to shine.

The inside layer of the cloth was woven loosely, to be soft against the skin. Outside, the fabric was so tightly woven that even peering closely, Tristan couldn't distinguish individual warp and weft threads. He did spot tiny runes of silver broidered about the neck closure and the edges of the fur-lined hood, almost too small for his sight. He could not imagine a needle putting them there. Too small for decoration, they must serve some magical purpose.

He wondered if the cloth had been woven upon Welslin's loom from the tufts of wool her white doves brought to her. He stubbornly refused to believe that he'd imagined or dreamed his climb up the tower—and whenever he became inclined to do so, Tristan had only to remember the apricot-colored pebble tucked among the other stones and feathers in the magic box hanging at his belt. No. Welslin was real, if engimatic. And upon her ensorcelled loom, all the clothes could have been swiftly made, as rapidly as they must have been made.

"Cloaks will not keep you warm in the mountain winds and may hamper you. Garbed in these, you will not miss a cloak's warmth while you walk. Better to pack the cloaks and save them for blankets of a night, to bolster the wool bags' warmth," Ambere was saying.

Tristan had been pleased to discover that his cloak had escaped the bonfire Polassar had made of the rest of his clothes. It looked nothing much as it had when he'd first worn it, but it had been new and a gift, and he didn't like to part with it. The sea had muted and blurred the colors a trifle, but that didn't trouble Tristan. His clothes had never stayed fine for very long. Elisena had worked the salt-soaked wool soft again, presenting it to him this very morning with a flourish, and Tristan thought that his pleasure about it had rather surprised her.

Ambere began to inventory their other gear, as if to assure himself that he had forgotten nothing. There were the thickly padded woolen bags for them to sleep snug in, the clothes, and the climbing tools. He was providing them with great coils of light rope, for they would certainly meet with country too rough to be climbed without such aid.

Beside the coils were metal spikes, which Ambere said were also to aid in climbing. He explained carefully to Polassar how they were used as anchors for the rope, being driven securely into cervices in rock or solid ice. There were hammers as well for that purpose, one for each of them to carry. Tristan paid careful attention to the lecture, hoping all the while that they wouldn't need any of the stuff. He was glad to see Polassar looking flattered at his being singled out, for a change. The man surely thought that Ambere considered him the only member of the party with a sufficiently practical turn of mind to profit by the instruction and agreed wholeheartedly with the judgment.

As to food, they'd carry little at the start—only such as would accustom them to climbing with loaded packs. The birds would supply them day-to-day, as they reported to Ambere of each day's progress. When they at length reached the point beyond which even the great eagles could not penetrate, a last, large drop of provisions would be arranged. Till then, they'd happily dispense with the extra weight.

The food they would carry in case of emergency or bird-delaying storms had been well dried to lighten it as much as possible. Jerked meats made up most of it, but there were many squares of a sort of cake as well. Ambere insisted that each pack must contain a share of the mixture of grains, nuts, and dried fruits. He contended that a single square could sustain a man for well over a day.

Polassar had seemed more ready to accept Ambere's word on other subjects, but that claim tested him sorely. He regarded the squares skeptically as Ambere expanded upon their usefulness. If they should by any chance become separated . . .

A shiver slid down Tristan's spine at the thought. Being caught all alone in Channadran . . . To cover his too-vivid imagination, he leaned forward and touched what looked to be a section of charred rowan wood. The chunk was about as long as his arm from wrist to elbow and not much thicker. No charcoal soiled the finger he'd brushed against it. Thomas, eyes wary still for low-flying birds, jumped to the table and sniffed with equal curiosity.

"You run ahead." Ambere said, behind him.

"What is it?" Tristan asked, having failed to learn anything from his own or Thomas' examinations.

"Warmth, to keep your blood from freezing when the sun does not shine and you are too weary to walk. You'll find no wood on Channadran's slopes either." Ambere recited a phrase, and the log burst into flames where it sat, putting a coil of rope in some jeopardy. Thomas leaped backward with great agility, missing the table's edge and rebounding from Tristan's chest to the floor.

Ambere said a second spell and made a gesture of dismissal. The flames died, and the wood was no further consumed than it had been before he spoke. Thomas hissed and slunk off to settle his fur and his nerves.

"You will each practice the keys to this until you have them by heart. And take good care of this—it is far from an easy device to craft."

Tristan rehearsed Polassar in the spell that night, intermittently brightening the nearly dark room, to Thomas' irritation. It was slow work. Polassar's big fingers had infinite difficulties in mastering the fingerplay of the passes, and he had still more in recalling them. Tristan, mindful of his own difficulties in commanding certain spells, had less trouble being patient than Polassar did.

"Plague take this foolery! Can we not just carry sea coal?"

"No." Tristan knew better than to give in, even in jest, and he swallowed his smile. Ambere's command had been firm and sensible. "This is better, and it's not *that* difficult. Try again. Cock your thumb back more this time."

"Art trying to ruin my sword hand, Wizard? 'Twon't *go* farther."

"Oh, it will." Tristan swallowed another grin. "Trust me. And on the cantrip—stress the second syllable less." Tristan spoke the troublesome word both ways, slowly. "Hear the difference?"

"Aye," Polassar answered doubtfully.

If nothing else, Tristan supposed, this night would wring a respect for wizardry from Polassar. Pity it came so late. He could have used a bit of that respect the time he'd first met Polassar, when they went questing after Allaire and her rings. Even a little would have made his life so much easier, then.

"It's maybe a little harder than it looks," he suggested sympathetically. "Takes a while to master any new thing."

Polassar snorted. "I keep telling you, Wizard. Swords are cleaner than this skulking about in the dark."

Tristan finally let a smile out and motioned the man to try once more.

By the time they all bedded down, Polassar could light the magewood on about half his tries. Tristan had decided that the progress would have to be good enough for the present moment. They had to rise early in the morning, and a later night would make that unpleasant. Tristan lay back among the bed furs, wondering if he'd sleep soundly or if he could expect to see big fingers waving and hear mangled words in his mind all night long.

He *did* hear them, Tristan realized moments later, though the syllables were considerably blurred by snores. The realization dragged him back from the fringes of sleep. Tristan sat up.

The sound faded, then came again as he listened. He was able to put a direction to it—the spot where Polassar had spread out his pallet. Tristan rubbed at his eyes, trying to sharpen his vision to match his hearing.

Polassar lay on his back, exactly as he'd flung himself down while still flushed with his last triumph, his limbs sprawling every which way. His lips moved, and the words came forth again, clear as bell notes. They disappeared under another reef of snores, but still better than anything he'd done awake.

Tristan's eyes widened. Luckily the man's hands weren't moving in time to the spell—at least Tristan thought not. In the dim firelight, it was hard to tell, and he was more asleep than awake himself. But why should he be so relieved? Tristan would have staked what little reputation he had that no one could work a magic without consciously willing it. Certainly not such a one as Polassar.

After a minute of anxiety which he didn't care to have extended over the entire night, Tristan slid out from under the furs. He limped across the chilly flags, cursing under his breath, and rummaged about until he found the pack he sought. He lifted out the chunk of magewood and put it safely on a bare spot in the middle of the floor, away from anything burnable. Appeased, if sheepish, he climbed back into the bed.

Elisena stirred, rolling over to lie against his side. Tristan looked down at her a long while, thinking how seldom such a chance came, when she was not up earliest and latest, tending to anyone's needs but her own. He would have been wiser to sleep while he could, too, but Tristan relished the protective feeling enough to ignore such good sense. He felt absurdly grateful to Polassar for wakening him. And if he tried to hold the moment so as not to have to look ahead into the dark—well, a corner of his mind saw through that subterfuge, and that was quite sufficient.

In the morning, they all donned their new garments, slinging on belts and other such gear as suited each of them best and settling straps and pouches as comfortably as might be until the clothes were well worn in. Polassar overlooked his, and grumbled profusely about having to disrobe and start over, but Tristan was pleased at the knitted wool pieces that went under the other gear. The pieces fitted close, while the outer things fitted loosely, resembling sweaters and breeches, warm just to look at. In the mountain cold, they'd be doubly welcome—and Am Islin was not all that warm, at daybreak.

While the dressing went on, they snatched mouthfuls of oatcakes drowned in honey and great planks of fish browned smoking hot in seasoned crumbs. There was ale, rich stuff with a fine, nutty flavor, served up in tankards made of great horn-shells. Polassar's spirits rose remarkably, and he left off fussing over his tunic fastenings to address his mug properly.

Watching him, Tristan glanced at Reynaud's place, saw his set of clothing still folded neatly upon a little stool by the fire, just as they'd been left the night before. Reynaud didn't look to be in any hurry about getting into them. He still wore his familiar black, with all the gold and scarlet embroideries upon the fitted undergarments. Tristan had been too busy dressing himself to note that Reynaud had not followed suit. Now he gave the matter his full attention. Could it be—dare he hope?

"Have you decided to stay at Am Islin, then?" he asked,

his voice a shade more hopeful than he could reasonably expect Reynaud to overlook.

Reynaud arched a brow at his transparency. "Hardly so. Why ever should you think that?" He marked Tristan's pointed glance at the pile of clothes. "Ah. Those things are of little interest to me. I am used to my own garments and shall keep them."

"I hope you're used to cold as well," Tristan commented nastily, disappointed.

Reynaud draped his cloak back carefully, fussing with its artistic folds. "Don't trouble yourself on my account, my lord. This cloak will suffice me. It's extremely ... adaptable."

He flicked one finger, a movement so small that only another wizard could have guessed at it as magic, and the black fabric rearranged itself instantly, wrapping Reynaud snugly yet leaving his arms unhindered. Another finger flick and the cloak resumed its former elegant draping, settling back down like some exotic bird's plumage.

"A small matter of sorcery," Reynaud explained negligently into the taut silence that ensued.

If anyone besides Tristan felt that Reynaud was unwise to scorn Magister Ambere's gifts, they kept quiet about their doubts. Nor did Ambere himself remark upon the matter when he came to see them off, an omission which left Tristan utterly baffled. Ambere seemed uncharacteristically forbearing, and surely even Reynaud couldn't value a chance to show off his skill so highly?

The wizard would be sorry soon enough. Tristan looked forward to that satisfying moment. They packed the extra clothing as spares, so there was no real danger to Reynaud—except to his overweening pride, when the man came a-begging, shivering, as he needs must.

the First Steps

THE SKY ABOVE THE TOWER WAS THE DULL COLOR OF lead, and the osprey upon Ambere's shoulder stood out as whitely against it as did the tower itself.

Somewhere within Am Islin, Minstrel was beating his wings wildly against the bars of a cage—the first cage Am Islin had ever seen. Tristan heard that pitiful struggle with his mind, if not his ears, and his heart was fully as heavy as his resolve. He had made the cage himself, and Ambere had not refused it.

Ambere was scarcely more communicative than the sea-eagle that companioned him as he watched them on their way. Any words of counsel they might have hoped to have were listened for in vain. Royston Ambere bore a great staff of what looked to be driftwood, but it had never been wrought by sea alone. He spoke to it, his tone so low that none could catch his words. Tristan wished he'd dared to examine that staff more closely. He knew he might have learned much from the opportunity, fleeting as it was. He had more questions in his head about Ambere than ever; some answers would have been welcome to complement them.

He got no answers. His face, like the faces of the others, was turned at once toward the mountains, and Tristan left his questions behind. It was simpler so—and best that he travel light.

The tongue of the Winterwaste that they needed to cross was narrow, and perchance Nímir's power did not run so strongly when it clashed with Ambere's domain. Or mayhap the tongue was but a recent outreaching of the Waste, not yet ancient enough to have acquired the usual number of baleful inhabitants. The air was dry and cold, the winds incessant and tricky, but snow fell only intermittently, never so heavily as to confuse all sense of their course. The little party met with no perils of any other sort. In two days they were out of the Waste, though, as Ambere had predicted, the country looked scarcely different. The distinction was one of maps, not of landscape. They tramped till another sun-fall.

The first change in terrain came when they reached hills, which broke the winds and let a sparse few scrubby plants take hold. It became possible to find relatively sheltered spots in which to sleep at night, for which Tristan was grateful. They had rested one night while crossing the Winterwaste, not finding it safe to move there in the dark, but Tristan doubted that the others had slept any more or any better than he had himself. Their woolen bags were warm enough and could be laced tight to keep out all the cold air, except what was needed for breathing, but the whispering, teasing rush of the wind had made sleep either impossible or unrestful. Tristan walked in a sort of a daze for hours the next day, uncertain whether he was depressed or merely half-asleep on his feet.

At night, the four of them resembled four lumps of gray rock among the sere grasses that grew between the wind-stunted bushes. It was good camouflage, if such had been intended, but Tristan suspected that they were unmolested rather than ignored or overlooked. He had a keen sense that something waited for them far ahead, something that was content to wait so—for a while yet. He didn't sleep well the night he thought of that, either.

Falcons soared ahead of them by day, marking their route, lest there be any doubt, and seeking decent campsites for the night. Later, owls sometimes appeared like ghosts, soundless fliers that they were, their eyes glowing in the light of Ambere's magewood. Food arrived with them, a fresh-killed hare, perhaps, or a marmot and once salt fish with a faint smoky flavor which Thomas much relished. Tristan had as little appetite for food as for sleep, despite all the exercise, so Thomas easily got a bit more than his rightful share of such dainties.

Watching the birds come and go, Tristan found himself listening for the familiar whir of wings beside his ear and, when it did not come, missing it dreadfully. His heart did odd, hopeful things every time nearby wild birds began to sing. Under stress, his spirits remained as buoyant as lead, though he never once regretted having left Minstrel behind. The canary had the best home he could ever hope to find, even if that was not of the slightest comfort to his lonely master. One life, at least, was not hostage to Nímir.

Walking, at least till late in the day when they began to grow weary, was much more conducive to conversation than riding had been. They stayed closer together, especially after that first, haunted night, and the scenery was so dull and unvarying that they badly needed some way of passing the time. They rapidly developed a regular pattern for it.

Talk began usually when Reynaud or Elisena spotted some herb growing tenaciously by the trail and fell to discussing its rarity, the spots where it was more common, and the uses to which it might be put. Having opened matters thus, Reynaud might go on to discourse at length of his student days or his wide travels, never seeming to care whether his anecdotes were attended to by anyone save Elisena.

At first Polassar was bored enough to take recourse in the chanting of his forefathers' marching song under his breath, until he had all of them humming the measure—which was maddening at times. However, Reynaud soon discovered Polassar's fondness for tales of marvels and heroes and he craftily began to confine himself mostly to those subjects. The chanting dwindled and ceased.

Tristan suspected that most of the legends were invented at the moment, strung together word by word, but he never challenged a tale, not wanting to seem churlish. Polassar questioned nothing, however extreme, leading Tristan to suppose that the man's education must have consisted solely of legends read from wonder books. He considered Polassar's manner of speech, the rich blend of common talk and archaic usages, and thought that his idle guess was very likely quite correct.

At night, whenever it wasn't cloudy, they sat with backs to the fire and its light and heard the tales that were told in Kôvelir about the stars—of the great black wolf Valint, whose eye the green Wolf Star was; and of Cirilyn, who wore a tiara of gems beyond the hope of any earthy queen. Adares, her lord, searched the starfields for her cease-lessly, but the very seasons conspired to keep the lovers apart—there were never both their sets of stars in the sky at one season.

Tales were told of the Kings and the times before them, sketchy as that information necessarily was. Having read so many of the chronicles of his kingdom, Tristan was able to comment as often as he cared to, which was not frequently. He was still nervous about Reynaud and not anxious for his fellowship.

Nonetheless, the two of them spoke a good deal about magic. Constant contact had failed to lessen the friction between Reynaud and Tristan—they were no more easy together than flint and steel, and likewise always striking sparks—but they did talk. The fault of their quarreling lay with both of them, shifting impartially from one to the other with fair regularity; and they were both quirky enough to begin pining for speech just after they'd sol-emnly sworn to hold silent. Resolves like that tended to go by the boards quite often.

Tristan was too ready to see mockery and insult in Reynaud's jests, and Reynaud was far too eager to bait him. Day after day, it was the same—peace for a while and then sarcastic words, quiet talk and then silences so acid they would have eaten metal. Elisena watched it all with troubled eyes and sometimes a set mouth.

"Magic is an art, and as such has fewer hard-and-fast rules than you might suppose or have been taught," Rey-naud pontificated, chewing at a bit of rabbit. "Much is merest usage. In some lands there are mages who claim they conjure something called Daemons to work their will."

"And do they?" Tristan barely concealed his skepti-cism.

"I doubt it." Reynaud shrugged, and firelight flashed red and gold from his clothes. He had never yet com-plained of so much as a chilled toe, to Tristan's disgust. "They believe they can work no sorcery without the prac-tice; but of course they are in error. The rules, whatever exactly they are, should be the same everywhere, regard-less of local superstitions. I've heard it said that more depends on a wizard's will than on his trappings. Observe—with this gesture I light fire."

Flames crackled between Reynaud's feet in response to his fingers, till a little clump of dry grass was consumed.

"Yet how often do a man's fingers align themselves so by chance, and no flame occurs? The intent seals the spell. To confuse things the more, half the common magic is no magic at all, but thrifty profiting by the happenstance of the moment. Yet there is skill to be considered, and Power, and those two go not always hand in hand. Skill may be learned with persistence, but true Power is beyond our understanding, if not our use. Thus we study always, while we live." He quenched the fire between his boots finally, with a gesture even more negligent than the one he had used to light it.

Tristan said nothing. Blais had always been a little impatient with the Theory of Magic, and thus his pupil didn't feel safe enough in it to dispute with Reynaud, graduate of Kôvelir's illustrious Academy. Tristan congratulated himself that he was no fool. Thomas sighed and shook his whiskers.

"I have always been fascinated by Power," Reynaud was going on. He seemed like to do so all night. "I was led to magic, seeking it. I thought the mastery of a few tricks would give it to me, at least over such simple folk as are easily swayed by that sort of mummery. I found to my amazement that there was Power *in* the magic, the magic itself, and from that moment my life changed. I like to think I have been a faithful lover, giving as well as taking."

He was quiet a moment, then seemed to toss off the mood as perhaps inappropriate.

"But what of Blais' apprentice? You've never told us what set you on this course."

Tristan looked up from his task—he was grooming Thomas, carefully working the travel snarls and balls of ice out of the cat's dense belly fur. Wizards' fingers were agile, useful for more than sorcery. By then Thomas was dead asleep from a surfeit of ecstasy. Tristan shrugged at the question.

"I was raised by a wizard," he said. To a casual listener, that would have explained the matter well enough, or at least communicated that he wished to say nothing more on the subject.

"And that's all there was to it? Come, sir, that's too dull!" Reynaud wasn't to be put off. "Did he just train you for a hobby or was it by your own choice?"

Tristan tilted his head back, easing cramped muscles. He'd caught the pleading look Elisena was wearing for his benefit. He sat so a moment, remembering, seeking understanding.

"My choice," he said at last, very quietly. "I wanted to be what he was. It was natural enough. I'd never seen anything else. He was all the family I had, all the world I knew. Blais could do the most wonderful things, fascinating things. What child wouldn't want to live with a wizard?"

Polassar snorted, but Tristan didn't hear.

"I saw him change a stone into a toad once. It's one of the very first things I really remember. I followed that toad everywhere for a whole day, trying to figure out how he'd done it. Finally it tried to cross running water and turned back into a stone." He smiled ruefully, recalling how heartbroken that long-ago small boy had been that day, the day that Blais had finally, in desperation, begun to teach him wizardry. "Do you know, I still can't make that particular spell work," he added wistfully.

"That's a long time to be bothered by an illusion," Reynaud said.

"Ah, but it was a very *good* illusion. Blais was a craftsman."

Reynaud made a disgusted noise. It drenched reverie like cold rain.

Tristan sat up so straight and so sharply that he jarred Thomas awake. He checked the movement at once, but there were muscles jumping in his jaw and sword hand, past his control.

"I meant no disrespect to Blais," Reynaud said blandly, not having missed the signs of tension.

If there had been anywhere to go, Tristan would have gotten up and walked away from him. He told himself that, even as he began to speak into the silence that had fallen like a weight upon them.

"Then perhaps you'll tell me just what you *did* mean." His voice was frighteningly formal.

"Of course."

Watch it, Thomas said in alarm. *How did you manage to start this up so fast? Can't I snatch a minute's sleep in peace?*

"Don't take such ready insult," Reynaud said, his very tone another slight. "I was thinking of something quite other than Blais' abilities. I would not presume to criticize one whom Master Cabal held in such high regard, certainly not a man I never met."

"*You* studied with Cabal?" Tristan asked, startled nearly into forgetting anger and pride.

"Yes," Reynaud said amusedly. "I, too."

Tristan looked away from him. The memories of his own studies with Cabal and his rather spectacular failures, were still too raw to be bearable. He knew he ought long since to have put them in perspective. He hadn't been in Kôvelir to study; he had been tricked into it by his own reluctance to hurt Cabal and hadn't had time to devote to an art which consumed all one's hours or none of them. Still, he'd failed—miserably. A further horror occurred to him. Could Reynaud possibly know as much about that as his smile indicated?

There was nobody in Kôvelir who would have known except Cabal and possibly Bleyvr, but Reynaud had his own ways of finding things out. Tristan began to fidget nervously, his fingers unable to remain still.

Luckily, he'd removed them from Thomas' fur. It was lucky, because he was past noticing what they were doing, and he didn't realize what was going on until the tiny pile of cat hair combings beside his right boot burst into magical flame.

Tristan cursed his memory, which would desert him at the most critical times and yet now could pick up perfectly the threads of the spell he'd barely noticed Reynaud casting—not only pick them up but repeat them flawlessly. Polassar, of course, thought he was just cursing because he was getting scorched, but everyone else present knew the truth, multiplying his humiliation. Tristan tried to stomp the flames out, but they only coiled around his boot and threatened his breeches. The quenching-spell, which naturally he could only remember partially, didn't work on the first two of three attempts.

Tristan sat down again. No one said anything—the

silence was as suffocating as the stench of burned hair. Over and over, Tristan reminded himself that he ought to be used to that sort of thing. It no longer mattered whether Reynaud knew about Kôvelir. He wanted to sink through the cold ground.

The moment might have passed, however awkwardly, if Reynaud had permitted it to. He did not.

"I've often wondered at your charming modesty about your magical accomplishments," he said mildly. "Hardly realistic, despite this obvious block you seem to have. 'Ware letting little mischances overshadow true accomplishments. You have more ability than you've taught yourself to expect. At Radak—"

"Oh, yes," Tristan answered, wanting a quarrel by then. "Thank you for reminding me. I've been curious about that a long time. Why *did* you let me go?"

"Do you suggest I could have detained you?"

Tristan gestured at the blackened spot by his feet. "I wouldn't think you'd have had much to worry about. Even less then. And don't bother claiming any noble feelings toward a fellow wizard. You tried to kill me not long afterward."

"That's past," Reynaud insisted strongly.

"Yes. Maybe. But nonetheless, I want an answer from you. It might shed some light on future questions." Shame had curdled into anger.

Polassar shifted uneasily, firelight glinting golden from his arm band as he moved. Those two looked certain to come to blows, and he ought to take steps to prevent such a disaster, for all their sakes, but he was mortally uncertain which of the two of them it would be least unwise to lay hands on.

"Do you mean that if I answer satisfactorily, I'll win your trust, now?"

"I doubt that, but you're welcome to try." Tristan swept a hand out, offering Reynaud free speech.

Reynaud shrugged. "You won't believe the truth. I told you that once before. Why did I let you go, when I more or less had you in my power? I had no choice. I could not have held you there. And I wanted no part in unleashing what I sensed in you. There was a quality to your despair that night. I feared it, feared to push you too far. I spoke of the power of a wizard's will before. If you ever lose hope entirely, I think you could rip the roots of this world apart."

Tristan laughed. It was all the response he could think of to make.

"It's not a matter for joking," Reynaud said sternly. "You don't understand. I told you you wouldn't."

"No. And next you'll confess to me that you're frighted of the dark, and I expect my reaction will be the same. What sort of fool do you take me for?"

Reynaud shook his head angrily. "You asked me for an answer. I've given it to you. Accept it or not, as you like. It's all one to me."

"I doubt that."

Polassar gave Elisena a desperate look. He wasn't even following the point of the fight anymore; they'd lost him a long way back, but the anger was so thick that he could smell it over the burned fur. He'd seen men kill in calmer moods.

"You doubt everything." Reynaud's voice was smooth as a snake's skin. "If I'm ever proved right, I trust you'll remember."

"You must have had a time explaining yourself to Galan," Tristan said musingly.

"Indeed, no. I simply never tried—I was wiser then. I permitted him to think that I was too busy saving his life to stop you as well. I could have done both, of course. He was never in *that* much danger from that wound— but he didn't know. I left the revenge-cup for him to drink; he relished the taste of it more. Nothing I've seen since makes me regret that decision."

"For a man who asks trust, you're awfully proud of your double-dealing."

"One does what one—" Reynaud snapped the train of words as though they'd been a knife blade bent too far out of line. "You're playing at word games with me, because you're afraid and because you think your magic doesn't measure up." His eyes flashed. "You, with your talent that you don't understand, can't even *see*! The little magics may slip through your fingers, but the things you *do*! You create spells as you go, improvised for the moment—so simple and direct that they're only virtually impossible! That kind of magic can't be learned or memorized, only honed by the kind of training and polishing that Kôvelir excels at. You've got a gift, you fool, a gift most of the mages of Kôvelir would gladly trade an eye and a hand for. And you behave as if it's *nothing*!"

Tristan sat stunned a moment, then said with deepest suspicion, because that was the best thing to cover hope with, and he was determined not to be that helpless in front of Reynaud, "If it's as you say, then explain why, with this great talent, I can't cast the simplest spell straight half the time! Now who's playing at riddles?"

Reynaud arched one dark, thin brow.

"*I* don't know why you can't. Perhaps you do. You scourge yourself endlessly over an illusion you can't turn and you grieve over children's tricks. Illusion, charades, formulas—magic-by-rote! It's beyond me why you even *care* about that drivel. Does an eagle lust to build a wren's nest?"

He's such a snob, Thomas said, rolling over again. That seemed safe. The urge to fight had gone out of Tristan, replaced by something that was probably worse, but at least was quieter. The crack about his magic not measuring up had hit home, the more so after the appallingly graphic demonstration. Thomas doubted that Tristan had really heard anything that was said afterward, though it was very like him to have kept on arguing anyway, saying words that tumbled out of their own accord.

Reynaud's voice had an odd quality to it, just for a moment. Thomas was surprised when he placed it, finally, as gentleness.

"Whatever blocks you, it's somewhere very deep," the wizard was saying to Tristan. "You're afraid, and that makes you hold back even when you don't realize it. It works that way—fear becomes a habit, and then you have a barrier of your own making. If it's been there long enough, you won't even be able to see it. It could take a lifetime to discover where it is or why it grew there. I'm not sure you want to try. You get around it well enough when you really need to. Strong emotion helps, as you've probably discovered already. Anger, fear, or despair."

Tristan said nothing. He was afraid—afraid to hope, afraid of a trap, afraid Reynaud was only setting him up for some final humiliation.

Elisena took breath to speak, then held back. The conversation had taken a nasty tone from the very first, but there was hope in it, too. Tristan and Reynaud might, against all likelihood, bridge the gap between them. That could happen in an instant—if they didn't come to blows first.

She didn't much like the look on Tristan's face. He was close to tears, under his anger and wariness. Maybe he was tired at last of walking tiptoe around Reynaud and exhausted from the no-longer very private agony which she'd mistaken for the lack of sleep affecting them all to some degree. His hands were shaking ever so slightly, and he looked at them wildly once, as if he expected some new catastrophe to slip through them. Elisena wished she knew more precisely what his emotion was. Walls must break to come down, and this was one she'd be happy to deal a good, solid shove, but not if doing so risked breaking Tristan as well.

"It may just be that some part of you recognizes how basically worthless the little magics are," Reynaud went on thoughtfully. "You don't want to waste time with them. That would be sensible. Why pine to exchange the gold you already have for the glitter anyone can acquire?"

"So, amid all that glitter they gave you at Kôvelir, is there a cure for this? An answer?"

His tone was sarcastic, but there was a forlorn helplessness under it, a longing in Tristan's voice that wrung Elisena's heart. She'd been wrong in her hopes, and this had gone on long enough—too long. She reached out to him, but Tristan didn't see. His hollow eyes saw only Reynaud.

"Answers? What would you have me do—take you back to your basic lessons and retrain you? No. The answer you require is one you must find for yourself. I can't give you mine." Reynaud looked troubled. He was about to say something more, or seemed to be, but the bridge was breaking when it had scarce been begun, dropping away into the chasm below.

"I didn't think you'd tell me," Tristan said bitterly, and turned away into the night.

the High Pass

ONE THING WAS NEVER DISCUSSED, NOR DID IT NEED
to be. In that sort of country, it was not easy to forget
where they were bound. For a sevenday, they did only
rough walking, with no climbing worthy of the name; but
the rising ground grew more and more bleak, and Channadran's peaks rose always in front of their faces, in case
anyone needed reminding. The air was chill, colder than
season or altitude warranted.

Elisena walked by Tristan. After a while, he noticed
how seldom she joined in their conversations and how far
away was the look in her eyes. He couldn't presume to
guess that her thoughts matched his own, so he only walked
by her side, offering her that little comfort and remaining
silent most of the time himself.

Ambere's eagles brought evil tidings—reports out of
Calandra itself, relayed by lesser birds escaping it. Great
masses of cold air flowed down upon the land from the
Winterwaste, and an icy rain fell almost daily. The crops
were dead, rotted in the fields before harvesttime. Snow
had not fallen on the wreckage yet, but it was daily
expected. In Esdragon, farther from the Waste, there had
been some grain reaped, but great storms had come in
from the sea, wreaking much destruction. Famine, not
yet quite inevitable, was not far off.

Such news desolated all their hearts. Even moving at
their fastest pace, they would barely be into Channadran
when winter sank its fangs into Calandra's throat. There
was no haste or craft by which they could spare the land
this season of destruction. It had been folly to hope seri-

ously that they might, but there was no one of them that had not secretly cherished such a dream. Even Reynaud's usually mocking face was shadowed with that shared despair and took on the determination the rest of them felt, though Tristan suspected that it was mostly show or protective coloration.

Tristan took a wand from his pack. It was not a magical tool, only a bit of peeled willow twig, but it was valuable all the same. He laced it through the fingers of his right hand and began to slowly twirl and manipulate it, using four fingers only, permitting no help from his thumb. Later, he'd restrict himself still further.

He twirled it forward and backward, then repeated both ways with a variation that used three fingers only, skipping one and picking it up again on the next round. The muscles in his forearm began to ache. Obviously, he needed the practice. He'd scrimped on it too long, having been lazy as well as busy. He could nearly hear Blais chiding him on that account.

After a bit, he began the drill over again, using his left hand. He was pleased at his progress—his muscles might be recalcitrant, but he hadn't yet dropped the wand or been unable to move it. Blais would have grudgingly approved. There was no sign of any block in his finger-play.

Why was he thinking of blocks? Dwelling on them only made them worse. He cursed Reynaud's bringing the subject up in the first place! Tristan sat staring into the fire; but though the yellow flames flickered across his eyes, he did not blink or otherwise react to the changing light.

Reynaud, noticing, called his name softly. He got no response. *Self-wrought trance.* Reynaud's lips curved in satisfaction. He had not expected the process to begin so easily, and so hard on the heels of his words the night before, but so quick a response was not unheard of. Get a man thinking about a problem of this nature, and quite often the mind took over without conscious attention, to solve the riddles that the man would shy from, if fully aware. Something like that must be going on in Tristan's mind.

Still, so rooted a problem would not be cured by trance alone, or it would long since have been resolved. Like a man caught in a marsh, Tristan would need to be guided to safe ground. Reynaud stretched out his fingers. Let there be the lightest of contacts between them, skin to skin, and he'd be able to read the trance like the clearest-lettered scroll. And with what he could learn, he might shape a cure. His fingers brushed Tristan's cheek.

For Tristan, the sensation was like coming awake—or beginning to and not quite making the whole journey— and so he was caught between for what seemed an endless age. A blinding light flooded his mind, with a hint of green to it that somehow terrified him. Something was stirring like a wind, and something else was *hopping—*

He struck out wildly, only wanting his hands free to cover his face and shut away that awful brightness before he remembered— His hand hit something, and the light died.

No, his sight simply cleared. Tristan found he was looking straight into Reynaud's eyes, as if he and the wizard had been conversing closely, but he couldn't remember anything they might have talked about. He felt more as if he'd just screamed, but the mountains gave back no echoes, and no one was reacting as if he'd done anything so odd as crying out. Reynaud looked puzzled, but that he could cheerfully ignore.

Must have dozed off, Tristan thought, wondering how he could have done that with Reynaud so close. He felt stiff from exercise and sitting still so long, perched on a cold rock. Tristan stretched, coming back to himself. He certainly must have dozed and begun to dream. The dream was gone, but shreds of it remained, teasing him. Facts fled, but emotions stayed. That must be why he felt so odd.

Why should a dream upset him so? Nothing that he remembered of it was frightening—just light, grass waving, and water sparkling. It should have been rather pleasant. And it was pointless to wonder about it. Far better to let it all be forgotten. He discovered the wand in his hand and put it away.

That night, after the eagles had brought the doleful news, they all seemed to sink into thoughts as chill as the great ices of the Winterwaste. But in the morning, they did all that they might do. They went on.

Their course had begun to veer sunward a couple of

days earlier as they made for the pass Ambere had recommended to their use. Now they pressed on with greater
speed, always uphill. Those hills took the sharpest edges
off of their determination, whittling away with the keen
blade of exhaustion. By then they were scrambling more
often than walking.

There had to be a gap between the shoulders of the
peaks before them—Ambere's birds could not have been
mistaken about that—but it was days before they had
that gap in sight and days more before they were in reach
of it.

Ice had indeed filled the pass, but not so deeply as
they had feared to discover. It was possible to climb above
the glacier, on the skirts of the mountains, without going
very much higher than they were. They found ways enough
among the rocks, mostly swept bare of snow by the same
winds that were wreaking havoc upon Calandra. The way
was never easy, but it was possible, even when it didn't
appear so.

Rockfalls often blocked their way, or ridges thrust down
across their path. Not liking to trust the ice below, which
was full of deep crevasses, as could be seen from above,
they learned the use of their ropes. As Ambere had predicted, the mountains taught them to climb. So, at last,
they forced Channadran's postern gate; if any guard posted
there gave alarm, they heard nothing of it. The hawks
went as always before them, eyes alert.

Still on the slopes beside the ice-clogged valley, they
turned yet farther to sunward, moving around the flank
of the peak they had just passed. The highest peaks lay
in that direction, and that was compass enough for any
of them at that moment. A gyrfalcon's dark wings marked
out the way in the sky above.

Snow sifted down, picked out briefly by the firelight,
then fell on past their ledge and vanished. It had become
difficult to find campsites which were more than narrow
shelves upon the mountainside. For several days, one
camp had been much like another in a dead land of ice
and snow, except that each was a bit more cramped and
a bit less convenient than the last.

Flakes settled on their clothing and gear, as well as on

the rocks. They covered Elisena's bare head as she spoke, glistening like the stars of Cirilyn's crown.

"Once winter was a time for sporting and frolicking. Men fastened staves of bone to their boots and skated about on the frozen rivers. And there were sleigh races, with bells tied in the manes of the horses. Half the designs that the weavers and embroiderers use were once snowflakes. They were considered beautiful, miracles like flowers, beauties which lasted but for an instant and then were gone, and so needed to be remembered." Elisena sighed and leaned her head against Tristan's shoulder. He brushed the flakes away from her hair.

"In those days, winter was but one of the natural seasons. We could depend upon it to end in its proper time. Then we never doubted that spring and life would return. I wonder if our folk will ever feel lighthearted at the sight of snow again?"

No one answered the wistful question. Tristan watched Polassar, who was hunching over against the cold. He had taken off his arm-ring and turned it round and round between his big hands, the meaningless motion as soothing as the remembered touch of Allaire's white hands.

Once they had rounded the peak that guarded the pass, looking back became fruitless—only mountains could be seen in any direction. The lowlands might never have existed. Perhaps, Tristan thought, remembering the glacier thrusting through the pass and the news from Calandra, they no longer did, but had been crushed and flattened to frozen mud. So, there were no backward glances.

Tristan stared ahead apprehensively at still loftier peaks than the one beside them, peaks whose tops were lost among clouds. When snow fell thickly, all the farther mountains vanished, and even the nearest slopes were muffled to charcoal-colored smudges against the sky. Unfortunately, that brought no relief. He didn't need to see the mountains to know they were there and waiting.

The wind played without ceasing between Channadran's heights. It could be heard always, though felt only occasionally and not in its full force, for it was blocked and thwarted by the maze of mountain sides and rock walls. That was fortunate, offering the party a small respite while still keeping the trails they must use more or less clear of snow.

On the day they reached the pass, no snow fell, though clouds were massing. The nearer of the great peaks could still be seen, its rocks black fangs with the snow's white poison dripping from them. Tristan coiled up the ropes they'd used getting up a steep, boulder-strewn slope, while Polassar and Reynaud went ahead to scout out the next bit of the way. Tristan was slow at the task, not only because Thomas insisted on playing with the rope, but because his eyes kept straying from his work to the great chain of peaks that lay smack across their path.

"This frightens me," he confided quietly to Elisena, who was helping him manage the ropes. Her questioning silence drew him on. "I suppose this is the first time I've let myself think about what we're doing here, and now I'm terrified! I can't help wondering if whatever victories we've had have only been won because Nímir wasn't quite paying attention to us. Mostly it's been luck and accidents. To go into Channadran now to his very doorstep—Nímir won't ignore us any longer. He's going to start taking us seriously. He'll have to."

Tristan lifted his eyes to the distant peaks again. The sheer pinnacles were ribbed with ridges like strong-grained wood. Even as he watched, a great field of snow avalanched down the shoulders of one peak—a vast slide indeed, to be so plainly seen at such a distance. "How do we dare? How can we ever hope to best him? And why us, why this way?" He knew the questions weren't fair. He hardly knew he'd put them into words at last. They'd been hiding at the back of his mind for a long time.

"Suppose you want to get a sword," Elisena said softly, as if not to startle him. "You know all that involves, beyond simply going out and buying a blade. There is the metal to be dug, the wood to be burned to purify the metal and then forge it strong. And even when the blade is balanced and bright and true, still it must be tempered, sharpened, and hilted before it is ready to be put to its use. In all that time of its making, what does the iron know of the reason it was plucked from the ground? Or for whom? A weapon strong enough to be used against Nímir must be wrought with even greater skill and must be longer in its making. Metal will not serve for this weapon, but only human hearts—nothing less." She put a hand on his arm.

Reynaud had said that answers were what one found for oneself. Tristan must search out his own answers and not be a child begging for comfort where there could be very little. Like it or not. He deposited Thomas in his pack, slung the coils of rope over his shoulder, and gestured to Elisena. They set off after Polassar.

"Mark yon storm clouds, Wizard." Polassar jerked his head sideways, though the clouds scarcely required the indication. The whole sky boiled black with weather, dark almost as night, though it was just past sun-high. "Full of snow, aye, and all for us, if we don't move like quicksilver. We've got to be up that ridge and through yon gap before it hits us, or we'll never get there, not in this life. It's a rough way."

"Think we can make it?"

Polassar shrugged, eyed the clouds again, and flipped an imaginary coin into the cold air, then mimed catching it. "Long odds, Wizard. Let's be about it."

Ambere's birds reported the pass itself to be short and clear of serious obstacles. Once through it, they could go below the storm again, finding shelter on the lower slopes with fair ease. If they could get to the pass . . .

The wind picked up. The hawks departed in haste, lest sudden gusts smash them upon the rocks of the cliff side. They'd be back, once the storm had passed, to pick up the trail once again, if there should be any reason for them to do so.

Most of the way ahead was a rough scramble, always upward, over slopes of rock shattered to gravel. What must have done that shattering, Tristan did not like to guess. Better not to think about it. They made the best speed they could, trying not to waste time watching the sky, but with one eye always on it anyway. The clouds were still sweeping in endlessly and very fast.

Polassar topped the ridge and staggered to a halt. Tristan, not expecting the pause, bumped into him, lost his balance, and slid halfway back down the last slope before he got his footing back. His boots were sunk to the ankles in fine gravel.

"What?" he asked, as the sound—not faint—of Polassar's curses carried down to him. Polassar didn't answer him, so Tristan struggled upslope again with Elisena after him, well to the side of Polassar and out of mischance's way.

Reynaud was there already on Polassar's other side. His cloak flapped once against his ankles as if surprised, then hung limp once more.

"We'll never get up that," Reynaud said, his voice flat as slate.

Rising above the ridge where they stood was a thirty-foot-high cliff of sheer granite, its face as smooth and sharp as knife-sliced cheese. It dropped down from the pass almost to Polassar's feet. Once up it, they'd be on their way, free and clear, but the cliff offered not the slightest foothold and not the least relenting of its steepness. There was no spot at which they might claw their way up. They could see the pass above them, but that sight seemed to be as close as they'd ever get to it.

"We'll have to seek shelter farther down," Reynaud went on.

"And come back all this way when 'tis covered with rime and frost?" Polassar's arm-sweep generously took in the whole way they'd just come, with rocks of all sizes. They'd have to retrace a league at least to reach shelter.

"Unless you think Ambere can lend us his birds' power of flight, we'll have to," Reynaud insisted. "And the sooner the better." Big flakes were starting to fall.

Tristan's heart sank. There'd been no prophecy about it, but somehow it seemed to him desperately wrong that they should turn back or give up one foot of ground, once they'd covered it. That made about as much sense as a child's fear of stepping on certain "unlucky" colors of stones, but the feeling was there and strong. Tristan paid it more heed when he realized that it had come to him as his hand rested upon his sword hilt. They should go ahead only, never retreating by one single pace, or they'd forfeit what little luck they had. The hilt felt warm under his cold fingers.

What's all the fuss about? Thomas' head popped out of the top of the pack, just behind Tristan's left ear. *Oh my!* His head disappeared again.

Tristan considered the need for retreat. Maybe Elisena could shelter them by hardening a shell of air around them. He knew she could do such things, but she'd used no magic of that sort thus far, and there might be a reason for that, he supposed. And if she were disposed or able to use her powers in such a way, she was saying nothing about it. Surely the suggestion ought to be hers.

He rejoined Polassar in making a closer inspection of the cliff face, while Reynaud fretted and argued with Elisena, since Polassar was ignoring him. The cliff wasn't perfectly smooth, of course. There were plenty of fissures running down it—unfortunately, none of them seemed to promise secure footholds. If they chose to climb, they'd need to go fast. In fact, if he and Polassar didn't locate something very soon, Tristan knew he'd have to resign himself to turning back, whatever his sword insisted.

"Ha! Wizard, it looks like our luck's not left us just yet! See?"

Snow was falling more thickly. Tristan had to squint through it to see what Polassar was pointing at. To him, it looked like just a slash of shadow on the cliff—then he realized that the overcast sky wasn't bright enough to cast such a shadow. He went closer, right at Polassar's heels.

What Polassar's sharper eye had spotted was a broad crack running vertically through the rock, broader than his own shoulders by at least a little. It ran the whole way to the top of the cliff, Tristan could see that by the way the snow-melt had run in and frozen along the sides. Polassar went closer, craning his neck to make sure. Yes, it was open to the sky at the top, save for a few boulders wedged in. Those could be gotten around.

"We'll climb it like chimney sweeps, Wizard. Backs to one side, boots to the other. And a rope rigged, just to be safest."

Polassar stepped into the bottom of the crack, head still back. "Looks like she widens a bit, toward the top. Might be nasty. Ropes for sure."

"To get round those rocks, anyway." Tristan unslung the coil on his shoulder and passed it to Polassar. The man tied a loop in it carefully and gauged a spot to try his first cast of it. Elisena and Reynaud came up to them just as Polassar made his third try, missed a third time, and reeled the rope in once more for another.

He kept on trying, undauntedly, tossing the looped rope up with surer and surer aim, but it obstinately refused

to catch on the icy rocks above. A grapple might have
worked, but they'd nothing they could rig into one. There
were Ambere's spikes, but their shape was wrong for such
a purpose, and there was no magic to be worked upon
cold iron to alter them. Polassar, swearing steadily—his
own brand of incantation, Tristan thought—tried to pitch
the rope farther in, hoping to snag something farther back
than he could see, but his only reward was a slightly longer
interval before the rope slid back to slap him in the face.

"If my lord will permit—" Reynaud stepped in and
seized the rope's end.

He whispered a charm to it and set it down before the
cliff face. The rope rose carefully, higher and higher as
more of its coils followed the loose end, like a snake rising
to strike. Polassar's eyes widened, and Tristan struggled
with a bitter taste of jealousy.

He need not have bothered fighting the feeling. The
wind was too rough, and the ensorcelled rope could not
rise and fight it at the same time. It quivered, gaining and
losing inches at a time. Finally the spell failed, and the
rope dropped back at Reynaud's feet as it had at Polassar's.

Reynaud seemed untroubled. He drew his silver dagger
and pressed the rope's end to its pommel. The silver flowed
obligingly about the rope.

Again, it was for naught. Reynaud hurled the dagger
skillfully, and it took the rope with it; but away from its
master's hand, it lacked the power to soar to the cliff's
top. Its blade chimed faintly on the rocks as it fell, but
Reynaud's long fingers scooped it up before it tumbled
the last of the way to his feet. He regarded it a moment,
as if searching for hurts to the metal, but finding none.

"Well," he said unemotionally. He bent to pick up the
rope again. Thrusting the end of it through his belt, he
sidled past Polassar and entered the bottom of the chimney.

"Going to try flying up with it, sorcerer?" Polassar
asked sarcastically. The rope's intransigence had done
nothing for his temper and less for his self-control.

Reynaud turned, smiling coldly. "I wish I might. Try
and keep the rope from tangling down here."

Tristan watched closely, puzzled.

Reynaud thrust the silver dagger deep into a crack

between rocks, as high above his head as he could reach. He spoke sharply to the blade, the sorcerous words hissing like sleet falling into flame. The red and yellow threads upon his clothing gleamed fitfully. Getting a good grip on the dagger with both his hands, Reynaud pulled himself up and wedged himself between the rock walls, pushing out hard with his boots to keep his back firmly against the wall behind it. Thus secure, he bespoke the dagger again, pulled it free, and jammed it in at another, higher spot.

He worked his way up, first to the dagger and then to the next anchoring place he made with it. That slender silver blade should not have been able to take his weight, but it did easily. As Reynaud found other holds for his fingers and toes, a word to the knife sent it winging higher to lock in the place where he'd need his next grip. He reached the jammed boulders.

Tristan held his breath. Any of them could have gotten that far, even without magical help. Above, silver flashed, and Reynaud twisted with more than his usual agility. Polassar paid out rope steadily. After a while, all they could see from below were the soles of Reynaud's boots, and those disappeared next, as Reynaud reached the top and heaved himself over. The rope shivered down its whole length as he tied it off above.

Reynaud appeared at the cliff top, waving a hand in a theatrical gesture, sweepingly offering the secured rope to their use as their gateway to safety.

"Always the show-off," Tristan mumbled. He could as easily have thought of doing the same. Why hadn't he? He even knew a rope-charm, perfectly adaptable. He told himself that in another moment he'd have been bold enough to use it, knowing all the while that he lied.

Polassar looped the rope's end, tied it carefully, and passed it over Elisena's head and under her arms. "You're next up, Lady. Just you keep a tight hold."

Tied so, she couldn't properly climb, but it was plain Polassar didn't wish her to. Reynaud pulled on the rope from above, and Elisena made what use she could of her feet on the rocks, trying to walk up the chimney as far as possible, supported by the rope. Footholds were fewer than Reynaud's passage had made it seem. Her boots continually slipped on icy patches. Tristan kept catching his breath, till he finally saw how equably she recovered from each slip.

The rope began twisting as she moved higher and as Reynaud hauled at it, turning Elisena first one way and then the other. Soon she could no longer keep her feet to the rock, not being so tall as Reynaud. Soon she couldn't get her back against it, either. As she neared the top of the cliff, Elisena's efforts were mostly confined to fending off the rocks, as the rope's swings carried her too swiftly toward them. The swings were shorter but faster as the rope above her drew in, and Tristan winced each time she swung toward the chimney's sides. In narrow spots, if she caught the rock with her boots, she'd simply bounce away from one wall and slam backward into the other one. Her padded clothes seemed to muffle the blows, Tristan was thankful to note, but still his mouth was as dry as his helpless hands were damp.

One last struggle upward, one more good foothold, and then Elisena vanished exactly as Reynaud had done, to return an instant later on the cliff top a pace or two from the chimney. She waved jauntily, and Tristan sighed his relief. That left just him and Polassar.

Polassar required other tactics. He'd have to climb. Reynaud probably couldn't drag him up, even if Polassar might have suffered him to or trusted him so far. He moved into the chimney and looked doubtfully up it, wondering probably how best the two of them might get up. Based on what they'd just seen, some spots were too wide to negotiate without the rope, but the narrow bits made the rope difficult to manage handily. Tristan could almost see Polassar measuring the narrows against his own girth. That was another complication, but one he himself needn't suffer.

"If we anchor the rope down here, you won't swing," Tristan suggested. "That should make things easier."

"Aye, but we'll have need of it again. No saying what we'll find ahead. If you weight it down with something, how will we get it up again?"

Tristan took hold of the rope. "*I'll* weight it down. I'll hold it for you. Go on up."

Polassar had obviously been assuming that Tristan would be the next to climb. His brows knitted as he pondered the wisdom of revising that. "How will you get up, then?"

Tristan glared at him. "I can go up the same way Reynaud did, if I have to! He's not the only one can work magic, you know."

Jealous? Thomas questioned in a surprised tone. *I hope you're not going to try something stupid just to prove you can do it.*

Tristan bettered his grip on the rope's end and pulled it taut. "Get going before this wind picks up. It will be worse up higher."

Polassar still eyed him doubtfully.

"Art sure—"

"Yes!" Tristan snapped. "Toadstools, I'll have the rope. If I get into any trouble, you can *drag* me up. I'm narrower; I won't stick in the tight spots. Get going."

The rope heaved in Tristan's hands like a live thing struggling against him, but at least Polassar was soon up, so he didn't have to fight it for long. The big man did nearly manage to wedge his shoulders in the narrowest spot, but a lot of grunting and twisting saw him through, his mail shirt ringing on the rock. In a moment, another grunt signaled triumph.

Polassar had scarcely gained the top when he began loudly urging Tristan to make haste in following him. From his high point of vantage, he could probably see many more of the approaching storm clouds. The wind Tristan had warned Polassar of had arrived in full force. It made the rope hum and shake in his hands.

Tristan used his teeth to tug off his mittens and rehearsed in his mind the spell that he wanted to use—just a small incantation, to give him slightly better traction while his boots were on the rocks. He'd been using it for days on difficult bits of the trail, with fair to middling success. It was just what he wanted here, if he modified it slightly to include a surer grip on the rope. He made the requisite asses, said the words, and, satisfied, started to climb.

He ought, before beginning, to have tied the rope around his waist, Tristan supposed. But at first he'd forgotten, and then it suddenly seemed a matter of grave importance that he make the climb on his own and not look as if he expected to be dragged to the top at the slightest hint of difficulty. Besides, if he put the rope around his waist, a loop would form below him as he climbed, maybe tangling his feet. In this wind, that was likely. There was no sense taking the rope's end up with him; he could easily haul it up once he got to the top.

Now who's showing off? Thomas asked worriedly. His twitching whiskers nearly brushed the rock wall.

Tristan paid the cat no mind. He was busy. Hands for the rope, boots for the rock. Simple! And at first it was simple and easy, until frost-rotted stone started crumbling away wherever his boots sought a purchase on it, breaking up just when he needed footholds worst. Whenever that happened, his motion swung him outward so that he dangled, unable to reach the rock.

It must be just the rope, then, for a bit. Tristan wasn't unduly concerned. This was what the rope was there for. The spot where Polassar had met his worst trouble wasn't too far above him. Once he reached that, he'd be all right again, able easily to touch both walls. Till then, he could manage to climb with just his hands. Tristan decided to take the traction-spell off of his boots and transfer it to the rope, just to be safe.

The wind twirled him right around again, distracting him from the work. He had to start the spell fresh and took one hand from the rope briefly, to make the gesture the charm required. It was harder than he'd expected. The rope's swinging motion was making him queasy.

Think a little less about looking like a wizard and a little more about climbing, Thomas cautioned.

Tristan ignored the cat again and finished his finger-play, beginning to speak the short summation. At least it had seemed short enough when he'd recited it on the ground. Now was another matter. His fingers were getting tired and were cold from the wind, but he was still safe enough. His grip would increase in strength once the spell took hold and he had both hands for it.

Yet the spell broke again when a fierce wind gust blinded Tristan with icy snow and flung him hard against the side of the chimney. His summation was cut off in mid-word. Even through the padding feathers in his jacket, the blow was hard enough to drive all the breath from his body. Thomas, less battered but nonetheless scared, squalled with distress.

Tristan hung on grimly. His whole weight was supported by his increasingly numb fingers, but each time his feet found a welcome hold, it crumbled away, or else the wind shook him loose again. His sword tangled his legs. He wished he'd thought to strap it onto his back, though he hadn't been troubled by it previously. If he was still moving upward, he was gaining only inches.

Wind-blown snow obscured everything. Tristan couldn't tell how much climbing he still had ahead of him. He wasn't even aware of his closeness to the rock until he was swung into it again with a jolt, with the impact catching the side of his face and one shoulder. Tears of pain froze Tristan's eyes shut faster than he could open them. His fingers started to slip.

Desperate, he tried the spell again, then grabbed for the rope with his spell-casting hand when someone above belatedly realized he was in trouble and tried to hasten his ascent by hauling him up, rope and all. The rope twisted snakelike in his hands, just as Tristan was trying for a better grip. And by then it was sheathed in ice from the melting snow...

His fingers slipped in earnest, and Tristan tried to grip the rope more firmly, but his frozen hands wouldn't respond, nor could he wrap his legs about the rope. He almost trapped it with his knees, but he missed the grip. In another instant Tristan was at the end of the rope, feeling the heat of it burning his palms. Then he was past it, falling right down the chimney.

He didn't fall far. There wasn't time to stop himself with a spell—not even time to think of one. There wasn't time for Elisena to make the air beneath him thick enough to bear him up, or for Tristan to wonder if she could do that sort of thing. There was just time enough to fall, knocking against the rocks and trying to slide along the stone, in a vain attempt to slow his descent.

Tristan hit bottom with a fearful jolt, feet first, to end up half lying on his back, or on the padding of his pack at least, propped against the back of the chimney. The hitherto nearly invisible runes on his clothing glowed incandescently, but Tristan didn't notice. There was a moment's silence, before the echoes of the bits of rock that had fallen with him came floating up.

I landed on my feet, Tristan thought incredulously. *Just like Thomas.* It was the worst jarring he'd ever had in his life, but he felt unhurt where he'd expected to be well splattered. Tristan's eyes widened in amazement. Maybe the fall hadn't been as great as it had seemed . . .

"Tristan!"

"Wizard, art hurt?"

"No—" The intended happy denial came out as a gasp of pain and disbelief as Tristan discovered how terribly it hurt him to draw a deep breath. Nevertheless, he pushed himself fully upright and took a step, wincing. It was just his luck to have turned an ankle. And all that climb still had to be done over. Tristan took a second step, back toward the trailing end of the rope dangling in front of him.

Pain stabbed from his ankle clear to his hip, his chest caught fire, and night fell with astonishing swiftness.

"He hadn't even tied the rope! Lady, I know not what evil mood took me to let him come up last and alone when I couldn't make sure of him—"

"An evil possession perhaps," Elisena said uncritically. "A bad choice may be only a simple mistake, an accident a mere mischance; but in this place, we might expect Nímir's hand to be in it as well. I didn't think either, Polassar, or I would not have allowed this."

The voices floated into Tristan's ears like smoke, and not much more substantial. He tried to open his eyes when he felt hands on him, but found he couldn't. His lids were heavy as solid rock.

"Two ribs cracked, besides the ankle bone." That sounded like Elisena again. It was her touch, too, trying not to hurt him. She didn't quite succeed. Tristan drifted off again, not of his own accord, but not altogether unwillingly.

"Can we rig some manner of sling to carry him, Lady? I know you'll mislike to move him, but we dare not linger here. If the snow seals yonder pass before we can get through it—"

Reynaud, leaning out perilously over the rock face, asked if he should come down.

"Stay there! We may need your help getting him up there." Elisena's brows were drawn tight together, as she felt Tristan's throat for his pulse again and found it comfortingly strong. "Polassar, I think I can heal his leg well enough so that he can walk a little way. You must hold him still, while I straighten the bone—*no*, not at the shoulders. I need to pull, and that would hurt his ribs worse. Try at the hips." She positioned his hands. "Yes. Just there."

"Lady, we've swords to use for splinting," Polassar offered. He was steady, used to dealing with battle injuries, though he needed a healer's advice for guidance.

Elisena made no reply. Tristan moaned as she carefully began to straighten his foot. She could feel the swelling inside his boot already, through the leather under her fingers. Tristan's eyelids twitched. Elisena put a hand on his forehead and spoke softly, words of magic and mercy.

"I'd just as soon you stayed unconscious till I've got this done," she added. "I don't want it to hurt more than it needs to." Tristan quieted obediently and was still once more.

"He's lucky it was only the one ankle. Now, hold him steady."

The sharp pull she gave his foot produced no reaction from Tristan, though Polassar went a shade of white that looked most odd next to the bristling color of his red beard. Elisena's fingers probed the leather of Tristan's boot delicately once more, acting as her eyes for what lay beneath it. All seemed to be in proper place once again, with the snapped ends of bone all neatly aligned under the puffed flesh and the twisted ligaments lying where they ought.

Polassar was starting to draw his blade from its scabbard, but Elisena paid him no heed. Turning her hand over as she went, she traced a line about Tristan's ankle with the ring binding the smallest finger of her left hand. Many tiny spirals of silver made it up, their coils interwoven and linked like the roots of growing plants or the tendrils of pink-blossomed bindweed. Day's light was fading fast with the approach of the storm, but the ring gleamed bright.

Elisena moved finger and ring slowly, tracing precisely the jagged line of the break in the bone. That done, she repeated the action with the same finger of her right hand, in the opposite direction. The ring nesting there was a chain of linked hearts, its silver warm as her love, even in the cold air. Elisena spoke all the while, the tiniest whispers of sound. like new plants springing from seeds in the spring, breaking the soil's crust and thrusting into the sunlight. Presently, she left Tristan's ankle and tended to his ribs, repeating all the actions except the bone-setting, which they didn't require. Luckily, he'd done no worse than crack the bones there, not snap them entirely. Polassar quietly slid his sword back into its sheath.

The ring on her right thumb was set with a water-smoothed bit of pearl shell, the silver around it sculptured to match the shell's flowing lines. Elisena laid her palm on Tristan's forehead once more, and drew that ring gently across his eyelids, one after the other, light as the touch of a breeze. Tristan's eyes opened at once and fixed on her after a moment. His expression was bemused.

"It doesn't hurt anymore." He lifted his head, trying to see what she'd done.

"It wouldn't have hurt at all if you hadn't tried to walk on it," Elisena said gruffly. "Lie still now and let the spell finish its work." She knelt by his feet once more, checking her healing's progress. Where the silver rings had moved, they had left behind a trail of white light. That coiled about his boot was softening now as it began to fade inward. She knew without further probing that the swelling was fading as well.

"That's very handy," Tristan said, lifting his head again. "It really does feel much better."

"You'll be standing on it in a moment," Elisena assured him, turning to gather up her healer's tools.

A soft *plop* sounded as Thomas jumped down from something to stand beside Tristan's ear. The cat was disheveled but unhurt. There'd been enough soft stuff in the pack to cushion him, though even Tristan realized what a great wonder it was that he hadn't smashed both cat and pack flat in falling—not to mention himself.

People aren't supposed to land on their feet, Thomas said, in shocked tones. *You deserved to break both legs.*

Tristan tried to shrug, unwisely as it happened. Elisena hadn't dealt yet with minor bruises and strains, and he had plenty of each. "I didn't think about it at the time. Sorry to usurp your prerogatives." The attempted jest was quite as feeble as he was.

He grew drowsy. Elisena's hands were moving over him again, probing for those other, lesser hurts. Her touch was soothing, even when it hit bruises. Tristan shut his eyes as the magic worked and relaxed as miscellaneous pains faded. He felt warm and snug, as if in a feather bed.

Presently Elisena's voice jogged him out of it.

"Tristan, I'd like to let you sleep, but we can't stay here. We've still got to get through that pass before the storm comes. Do you understand?"

Tristan blinked at her and made to sit up. Polassar's strong arm arrived behind his shoulder at a crucial moment, holding him till he had his balance.

"Wizard, I'd let you rest if I could, but 'tis move or freeze for us now. Not much of a choice. Art ready to try?"

Tristan nodded and blithely gathered his feet under him.

Polassar was doubtful of the outcome, though, and held himself ready. He'd *seen* the angle at which the Wizard's foot had been twisted. Tristan would never be able to stand on it, however skillfully the lady had stopped or masked the pain of the broken bones—not with the break unsplinted. Well, she might not want the steel swords bound to him, and if 'twould truly poison him, very well, Wizards were queer folk. But Polassar doubted that the spell the lady had used instead could stiffen the wizard's boot enough to let it bear his weight. The man would scarcely be able to stand alone. Without pain to deal with, they might have an easier time of moving him, but as for walking—as soon teach a cow to dance.

Tristan, with utmost confidence—enough to make Polassar guess that he must have banged his head while falling—took a step the instant he was heaved onto his feet. Polassar's grip on him tightened convulsively, heedless of cracked ribs, anticipating the broken leg's wobbling out from under him.

It didn't happen. Tristan took two more steps, and the leg still supported him firmly.

Getting Tristan back to the cliff top was no great matter. Reynaud shifted the rope away from the chimney. Polassar tied its end around Tristan and Elisena both, then scrambled up to Reynaud. Once there, he proceeded to haul in the rope, and the two below with it, as if they were a basket of eggs. His muscles bulged until even

Ambere's magical garments could scarcely accommodate them; but with more weight on it, the rope swung scarcely at all, though it creaked and complained, and the task was quickly accomplished. Thomas remarked acidly upon Polassar's wisdom for doing at last what he ought to have done in the first place. Why let all those well-schooled muscles go wasted?

Bodily, Tristan was perfectly well by that point, the healing spell having been fully effective, but he was still so jolted, dazed, and bewitched that he could barely control his legs, though they were whole again. He'd have fallen once more—though only to his knees—had Polassar not kept hold of him while removing the rope from around his waist. He was so pale that Reynaud began to search through his baggage hastily, seeking herbs to stop him fainting.

Elisena waved Reynaud off. Tristan would be able to move well enough with someone on each side to guide him, she thought. At that moment, there was nothing herbal remedies could offer him. He needed rest and sleep, and he'd get neither for hours, so they had best start moving, to reach that rest the sooner. She knew well how desperate Tristan's need for sleep was. Looking at the sky, she knew better than he that the need must be denied for a space.

She pulled Tristan's hood up gently. She'd only intended to keep the snow from his face a little, but it helped her catch hold of his wandering attention, too, since Tristan could see nothing then except her face directly in front of him.

"Just follow me," Elisena instructed him. "Only for a little way, I promise. We'll stop just as soon as we possibly can."

She thought Tristan nodded in agreement, but it was hard for Elisena to be sure. The light was failing rapidly, and he said nothing.

Elisena lit her rings and went ahead before Polassar, for the snowclouds had brought an early night with them. What little they might have hoped to see in the gloom, wind-swirled snow hid behind a wall of gray, as the storm claimed the pass for its own. Winds rushed eagerly through it, buffeting the travelers sorely. Often, as they rounded some upthrust of rock, even mighty Polassar was unable to proceed farther, because the air held them back like a solid wall. There was no returning to the lowlands by then.

The way was rough and winding, for the pass was little more than a low spot between two peaks. There had never been any sort of a trail there, nor travelers to make one. There were great boulders to be skirted and gullies where ice had split the rock as if with wedges, leaving deep slashes across their way. They proceeded slowly, lest the warnings Elisena's rings could give them should not be quite timely enough.

Polassar and Reynaud each kept a hand on one of Tristan's elbows. He stumbled often, though never because of his hurt leg. Tristan was keeping his gaze fixed on the light of Elisena's rings—the only light left in the world, it seemed to him. He dared not look elsewhere than at his beacon, even to watch his own treacherous footing. He might lose Elisena and never find her again, like a tiny star seen through a powerful spyglass.

The ground below confused his eyes too much, anyway, making him dizzier than he already was. A thought nagged at the back of Tristan's mind; there was *some* reason it wasn't quite right for him to be walking as he was. He couldn't hold onto it tightly enough to make sense of it or to any of the encouragements Polassar assailed his ears with. He kept his eyes on Elisena, and the world was simpler.

Darkness, blowing snow, and walking, endless walking! The wind howled loud in Tristan's ears, drowning out Polassar's voice and muffling even his own heartbeat. Once or twice there came a respite, or at least a change, as they descended steep slopes and were sheltered by rocks. The hands on his arms tightened then, and other hands guided Tristan's feet from one spot to the next, steering him until he was on level ground once again. Someone was being very careful of him. Tristan wondered why. He could walk perfectly well on his own. Wasn't he proving that with every step?

"This is madness!" Reynaud shouted desperately, as if he'd long nursed the words. "The air's black as the inside of a tomb! We're as apt to walk off a cliff as not."

"Stop moving and we freeze. Wouldst prefer that?" Polassar's heavy hand jerked at Tristan's arm painfully.

Tristan tried to protest, but no one heard him, it seemed. The icy air hurt his throat, and he fell silent. Reynaud went on arguing with Elisena then, but he pulled at Tristan as he did.

"Lady, cannot your rings still this wind for a little? Enough to shelter us till first light; if we could but see—"

Tristan didn't hear whatever answer was made. The wind blew the words of the rest of the question and Elisena's reply past his ears too quickly for him to sift any sense from the tangle. He suspected, though, that Elisena's rings could never turn this ravenous storm, not all alone, though Elisena spend her life trying—not that she would. At this point, that would be no gamble, but only a waste. Elisena was too practical for that, and not half such a fool. Tristan was proud to be able to think so clearly, and a little surprised. He wished he had the strength to express the thoughts aloud.

All the while, Polassar kept him walking. After a few moments, as the wind began to hit him with less force, Tristan knew that Reynaud must have fallen in at his other side once again. Tristan's eyes were for Elisena's rings alone, but his other senses could tell him well enough what his companions' positions were, at those rare intervals when he cared to know.

Drifted snow was packed hard as stone between the rocks. That made it impossible sometimes for them to continue three abreast. They shifted to a single file, keeping Tristan safe in the middle, but found he fretted there, if Polassar's shoulders cut off his sight of Elisena; and he kept bumping against Polassar's back, trying mindlessly to get past. Elisena's rings drew Tristan on like a lodestone, which at least kept him moving, but his stubborn insistence was frustrating. Patiently, Polassar kept Tristan on his feet and in his place.

What kept Elisena moving, always first into that bone-cutting wind, was impossible to guess. Hers was the greatest burden, for she must see every cliff or crevasse that lay in wait for them and discover every spot where supposedly solid rock dropped suddenly away into a snow-filled pit. There was one whole long slope like that, all great boulders covered to their very tops with snow, so that the hill looked smooth and easy. They floundered down, discovering the truth and bruising themselves badly. There was no help for the collisions; they were threading a maze, blind. The snow reached sometimes to their chests and sometimes nearly above Elisena's head, and they swam through the stuff more than walked. Polassar led that stretch; none of the others had the strength necessary to break such a trail. He dragged them all through by what must have been sheer stubbornness, till they came to shallower snow and, at last, bare rock. Elisena took the lead from him once more, weary but unfaltering.

Their path turned onto a ledge, dwindling to next to nothing after a few paces. Reynaud made to turn back, but Elisena bade them turn their faces to the rock, and they inched along sideways, cheeks pressed to the cold stone, fingers splayed out to gain what holds they might. The wind whipped and tore at them with eager, gleeful cries which altered to pathetic disappointment as they reached the place where the ledge widened once more to safety and refused to be thrust back into peril by vicious blasts. They staggered on.

Reynaud tripped over a frozen snow ridge and fell flat on his face. He was so cold by then that he only felt the impact as a welcome cessation of movement. He'd been starting to imagine faces in the wind as well as the voices he'd been hearing for hours—fair faces that entreated him to remain behind with them. He would have obeyed and stayed where he sprawled, but he somehow didn't want to be left alone with them, lovely as they were. Reynaud got to his feet doggedly and said a spell that wrapped his cloak tight about him once more, shaking the snow from its ebony folds. Floundering, he caught up to Tristan at last.

Tristan's hood had fallen back from his face, or else he'd put it back, not aware of what he was doing and forgetful of the cold. There was ice in his hair, on his brows, and even on his eyelashes, and he was staggering a step sideways for every two he took forward. Even in the dark, Reynaud could see how his knees wobbled each time he set a foot down into the snow. Icy spots nearly undid him, for he couldn't keep his precarious balance long, even on safe spots. Reynaud, in scarcely better shape himself, grabbed Tristan's left arm and flung it over his own shoulders. Tristan made no attempt to pull away from him.

That was not a good sign, Reynaud thought, though such pliability was convenient. From the top of Tristan's pack, two green eyes glared lambently at him from his own eye level, but Thomas made no more protest over his proximity than did his master.

Abruptly, the wind dropped. More precisely, it continued to roar, but some feet above their heads. Some sort of outcrop sheltered them, however briefly. Polassar almost walked into Elisena, who stood pressed close to the rock, trembling with weariness.

"A minute," she requested faintly. "I can't face that blasted wind again just yet."

Reynaud, able to get his breath at last, spoke urgently while he had the chance, renewing his protest. "Elisena, we've got to stop. I think Tristan's out on his feet, and I'm not sure I can walk much farther myself. Come morning—" he broke off his plea as Tristan, unable to stay both immobile and upright, sagged limply against him.

"Give him here, sorcerer," Polassar growled, shattering ice in his beard. "I'll carry you both if need be, but you'll walk while you can, and that will be some farther, I vow. You've the stomach to outlast a man with a broken leg, surely?"

I think you've finally managed to impress Polassar, Thomas said sarcastically into Tristan's ear. *Who'd have thought it would be so easy?*

Tristan didn't answer. Thomas leaned forward and rubbed his whiskers against Tristan's ear, but he got no more response to the tickling than he had to his taunting. The cat mewed worriedly. This was serious. Tristan didn't need anyone fighting over who was going to carry him. He didn't need to be carried. He needed to lie down out of the wind in some warm place, at least till he could collect his wits enough to appreciate a joke again. *Come on. Wake up a little. If you don't, I think there's going to be nothing left here come morning but one very large wizard-shaped snowdrift.*

Still there was no reaction.

It was time to put sharp eyes to use, Thomas thought. He saw better than any of the humans in the darkness of the storm, though, with all the stuff still blowing about, mostly all he saw was snow. If he could only spot a little trifle of a ledge, or a hole in the rock, something that would shelter them . . . This bit where they'd stopped wasn't bad, but it was narrow, and a shift of the wind would leave them at its mercy and without space to retreat. They needed something snugger. Give them a corner to crawl into and they'd be warm enough in their wool bags. He knew, sharing Tristan's as he had been.

Tristan must be terribly cold, besides being exhausted. A tear welled out from between his eyelashes, but it had only tracked halfway down his cheek before it froze. He wouldn't last much longer. Thomas scrabbled to find footholds on the stuff under him in the pack and gained a few inches, enough so that he could see past Reynaud's shoulder. It looked as if they might be pausing for a bit, so he'd best have a good look about while he could.

He hadn't much time—they were all leaning against the rock, back out of range of the snow-laden gusts, too weary to risk sitting. They'd be moving on soon, before anyone got stiff. Thomas dared not leave his perch in the pack. Tristan wasn't in any state to notice his departure, and he would be left behind for sure if he disembarked.

That tumble of rocks yonder! Might there be a space behind it? Those boulders didn't look as if they were lying hard against the cliffside. If they could get in there and put their cloaks overhead, like a tent roof—not a bad thought, Thomas complimented himself. Now if someone would only listen to him . . . Tristan was his best bet for cooperation, but the man was hardly accessible—

Just then Elisena raised a be-ringed, glowing hand to brush snow-soaked hair back out of her eyes, and one of the boulders vanished. The extra eyelid that cats were gifted with flicked over Thomas' eyes, a surer sign of surprise than even full blinking. He strained to see more and stretched prodigiously, clawing higher in the pack. Finally he overbalanced so badly that he fell off Tristan and onto Reynaud, who cried out as if he'd been struck with a dagger instead of fur.

Thomas paid no heed. He was making straight for what he alone had seen among the shadows of the cliff.

The opening in the rock was as high as Elisena was tall and as wide as Polassar's shoulders at one point, though the gap was roughly triangular and much narrower in other

places. Elisena's light had not been reflected back out of
it, but had been swallowed or soaked up, which meant it
went deep.

Thomas scarcely paused to test the hole with his whiskers. One never wisely measured the tail of a gift mouse,
and he felt lucky. Even before he ventured in, Thomas
knew that the cave would be large enough to shelter them
all.

Haven

POLASSAR PROBED THE WAY DAINTILY WITH HIS SWORD
blade, till Elisena's fingers plucked at his sleeve and drew
his arm back.

"There's nothing hurtful here. Thomas would know.
Come."

Polassar frowned, hurting his frozen face. "Lady, I can
remember yon cat strolling into Darkenkeep, easy as if
'twere his own home! I'm wary of this sudden good fortune."

"Yes. I'd observed." That was all the notice Elisena
took of his feelings, as she brushed past Polassar and
turned sideways to pass the narrow opening, all her rings
alight. Polassar, with a despairing curse directed at
womankind generally, followed her, dragging Tristan.

The hole in the rock was tiny, scarcely large enough
for the four of them to stand, pressed close. Reynaud,
searching the walls with a lighted crystal held high in
Thomas' wake, was partner to the discovery of a sharply
angled fissure in one wall. It was narrower still than the
entrance to the cave itself, but the chamber it gave access
to was larger than the first, and two turnings out of the
wind's reach as well. Polassar had to duck and squirm
and finally shed both pack and longsword, but shortly
even he had safely made the passage.

The stone floor was cold, as the bones of mountains
were by nature. Polassar cast one of the wool bags down,
before lowering Tristan to the floor and propping him
against the wall. The wizard looked ghost-touched, Polassar thought, so white was he with cold and snow, but he

managed to nod what was probably intended as thanks. Polassar accepted it as such.

Thomas ran to Tristan, dusted snow away with his tail for a brush, and settled contentedly upon his lap. In a moment he had begun to purr, loudly praising his own finding of their shelter. Tristan tried to smile.

Reynaud got the chunk of magewood lit, rattling through its incantation faster than any other of the company could have done, his fingers blurring to match the whispered words. He managed, by heroic effort, to keep his teeth from chattering together until he'd finished, another motive for speed. With the fire's flaring, the cave's walls shot back, then drew in again, though not so closely as before. Reynaud stayed by the fire barely the moment he needed to be sure the spell held, then gathered their copper pots and went out to fill them with snow, so that they might have water. There was no use waiting longer to get warm— he'd only feel the cold worse when he finally went. He had to squeeze past Polassar, who was nervously pushing the packs they'd shed back against the walls, clearing the floor as much as might be and eyeing the roof as if he expected it to fall the second he began to trust it.

With a fire lit, the tiny space quickly warmed, though the rocks were still chill. Snow dripping from Reynaud sizzled as he set the pots by the edge of the flames to start the snow melting. The hiss of sleet outside was covered by the crackling of the fire.

"Think you that will be safe to drink?" Polassar asked irritably. He'd decided to pile the packs against the cave mouth, so nothing could get in—anything so foolish as to try to pass the wards Elisena was setting so busily. He'd had to wait for Reynaud to return before he could proceed with the job and was cross on that account.

Reynaud shook his head at the man, not even answering. They had a roof above their heads, beyond all expectations, and walls against the wind; they needn't spend strength or magic securing either. They weren't going to freeze to death on a wind-swept slope. Polassar couldn't expect to find a spring of sweet, unfrozen water as well, surely? How much could the man presume? Reynaud took dried meat and barley bread from one of the packs, earning a glare from Polassar. He set the food by the fire to warm, then doffed his cloak and spread it to dry. As an afterthought, he shot a spell at one of the pots, and the snow melted to water and began to boil at once.

Tristan had finally managed to drag his frozen mittens off and had stubbornly teased at the straps of his pack until he got one of the buckles undone. The pack had started to slip off sideways before he was able to undo the other strap, but he'd disentangled himself from it somehow. Now he was trying to get his wool bag out of the pack's top, but his fingers had little strength, and the bag fitted the pack too tightly. He couldn't lift it clear.

He kept trying, grimly determined or else moved by the deep-grained habit of making camp. It would have been so much easier if he'd stood up, but he couldn't trust his legs any longer.

Tristan barely knew what he was doing, Elisena thought, marking the blank look of exhaustion on his face when she came over to him. He'd set his fingers to a task, and they'd kept on mechanically trying to accomplish it until she knelt down by him and moved the pack out of his reach.

"Let that be for a bit. Look at me, now."

His eyes were enormous, the black of the pupils nearly obscuring the green, and there were great shadows under them, as dark almost as the ugly bruises on his jaw. Tristan's pallor accentuated both disfigurements.

"*Tchh*, I certainly missed that one." Elisena set down a bowl of hot water and a bit of clean rag. Tristan's eyes inspected her, slowly.

"My own fault," he said through wind-cracked lips. "Showing off. Toadstools, you'd think I would learn—" A drop of blood welled from the middle of his bottom lip, but Tristan didn't look as if he felt it.

Elisena began to sponge his face carefully, her fingers whisking always with a bit of spell just ahead of the rag, to take the pain away before he could begin to notice it. His dazed condition made that relatively easy.

"You're only guilty of stumbling into a trap," she said. "You didn't set it."

"Nímir?" Tristan shivered, then looked even more ill, as a thought occurred to him. "He's seeking me out, then? Because I'm our weakest link."

"I would doubt that very much, if I thought you were in any shape to pay attention to me." Elisena bolstered her spell a touch on finding a white spot of frostbite on Tristan's right cheek. "Don't you see what this means? If Nímir *is* striking at you with such persistance, when he's left the rest of us alone, why else but because you're a danger to him? It would mean we *can* succeed. He's afraid of you."

Tristan frowned. A trickle of water ran down his neck. "I don't know about that. I get the feeling that he knows me now. It's getting easier for him to trick me."

"Then be on your guard." Elisena laid a scrap of cobweb on his cheek and charmed it into place. The frostbite vanished.

"I thought I was," Tristan answered. He shut his eyes. Not with weariness, Elisena thought, but for protection. He didn't want to meet her eyes any longer. She reached out to reassure him.

Outside, the wind cried like a raging wildcat, disappointed of its prey. Thomas raised his head, looked ready to warn it off. His eyes blazed wide, pupils such thin slits that he could have seen nothing—at least, nothing in the cave. The wind died, and the cat relaxed back against Tristan, satisfied.

Elisena felt a strong desire to fling her arms around Tristan, whether the clasp might hurt him or not, just because she was grateful that he was still alive. She resisted, rightly guessing that such an outburst at that moment would probably frighten Tristan out of whatever wits his ordeal had left him. Instead, she eased his boot off and reviewed her healer's work.

The ankle was as bruised as Tristan's face, but at least was straight and unswollen.

"You must tell me if anything else pains," Elisena said, as she slipped the boot back into place and laced it loosely. "I had to work so quickly, I'm sure I missed more than that bruise on your face."

Tristan said nothing.

Reynaud brought a cup of tea, the boneset, and speedwell she'd asked for. He'd put no honey in to mask the bitter taste of the medicinal herbs, but Tristan drank the posset without protest. The bedding was unpacked, and he was soon wrapped in most of their cloaks as well as his own wool bag.

He'd said nothing for a long while, and Elisena began

to wonder if she ought to have added something to the tea for headache. She had an irritating trace of one herself, from exhaustion and cold; Tristan's would probably be much worse.

Polassar squatted suddenly beside her as she considered, chewing at a breadcrust. One side of it was black, having got too close to the flames. Polassar swallowed a bite of it by mistake and grimaced.

"Wizard, I've never seen a man so ill-wished." It was hard to tell whether Polassar was awed or annoyed. "Next time, mind you remember what we brought those ropes for. Or don't wizard folk learn to tie knots, having their minds so full of other high matters? You'll be more careful, mark me."

"Done." Tristan held his right hand up. Polassar spat on his own palm before clasping it. Bargain sealed to his satisfaction, he went off to have another look outside, muttering and stamping.

Elisena adjusted the piled cloaks so that no great weight would rest on Tristan's injured foot to cause him more pain. Healed it might be, but she thought the leg would still ache for a good while. There was no escaping all the consequences of such a fall as he'd had, even magically.

Tristan was watching her again when she looked up. His eyes were a trifle clearer, a sign of recovery that she welcomed.

"I'm not going to wake up in the morning and find out that it's still broken, am I?"

Elisena smiled, relieved further by the half jest. "No. That was an authentic healing, not an illusion. And it will stay healed, if you let it."

"You must be a terror at mending crockery." Jest or not, the words began to slur with exhaustion.

Elisena brushed a finger across Tristan's lips. "Shhh. That mending took almost as much out of me as it did out of you. Go to sleep now, so I can do the same."

Polassar and Reynaud had already bedded down. Indeed, Polassar's snores had begun some moments before, while she still fussed with Tristan. Elisena raised a brow at the noise.

Better go to sleep while we still can, Thomas said, his eyes narrowing crossly. *Before the roof comes down.* He pushed his way down into the warmest folds of the cloaks,

still grumbling faintly as he dropped off. *Never a word of
thanks, you know. As if there were a cave handy wherever
you looked here.*

Tristan, smiling, tried to reach down and tweak the tip
of the cat's tail, but he was too far into sleep to do much
more than think of it.

Elisena slipped inside her own wool bag and spoke a
word of command to the magewood. Its flames died to a
gentle cherry glow, still casting plenty of heat, but leaving
the cave darkened enough for comfortable sleeping. The
dim light made the rock cupped about them seem warm
and as safe as cottage walls. Tristan blinked, surprised
almost back to wakefulness by what he'd seen. He hadn't
suspected that Ambere's spell could be so modified.

Elisena slept badly. The magewood burned quietly, but
she heard every least crackle that it gave off. The ever-
rushing wind outside sang as if the mountain peaks were
harpstrings, and the cave itself vibrated like that great
harp's sounding board. The noises held her just at the
surface of sleep for a long while. Elisena kept opening
her eyes, as if her sharp ears alone weren't to be trusted
to report to her that Tristan was still breathing.

His face was white and pinched, even in the fire's warm
light. He looked worse than either the fall or the long hard
walk in the cold could answer for. The healing had been
harder on him than she'd expected, Elisena thought—
though there'd been no choice about it. Tristan was hardly
an ideal patient—he had no reserves to fall back upon.
Every scrap of his strength was used up by Channadran.
And it wasn't sufficient that he was exhausted and hurt,
but he must take it into his head that Nímir was concentrating attacks upon him personally.

He was probably right. That thought kept Elisena awake
far longer than fretting over Tristan's health. She wondered how she could allay Tristan's undeserved guilt without outright lying to him—and still safeguard him.

Someone touched her shoulder, a grip of some urgency
or at least persistence. Elisena was startled to realize that
she'd slept deeply. She turned her head on a neck that
felt stiff, opening heavy eyelids.

Firelight flickered across the cave's low roof, too dim

to make Elisena blink, but more than bright enough to limn Reynaud's crouching figure clearly.

"Lady? I didn't like to wake you, but—" Reynaud gestured at Tristan, or at least in his direction.

Elisena sat up quickly, looking past Reynaud as if he had instantly ceased to exist. Tristan had managed to work his way out from under most of the cloaks and had shoved his wool bag back as far as it would go with him still lying in it. He was tossing restlessly from side to side, as if in the grip of a strong dream or a fever. Elisena felt his forehead, alarmed. The skin was warm, but not dangerously so.

Tristan did not wake at her touch, though he turned his head away as if bothered. His hands were moving, his fingers weaving freely above the wool bag. His cracked lips worked, too, almost but not quite silently. At about every third word, the fire about the magewood flared up to lick the roof.

"Every time he does that, it gets a little hotter in here," Reynaud explained, kneeling beside her. "Not to mention brighter. I can't say how long he's been at it. It only woke me about a quarter of an hour ago, but he's been getting steadily better at it the whole time I've watched. I was afraid he'd set someone alight next."

"He's getting no rest from this sleep." Elisena was deeply concerned. "You did well to wake me."

Pictures flickered in the flames. Elisena saw tended plants, ancient trees, and a thatch-roofed building. Tristan spoke again. A flame licked up. There was a loud pop, as of a coal cracking in the fire, and a shower of apple blossoms drifted softly down. Thomas sniffed in surprise, then stretched himself out to enjoy the warmth as it deserved.

Reynaud lifted both a scented petal and an eyebrow. "Fever?"

"No. Dreams, I think." Tristan managed to move his fingers again, just a bit faster than Elisena had reached to catch them. The fire flared again, and a wave of heat washed over them, uncomfortably hot.

Elisena chuckled, as she successfully captured Tristan's hands at last. "I suppose I shouldn't really be surprised. You've been terribly cold all day. You want to be warm now, and wizards' wishes always come true. But it's quite warm enough in here, and you're going to wake Polassar next. We can't have that."

She put her left hand against Tristan's face, and he promptly, predictably, rolled his head away from her. His left cheek met Elisena's right hand, which was waiting. Elisena drew her right thumb, with its ring set with pearl shell, gently across Tristan's eyelids once more, then his forehead, stroking him as she would have gentled Minstrel.

Tristan didn't succumb at once, but fought her ministrations with all the slight strength he had left. He struggled without success; all at once, the bright fire subsided into a semblance of heaped coals. The cave darkened. Tristan relaxed back against the pack his head was pillowed on, eyes tight shut. Elisena continued to soothe him. Thomas sighed and went back to sleep, deep in the fabric heap.

"I know a dozen wizards in Kôvelir who'd give right hands to do awake what he just did asleep," Reynaud whispered.

"He probably can't do it when he's awake, either," Elisena answered absently, feeling the pulse slow and steady at Tristan's throat.

"That's what I find so fascinating about this blockage of his, wherever it comes from. He never had any sort of an Examination, did he?" Reynaud scarcely waited for her answer. "I thought not, though he must have been nearly of an age for it when Blais died. So unfortunate. He's been left with no objective way to judge his skill. From Tristan's point of view, he's stuck permanently at the apprentice level. He has no idea how much he knows and sees lack of rank as a failure, a self-fulfilling prophecy. Blais picked a bad time to get himself killed—not that he had a choice."

Reynaud looked down at Tristan's still face. Tristan would have been astonished, could he have seen the concern carried in that look. "I wonder, if we—"

"Don't start poking at him, Reynaud," Elisena cautioned sharply, brooking no dissent. "Whatever his trouble was, it's buried deep now, and he's learned to deal with it, as you yourself told him. Would you grind a pearl away, to find the grain of sand that began it?" She might not understand Reynaud's obsession, or guess why it should be stronger than Tristan's own, but Elisena recognized it and its dangers.

"I wouldn't hurt him, Lady. *You* must know that, even if he wouldn't believe it. And it might help him." Reynaud looked at her pleadingly.

"Only if he trusted you," Elisena answered sternly. "And as you admit, he doesn't. You'll only frighten him, and that's one burden I won't have put on Tristan. He's carrying enough now." And perhaps Tristan did well to be wary of Reynaud, after all, she thought to herself.

Reynaud inclined his head, accepting reluctantly. "I'm a little afraid of *him*, if you want honesty at this time of night. Wizards don't *do* some of the things he does—that iceberg, just for instance. You know as well as I do that it should never have worked, and it's terrifying that it did." He shook his head. "Oh, you needn't worry, I won't let *him* see that. I know it would just upset Tristan, coming from me. He wouldn't see it as a compliment! But I'll tell you this—he asked me once before why I let him go that time at Radak, and I lied to him, saying he wasn't worth my bothering about then. Nothing could have been farther from true. I was afraid of him then, that long ago, when he knew even less what he was. I've seen more since and I'm still afraid."

Reynaud started to turn away, then spun back again and stood quietly, looking down at Tristan with hooded eyes.

"What is it that you lock away? What fetters your magic, tangles your fingers, and trips your tongue? The more leisure you have to shape a spell, the more careful you are of it, the worse it comes off. And yet... there are times when I shake with terror, watching you. It's a positive wonder you've not lost all your confidence by now, instead of just most of it."

Thomas' head popped up, the better to catch the amazing monologue.

"You're like a man in a maze of glass. You can't see what you're doing, you can't see the barriers when you do find your way past them, and you can never trace out the same path a second time. What happened? Did something convince you that magic was unnatural and make you suspect your gifts? Or did something you just weren't ready for put down those roots of pain? You're looking for answers and you need them, even though finding them may kill you. A poisoned wound will never heal till it's cleansed, and you need to be whole. For all my skill, I can't do a thing for you, because you won't let me touch you. Alas."

He was in no way speaking to her, Elisena realized, and was indifferent to the fact that she overheard him, so she said nothing. Speech would have been an intrusion. Nor would she pass those secret, impulsive words on to Tristan, though she dearly wished she might.

After a moment, Reynaud went back to his own sleeping place, with the black cloak lying casually across it. He'd been sensitive enough not to offer it to Tristan along with the others. There was no sense in furthering mistrust or provoking a scene. Now the cloak's folds settled over Reynaud like night falling, comforting though their warmth wasn't needed. He turned his back, after one slight movement that might have been a wince at Polassar's still-noisy breathing.

"A deeper sleep," Elisena whispered into Tristan's ear. She found that her throat was aching and she knew well why. The feeling surprised her. She had never thought to grieve for Reynaud in any way. As for Tristan—tears were hardly the most useful thing she might offer him. Her fingers moved slowly against his forehead. "Sleep deeper than dreams, so I can be sure you'll rest untroubled."

Her left hand scribed monotonous patterns in the air as she spoke, repeating and restating. "Deeper than the sea, with its surface of storms. Deeper than the sleep the mandrake brings, but with no taint of its poison. Deep as a seed sleeps, waiting for the spring. Safe and warm, as a seed is safe in the haven of the soil. Sleep."

Thomas yawned wide, showing all his teeth and curling his tongue as dogs do. His whiskers folded back into their places slowly. From the other side of the cave, but a few feet away, Polassar's snores reached a mighty crescendo, then died off gurgling before beginning again. *As if anyone could be expected to sleep through that. No wonder he kept looking to see if the roof was sound.*

Somehow, their sleep did seem to survive the racket, for what must have been many hours. It proved difficult to reckon time by the sky outside. Reynaud, stretching and then shivering like a nervous horse, once he'd squeezed back into the cave, reported that nothing was visible at all save the snow, which was either blowing about or piling up on the narrow ledge outside. Polassar awoke, heard the gloomy news, and promptly went back to a sleep which Tristan had never left.

They each did more or less that same thing, like animals huddled in a hole, getting through a bad time by sleeping it away, conserving strength and refusing thought or worry. Till the storm released them, their actions were strictly limited; there was no sense straining at them. When sleep had been exhausted, there still was little conversation. Polassar mended gear, oiling boots, checking over all the ropes for worn spots, and sharpening pitons that rock had dulled. Reynaud took out the map he'd copied from Ambere's sand sculpture and began another in his black book, based upon it and his own careful observations along the trail. In his corner, Tristan continued to sleep.

Elisena inventoried their supplies and cooked a hot meal, better than any they'd scraped together in their previous camps among the icy rocks. She had reason to be creative with her herbs, for of the food itself she must waste nothing, no least crumb. Until the storm abated, they dared not leave the cave's shelter; and until they did so, Ambere's birds could not find them, even if some managed to survive the storm winds. What they had must last, though they were in no danger—*yet*.

She made a stew, for water would turn to broth, a thrifty addition to meat and vegetables. Then dried cherries were set simmering for hours until the fruit softened and waxed sweeter than when fresh-picked. Tristan deserved to have his sweet tooth catered to just for once, Elisena thought. The cherries would please him, and a hot meal would do him more good than any of the rest of them—and they needed it badly enough.

Elisena looked for the aroma of the cooking cherries to wake him, but Tristan never so much as twitched a nostril. He'd turned onto his side during the night, pressing his cheek against the rough fabric of his pack, and he had stayed so, not moving again. Elisena kept a close eye on him, for even the deepest sleeper shifts often. Tristan's breathing was deep and reassuringly steady—apparently the healing done on his ribs had been completely suc-

cessful, which was one concern the less. Elisena studied
him a while longer, then went back to stir the cherries
once again. They'd nearly turned to jam.

She dropped in a pinch of cinnamon. *That* might do
the trick. The scent of spice filled the cave, a smell redo-
lent of feast-days and celebrations. Reynaud glanced her
way, smiling approvingly, and Polassar's belly gave a rumble that seemed to be agreement. Disappointingly, those
were the only reactions.

Why not just put a pinch under his nose? Thomas suggested, stretching fore and aft. *That should wake him
quick enough. Given his nose, you'll only need the tiniest
bit.* He sniffed at Tristan's ear and tapped a paw on the
topmost layer of the blankets.

Elisena dug out a thin strip of dried meat and held it
out to the cat.

"Here. Chew on this and leave Tristan alone. He'll
wake when he's ready to, without you pestering him."

Polassar put a fresh pot of snow by the fire to melt,
and dropped gobs of half-melted flakes onto the floor.
Thomas, gnawing at the dried venison, hissed irritably at
him and removed himself to the far, dry side of the cave.

"Still snowing?"

"Oh, aye. Like 'twill never stop." Polassar opened up
his jacket, to let the heat of the fire reach him the quicker,
and tossed his wet gloves into the corner. Thomas ducked
and came back up glaring murderously. Polassar paused
to look down at Tristan, or at least at his back. "Lady,
heal-craft's not my business, but shouldn't he have waked
by this? 'Tis two days at the least, even if we did lose
some count of 'em. Mayhap we ought to try rousing him."

"Oh, let the man be." Reynaud looked up from his
mapwork, then tapped the page with one finger. "The way
from here will be worse, not better. He'll need whatever
strength he can gather now. And so long as we're bottled
here, asleep or awake's pretty much all one." Conversation ended, he dipped his pen again and continued writing without another glance at Polassar.

Polassar glowered at the interruption, then chose mag-
nanimously to let it go by. He looked to Elisena again.

"I'd rather Tristan woke up long enough to eat something," she admitted. "But otherwise, Reynaud's probably
right. Getting here exhausted all the strength Tristan had,

and sleep will do him no harm. There's no reason to trouble him yet."

"Lady, he's not even moved!" Polassar's concern was breaking through increasingly, in spite of Elisena's assurances.

Reynaud laughed. "By the lightning, Polassar, hasn't he been on the move long enough to suit you?"

While the two men squabbled, Elisena looked at Tristan once again. The noise level rose, but he gave no sign of being disturbed by the argument on his behalf. She went to him and touched his cheek lightly, hoping that she had been gentle enough when sending him to sleep that night and that she hadn't pushed him so deep that Tristan might be having trouble now finding his way back out of it. His temperature seemed normal, and his color was finally better.

Tristan was sound asleep, nothing more or worse. Elisena decided to be convinced of that. She turned him over onto his back, and he rolled without resisting, but didn't wake.

The sounds sifting through Tristan's dreams were nothing like Polassar's grumbles or Reynaud's sarcastic remarks, nor was there any hint of the hunting cries of the mountain winds. The notes Tristan heard were as measured as the rising and falling of the sea, as familiar as a heartbeat.

Far away, on the edge of the sea-lapped world, a tower rose among storm clouds. Within its shell-white walls, a woman sat alone, listening as if to a tale of marvels being told her. She smiled, her lips rounding with a deep contentment, and she fed her shuttle through her loom delicately, sparing fragile-woven warp threads till more interlacings of the weft could support them.

By morning, Tristan had been asleep for nearly three full days and had still shown no least sign of wakefulness. That, Thomas uneasily concluded, couldn't go on. He was properly fond of indolence himself, but he knew perfectly well that one couldn't spend all one's time sleeping, unless one wanted to lose hard-won muscle tone. Not that Tristan's began to compare with his own, but if the man stayed immobile much longer, considering the bruising fall he'd so recently suffered, he'd scarcely be able to move when he finally tried. And stiff wizards were too cross to share such close quarters as they must while the storm continued.

Polassar and Reynaud had begun dicing to pass the time, restless as they grew better rested. Reynaud's every win infuriated Polassar, who was certain the man was magicking the dice. To save bloodshed, they'd switched to draughts, that being less a game of chance and thus presumably less susceptible to sorcerous trickery. Reynaud had obligingly limned a board upon the floor, and Polassar was puzzling over the grid, trying to fathom the means by which Reynaud had both foiled his own schemes for a swift victory and captured that victory himself, along with the cracked pebble serving as Polassar's king. It was the third time running that the unlikely thing had happened. Thomas thought scornfully that Polassar ought to be used to the outcome by then and not so surprised, but he refused to profit from bad experience.

Shouts of victory and quarrels over losses had done no more to rouse Tristan than any of Elisena's previous ministrations. She was consulting Blais' grimoire now, concerned both that her remedies had failed and that the removal of the book, which had been in the pack Tristan's head was pillowed on, hadn't disturbed him, either. Pages crackled impatiently under her fingers.

Thomas prodded Tristan's nose with one velvet paw. *Wake up, won't you? Don't you know you're worrying her half to death? She thinks she hurt you.* Thomas wasn't sure it would be wise to subject Tristan to any more magic just then, even Blais' spells. Tristan had quite enough to cope with these days. Perhaps Elisena felt the same way, or else the grimoire offered her no likely remedies. Otherwise she'd have tried something else, instead of looking so grim. Thomas shifted his stance to Tristan's chest, for easier pawing.

You were so proud of having landed on your feet—but anyone would think you'd landed on your head. Must you be so stubborn about everything? Thomas kept patting at Tristan's face, his blows a little harder now. Sooner or later, he'd get some response.

"Thomas! You stop that!" Elisena had glanced up from the grimoire. It wasn't quite the response Thomas had hoped for. He'd expected her to overlook him longer. And no feigning of innocence on his face would make her forget him soon. What rotten luck! He measured the distance between them, guessed how long Elisena would take to reach him, and took his chance. Thomas' paw hit Tristan on the cheek again, this time with the tips of the claws just barely extruded. Tristan woke with a blanket-choked yelp of pain, or maybe of surprise.

"Thomas!" Elisena had the cat by the scruff of his neck almost instantly. She'd moved much faster than he'd calculated. Bad judgment, that. He was getting sloppy. Thomas writhed helplessly in her grip.

"I told you to leave him *alone*—"

Tristan sat up, blinking and rubbing first at his cheek, then his eyes. "It's all right," he said groggily. "He usually *bites* me when I oversleep and miss getting his breakfast." He turned to face Elisena and groaned as his joints protested the twisting. "Toadstools, why did you let me sleep so long?"

Elisena and Thomas exchanged glances. She put the cat down far more gently than she'd lifted him up, and Thomas quickly set to work grooming his mussed fur.

Tristan yawned and winced when it hurt his jaw. He shifted around, trying to find a comfortable way of sitting. From his expression, there didn't seem to be one. He looked as if he wanted to stretch and was afraid to try.

"I'm hungry," he said then, as if he'd just discovered the fact and was much surprised by it

"You should be," Elisena said. "You haven't been awake long enough to eat for three days."

Tristan's eyebrows went up. His head came up, too, and he winced again, clapping a hand to his neck. His rubbing at it didn't help the stiffness, as his woeful expression showed. "Three days? I was asleep that long?"

"Aye, Wizard. Thought you might be going to sleep the winter away, like a bear." Polassar had forgotten or forgiven the loss of the draughts games in his relief. Reynaud stretched his lips in what might have been taken for a smile and set up the board again.

"A bear would sleep a long while up here," Tristan said. He ran a finger along Thomas' back, and the cat raised his tail, inviting the tactile pleasure to be extended to it as well. As a coin of thanks and reparation, stroking sufficed very well.

The depth of the snow outside appalled Tristan, who had assumed they'd be on the move as soon as he'd eaten—or when morning came, he amended, not having figured out at that point whether it was day or night. He couldn't share Polassar's confidence that the wind would quickly clear the trails they'd use. There was an incredible accumulation after three days of unrelenting storm. Small wonder Polassar had chuckled over his asking when they were leaving.

There'd been little to see, before the gusting wind had thrust him back from the outer cave mouth. It seemed to be day, but there was no sun in sight, just a grayness everywhere. The wind was thick with snow, like the ground. Tristan cursed his clumsiness, which had got them stranded—then realized that they were better off this way, out of the wind, than if they'd been shelterless among the rocks. It was really lucky that they hadn't been able to move farther.

Good. You finally begin to show some sense. Thomas lay close by the fire, soaking up heat.

Gritting his teeth, Tristan worked his way through a set of fencer's exercises, trying to limber himself enough to move without racking pain. It was hard trusting his bad ankle, though he'd walked on it and knew it to be sound, but he hurt so fiercely almost everywhere else that he was soon able to forget about it. Tristan stretched, strained, bent, and twisted this way and that, not having felt so sore and ill-used since Blais had first begun to teach him swordplay. By the time he'd finished, he was soaked with sweat, limber perhaps, but too weary to move again.

All the stretching was repeated a couple of hours later, under Polassar's approving eye. Tristan found the exercises easier the second time, though not much. He stopped when Elisena tempted him away with the last of the stewed cherries, but considered it was probably not wise to overdo the thing, anyway. He felt able to move freely by then, but getting himself to that point had left him too worn out for anything beyond sitting still and paging through Blais' grimoire. Elisena rubbed his back, and the pleasant treatment sent him back to sleep rather more swiftly than either of them anticipated.

The next day and the next were more of the same. Tristan felt steadily stronger, but the snow fell just as steadily outside. He spent much time reading. It was the most study time he'd found since his crowning, and he should have been grateful. Tristan reminded himself of that repeatedly, whenever listening to the wind outside made him restless.

On the Transmutation of Lead into Gold, he idly read, wondering for the dozenth time why, if this spell worked at all, he and Blais had always been poor as hedge mice? Maybe the necessary weather conditions—seventy-seven successive days of bright sunlight—had simply never occurred in Calandra during Blais' life. Such a procession of fair days would have been worth more than the gold, anyway. As to the rest of the spell—dandelions and buttercups gathered under the light of the full moon surely hadn't been the problem.

It was a foolishly fanciful sort of spell, whether it worked or not. It might not be meant to be taken seriously. Every book of spells held a share of blinds, double-blinds, and red herrings. Some mages worried more over protecting their lore than others, but they all subscribed to the practice to some extent. It required a certain amount of magical experience to sift out the tricks and traps, and the uninitiated did well to let grimoires alone—which they mostly did without being asked.

Tristan skipped over a section of love philters—most of those were also extremely fanciful, though a surprising number of them worked—and came upon Blais' shortbread recipe. That section wasn't where it belonged—but the page was a wandering one, apt to pop up at odd times, as if it wanted to be baked. Tristan licked his lips at the remembered taste, then shook his head sadly. "No butter." He turned another page.

A whistle distracted him, and Tristan looked up to see a white tendril of wind-urged snow snake into the cave, past the piles of rope and gear. Elisena flung it back with one stern word of command, and the storm was not so bold again.

Quite a lot of Blais' spells dealt with weather-witching, as was typical in Calandra. There were incantations for fair weather, for rain, and for lightning and thunder. Tristan had most of them by heart, even one for snow, which no Calandran wizard in his right mind would ever use. Or was the spell folly? If it were possible to work out a reversal of such a spell, it might have incredible potential. Tristan knew he couldn't hope to dismiss a storm with Elisena's authority, but he might yet be of help to her. It would be heartening to think so.

He wouldn't touch that storm outside, though. The wind still raged, and imagination and memory supplied a picture of what the world under the wind must look like. Tristan searched hastily for some warmer spell to take his mind's eye away from that picture.

Taming dragons! That *had* to be a false trail, for no wizard so stupid as to get close to a flame-spewing dragon with taming in mind would be smart enough to survive the encounter and scribble down the spell. But it might be diverting.

Another spell was labeled *Consorting with Griffins*. Tristan doubted very much that Blais had ever seen a griffin. They weren't native to Calandra, even magically. Probably the page was copied, at Blais' own master's direction, from some older source. He would have done the same sort of thing himself, if Blais had lived a few months more and taken Tristan's training to the stage of crafting a personal grimoire.

Tristan flipped through the fables to a section he was more familiar with and read quietly for a time, listening to supper bubbling in the pot and Reynaud humming as he spliced a rope. Coming to some notations for finger-play, he practiced those, though he wasn't so bored or so foolish as to practice an actual spell with Reynaud sitting practically on top of him.

There was a bone stylus in his pack somewhere and a small board coated with wax that went with it, Tristan recalled. If he liked, he might also work on his rune-casting. He'd have preferred privacy for that, too, but there could be none. Tristan supposed that he might have braved the cold and gone into the outer cave for a while, but Elisena had beaten him to that. Whatever consulting she was doing with her rings, he wouldn't disturb her with his idle study. He'd sidetracked her enough already with his clumsiness, making her worry about him when she'd already had enough other things to fret her.

You're moody as a moulting hawk, Thomas informed him helpfully.

Tristan sighed, agreeing with the charge, though there was not much he could do about his state of mind.

Picking up the intricately carved wooden box that kept his stones and feathers safe, Tristan dumped the contents out and began idly repacking them. He doubted that he'd find any pressing use for his rain-making paraphernalia in Channadran, so those gray stones could shift to the bottom of the box now. He liked to keep his firestone on top, though, even if he didn't need it so long as they were using Ambere's magewood. And his crystal should be there, too, handy. When one needed magical light, Tristan had found that one generally needed it rather quickly, and even a wizard couldn't reliably summon it out of thin air. The crystal gave a tangible focus and reliable results, even for him. Well, mostly that was true.

Tristan arranged the pebbles in the box with care and laid the feathers by the sides where the wood of the box would support them, keeping them unbroken. One feather clung stubbornly to his finger. It was small and white—Tristan saw a spot of blue-gray along one edge and realized with a pang that the feather was one of Minstrel's, shed unnoticed and fallen into the box. In a rush of memory, he heard Minstrel singing in Darkenkeep once more and knew the bird would have filled this cave with song and spring, to put hope in all their hearts, where now there was only waiting, boredom, and a gritty determination to see this sad trek done. He would have done better to bring Minstrel along, but it was too late for that regret, along with many others.

He couldn't look at the feather any longer. It made his throat ache inexplicably. He'd asked Ambere to make Minstrel forget *him*—he should have requested that the spell work both ways. Tristan tucked the feather back into a corner of the box, safe and out of sight, and wondered how many minutes it would be before he forgot and began listening again for the soft, familiar sound of wings beside his ear.

All the stones were stowed away save the pink and ivory pebble Welslin had pressed upon him. Tristan held the stone, wondering, almost hearing the sigh of the sea upon a beach and the crying of gulls. He shook his head. It was only the wind. Thomas was quite correct as to his state of mind.

"Where did you pick that one up?"

He hadn't realized that Reynaud was watching; but sunk in his thoughts as he was, Tristan didn't think to resent the question.

"Ambere's daughter gave it to me." Tristan laid the pebble in the box with the others. It found a place for itself easily.

Reynaud's hand had been half extended toward him, as if he had expected to examine the stone. He snatched it back, his long fingers sketching an ancient sign against evil, while the skin of his face went several shades paler. He had let his brush fall, making an ugly blot in the middle of his map, which he never noticed.

"What's the matter now?" Tristan snapped, irritated that he obviously couldn't continue to ignore Reynaud's intrusion. What sort of unpleasant game was this going to be?

"You haven't heard the legends?" Reynaud's brows wavered between surprise and frown. "You've been carrying that thing all this while, not knowing?"

"*What* legends?" Now Polassar was staring at him, too, aroused by the extraordinary tone of Reynaud's voice. Maybe it was just as well. Polassar was going to have that great sword of his polished away to a sliver if he kept worrying at it much longer.

"The legends about Welslin Fateweaver." Reynaud had stopped his fingers and voice shaking, but his eyes still escaped his control. That won him Tristan's full attention, as nothing else could have done. Reynaud rattled? And so badly? Tristan had never seen the man so much as surprised in all that had befallen their quest.

"No one sees her," Reynaud was saying. "Even those few who journey to Am Islin and are permitted entrance. Sometimes, from the bottom of the tower, the clack of her shuttle has been heard, or the whisper of the thread she spins. It's said to be a sign of destiny. But no one sees *her*."

Polassar was thoroughly awestruck. He looked exactly as he would at his own hearth, listening to his bard sing of marvels on a winter's evening, and Tristan was hard put to stop his own mouth quirking. How like Reynaud to be having them both on!

Reynaud's eyes, though, spoke of a deadly seriousness. There was no slightest hint of mockery in their stern expression.

"If you saw her, if she gave you—that, then it's a sign. The fate of our journey's sealed."

"That was so in any case," Elisena replied matter-of-factly. She knelt to warm her hands at the fire, and her rings reflected back jewels of red, gold, and sapphire. Her face was pinched with cold and her nose was red.

"It means this is truly an epic venture," Reynaud insisted. "Vaster than Calandra alone."

"Did you doubt that?" Elisena asked, so normally as to make light of Reynaud's agitation.

"The kind that's sung of?" Polassar interrupted eagerly.

"The sort never spoken of," Reynaud said, his voice dark as nightfall. "There are things even the mages of Kôvelir won't commit to writing. One hears things, never much, never all at once. And late at night one remembers, and pieces begin to fit together. Some of those things are Welslin Fateweaver's dealings with mortal men."

Tristan found it impossible to smother a wholly inappropriate laugh. All this fuss over a shy girl weaving in a tower? He'd never thought to see Reynaud so discomfited—and over so paltry a cause.

True, Welslin had had a weird effect on him, too, at the time, but he'd been ill and admittedly easily confused. Tristan had hardly understood half the things she'd said to him at the time—and had forgotten most of them since. Whatever her urgency at giving it to him, the stone was only a pebble, possessing some power, maybe, but not so strong that he was moved to search for a spell to tap it. A girl who seemed much more than half a dream, and a smooth stone that was ordinary enough, if prettily colored—what did either one of them mean, even as bits of a tale told in the dark in a far-off city? Less than nothing, Tristan thought.

He looked at the stone lying on his palm with the firelight beating on it and wondered fleetingly if he ought to be so sure of that. He didn't remember picking it up again. How had it got from the box to his hand? He must be growing pitifully absent-minded. He ought to be explaining Welslin to Elisena, lest she misunderstand, but there'd be time for that later.

Reynaud was furious and not doing much of a job of hiding it. In a moment he was going to speak whatever was on his mind, Thomas thought worriedly. They were all of them bored and edgy. A fight would only make bad things worse, and the cat was certain he wouldn't be able to keep Tristan out of it this time. Tristan's resentment of Reynaud, however baseless, was long since ready to boil over, likely at the very next word Reynaud uttered. Thomas sensed that Tristan's mood had shifted again. After all, the stone and the incident it represented were both intensely private. Reynaud's prying must therefore grate.

There was no hope that Reynaud might keep silent, either. Thomas sought frantically for some diversion. Short of jumping into the fire, he could think of nothing, but fortune smiled. He was handed a distraction at the last instant when it might yet do some good.

We have a visitor! Tristan lifted his head, and Reynaud turned his with a jerk. Thomas crouched by the opening to the outer cave, warily facing a large and considerably wind-tattered gray gyrfalcon. The bird half spread its strong wings, beating them against the rock, then settled once more and gave several shrill cries, fierce as the tumultuous mountain winds that had brought it.

"The storm clouds move south," Elisena translated. "The winds that drive them are clearing much of the rock as well. We'll be able to move on, come morning."

The gyrfalcon's dark eyes swept them all as the bird turned its head in little angry jerks to fix on each of them in turn. It might have been counting. Then it gave another cry and opened its wings, turning about among the rocks with an amazing control. Thomas sprang back. The falcon was airborne and out of the cave by the time Tristan got to the outer opening, lost against the white of the storm outside.

"It will report our position to Royston Ambere," Elisena said, "and assure him that all is well with us."

Tricks of the Light

IT FELT GOOD TO MOVE MORE THAN THE THREE SHORT paces he had needed to cross the cavern, Tristan thought gratefully. His legs welcomed the chance to stretch out, and he was glad to be out in the fresh air, cold as it was.

See how you feel about that in an hour, when you can't feel the end of your own nose. It's colder up here since the storm, Thomas pointed out. Tristan felt the cat burrowing deeper into the pack, seeking the warmest spot, his paws occasionally bumping Tristan's back.

Thomas was quite right. The air was frigid, and the wind was still as sharp as a sword blade. Tristan had fastened every hook, button, and thong on his clothing, and yet that wind found ways to reach his skin. Spells were useless for keeping it out. His breath hung as a continual cloud in front of his mouth—unless the wind tore it away along with all the warmth in his face.

There were no clouds to be seen, other than those before the mouths of his companions. Each of Channadran's nearly numberless mountains was plainly visible, sharp-etched. It was hardly possible to appreciate the distances between them, when even the most distant were not blurred by impurities in the air. The travelers were doubly grateful to Ambere's birds for the guidance they gave as well as the food they brought. Tristan couldn't tell from which direction he'd walked, far less which they were expected to continue.

Whenever they rested, Reynaud was busy with his map, taking advantage of the clear view, no matter how exhausted he might be. The ink blot had been meticulously scraped away, Tristan noted, but Reynaud had to mutter spells continually to keep his ink unfrozen. His temper hardly invited questions as to course.

Despite Reynaud's whipping out his map, they'd only paused to recover a trifle before negotiating a bit of down-slope that looked even more impossible than usual. They would need their ropes and have to search out footholds with feet they could scarcely feel, even in Ambere's warm-crafted boots.

Stamping to restore circulation to feet and toes was of little use. Indeed, Tristan wasn't altogether sure that feeling would be welcome. His feet would only be outraged again by the cold, like the rest of him. Nonetheless, he kicked about in the snow as he got the ropes ready and beat his mittened hands against his body, hoping forlornly that his fingers wouldn't break off. When the action began to be painful, he took heart a little and stamped harder.

His face felt frozen as well, but there was nothing to be done about that. If he tried to slap feeling back into his cheeks, he'd probably knock himself silly. His hands in the clumsy mittens felt as easy to manipulate as a seal's flippers.

The climb was nightmarish, and the level ground that they reached at the end of it was perilous. The thick-fallen snow—not wind-cleared at all—looked white and invit-ing, soft as feathers to topple into. It beckoned, clean as oblivion, and Tristan had to caution himself to remember the stark blackness of the rocks beneath and force himself to recognize the danger of a color scheme that cried out for the addition of a spatter of crimson blood. His knees wobbled, still locked as if by an ensorcellment, and the exposed skin of his face tingled, vulnerable to those sharp rocks and knowing it.

Every step seemed a disaster narrowly averted, a rest reluctantly postponed. Only after some moments did Tris-tan's head clear fully, when he apparently passed out of the spell's zone of influence. He was foggily grateful, hardly sure just what had happened to him. What sort of spell would it be—a confusion or something worse? Eli-sena or Reynaud might know, surely ought to.

But whether anyone else had been so affected, Tristan couldn't judge. He supposed his perceptions were still skewed or that he ought to expect them to be. He'd have thought the trouble all in his own mind, if other things hadn't also been more than ordinarily wrong.

Polassar and Reynaud were openly snarling at each other, quarreling first over the condition of the ropes and then about some gear which each accused the other of having left behind at their last camp. Elisena uncharacteristically said nothing, and Tristan was appalled as he listened more closely and at a loss as to how best to resolve the mess.

He located the missing gear at last—part of it was in his own pack, the rest in Polassar's—but only time and carefully kept distance mollified the two combatants.

It was time for all of them to get well clear of the ensorcelled ground of the pass and out of earshot of its evilly whistling winds. Tristan hoped they were out of it and that he'd correctly guessed the trouble's source, for no one else seemed to be trying. By nightfall they were much as they usually were at day's end, too weary and cold for quarreling, but there had been words spoken that Tristan could not hope would be wholly forgotten.

His own overtaxed nerves helped matters not a whit. He answered a casual request from Elisena to light the magewood more crossly than he had intended and felt that every smoothing word he said later only compounded his guilt and her hurt feelings. Thomas' fur stood on end all night, crackling at a touch, which the cat didn't permit more than once, on pain of claws uncharitably used.

It would have been a good night for nightmares, had Tristan been able to sleep at all. He was weary, cold, out of sorts, and full of discord. Could whatever they'd run into that day be expected again? And why did no one else seem to be aware of it?

He spoke of it finally to Elisena and saw by her troubled look that she'd surmised the trap as well, but perhaps hoped no one else had. Deceptions of that type were hard to be sure of, she said.

The stars burned close enough to touch, and there were more of them than Tristan could easily believe. Familiar constellations were as thick with new pinpricks of light as a school of fish with fins.

The glitter of the stars did not seem friendly. There was no more idle telling of the legends of the constellations. Voices carried in the still air, and it seemed safest now that they should not speak lightly or often. New fears kept them quiet.

They came down from the shoulders of the outer mountains, entering what had once been a broad valley. Tristan thought it might once have been the size of Calandra itself, if not greater. Now the vast space was filled, rim to rim, with a white river of glacier. It looked dangerous, but safer than the mountain rocks. Those promised too much hazardous climbing with too little progress in return.

Days and nights continued clear, and now that began to prove a menace. There was no least scrap of cloud cover, and the glare of the sun on the white snow and ice was frightful. With eyes closed to slits against it and sometimes shut entirely, it was hard to see dangers in time to avoid them, and there were plenty to dodge.

Ice, being so solid, must flow rather poorly, Tristan supposed. When Nímir was importunate, forcing the ice ever downward and outward from Channadran, it had no choice but to move, but it did not do so easily. The shifting left the glacier's surface cracked and heaved up, as frost heaves up paving blocks, and it made an incredibly jumbled course to try to walk. Broken ice alone was not the worst thing they must contend with. Where snowslides had come down the mountain sides, there might be great fans of soft snow, leavened with huge chunks of ice. Crossing one such spot cost them a whole day of struggling. After that, Elisena led them around the snow, finding the longer way faster. They were always weary and aching by day's end, and their clothes were damp inside with sweat, despite the cold and Amber's kind sorceries.

Snow often covered fissures and crevasses, or what looked to be a safe bridge of ice over a chasm proved deceitful. Polassar broke through one such and floundered armpit deep in soft stuff. One chop with his ice axe gave him the leverage he needed to clamber out of danger before Tristan could uncoil a rope to throw to him; but had the crack been deeper than it was, it would have been another matter. The incident made up Polassar's mind, at any rate. Henceforth, he decreed, they'd rope themselves loosely together for safety's sake.

The idea's worth was proved the very next day when they nearly lost Reynaud to a crevasse none of them had seen. He broke through the lip of snow that overhung its edge and vanished from sight in an instant. Polassar threw his weight hard against the rope, or else Elisena might have been dragged in as well. She jammed her axe between two great chunks of ice and managed to stop herself sliding, but she could not have held Reynaud's weight as Polassar did.

Tristan, trying to help with the rescue, got too close to Polassar and was knocked off his feet as the bigger man began to haul on the rope. He got up slowly, more shaken than he wanted anyone to see, just in time to watch Reynaud being dragged out of the chasm like a fish on a line.

The rope was knotted securely about his waist, but Reynaud wasn't trusting that. His fingers were wrapped about the rope so tightly that Polassar nearly had to pry them loose, and Reynaud took several minutes to steady his breathing before indicating he was ready to continue.

Tristan had to force his own eyes open. He'd shut them, hoping to get a little relief from the glare off the ice, but it hadn't helped much. Now nothing came into sharp focus, and what colors there were looked wrong. He shook his head crossly and was sorry he did, because the movement started a fearful throbbing behind his eyes. That night he said the fire-lighting-spell over one of the copper pots in place of the magewood—mistaking both the shape and the red glow—and was thankful that no one noticed. Maybe their sight was as bad as his. Tristan said nothing about it, trusting a night's sleep to put things right.

Next morning, the going seemed easier, but, as the sun climbed, the glare increased once again. Tristan shut his eyes against it briefly, then found it hard not to keep them closed. That was dangerous, he knew, but he couldn't convince his eyelids of the peril. They kept dropping, as if he were fighting off sleep without much success. He had to force them open every dozen steps or so. At least, he thought he managed it that often. He could well have been wrong.

His head began to ache again, more cruelly than before. Walking jarred it, and when they stopped to rest and eat, Tristan dared take nothing more than a few sips of water. Solid food seemed an outrage his queasy stomach wouldn't tolerate. He wasn't even sure that the water had been wise. It lay cold in his belly for a long while, setting him shivering. That hurt his head even worse, naturally.

He was determined not to give in to weakness again, so long as anyone else could stand the bright light. If Reynaud could walk, Tristan thought, he could too—and he would. He gave himself no choice about it.

Worse than the glare was the strain of walking into dangers that couldn't properly be seen, knowing perfectly well that each step might be the one to plunge one of them into waist-deep snow or worse. There were chasms and crevasses everywhere, and Tristan was amazed when the snow held firm under his boots, instead of giving way and dropping him into emptiness, to be jerked up short by his rope and choked by its pressure on his chest. He was always expecting it. It happened often enough.

He grew dizzy. Tristan couldn't tell whether he was walking in the right direction or in circles. So long as the rope didn't bring him up short, however, he knew he must at least be going in the same direction as the others. Thomas could have reassured him, but he didn't have the cat for comfort or a second pair of eyes at that moment. Thomas was up ahead with Elisena, testing the ice bridges as they came to them. His slitted eyes, with their extra membrane and long pupils, stood the glare better, and Elisena trusted his eyes more than her own.

Tristan stepped to his left, around what was either a shadow on the ground or a crevasse in it, and banged hard against something solid. He stopped, startled, and tried to see what the obstacle was, while the slack in the rope got used up and he was nearly jerked off his unsteady legs. Whatever he'd hit was dark, so it must be rock, not ice. They had moved close to the edge of the glacier again, then. Cracks in the ice had led them a long way out from the mountain's shoulder during the morning, but they needed to head back toward it as soon as that proved possible, taking full advantage of the evening shadows which would fall first there.

Tristan couldn't judge how much farther they traveled after they reached the rock—only to the first sheltered spot, probably. But he seemed to have been walking for all he could remember of his life, wobbly-kneed and clinging to the rock beside him with one numb hand, barely able to open his swollen eyes. They were in shadow now, he thought, because his face felt colder, but the darkness didn't help. Still he could see very little.

Tears streamed down Tristan's cheeks and froze in the wind continually. His face felt flushed, sometimes, but the cold air stole all the heat away, and mostly it was as numb as his hands. He was still sick to his stomach and thankful that he hadn't eaten. His head ached worse every minute. He couldn't think straight and he was nearly too dizzy to stand, much less walk. He kept tripping, sometimes falling against the rock and sometimes against hands that snatched at him and heaved him upright again. Still, he kept moving, chiefly because he was too disoriented to remember that he could stop.

He went down on hands and knees finally, on what felt like either bare rock or bare ice. Nobody picked him up, or callously insisted that he get up on his own, so Tristan stayed where he was, his eyes still shut—or else open and totally blind. He would scarcely have known the difference by then.

A long while later, Tristan became aware of something cold resting against the back of his neck. At first he thought that his hood must have slipped back, but his head began to clear and no longer ached so badly as it had. Tristan blinked, and a face swam into focus for a few seconds, right in front of his own.

"This should help a little." Elisena was holding a lump of snow against the back of his neck. Her other hand juggled a cup against his lips, and Tristan managed a few swallows. He couldn't feel the liquid against his lips, but he could taste it well enough. It was nasty stuff.

"Can you see anything yet?"

"Some." Tristan got his own fingers around the cup, clumsily but able to control it. "It seems dark. Or is that just my eyes?"

"It's night on this side of the mountain," Elisena said. "I've sent a message back with the eagles, asking Ambere for hawkweed. I can make a poultice from it for your eyes, but his birds won't be able to bring it in before morning. The owls can't fly this far. We'll be right here for a bit—none of us can see well enough to risk moving any more. Reynaud's sicker than you are—Polassar had to carry him most of the afternoon. That did Polassar in, too, I think."

She guided Tristan's still-mittened hand up to his neck and placed it over the ball of snow. "Can you hold that there yourself? I've got to see what I can do for Reynaud."

Tristan sat quite still for a moment. Melting snow trickled down his back. He tried to open his eyes again. His sight cleared briefly, and he could see Thomas lying beside him. The cat was biting at his paws, teasing out balls of ice from between the pads. Tristan's vision blurred again before he could discover where Elisena had gone. He called hopefully in the direction he thought she'd taken, knowing she wouldn't be far enough away to be out of hearing.

"Elisena? I think I have some hawkweed in my pack. I keep it for the horses. You'll have to help me find it, though—I don't think I can read the labels."

Elisena didn't answer him. In fact, he couldn't hear her moving about or speaking to Reynaud as she would have been doing had she been nursing the man. *"Elisena?"*

Tristan put a hand out, letting the lump of snow drop. He tugged his mittens off. His chilled fingers met the edge of the fire first on their search. His eyes hadn't warned him of it—they'd gone nearly shut again. Tristan gave up trying to force them open and relied on his hands.

Next he touched the sturdy crockery of the cup Elisena had been holding and slid into a cooling puddle of spilled tea around it. By the wetness, he felt cloth, then the fur of Elisena's hood and the ends of her curling hair.

"Elisena! Thomas, where are you? What's happened to her?"

He felt the cat beside him, though his hands were still busy at Elisena's face and throat, searching for signs of her breathing. Thomas' fur brushed them as the cat pressed close.

Fainted, I think. It's no great wonder. She had to be first, through all that today. It was hard work.

By that time, Tristan had felt Elisena's breath, warm against his fingers. Her breathing was steady enough, and that calmed him as much as Thomas' matter-of-factness.

"All right," Tristan said—he hoped decisively. "Thomas, you'll have to help me. There's no one else.

Find the hawkweed bag, first. Oh, and did she brew this tea up in a pot? Is there any left? I'll need it." He'd already located the cup again and picked it up carefully. No less carefully and still working by feel, Tristan turned Elisena onto her back and propped her against him.

"Thomas?"

A little patience, if you please! It's on the very bottom, I think. A furious rustling came from the pack on Tristan's back, and he felt the baggage shifting with Thomas' weight.

"Thomas, I can't see a cursed thing. How does she look to you? Is she waking up yet?"

Not yet. Try to relax a little. You're going to spill that tea all over yourself, and it's still hot.

He couldn't remember dipping the cup into the pot. Trembling, Tristan put a finger against one of Elisena's eyelids. Her lashes fluttered slightly at his touch. He whispered her name encouragingly. Elisena didn't answer, but her head moved against his chest.

When she stirred again more strongly, Tristan lifted her head and put the cup to her lips as she had to his. "Just you lie still and swallow this. It will help."

Elisena drank obediently, then squirmed. "That's awful! What on earth is it?"

"Same stuff you just gave me."

"I apologize," Elisena said faintly, after a moment's silence. "I had no idea it tasted like that."

I think I found it. Thomas shoved a bag over Tristan's shoulder. It fell into his free hand, either by luck or Thomas' aim. Tristan took the bag, gave it a squeeze to crush a few of the topmost leaves, and sniffed it.

"Yes. There are some clean rags in the bottom of that mess somewhere. Did you see them? Fetch them for me, too." Tristan dragged out the nearest wool bag and rolled Elisena carefully into it. She tried to sit up, but he tucked the folds around her relentlessly. "You stay put. I'll do whatever I can. Thomas will help."

He got more water boiling and steeped handfuls of the dried hawkweed, adding marigold petals and rue. While the brew cooled a bit, Tristan stretched Polassar's cloak and his own across some of the rocks behind them to make as much of a shield as he could manage against the snow. Working blind, the task took him a long time, and he kept bumping into things, but under Thomas' direction he at length had a nearly weathertight shelter over their heads. He could have improved it by using magic, but Tristan had no energy to spare for thinking of spells, far less to spend executing them.

Polassar was snoring faintly, though he seemed to be still in a swoon. He was too heavy to lift, so Tristan finally laid a wool bag over him and put a poultice across his eyes. A louder snore assaulted his ears then, somewhat reassuringly. Tristan needed to do nothing else for Polassar, save to let the man sleep.

Elisena had fallen asleep by then, too, and she didn't wake when Tristan applied the next poultice to her eyes. Finally he wrestled Reynaud into a bag and felt the man go suddenly rigid when he woke to find himself being handled.

Tristan tried vainly to clear his own eyes again, not wanting to seem as helpless as he was in front of Reynaud. It didn't work. Blinking did no good, nor did rubbing. The most Tristan could make out of his surroundings was the glow where the magewood was—barely that.

Reynaud sat up, bumping against the stretched cloaks. "What—"

He sounded terribly ill, bad enough to make Tristan ashamed of his own wariness. His vision cleared a trifle, contrarily. He could see that Reynaud had cut his cheek, probably while falling into a crevasse. As the man's flesh began to warm, blood began to flow again. Tristan wiped it away with a rag. He put the cup of tea to Reynaud's lips and waited while Reynaud drank, juggling the poultice in his other hand.

Reynaud sniffed. "Hawkweed?"

Tristan nodded, then remembered he'd have to speak. "Yes."

"I can't see," Reynaud informed him flatly.

Tristan helped him to lie back again, then tied the poultice in place as gently as he could. "I can't, either," he finally admitted. "It doesn't matter—it's night now, anyway. Go to sleep. We should be all right in the morning."

"I thought I'd gone blind."

"Go to sleep." The last thing Tristan felt he needed was a long discussion of hawkweed's medicinal applications. There were probably plenty of things he could have done to make the herbs more effective, but he couldn't see well enough to try anything fancy.

Better use yours before it gets cold.

Thomas meant the poultice, Tristan supposed. He picked the wet bundle up, unrolled his bag beside Elisena, and lay down on it. He ached all over. Just lying still hurt, and he doubted he'd sleep, unless he was lucky enough to faint again.

Tristan laid the warm cloth over his eyelids, wincing as a trickle of water ran down toward his left ear. The stabbing in his head subsided mercifully. The herbs would cool quickly, but that didn't matter. For the moment, they were helpful. He'd leave the poultice in place until it cooled, but no more than that. Polassar would be hungry when he woke, and Tristan thought he almost felt well enough to scrape together some sort of stew. It could be only dried vegetables and melted snow, but anything hot would be welcome...

Ambere's birds woke him at first light—or rather Thomas did, chary of dealing with four eagles all at once on his own. Tristan didn't feel quite up to such an encounter either, but he managed, thankful enough that he could see all four of the birds. His eyes still burned as if he'd gone without many nights of sleep, but his sight was clear again.

He squatted in front of the foremost eagle, feeling awkward about standing and towering over such a proud sort of bird. The eagle didn't seem to note his consideration, and its expression of disdain never altered. After regarding him for a moment, the bird stepped back from the bag of dried hawkweed that had been under its talons. Tristan reached to take the bag, thanking the creature gravely.

Two of the other birds had brought meat—fresh-killed rabbits, both stiff as wood from their cold passage. The last eagle held another leather bag. Tristan assumed it contained more hawkweed, but the bird did not release the parcel when he put his hand out for it. Instead, it screamed several times, then snapped the hook of its beak above the bag. Tristan jerked his fingers back hastily, resisting the urge to count them.

He couldn't understand the bird's speech as Elisena could, so Tristan was thoroughly baffled when, after screaming again, the eagle stepped back from the bag and launched itself into the air. Its companions followed, their pinions stirring up loose snow. Tristan picked up the sack warily, still looking after the four departing eagles.

The sack was light, though it seemed to be full enough. Tristan unhitched the laces. Black powder, probably charcoal. A medicine? It wasn't a specific for eyesight or anything Tristan could think of, except for some poisons.

The one that almost took your hand off said something about eyes, Thomas informed him. *I think you want to rub that under them to cut the glare. It might work.*

Perhaps, but probably not well enough, Tristan thought. The sky was still clear, and he knew that, hawkweed or no, charcoal or no, they dared not risk another day's travel like the one just past. They'd been mad to continue. It was just past dawn and already the light hurt his head and eyes. They might just as well lie down and die where they were, where they could be comfortable about it. If there were only a *little* cloud cover.

So many years of watching Blais witch weather, and nothing comes to mind?

Nothing seemed to, Tristan thought with shame. He was half-relieved, as he felt rather incapable of any magic. Unless—

Tristan opened the bag of charcoal powder again and dumped a little of the stuff out onto his palm. It was ground so finely that his breath on it sent little curls up into the air. Maybe matters weren't so bleak after all. Tristan glanced back at the makeshift tent.

No one else was stirring yet. He had privacy, at least, and an idea that it wouldn't hurt to try. Or so he thought. He'd tried no magic in a long while. He heard Reynaud's voice as if in his ear, saying, "Blocked..."

Tristan knelt down at the first flat spot he found, heedless of the snow that still drifted over the rocks. Drawing his brass dagger, he scribed out runes on the snow crust in front of him, arranging the words in delicate lines, arcs, and spirals. He'd best be very careful with this one, Tristan cautioned himself, or he'd get a fog instead of the clouds he wanted. He was good with fog spells, or had been, and the distinction between a fog and a cloud was only one of height, not of kind. He'd need all his skill and confidence. It would have helped if he'd been feeling clearer-headed.

His knees were cold already—matching most of the rest of his body. Tristan willed himself not to shiver. He dared do nothing that might throw his delivery off, once he actually began the spell. He reminded himself that he had endured worse discomforts.

Tristan set the bag of charcoal on a blank spot he'd left in the middle of the rune pattern. Reaching into the pouch he wore at his belt, he located his magic box and felt down to its very bottom, where he found a heavy gray pebble. He weighed it in his cold fingers. It should do. He generally used it as part of a rain spell, so he knew it was reliable and perhaps cloud-linked, from many uses. He stroked the stone a few times, instructing it. Thomas watched, tail switching, eyes bright.

Tristan began to speak the spell. When he was halfway through the words, he began to loosen the thongs at the top of the charcoal bag. Putting a hand on each side of its neck, he opened the bag's mouth as wide as it would go. Then he lifted up the gray pebble once again, cupping it between both his palms, as if it were extremely weighty for its size. Tristan spoke the rest of the spell, the summation. He opened his hands to let the unbearably heavy pebble fall.

It dropped straight into the open neck of the charcoal bag, sending up a thin plume of black dust. Tristan sat back on his heels, being careful not to breathe any of the powder. Like smoke, the black tendrils continued to rise from the bag. The effect, as they wove around each other on their way skyward, was almost hypnotic. Tristan forced himself to keep watching the tendrils, not the sky, while his words droned on. After a few minutes he reached out and squeezed the neck of the bag closed, estimating that the spell had run long enough for his purpose. A little of the powder sifted over his fingers.

Tristan stood, wobbling more than a little. He'd been kneeling in the snow a long while, a good way to take an ague. His feet were quite numb. Tristan turned back toward the camp and the promised warmth of the fire—then realized that he was casting no shadow. He finally remembered to look at the sky.

The sunrise edge of it was lit with a pale yellow glow.

The sun climbed as Tristan watched, and the light increased, but never burned through the thin cloud cover.

Good job, Thomas said offhandedly, and made for the warmth of the makeshift tent.

Elisena sat up at once when she woke, despite Tristan's protests.

"I'm all right now." She fingered the hawkweed poultice. It was fresh, as Tristan had just finished changing the dressing. "You did find some hawkweed?"

"And Ambere's birds brought more this morning," Tristan answered. "Want some tea?"

"Ah . . . that depends. What kind of tea?"

Tristan grinned, understanding. "Peppermint. With honey. There's going to be some stew in a little while. It would be ready now, but it took me a while to figure out how to skin a frozen rabbit."

"Where are the others?" Elisena took the cup he held out, sniffing it first with concealed suspicion, then with appreciation.

"Scouting a little way ahead. I hope Polassar keeps a sharp eye on Reynaud—he looked almost as bad as you did, but he insisted on going."

"It's that damned glare." Elisena rubbed gingerly at her eyelids. "I should have tried to pull a cloud-spell together, but I couldn't. I thought my head would split open."

"Stop rubbing. I tried that, and it doesn't help."

"Yes. Did you know your nose is sunburned?"

"It is?" Tristan brushed at the spot unwisely and winced. "First time it's ever seen so much sun, I guess." He said nothing about the clouds outside. Let them be a pleasant surprise.

"I'll put some salve on it for you."

"That you won't. We're not going anywhere until Polassar and Reynaud get back; and in the meantime you're going to rest and have something to eat."

"Scared you, did I?" The corners of her mouth twitched.

"Yes. And I didn't much like it. Are you warm enough? I wish we had some wine. I think the birds try to bring skins of it in now and then, but it probably freezes on the way. The rabbits certainly did." Tristan paused a moment, thinking. "I wonder if Reynaud has a flask? I wouldn't put it past him—"

"That's all right. The tea was enough—not that Polassar would agree."

Tristan shrugged, then began to stir the stew once more.

"Think you could do that from over here?"

Tristan glanced over at Elisena, then returned the smile she sent his way. They hadn't really been alone together, since leaving Crogen, unless time could be counted in minutes snatched. Polassar and Reynaud had only just left and might well be gone a decent while.

He settled himself against the rock and Elisena's shoulder. Tristan realized that he could no longer reach either the pot or the spoon, but for once his fingerplay was sufficiently adept to permit his handling the spoon without physically touching it. So long as he didn't get too preoccupied, the stew wouldn't scorch.

Reynaud's silver knife flicked deftly about his face, keeping the edges of his beard in perfect trim. Firelight flashed off the blade as it turned this way and that, but Tristan tried not to let it draw his attention. He was also trying not to seem envious as he cut away those few hairs on his own face that he needed to bother with. His beard grew too erratically to offer him any protection from the cold, even should he be willing to forget how miserably unkempt he'd looked when last he'd tried to grow one. Luckily his hood was fur-lined.

Polassar was as hairy as the bear that had given up its skin to line his cloak. Normally he shaved away all except his long moustaches, of which he was vain, but he'd let the whole beard grow in since they'd reached the mountains. It crackled in the dry air the same way Thomas' fur did, and he was never seen to touch a blade or comb to it. Polassar looked somewhat scornfully upon Reynaud's careful toilet, but loftily said nothing.

Maybe he still thinks he might get changed into a toad. Thomas completed his own toilet, more finically even than Reynaud, and sat daintily by Tristan's boots.

They were quite deep into Channadran. Soon they'd reach the point beyond which Ambere's birds could not guide them, and would then lose both their guides and their supply line. Their situation from that point would be grave, for none of them had any idea yet of how they ought to proceed then. And there was no telling how much longer their journey might take.

Tristan could feel their momentum and their sense of collective purpose slipping away. He felt as if he'd been walking and climbing all his life and he found it sometimes hard to recall that all the agony was but a means to an end which seemed by then as distant as its far-off beginning. It would have been very easy to live only in the present moment—could they have afforded such a luxury.

Tristan had seen the mountains in all their colors by then. It seemed odd to him that such a dead place should have colors other than black or gray; but as the light changed, so did the appearance of the peaks. Depending on weather and time of day, they might be indigo, pink, or purple, and the sky behind them could be only a slightly differing shade of the same hue. At sunset, the far-off valleys were black and purple, the peaks above them a dripping blood-scarlet. Sometimes the world was all moonlight white—peaks, glaciers, snow ridges, fog, and sky.

The mountains did odd things to the light. Just now, the ridges all were dark; but far away, one valley was yet filled with light, brimming with it like a golden bowl of wine or some promised land. Tristan, thinking of home, blinked hard and told himself that his eyes still tired easily, and in consequence watered much.

His sword lay across his knees, along with the oiled rags he'd been using to tend it. The blade looked dull and lifeless to Tristan's eyes and certainly it did not sing at his touch. The sword was a long way from its home, too. Mayhap that robbed it of something vital. How he longed for the sight of a flower or a fruit tree ready for harvest! Those things he thought never to see again, and Tristan missed them so sorely that he could scarcely conjure what they looked like, even to his own mind.

The sword might be mirroring Calandra's condition, indeed. They'd been gone a long time—precisely how long, Tristan wouldn't know unless he humbled himself and asked Reynaud, who was keeping their records along with the map. If, in all that while, Calandra had borne Nímir's attacks, there'd be very little left alive there by this time. The home he longed for so desperately might no longer exist.

Nímir had left them unmolested for a few days, which was certainly puzzling. He would not be trusting to his mountains entirely, since alone those were but rock and ice—in theory, penetrable, if with difficulty. If Nímir bolstered his mountains with nothing sorcerous, that might mean they'd failed in their hope to divert him from Calandra itself. Or else, as Elisena thought, Nímir had simply become curious. He'd permit them to come close to their goal before moving again to crush them. They'd proved the seriousness of their intent by their persistence. Conceivably, if they gave good sport they'd be let live longer, to give that sport for a longer while. Tristan shivered. He thought he knew how a mouse must feel when stalked by a cat.

You do not. Thomas began pawing at a little bag one of the eagles had dropped off that day, batting it about atop the rock he was lying on. *They don't think nearly so much. It's simpler for them.*

Tristan rescued the bag. He'd assumed it held cornmeal, but it hadn't behaved that way while Thomas played with it. He opened the drawstrings, wondering. Maybe Ambere had sent them something new. Thomas was right—he did think too much, and that led to melancholy.

The stuff in the bag was the color of jerked beef, but heavier and not so grained. Tristan sniffed at a bit of it. It wasn't meat. Some spice? Its smell was sweet. He had no idea what it might be, and neither had Elisena, when he asked her opinion.

"Some medicine, maybe?" The stuff was soft, Tristan could scratch it with a fingernail. And it had grown sticky where his fingers had warmed it, like resin.

"No, it's a sweet," Reynaud said. He reached into the bag and drew out a piece, nodding at it. "Yes. I have heard of this, though not seen it. A sweet, but it sustains better than most such. It's rare and costly, and its source is far away from even Kôvelir, though maybe not so to Royston Ambere."

Tristan nibbled at his dark-colored piece gingerly. There was a bitterness, mixed with the richness and the sweetness his nose had told him of. It was an altogether agreeable flavor. He'd never tasted its like before, but he wished to again. He took a second piece and smiled at Polassar's scorn of such "lady-food." True, the stuff didn't look capable of satisfying a man long, but it tasted as if it just might, and Ambere would hardly have bothered to send them something useless. Knowing such a taste waited at mealtimes might make walking more palatable, too.

They pressed always, as they had been bidden to, into the worst country, following the birds. Where they could, they used glaciers for roads, despite the dangers, for those offered an easier way, with less climbing to do. It was hard to sleep there—the ice groaned and grumbled in the night, moving always. Whenever possible, they camped on rock, even if it was not convenient to reach, because it seemed more secure.

It was near to day's end. They were climbing a ridge, which caught the sun longer than the glacier below, but they'd be making camp soon. All were weary, and they'd strung out in a straggling line. Tristan was in the rear— well back, since he lost ground as he paused to scan the slopes about them, hoping vainly to discern some response to them in his sword—some clue as to their ultimate goal. It didn't matter if he lagged a bit, he thought—the way they must take was plain. They'd met with no rough climbing that day, so there were no ropes strung between them to nag him on.

The sun was sinking, tinting the snows pink and gold as it bade them farewell. There were red slashes like claw marks across the sunward sky. All the shadows were deep blue. A sudden flicker of movement caught Tristan's eye. He looked closer, saw nothing, and decided that the motion probably was just snow sliding across the rocks. There was nothing else up there to move. But he had an insistent feeling he'd seen *something*.

Might it be one of Ambere's birds? This late in the day, a bird would have to fly hard if it hoped to reach them with a message and still return to Am Islin. Such a bird might easily overfly itself. Tristan thought he'd better see about it. Looking after Ambere's birds certainly wouldn't hurt, and would keep them in Ambere's good graces.

The movement had seemed to be near an overhang of snow, and the shadow cast there was heavy. He'd have to get closer; he couldn't see a thing in the darkness. No matter, the slope was gentle enough, and the snow on it no more than ankle deep. He could manage far worse, and had done so every day.

Tristan climbed away from the trail, looking and listening for the flutter of wings. He'd have to be careful if he did find a bird—one the size of Ambere's eagles could do a lot of damage when it was hurt or frightened. No wonder the shadows were so dark. He'd reached rock, and there was rock overhead, too, a ledge that supported the lip of snow. Tristan eyed the overhang, but it looked solid enough, and he was getting better at judging such matters.

He still saw no bird, and the others were farther off than Tristan supposed was wise. He'd have to go back down. The only reason he wasn't being nagged about it already was that Thomas was sound asleep in the pack, and no one below had noticed his detour yet. He'd better get back before they did miss him.

Tristan turned to retrace his steps. It was easy; his footprints were as clear as if they'd been carved there on the snow. He found the spot where he'd turned to look back the first time. There were a lot of tracks, more than he'd thought he'd made. It was funny how many steps a man took daily, never thinking about them because they normally left no trace.

There was a dark lump in the snow beside one print, not much bigger than his fist. Tristan bent to pick the object up and didn't know whether to curse his carelessness or rejoice in his luck. The thongs of his belt-pouch must have come undone as he climbed to let it open and spill out his box of magic stones. It must have happened as he scrambled up the last bit of slope, and it was a wonder it hadn't happened somewhere else in the day's march, when he wouldn't have been backtracking to notice it. He moved to stow the box away, more carefully this time.

His leather pouch was laced tight shut and was already full! Tristan stared at the carved wooden box in his hand. It wasn't his own, he saw as he looked at it better—but it wasn't strange to him either. It had been the pattern he'd made his own box from, following the ancient custom of apprenticeship and making one's tools oneself, under the master's guidance. Where Tristan had chosen—and somewhat crudely executed—a design of flowering herbs, his master's box had borne a bird with outspread wings, beautifully carved. Tristan hadn't seen the box since that day when he'd come home to find Blais dead and all his tools missing.

Now, he'd found that very box. There was no mistaking it. Tristan knew it as well as he'd known Blais' seamed face, with the smudges of dirt the mage had collected like a small boy in the course of his varied, often absent-minded experiments. It was the same box. Tristan knew precisely the stones he'd find within if he opened it—the big firestone and the elegant drops of clouded crystal that Blais had used to weave rainbows as a special service for just-wedded couples.

But how came it to Channadran? The box had never left Blais' side, any more than Tristan had ever been willingly parted from his own tools.

The thought struck with a force that took Tristan's breath. He'd simply assumed that Blais *was* dead, for his master had lost his duel with whatever creature Nímir had sent that day to deal with an upstart wizard who dared to meddle in great affairs. Suppose, though, that he'd been wrong and had jumped to one conclusion too many? All that Nímir touched did not die. There was ample proof of that. Elisena was alive and free, and Allaire was none the worse for her years of captivity in Darkenkeep. Suppose—

The sunset thrust fingers of light into the dark space beneath the overhang of rock and snow. It was deeper than Tristan had supposed at first. Peering into it, Tristan now saw the ashes of a fire, a cookpot sitting on them, and a rolled bundle of cloth the size of a bedroll. He stepped nearer.

As he moved, a shadow within the shadows did likewise, and what Tristan had previously taken for a rock was suddenly a man with an old and familiar face. The light found his eyes and he blinked, dazzled, looking at first astonished and then welcoming.

Tristan was no less astonished. He took another step forward, then stopped. His mouth had opened, heedless of the pain of the cold air against his teeth. He had to close it and remember to breathe, before he could speak.

Even then, he only managed a whisper, nearly choking on the emotion behind it.

"Blais?"

Elisena, on the trail below, turned back and searched the slope for Tristan. He'd been falling behind all afternoon. She hoped that didn't mean that his leg was bothering him. Such rough travel strained the healing greatly, though he'd said nothing of any pain. Elisena was concerned and intended to speak to him about it.

Tristan wasn't on the trail or even to one side of it, floundering in deep snow he'd slipped into, but she spotted him swiftly nonetheless. He was looking at something, but all Elisena could see was a shadow among rocks that looked like a gaping mouth. There were fangs of ice hanging lower from its lips, and Tristan was moving toward it eagerly.

Elisena's eyes widened. "*Tristan!* Polassar, *stop him!*"

Polassar had whirled at her first shout, anticipating trouble, and he moved with more speed and agility than such a big man should have been capable of through rock and snow. He reached the slope, just as Tristan vanished under the overhang, and struggled up it, but he was hampered by a heavier pack than Tristan carried, and the coil of rope over his shoulder slowed him, too. Snowdrifts that Tristan had somehow missed dragged at Polassar's boots maliciously. Polassar cursed and shouted at Tristan's back.

He had the wizard in sight at last and only a few more yards to go. The wizard was paying him no attention, but he wasn't too big to be dragged out of there, willing or not. Polassar was firm on that. The spot was evil. His own eyes told him that, as did Elisena's frantic command.

Something rumbled overhead. Polassar was minded not to heed it, but the noise got louder. He skidded to a timely halt, just as the overburdened overhang let go. Rock, snow, and ice came crashing down in front of him. Tristan vanished.

A Trap Sprung

DARKNESS SEEMED TO STRIKE TRISTAN A BACK-handed blow between his shoulderblades. He staggered and fell to his knees. For an instant, he felt as if the mountain had fallen in on him—not physically, but he was aware of the crushing oppression of its weight overhead. And it was freezing cold, colder than the air outside had been. He felt as if his mind were going numb.

Tristan made his fingers reach for his crystal, wondering even then if he'd be able to light it. The requisite spell seemed to have fled his mind, which was no fit home for spells at that moment.

Sternly, Tristan told himself that he'd worked the crystal well enough in Darkenkeep, where conditions had certainly been worse, but he was still baffled, blank, and empty. The blackness about him seemed full of shapes, glowing spots, the rattle of rocks falling, and other sounds like shattering glass. He wasn't sure about the sounds, but he thought the shapes and spots were illusions, tricks his eyes played while bereft of light.

Tristan shut his eyes, finally, surprised to find that so simple a stratagem worked so well. The familiar dark behind his eyelids somehow held none of the terrors of the dark outside. Tristan's fingers flickered unseen, and he whispered the magic words. His breath began to come a little easier. The insides of his eyelids turned faintly orange-red. Tristan opened his eyes.

His crystal glowed feebly between his thumb and forefinger. It couldn't make much of a dent in the darkness around him, but what Tristan could see was confusing enough to him. There was a jumble of ice and rock all around him, and no sign of Blais whatsoever—not even the cookpot. Tristan took in the sight numbly. That overhang must not have been as solid as he'd thought, and his misjudgment had been close to disastrous.

"Blais? *Blais?* Thomas, he's not *buried* in this, is he?"

Huh? What have you done this time? The pack bulged as Thomas turned himself around and jumped out of the top of it.

"Maybe he was frightened. This would scare anyone. Or maybe he jumped to the other side." Tristan got to his feet, almost bumping his head on the rock not too far above it. "Maybe he didn't recognise me—or thought I was some kind of trap. If he's hiding from Nímir, that would make sense. We've got to find him!"

Find who?

"This is the only way he could have gone." Tristan had found a gap between two stones, almost a passageway. It was a narrow squeeze, even for him, but Blais was also thin and could have passed the gap easily. "This has to be it. Everything else is snow. I know he didn't go past me. Come on!"

Down there? Have you finally taken leave of whatever little was left of your senses? Just where are we?

Tristan was through the gap, paying no attention to the cat, and taking all the light with him. Thomas had to bound to catch up.

"How long can a man live, buried like that?"

Polassar and Reynaud were hacking at the snow with their swords, careless of breaking a blade upon rock. Their work showed little effect. The snow was too light and too deep. Polassar's frantic arm-sweeps were more useless than if he'd been cutting a path through feathers.

"I've heard as much as a day, if the snow is not packed down hard," Reynaud answered. "But we haven't that long. The temperature drops when the sun does. He'll freeze before he suffocates. We must be quick."

"*Wizard!* If you hear me, make answer!"

"I doubt he can."

Polassar turned on Reynaud with a snarled oath, but the man paid no heed to the sword leveled at his chest. There was no scorn in his voice.

"I don't mean he's dead, but look at that mess! If Tristan's not actually buried in it, then there's too much of it between us for him to hear even you, Polassar."

"He still has the sword," Elisena said, dazed yet by the sight of those jaws of ice closing over Tristan while she stood helpless. "It's seen him through thus far."

"Lady, magic or not, no blade's proof against a mountain falling in, and cold iron won't breathe for him. We've got to get him *out*."

Shuddering, Elisena shoved her hair back from her face with both hands. "This place—he was trapped purposely—" Her eyes stayed shut until her breathing steadied, and when she spoke again, she was calm enough.

"We won't dig him out this way. There's too much snow, too many rocks. Reynaud, assist me."

Elisena bent close to the stones, touching certain of them. Reynaud stooped, laying the iron of his sword down well out of his way. He discerned a pattern which Polassar could not even guess at and knew the signs that Elisena's swift fingers scribed into the snow between the upthrusting rocks.

"Lady, be careful," he said with professional concern. "There's been magic here already. Whatever happened was no accident."

"I feel it. Danger or not, we have to try."

"Whenever you're ready." Reynaud shrugged off his fears, whatever they were, not caring that Polassar was frowning at a conversation he couldn't fathom. Reynaud knew what she wanted done. "This is work for two. Shall I do the incantation?"

"Yes. Start slowly. I will match your tempo."

Reynaud glanced around critically. "Polassar, stand back a little. This might get violent."

Polassar took one look at the set of Elisena's chin and did as he was told without a single word of dissent.

Elisena stood with her beringed hands still at her sides, as Reynaud began chanting in a tongue which fairly screamed of its magical power. At about his tenth word, her fingers began to twitch and then to make patterns between them, as if she played at cat's cradle. Elisena held no string. She held *something* between her hands, however. The witchery began to take shape.

Stones lifted themselves free of the ice and rolled aside,

bounding unnoticed down the mountain past Polassar. The greater boulders remained in their places, but a way was slowly opening between them, like a door on hinges of ice. Polassar leaned forward eagerly, seeking some sign of Tristan, whether a weapon or scrap of clothing.

The door slammed shut in Elisena's face, without warning. Reynaud was cut off in mid-word. Polassar could not see quite how. There was a great gust of wind that nearly knocked him off his own feet; when he could see once more, the snow had settled, unmarked, back over the spot where they'd begun to dig. There was no sign of any of their work now, except for Reynaud lying flat on his back, with Elisena kneeling beside him.

"Reynaud, forgive me. And you warned me, too—"

Reynaud sat up, his hands pressed to his temples. His face between them was bone-white. More than being wind-tossed ailed him. "We were almost through," he mumbled. "We can try again. I can strengthen the second passage—" He made a game effort to get to his feet and failed.

"It would kill you next time, and quicker," Elisena said. "No. You were right in the first place. This way is guarded too well. There is purpose behind this."

At that, Polassar broke free of the shell of fear and awe that had hitherto held him still. He came out of it with a great cry of rage and leaped upon the snowy spot they'd been laboring over. His longsword rose and fell furiously, as if he could win his way through where even Elisena had failed by the pure force of his anger. He got a fair way, though not nearly far enough. The snow and the smaller rocks kept sifting back down to frustrate his efforts; after a point, the hole's depth remained constant no matter what he did.

Elisena let him go on for a time, then started to call him off before he should exhaust himself utterly. Polassar's strength would do them more good if they could bridle it and think how best to put it to use, though Polassar would be hard to convince of that at the moment. They had no time to waste, thinking or arguing.

She held tight to what calm she could. Tristan was not dead. If he had been, the magic guarding the slope would not have bothered to keep them from him. There would still be time to get to him, but not this way. She swallowed panic like a bitter medicine.

Elisena stretched her hands out before her, and her rings flared once again, but softly, to rouse no other guardian spell or wind. She did not ask them to tell her much and so she got the answer she sought, where a greater questioning might have gained her nothing.

She sensed an emptiness behind the veil of snow and ice, not the feeling of constriction there would have been had Tristan been pinned there, slowly smothering. He was still able to move, then, and had apparently done so. Another comfort reached her—a memory of Ambere's protective runes, the same that edged all their clothing. Neither would Tristan freeze to death—not for a while.

Polassar's sword hit rock, the blow numbing his arm to the shoulder. He switched the blade to his left hand automatically and carried on doggedly. He was still nowhere close to the spot where Tristan was last seen. They had been nearer before, when the spell had begun to part the snow. If he went farther ahead and dug straight down—

Finally, the surface of Elisena's mind touched what her rings had been suggesting to her all along—what she would have seen long before if she had been looking at anything other than Polassar trying blindly to dig his way down to the spot where he thought Tristan was. She looked this way and that at the top of the ridge and the rocks thrusting up through the ice. Some of them were the size of tall trees, yet the ice rose nearly to their tops—but on one side only. Looking into the crystal that hung from her thumb, Elisena saw what she had begun to expect: a maze of rocks under the ice, and spaces between them. It was nearly a cave, but roofed over with ice instead of rock. As if she had eyes to pierce the snow, Elisena saw that there would be other openings to the labyrinth in other places.

Thomas was beginning to figure out what had happened. Each new crumb of understanding firmed his resolve never to sleep again while Tristan was awake.

They were traveling along a tunnel that was half ice and half rock. There was no light, save for the crystal Tristan carried in his left hand, and all of Thomas' six senses complained stridently of danger. He'd have thought they were in Darkenkeep, if he hadn't been moderately sure that that place was far off, too distant for even Tristan to have stumbled upon.

"He's got to be here somewhere, Thomas! Can you hear anyone else moving?"

Thomas hadn't quite decided why Tristan was suddenly looking for Blais. That sort of idiotic behavior he might have expected months earlier, when the shock of Blais' death was still fresh. Maybe Tristan had just been too busy then, and it had taken him this long to be bothered by the fact that there'd been no body for him to bury. Maybe, without that, Tristan couldn't accept Blais' death for what it was, but deep down only saw it as a disappearance and was harboring false, foolish hopes. If so, those hopes had picked a witless poor time to surface!

But Thomas had no more time for analyzing. He'd have enough to do just getting them out. No rock gap was so narrow but that Tristan would try to wriggle through it. Thomas kept hoping that he'd stick fast in one of them. At least that would slow Tristan down long enough to have some sense talked into him.

"Thomas, I wish you'd been awake and seen him! Maybe then he wouldn't have run, though I can't blame him, with the whole roof coming down like that. I was amazed to see him—after all this time, to find out he was only a prisoner. Thomas, come on, help me! You see better than I do in the dark; you're always so proud of that! We can't let Blais get much farther away, because we've still got to go back and dig our way out—"

Tristan kept rattling on, just when Thomas had hoped he was starting to make sense at last, realizing that they were still buried, even though they moved freely. Most exasperating!

Then Tristan cried out that he saw footprints, where all Thomas saw were scuffed places in the snow. They'd come to a sizeable clear spot—it was wide enough to let a man begin to run, and Tristan promptly did. Plainly, from the look on his face, he saw something he wanted to reach on the far side of the space.

Thomas saw nothing. Tristan called Blais' name obligingly, giving identity to his hallucination.

Then Thomas blinked. There *was* someone over there!

It didn't look much like Blais, but that didn't matter, because Tristan wouldn't reach him, anyway. Two yards in front of the figure, hidden among shadows but not from Thomas' sharp eyes, a crevasse opened up the ice floor. And Tristan, naturally, was running straight for it!

There was no time for niceties of strategy. Thomas hurled himself between Tristan's running feet. The right one put a toe hard into his ribs, but the cat got a claw through the lacings of the left boot, and that was all it took. Tristan tripped, couldn't recover on the slippery floor, and sprawled full length onto the ice. His padded jacket cushioned the fall a trifle, but his head still hit hard enough to make Thomas wince. Tristan lay still, and the crystal rolled out of his limp fingers. It stopped just before it reached the crevasse, and its light went out.

Thomas pawed at Tristan's face, with more urgency than gentleness. Tristan moaned and made a very fine attempt to curl himself into a ball. He put an arm over his bruised face, making sure Thomas couldn't reach it again.

Come on. I'm sorry. I didn't mean for you to get hurt, but it was the only way to stop you. Listen to me, now.

From under Tristan's arm, there came a muffled repetition of Blais' name.

Thomas found the crystal and brought it carefully back to Tristan. The spell was still operating—it glowed faintly once more when Thomas shoved it into contact with Tristan's fingers. The light did a little to rouse him. His arm moved, and Thomas could see part of his face. It was wet with tears. Above the wetness, Tristan's eyes were hurt, accusing.

I said I was sorry. And you nearly kicked my ribs in, you know. Now wake up. We've got company, and it's not Blais.

Tristan sat up slowly, the crystal brightening in his hand. At least, Thomas thought, he wouldn't have to struggle forming more arguments to convince Tristan that he'd somehow been tricked. Tristan's face had the look of a sleeper wakened roughly from a fair dream, with an expression of loss and longing which showed that he knew the dream was false, even while the last threads of it yet wound around him. Tristan looked fully awake, but utterly forlorn. Thomas was glad to see the awareness come back, though the pain was cruel and even plainer to see.

The crystal still didn't throw much light, but the space was not so vast that it could not touch the man who lounged, smiling, at the very spot where Tristan had just seen Blais turn to face him with a look of disbelief and happiness almost beyond hope on his old face. Of Blais, there was now no sign, and seemingly nowhere he could have gone without leaving one. There was just the man, leaning back against the rocks and laughing quietly to himself.

"When He gave you to me, He said it would be easy, but I never expected this—like a fly into the spider's web. Stupid with the cold, I suppose."

The man had a broad, heavy face, Tristan saw—one that might have been modeled from dead clay instead of sculptured on bone. The sculptor had carelessly squashed the nose as he worked, for it was broad, too, and flat, spreading across the middle of the face. His hair was of no special color, straggling like cobwebs around his face, but the man's eyes made up for that and for his other undistinguished features. They were a bright, hot blue, like the edges of flames—mad eyes.

Tristan didn't bother to ask the stranger where Blais had gone. Blais had never been there, except in Tristan's own longing.

"You don't recognize me, I suppose," the man said. "That's to be expected—we've never met what you might call face-to-face."

He reached into a pocket and drew out a wafer of ivory the length of a man's hand. Scarlet and green flashed fitfully on its back, as if the colors squirmed away from the touch of his fingers.

"Maybe this will jog your memory."

He turned Crewzel's card over, to show Tristan the face of it. The card was black.

Cheris

TRISTAN FELT AS IF HE'D HAD THE WORLD JERKED OUT from under his boots just one time too many. He wondered, briefly, how cold his blood had to run before it stopped his heart entirely. There was rock behind him. He slid back against it till he could move no farther and then sat, trapped, his breath betraying his panic as it puffed out rapidly in front of his lips. Thomas crouched, arching his back as if he intended to hiss and spit, but he made no sound. The cat had recognized the card quite as quickly as Tristan had.

"Surprised to see me?" Cheris asked. "But you shouldn't be—I'd be most remiss not to thank you for the opportunity you gave me. If it hadn't been for you, I might still be a petty conjuror in Kôvelir, aspiring toward higher sorceries. I'd never have entered the service of One who appreciates my peculiar talents—and has done so much to augment them."

"Oh, I expect you'd have managed to find each other," Tristan said through stiff lips. He dared not show any more of the fear he felt—Cheris would feed on it gleefully. He likewise couldn't afford a panic that would dull his own wits, because he'd have need of every last one of them. He wished, inanely, that he could know if this was Cheris' true face that he saw.

"You've taken a lot of trouble to get this far. Don't think Nímir has no esteem for you, just because he's given you to me instead of attending to you personally. It's a great honor for me, actually—and a sort of a test." Cheris licked his lips with a flick of his tongue such as a lizard

250

might make. "You *do* understand that he's given you to me? It's no good if you don't understand. The emotion of despair's very tasty. I should hate to lose it."

Thomas moaned, low in his throat, but not so softly that he wasn't heard.

Cheris flicked a glance his way. "He didn't mention you, little one, but don't fear. I've never been one to neglect your kind. Indeed not."

Tristan tried to use the instant of distraction to catalog his options. It was hard for him to make out the exits from where he crouched, though he was sure there must be some. Every shadow could be a means of escape—or a trap only inches deep. He'd run into several such blind passages on his way inward, and there was no way to tell which were false by sight alone—not from a distance. If he was going to run successfully, he needed to know precisely where he was going.

If there was a way out, Cheris would probably have planted himself squarely in front of it, to negate the chance of his quarry's escaping. Tristan would have to get past the man, then. But how?

Flare up the crystal, blinding Cheris, then damp its light entirely? No good. The cavern's ceiling dropped without warning, and there were sure to be more rockfalls like those he'd already climbed over. Even with bright light, going fast hadn't been safe, though Tristan thought he remembered running, like a hound on a scent. No, leaving Cheris blind left him blind as well, and he couldn't risk it.

The chasm in the floor? Could he try to tumble Cheris in? There seemed no way to do that without getting close, certainly closer than was safe. And Cheris was a master of illusion, who'd quickly see through any ruse attempted on those lines.

Tristan's muscles stiffened, and he slid back again without thinking about it. Metal chimed faintly against rock, as his sword hilt brushed the wall. He'd forgotten he was armed. Tristan's heart leaped and then sank, and Cheris saw neither expression on his face, since the man was still staring Thomas down, as if he hoped to frighten the cat beyond terror and into madness.

Tristan stifled a curse. There was no way he could get his sword clear of its scabbard, or even begin to do so, without Cheris seeing. Strapping it to his back as Polassar had recommended had kept it out of his way when he climbed, but it made for an awkward draw over his head. In his present case, that was impossible. He couldn't even reach the hilt unless he stood up; and if he tried grabbing the hilt with both hands and drawing fast, he'd still snag the ceiling before he could get the blade free.

Cheris laughed, when he could not seem to outstare Thomas. "Keep your pride, little one. I'll see with your eyes, before all's done—in the dark, like a cat. In truth, your little green eyes will help me to that goal, for you'll have no more need of them. Your familiar has an interesting disposition," Cheris went on, to Tristan. "Easy to see how you've come to this pass, if he was the best servant you could keep."

Tristan didn't answer. Let Cheris think him too terrified.

He'd gotten his fingers into both his pouch and his magic box. A tiny feather—the one from Minstrel—floated out and drifted across the floor, guided by Tristan's breath and will. It soon lay at the middle of the space. When it started to drift again, Tristan would know where the nearest opening lay, for if a draft of fresh air came from anywhere, it would be there. There'd be no such air from the blocked way he'd come. It was a frail hope, but he thanked Minstrel anyway for giving it to him. Tristan took his eyes from the feather casually, as Cheris began to address him once more.

"As I said, my puissant and generous Master has given you to me, wizardling, and I intend to play with you a while longer. There's no need to insult you by rushing, is there? Your friends are looking for you, but they'll be a long time at it. And there are secret ways here by which I can reach them quickly when I need to, so I've no cause to neglect you in haste on that account. I have time to attend to you properly. That will comfort you, I'm sure."

"Oh, very much." The feather wasn't moving at all. Tristan felt the stones in the box, more with his mind than with his fingers, for he dared draw no attention to what he was doing. There must be something else that would serve, if he could only think. Improvise!

"Imagine how glad your friends will be to see you again, so relieved that you're still alive. Too relieved to wonder how you happened to stumble blindly into them. Don't you think so?"

Cheris was smiling affably, but Tristan felt his own face go slack as he took in the man's meaning. If Cheris could impersonate Blais well enough to fool Tristan, the man would be able to do worse. Tristan hadn't been looking for Blais when he came into Channadran and had never before thought that his master might not be dead. He should therefore have been hard to deceive, but Cheris had managed it easily. Elisena and the others were certainly looking for him at this very moment, Tristan was sure, and in the frame of mind they'd be in, they'd never question—

Cheris continued to smile, seeing that Tristan had understood. "Perhaps I'll let them dig me out of the snow," he mused.

Tristan was probably expected to react by doing something desperate and stupid, he thought. If he didn't, it was mostly because he could think of nothing that offered the least hope of success in exchange for a ghastly risk. Blood surged in his ears, sounding like the wash of the sea, but Tristan sat still.

Cheris looked disappointed. He had to put on his good humor again, like a mask.

"But I'm wrong to expect gratitude, when I've yet done so little to express my own to you! I am remiss, and I promised you that I would not be. I ought to entertain you a while now, before I carry out my orders. Your journey has been so arduous, your zeal to reach this place so great, so admirably unswerving. Some wine, perhaps?"

A goblet appeared in Cheris' hand, out of mid-air. It was probably an illusion, the false cup covering a dagger, Tristan thought, but certainly it had been subtly done, the illusion as good as any conjuration.

"Thank you, no." He thought Cheris looked relieved, or at least glad. Well, if he died too quickly, there'd be little sport for the man.

"Probably you are not hungry either. Is there perhaps someone you crave speech with, one last time? Your master, perchance? But then you've seen me do him, haven't you? You should have something new and fresh. Repetition can be so tedious. Some other, then—a hero, perhaps, or one of the great mages? I have much larger scope now, you see. Once I could only mask myself in the semblances of bravos dead in knife fights over whores, or thieves who'd died on the red-hot spike. Such tawdry guisings!" Cheris' teeth showed like little needles as he smiled.

"Now the great, the powerful are mine, and it's fitting that you should have a showing of them, since you helped me to this service I bear. You and that slut Crewzel—though I can't find it in my heart to tender thanks to her, that harlot with her cards she pretended none but she could read! I'll give her share of the show to you."

When he starts to shift, jump him, Thomas suggested grimly. *It's better than listening to him.*

"You look so nervous, so tense." Cheris sighed. "You don't want to play. I don't think you have the wit to appreciate my art after all, wizardling. And I don't care for even the misguided to look down on me! You shall have no performance, then. It would be wasted on you." Cheris chewed at his thumb, like a dog at a bone. "That's unfortunate—for you. There are other ways I can take pleasure from you."

I'm going to create a diversion, Thomas said. *Try to run for it.*

Tristan clamped a hand down on the cat hastily. The feather still hadn't stirred. Either there was no way out, or else Cheris had indeed stationed himself smack in front of it. There was nowhere to run, yet.

Tristan withdrew his fingers from both belt and pouch. It was harder to do, for they weren't empty now. One flick of them, and a tiny gray pebble was hurled to bounce off the far wall. Cheris' head snapped toward the sound of it falling.

Under cover of that, Tristan's fingers flashed over the crystal in his other hand. Now the pebble's tiny shadow would be huge and, when Tristan moved the crystal, it would seem to leap. Thomas, Tristan knew, could be counted upon to howl uncannily as the shadow moved, acting as its voice. His fingers moved.

And nothing happened. No magic—nothing at all!

Cheris turned back toward him, smiling. "That was very, very naughty of you. And so pointless. *Shadows!* Is that really the best you can think of? I suppose it must be, or you'd hardly be here. I can't think why the Winter

King even troubles to stop you—you'd do the job yourself before you got another league." Cheris seemed to find his harangue amusing; at any rate, he began to chuckle.

"Since you're fond of toys, I've another for you. *This* one won't dissolve away into shadows, though, never fear. It's most delightfully solid—about the solidest thing there is to a wizard." Cheris untied a leather sack that had been tethered to his belt just beside his dagger. It clinked as he moved it. Cheris opened the sack and pulled a short length of iron chain from it. At each end of the chain was a thick cuff of hinged iron.

Someone hissed. Tristan thought it must have been Thomas—his own mouth felt as if it was lined with wool. He couldn't have spoken, even at the sight of cold iron. Those manacles robbed him of speech as surely as they would rob him of magic.

"Think on it, player with shadows—to be left here, chained with these most cunning bracelets of cold iron. Surely that will move you to speech. Did you think I intended killing you? You have misjudged me, you see. I won't harm you. I don't need to touch you, once these are on; and what you do after that is your own affair. I'll even leave your feet free." Cheris' eyes unfocused with pleasure, but their pupils were tiny, merest pinpricks.

"Of course, it will be rather dark in here, since you won't be able to use your little crystal light, and I'm afraid I've no food or water to spare you. I'll even have to take your pack—part of my costume, you see. I shouldn't worry, though. These will eat through to your bones long before you can starve to death."

"You can't use those," Tristan said, pleading and too frightened to be ashamed of it.

"Don't wager that I can't. I won't need magic to put these on you, believe me." Cheris snapped the chain playfully between his hands. "You're about at the end of your strength, aren't you? Note the ease with which I lured you in here. You've been beaten ever since, only you didn't know it."

The words were smooth and heavy, suspiciously like the beginning of a spell. Beaten, was he? Why waste good magic on him, then? Tristan knew that Cheris would, with iron in both his hands, dare use nothing stronger than suggestion. If his mind had been quite as clouded as Cheris seemed to think, it might have been enough. It wasn't though. Muddled his brain might be, but fear was lending wings to Tristan's thoughts.

He was, of course, under the same restraints as Cheris. There could be no magic while in touch with cold iron. They were closely confined, with not much room to maneuver. There was no spell Tristan could use which would not be as dangerous to him as it was to Cheris.

Tristan was on his feet by then. He tried to circle around to the spot where Cheris had been lingering and where the supposed exit was, but the crevasse blocked him. Cheris leaped across easily—the gap was narrower at his end.

"I hope you don't mind," he said apologetically. "This is actually the very same way I got rid of Giffyd. I'd like to be more original with you, but this way works so well, I think it bears repeating just this once. I promise you, I'll add some personal touches—"

Tristan's fingers went to the knotted thongs that held his scabbard to the straps of his pack. He'd drop the blade into his hands, scabbard and all, faster than trying to draw it from where it was, and he needed every second he could gain. He pulled at the thong, releasing the knot.

It held fast. The leather had been soaked with snow. Now dry, the knot in it was as stiff as if it were iron, like the manacles. It wouldn't untie. Tristan reached over his shoulder and found to his horror that he couldn't even reach the sword hilt. He'd tied the scabbard too low, or something—

Cheris was chuckling again. "Decided to play after all, have you? Very sporting of you, I must admit."

Tristan *had* to be able to reach the blade, he thought frantically. All those years of stretching and twisting his fingers and his wrists in the course of his apprenticeship to magic—had he gained nothing from that? Those skills were half the reason why a wizard could so seldom be successfully bound, except with iron—even without magic, trained hands could always wriggle free. He could stretch his reach another inch, surely!

And while he tried, Tristan didn't have even one hand left to defend himself with. Cheris aimed a blow at his middle, and Tristan dodged away, giving up trying to get hold of his weapon. The manacles, swinging from their chain, whistled over his head. They set the distance for the fight. If he got hit with them on the head or in the face, he'd be hurt far worse than if he were only punched or kicked. Cheris realized the advantage he had and slipped away when Tristan tried to close in. He stuck a foot out as Tristan went by, and Tristan nearly went into the crevasse in avoiding him.

Thomas moved fast and low, his tail streaming behind him. He sank as many of his teeth as he could manage into Cheris' calf, just above the top of the man's low, black boot. Cheris howled with pain and swung the chains at him. Thomas ducked flat.

That's one, if it matters, he said coolly.

Tristan fisted his hands together and chopped down at Cheris' back. He drove the man to his knees, but it felt as if he'd hit rock instead of flesh. Tristan staggered back, his hands almost useless. Cheris got up—there seemed to be something wrong with the way he moved, as if he hadn't quite been where Tristan had thought. Tristan saw that he'd dropped the manacles, and was warned that he could expect more illusions.

Cheris rushed him. Tristan jumped back to gain space to grapple and hit rock so hard that his sight started to close in. He was on his knees, struggling to get up, before he could see again. He could hear Cheris laughing once more.

"You can beat yourself black and never touch me! But do keep on trying, if it amuses you."

Thomas bit him again, more for spite than utility, and got kicked across the cavern for his pains. The cat hit hard, and Tristan couldn't see if he got up.

He remembered that Cheris had dropped the chain. Magic would be safe. He'd bruised his hands when he fell against the rock, though. They were half-numb, and he couldn't master his fingers. They didn't feel broken, but the fine movements he needed were beyond him, at least for a while. Tristan tried, anyway, and went down hard when Cheris hit him right through whatever he'd made of the spell. He got kicked, too, and rolled blindly away from the sharp boot toe, finding himself back by the crevasse. This time, he wondered what might be lurking down there. He could very well find out.

He got up and was hit again. Tristan wobbled into the

wall, unable to find his balance. His ears buzzed. If Cheris said anything more, he couldn't hear it. Missing the taunts was a mercy of sorts, one he hadn't hoped for. Tristan's fingers brushed stone, and he gripped the rock to steady himself. If he kept the rock to his back, at least Cheris would only be able to come at him from one direction, straight on. With a knife, he'd even have had a decent chance against the man, but his brass blade was somewhere in the bottom of his pack, out of reach.

It was no use anyway. Tristan knew he was spent; he had been when the fight started, and his luck had finally run out. He might have expected it, but the unfairness of the timing of it hit Tristan worse than the thought of dying did—worse than the pain of any of his hurts.

After all, he had been prepared to face death on his quest in many ways—drowning, freezing, being smothered in a slide of rock and ice, shrugged off the side of a mountain, or eaten by a glacier. He knew Nímir's power. There were plenty of tales and legends to inform him, as well as his personal experience. He had known that one slip might smash his bones, or drop him into a chasm of ice where he'd be shattered upon the fangs at its bottom. Winds, storms, and deadly frost he'd suspected and accepted. The odds had been long, and he'd accepted them. But to die like this! It just wasn't *fair*.

He might have died at any point, and it couldn't have hurt as much as being done to death by a gibbering mooncalf who'd been none too sane before Nímir had got hold of him. Anger flared, a warm, stubborn little flame. He'd sell his life dear, at least, so that Cheris might find himself in no shape to wreak harm on Elisena or the others. Tristan thought that he and Cheris could very well go into that chasm together. He could hedge his bet that far.

Where was the destiny that Crewzel had always spoken of as being his, now when he needed it? Tristan had put up with the discomfort of carrying it for a long time; he'd let it hand him a kingship he hadn't wanted and duties so heavy he thought they'd crush the life out of him. He was in Channadran because of following it. Had he suffered all that, only to end like this?

Tristan called himself a fool for expecting a fair fight. But this way seemed low and dirty, even for Nímir, an act not worthy of any respect. Was this all a King of

Calandra was, that his death was worth no better weapon than Cheris?

It's not worth any greater trouble, a voice agreed. Pictures formed in Tristan's mind, revealed abruptly as if a curtain had been yanked away. He saw blighted fields, flooded with cold, stagnant water, and barren heaths, where a scattering of leafless trees scarcely sheltered clusters of hovels with ragged children playing in the dust beside their doors. The vision grew dark, but a few lights burned. A dying horse dragged a half-empty cart down a muddy road toward a market in a gray town. *Compared to Kôvelir, it never was exactly a treasure.*

Tristan's own mind answered the vision back with surprising promptness, not denying but replacing and amending.

Crogen's foolish, ambitious towers rose, fine as fairy-work for all that none matched with any other and all were oddly pieced and patched with something that looked like white marble. Swooping away from them, like a swallow, Tristan remembered buttercups like a scatter of golden coins among dark green grasses beside a stream. He knew the water would taste cool and sweet and that the gravel it flowed over would be the exact color of the speckled trout that swam in it. Mint stems were so heavy with blossom that their tips drooped to touch the water, and the breezes stirred them, setting up an infinite, shifting pattern of ripples beyond any mathematics.

Calandra's loveliness was fragile, a loveliness that could easily be ignored by those who had no time to look and no spark of hope to make them see a sunbeam catching dewdrops, changing them into gems no wizard could hope to match. It was a beauty made of small, fleeting things, moments come and gone, flowers blown and vanished in an eyeblink of time, a note of bird song, a petal drifting on the wind, sunlight dappled by new green leaves, and honeysuckle twining about fence posts—and about Tristan's heart.

Tristan didn't need to close his eyes to shut Cheris out. He'd done so already, not even trying. His anger and fear were gone. The wonder he'd felt at his crowning replaced it, filling every crack in his battered spirit. *It was worth it,* he thought, amazed, though he felt his heart ripping apart with grief.

Something *was* ripping. There was a tearing sound, and his sword slid free of its ruined scabbard and flashed toward the floor, point down. Like a sleepwalker, Tristan moved his bruised right hand and caught the hilt, then felt the blade lift his hand to guard position.

Cheris, still giggling over the manacles and talking to them, almost ran onto the sword's point before he noticed.

"Oho!" he exclaimed gleefully. "The cub has teeth after all. You'd bite me, would you, like your poxy cat? We'll see about that!" He shoved the manacles through his belt, and sprang forward.

Tristan lunged to meet him, the sword moving as quickly as a glance. Then Tristan frantically turned the blade aside and fell down upon one knee, trying to stop himself, and still the blade was a palm's breadth from Blais' throat before he managed to arrest it. He couldn't...

Blais gazed at him sadly and began to say something in a disappointed voice—something about naughty apprentices—and Tristan, his face twisting with a pain past his bearing, let the blade pull his arm out straight. Its tip slashed for Blais' neck.

Cheris midjudged. Instead of jumping back, he shape-shifted to a smaller form below the aim of the sword. But the shining blade arced down to cut the tiny ice-lizard in two before its fangs could strike. The red poison sac at its throat burst as it writhed in its death agony, blood and poison spewing, and Tristan collapsed onto the ground as the spray hit him across the face.

Lizard's Blood

TRISTAN DROPPED THE CRYSTAL AGAIN, AND ITS LIGHT went out. He didn't notice. His eyes were shut. A torrent of blood seemed to have poured over him, from the feel of it on his skin. He wouldn't have thought so much blood could be contained in so small a creature. It seemed smoking hot, or else burning cold—he was uncertain which.

The blood was possessed of an unbelievable stench. Tristan gasped for air and found none. The colors in his mind shifted from violet to red to black and went darker still, swirling away like water out of a bath, dragging him with them.

It wasn't like fainting—more akin to drowning, as the skeining colors sought to work changes on him beyond any the sea could have essayed. What changes, Tristan was too panicked to guess. He strove desperately to resist, growing more lost in the tangles each instant. He felt as if he were bathed in fire—but how could fire not glow? How could it shed darkness instead of light?

Then even the darkest colors were gone, and Tristan finally fainted.

The blood-stench receded a trifle, taking with it some of the velvet blackness. Air began to find its way into Tristan's straining lungs once again. His fingers groped blindly until they touched the faceted surface of the crystal and fastened upon it. He made it light—mostly to find out if he could still see, not thinking to wonder about his magic.

The lizard's shrunken, emptied body lay only a few inches from his face. Tristan watched it a long while, expecting some new trick, but apparently this time the transformation was real and final. Cheris had shape-shifted for the last time.

Tristan must have been lying on the ice for a long time, he thought. He was cold to his bones, all the way in, and his muscles cramped horribly when he tried to move. Nonetheless, he got to his knees; since he couldn't stand, he began to crawl. It took him a long time to find Thomas, for the cat had fallen or crept behind a chunk of ice that was considerably larger than he was, and it hid him till Tristan was only inches away.

Tristan lifted him carefully. The cat made no sound, either of pain or relief. There was no blood on his fur; that was all the inspection of him Tristan was able to make. He thought all Thomas' bones were whole. The cat blinked at him once, vaguely, but his extra eyelid was drawn down over the eye nearest Tristan, so he probably saw nothing. Tristan switched the crystal to his right hand and cradled the cat gently in the crook of his other arm.

That left his left thumb and index finger just barely free for holding Minstrel's feather, which he'd found clinging to the back of his hand while he was trying to clean the blood off the tip of his sword. Tristan stood very still, watching the feather. It began to tremble, and the finest edges of it bent toward him.

Carefully, Tristan stepped across the crevasse, not looking down or behind him, and began to follow the feather's guidance.

He had to crawl much of the way. Sometimes the tunnel required it of him, so low-ceilinged that he couldn't stand or even crouch. Mostly, though, his own weakness kept him low. Tristan found he got dizzy if he stood up for too long a time and he didn't want to risk falling, in case he dropped Thomas doing it. He rubbed the back of his right hand across his face and found it bathed in icy sweat. His chest hurt, and he still wasn't breathing very well. He would have left his pack behind, for it had become almost unbearably heavy, but he wasn't sure he could get it off.

The going was hard. Tristan took a lot of false turns, when his sight blurred so that he couldn't read the feather's directions accurately. Once he thought they were stuck for good, because he couldn't seem to turn around in the narrow space he found himself in and he couldn't go on into solid rock. For a few other moments he had no sense of distance, and bumped helplessly against any wall he neared.

His tongue was swollen in his mouth, but he had no water to ease it. They'd been so used to melting snow as it was needed that none of them had carried a flask for a long while. Tristan dared not lick the ice all about him—even if it wasn't poison, his tongue would freeze to it for certain. After a while, he tried to eat some of the sweet that Ambere had so lately sent them, hoping it would strengthen him, but his outraged stomach heaved it up at once.

He couldn't tell if it was day or night—not that it much mattered, under and in the ice. Tristan wasn't wondering yet how he'd locate Elisena, once he reached the surface. Cheris hadn't seemed to think there would be any trouble. Tristan could hope the same. It was a thought, though, which could wait. He had no energy to think while he dealt with the greater problem of walking.

Thoughts came hard, but nightmares came easy.

Tristan dreamed of the dragon that had been Guardian of Darkenkeep and felt his terror of it afresh. But this time, he managed to turn his back on it and on dying Polassar. He took the frozen Allaire in his arms and carried her away. In the dream they both vanished, into the cold dark.

Tristan woke with a sour taste in his mouth and icy sweat trickling down between his shoulder blades. He felt tainted to his soul, as he guiltily remembered how close reality had come to that dream. It could easily have gone that way, and he still didn't know why it hadn't, or what had made him choose the right course by an act that still seemed insane to him. He could claim no credit for his valiant action and couldn't warm himself at the fires of remembered bravery. The seas of poisoned dreams closed over Tristan's head again and swallowed him up.

A breath of air touched his face. It had been so long since he'd felt such a thing that Tristan hardly recognized it. For a moment, his being so near the surface meant nothing to him. Thomas mewed faintly in his arms, smelling the fresh air, too.

It must, Tristan realized wonderingly, be day or close to it. He damped the crystal, and the wall before him still glowed faintly in spots. He put a hand out and felt slick ice and softer stuff where the glow was. There was a touch of air against his finger. He was almost out!

The tunnel's end was blocked with chunks of ice, and softer snow had covered them. The seal was incomplete, accounting for the inflow of air, but he'd still have to dig. It wouldn't be far, by the way the light came through. His trusty sword would do the job admirably. Tristan put Thomas down and went to work.

Once he could see daylight and was breathing untainted air, Tristan found that he didn't need to rest as often as he had before. Maybe it helped that, whenever he felt faintness returning, he could simply lean forward against the ice without fear of falling, letting his limp weight continue to push the blocks out. By the time he had cleared a way to the surface, the pale dawn he'd first seen was full day, or at least morning.

Tristan stowed his crystal away. There was plenty of light now, and soon he'd be out in it. He tucked Thomas safely into the front of his jacket—inside his sweater as well, so he'd be cushioned the more—and began to worm his way out of the opening he'd carved.

His sword went before him, chopping at knobs of ice that might otherwise hold him back. Those overhead were hard to reach—his pack caught on them, and he had difficulty getting it loose. Tristan didn't know whether to be glad or not that the straps held so firm. He wouldn't lose the pack, but he couldn't get loose from it, either, and was forced to hope he wouldn't need to.

The sword flashed and flared, as much with eagerness as with the faint daylight. Tristan squinted his eyes against its erratic brightness, trying to ignore the discomfort.

Snow sifted down his neck. Ice cut at him, but was impotent through his heavy clothing and so crumbled away spitefully beneath his boots, leaving them with nothing to push against. Nonetheless, Tristan squirmed ahead steadily.

He had worked his head and one shoulder free and was considering how he might best avoid rolling head over heels down the little slope that lay before him, when Tristan heard Reynaud's unmistakable voice raised in a shout of dismay. Apparently, he'd been spotted by the searchers. Good. He could expect some help. Finding his companions had been easy—he hadn't even begun to try! That was more luck than he deserved, Tristan thought gratefully.

Then he heard the rumbling, like far-off thunder, though the morning sky was clear. Tristan turned his head as far as he could, stared, and began a desperate scramble to get free of the ice. Above him, high on the slope, a great overhang of snow was pulling free of the rock below its bottom layer, shaken loose by Reynaud's echoing shout. The ice beneath Tristan began to quiver.

He barely got to his feet and took one stumbling step before the leading edge of the snowslide hit him, rolled him over, and buried him again.

Mandrake Dreams

TRISTAN'S EYES OPENED TO GLARING LIGHT THAT SENT a bright stab of pain shooting through his head. The hurt was sharp enough to make him cry out. He was surrounded by noise, not all of it apparently of his own making, for his numbed hands were being chafed roughly together, and someone was trying to get him to sit up. The forced movement hurt even worse than his headache.

Out of the confusion, he heard his name called. Tristan swiveled his eyes in the direction of the sound.

"Holly and ivy, heather and mistletoe! I can't believe you're still alive," Reynaud whispered.

Memory abruptly thawed out. Tristan remembered reaching fresh air after his long struggle; he remembered Reynaud's shout, the crashing fall of ice, and the smothering snow. He twisted frantically to get free of Reynaud's grip, afraid he was about to be strangled by hands about to finish what the snow had failed to do. He got his legs under him almost by accident. His footing in the deep snow was precarious, but Tristan didn't wait for sure balance before hurling himself headlong at Reynaud.

Reynaud shouted, only to find his breath choked off as Tristan's weight hit his chest. He scrabbled back wildly, with Tristan right after him. Both men toppled into the drifts.

The scent of revenge was hot and sweet to Tristan, all the guide he needed through the darkness that was dropping rapidly around him. His fingers found Reynaud's throat and tingled with unexpected pleasure at the lethal contact. Tristan hung on delightedly, despite the distrac-

266

tion of Reynaud's thrashing about, rolling them both through the snow and over chunks of ice. He was screaming accusations at Reynaud whenever he could get breath, paying small attention to logic, pouring out every suspected treachery and every questionable action he'd ever caught the man at. That, too, felt wonderful and strengthened him in his task.

Reynaud, frantic, nearly blacking out, got one knee onto the ice again and tried to turn over and stand. Tristan felt himself being lifted along. He tightened his grip. Reynaud's footing gave out under the double load, and they both pitched into the snow again. Tristan felt as if he tumbled into black feathers. Something solid reached up rudely out of their softness, smacking him so sharply on the forehead that he let go of Reynaud in surprise.

And then it was too late—Tristan sought the grip again, but his fingers would not obey, and he was helpless to grasp Reynaud again, or even to stop himself spiraling down and down, into the dark feathers.

"Ha! Wizard, there's no more snow to fight! We're all friends here, we've got you safe—"

Polassar blithely ignored Reynaud, still sprawled in the snow while clutching his throat and gasping for air like a half-drowned man. He lifted Tristan to his feet gently, handling him as he might have a child in a tantrum. Indeed, much amusement might be found at Reynaud's falling victim to Tristan's befuddled efforts to free himself from an icefall he didn't yet realize he was clear of.

Polassar's good humor lasted an instant more. Tristan shrugged an arm loose from his lax grip and landed a blow with an exactness of aim which would have been marvelous if he'd been trying for it. Polassar howled and almost lost the rest of his hold. Tristan tried to follow up his advantage and roll free.

"Curse you, Wizard, can't you tell friend from foeman?" Polassar's eye was starting to close. "Stop this thrashing, now—"

Tristan bloodied Polassar's nose and tried to blacken his other eye. He screamed something unintelligible.

He was heading for Reynaud when Polassar got hold of him once more, pinning him with a grip that Elisena feared would dislocate both Tristan's shoulders. She ran the last few feet to reach them, as she had run all the way to the icefall—then jumped clear of the brawl. She almost fell over Reynaud, who hadn't yet managed to stand.

Polassar cast frantically about for help, as Tristan twisted and kicked at his legs. This was sport no longer. Of a sudden, keeping hold of the wizard seemed more important than any risk of injuring him in the struggle, but Polassar still wasn't sure how long he could manage it. The man had the strength of the possessed.

If it was a mad fit, it should have ended by then. Tristan should have sagged back into unconsciousness, not gone on thrashing like a foundered horse. Polassar lost his footing in the churned snow, and both men fell jarringly. The jolt didn't seem to bother Tristan. He rolled free again and began to stand.

"Hold him!" Elisena called. She was clawing at her herb bag, discarding items heedlessly into the snow. A bottle and a cup came to her hand at last. She measured drops from one to the other with a skill born of practice.

Sprawling in the snow beside Polassar, she put a boot on one of Tristan's ankles and got a hand on his left shoulder. Between them, she and Polassar forced Tristan to lie flat, if not still.

There was no sense in his eyes. Indeed, little save the whites of them showed. Elisena forced the potion between Tristan's lips, thankful for Polassar's strength that could keep Tristan relatively immobile while she did so. The drug in the knobby bottle demanded precise measurement for safety's sake—and she wanted to be sure that Tristan swallowed the draught and that he did not spill the cup out of her hands before taking it all.

The cup shook dangerously. Elisena tried to calm Tristan with her rings and failed. Without the aid of Polassar's strength, she would have been able to do even less than the little she had done. She had not yet been able to examine him. Automatically, Elisena tried to remedy the oversight while she administered the sedative, the habit too deeply rooted for her to care that the attempt must be mostly useless while Tristan struggled so.

That he had stunned himself when he fell into the snow on top of Reynaud was plain. There was a blue bruise on Tristan's forehead to attest to a blow, and had he not been at least briefly unconscious, probably he would have finished throttling Reynaud before Polassar pulled him off.

The obvious injury had done no more than daze Tristan. And he'd gone after Reynaud at once, as if he'd never been interrupted. That injury, then, didn't account for his behavior. Elisena found herself relieved that she could justify with logic her intuitive seizing of drastic measures to quiet Tristan before he hurt himself worse than he already had.

The cup, finally, was empty. Elisena dropped it, to be free to add her strength to Polassar's. A moment or two later, the mandrake infusion finally took effect. Tristan went limp in the midst of the trampled patch of snow. Polassar waited a further moment before relaxing his grip, even after Elisena had signed him to let go.

They were both panting, even as Tristan had been. The rasp of their breathing was loud on the cold air. A few feet off, Reynaud was still trying to draw a breath deep enough to quiet his own tortured lungs.

Even oblivion guaranteed no safety. Tristan felt Reynaud's sorceries following him down as he fell, ready to resolve what the snowslide had left as a bit of unfinished business—his life. Panic struck him. He was helpless to defend himself on a magical level—he had no tools, no stones, no grimoire. Reynaud had stripped him of all those along with his pack, while Tristan was still stunned by the ice that had fallen on him. And he'd lost his sword somehow, probably the same way.

Weaponless, Tristan fought back as best and as long as he could, until the mandrake fumes sifting down robbed him of even that pitiful defense.

Elisena looked over the objects reclaimed from the ice along with Tristan—his pack, his unsheathed sword, a bit of crystal. The belongings were mute. She had not thought they would tell her much, and they had not disappointed her expectations, any more than Tristan himself had.

She was glad that Polassar had managed to drag him back to their makeshift camp, where she might work upon him with some efficiency. Elisena found she had barely strength enough herself to get Tristan into a wool bag and to settle him near the warm fire while she started more specific herbs steeping. Polassar looked as if he had questions for her, but the man had sense enough for once not to expect answers.

Hands shaking with weariness, shock, and a sleepless night catching up with her, Elisena sought signs of injuries or sorceries. She found bruises aplenty, to be soothed automatically, but she found nothing else beyond them— nothing to make sense of Tristan's mad behavior.

Perhaps he *was* mad. He might well be, Elisena told herself. Being buried alive would be enough to provoke that, even without Nímir's agency thrown in. And if it were so, there was little she could offer as a remedy for the condition. Of the only cures she thought might be effective, she had none at hand. Warmth, quiet, safety— she could promise Tristan none of those, not in Channadran. Elisena choked back a sob before Polassar could hear it, uncertain if it heralded fear or grief, refusing to grant either emotion power over her. Not yet, she vowed.

Reynaud came to her, moving carefully, not from the wariness she first expected, but walking slowly for the sake of the burden he bore—one last object reclaimed from the ice.

He held Thomas for her inspection, lent what help he might as she mended the cat's ribs, and paid no heed at first to Tristan's quiet, blanket-swathed form. Small wonder, Elisena thought with the part of her mind that Thomas did not demand. Reynaud had pulled the neck of his cloak high to mask them, but the bruises on his swollen throat showed plainly, and his voice was rough when he finally spoke, obviously painful to use.

Reynaud nodded at Tristan finally and tried to offer Elisena comfort while refusing the salve she offered for his hurts. "He's a touch frostbitten, but nothing he shouldn't recover from. And I suppose, if the same thing had happened to me, I'd be in no better a temper."

He held up a long-fingered hand for Elisena's inspection. "The cat bit me, too." Reynaud tried a laugh, but it rang flat as a leaden bell, and he did not offer a second.

Thomas' ribs were easily put right, but the shock which catastrophe had cast him into was less simple to deal with. Bitten Reynaud he might have, but the action was either reflex or a last-ditch effort at going out fighting. Thomas made no attempt to snap as Elisena worked over him. Gray tinged his lips and tongue.

She had already fed him boneset, speedwell juice, and plantain leaves. Shepherd's purse would staunch any bleeding the smashed ribs might have begun inside where she could neither see nor bandage. The gentle herbs were not enough—Thomas needed stronger physick, as did his master. Elisena's hands, with rings faintly glowing, traveled over those jars she had sealed with magic long before, lest any hand less skilled than her own confuse their uses.

Mandrake again, and black hellebore for mania. Henbane, poppy, and lettuce juice, powerful sedatives. Poisons, too, and she was careful with all of them, measuring drops for the cat and scarcely more for her larger patient. Tristan slept heavily, with only an occasional restless turning of his head. Had he dreams that even the drugs could not thrust out? Elisena stroked his forehead and whispered words she hoped would comfort, if he heard.

Tristan almost wished himself buried in the icefall again. At least there his struggles had produced results he could see, however slightly. Now none of his senses reported to him reliably, and he could stir neither hand nor foot. All the while, he was conscious of a dreadful peril, though its exact nature was unclear to his clouded mind.

After weary hours, the air around him seemed to lighten, as with daybreak. Tristan's eyes opened. Though he still could not make them focus, he could see well enough to make out Elisena's face as she leaned over him. Tristan smiled his relief, though perforce only inwardly. He'd be all right. Elisena would help him sort things out.

He began to whisper to her of all that had befallen him, of Blais, and Cheris, of Nímir's trap, and of Reynaud's nearly final treachery. She'd always been so much quicker than he ever was that Tristan knew she'd see the meaning behind all the separate events and discover fully the danger he could only tremble at the sensing of. Elisena would know what to do about that danger. He could rely on her, though he was too weak to do more than speak at the moment.

* * *

The hour was very early, but the first faint light in the sky overhead seemed to have roused Tristan. The drugs were wearing off as well, and Elisena did not feed him the fresh dose that sat prepared beside her. It was best to let him wake when he seemed so likely to. It should be safe enough.

Tristan's lips moved. Elisena leaned close and heard bits of words, all faint and neither alone nor in sequence making sense. It was too soon to expect coherence, Elisena cautioned herself. Tristan's mind and his tongue were still held at some little distance from each other.

Though Tristan might not speak, yet he was perhaps receptive to questioning of the right sort. Elisena flexed her fingers slowly, preparing to set to work. Her rings were better than any dream-sifter, for with them she might hope to cure as well as understand. The ten of them brightened upon her fingers as she breathed deeply, readying herself to begin.

Gently, she cradled Tristan's face between her palms and felt past the drug mists, brushing their traces aside like fog from a mirror.

She would have done better to allow them to remain in place—for they were the last of calm that she sensed.

Elisena's unspoken questions discovered a fear deep enough to drown in and met a searing rage coiled around that fear in a combination that she could only interpret as madness. Of calm, of any seed of sanity that she might nurture with healing, there was no trace. Elisena searched frantically, refusing to believe that there could be none. The ways she followed twisted and turned and led ever downward, into darkness.

All the way, Tristan fought her. He was stronger than she'd expected he could be with the drug still lingering in his blood. His anger brushed Elisena's mind like a scream. At its heart there was neither sense nor logic, nothing but itself. Elisena pulled back, trembling and reaching for the medicines she'd hoped not to need.

Still unconscious, Tristan moaned and twisted from side to side. His fingers stretched, then tensed as if he hoped to claw his way physically free of the mandrake sleep—or as if he'd strangle something. His eyes opened blindly. He sat up.

Elisena cried out with surprise, unable to reach for him and still keep hold of the medicine.

From behind her, Polassar moved with surprising dispatch for one who'd been deeply asleep an instant before, his battle training serving him well. He threw Tristan flat again and held him while Elisena shakenly poured her potion between his teeth. Tristan was weeping by the time she was finished. When he finally collapsed, Elisena nearly followed him into a faint.

She started when Reynaud touched her sleeve; the memory of the rage Tristan had shown toward him was still so vivid. Reynaud had brought her hot tea and he took the cup when she had gulped it hastily down, cleansing it with a handful of snow before stowing it in his pack once more.

The finicky housekeeping was meant to give her a space to recover and for the herbs to do their work and clear her head. By the time Reynaud spoke his inevitable question, Elisena found she was able to make him an answer, though she was none too willing.

"Did you find a cause?"

"No." Curse it, her voice still shook. Elisena ordered her throat to cease such disobedience. "I couldn't probe that deeply. And I think the intrusion frightened him—with the drugs, Tristan may not have recognized me." She sighed. "Mind-sifting's unsettling, when the mind doesn't want you there. There was no question about *that*."

"He fought you?"

Elisena had thought the answer obvious. "As well as he could. It wouldn't have mattered if he hadn't—Tristan's so afraid, it was like trying to run in a fog. I couldn't see much, only the closest things, and the answers I need are much deeper." Deeper than I can delve, Elisena added, but not to Reynaud, unless he guessed it.

Polassar was sorely troubled. He had to be, to question quietly alongside Reynaud without casting even one condescending look the man's way.

"Lady? You *can* mend him? Put him right?"

Elisena swallowed, willing her unproductive doubts to go down along with a bitter taste she could not rid herself of. "When that dose I just gave him wears off, Tristan *should* be much calmer. I'll have a better chance to answer you then."

Polassar thought, but did not say, that the wizard had been calmer, this waking. At least he was no longer raving about dragons in the ice and treacheries where any man might see there were none possible. Brain-twisting herbs might answer for his confusion and his blank looks. They would have passed off soon enough, if he hadn't been made to down more of the brew.

But the lady must know what she was about. And the wizard *had* fought her, plainly not yet accepting that he was safe and was back with his friends. If he truly *was* back with them. Polassar chewed his moustaches, wondering. He'd lost friends to death and mourned them meetly, but this was something other, something which both baffled him and rent his heart.

Elisena pondered the idea that many of a nurse's tasks owed their existence solely to the need to combat helplessness with action—any action that might keep one from sliding away into madness. She made such use of adjusting Tristan's wool bag and of making certain that he was neither too near the fire nor too far from it. She fussed with his clothing to be sure that his collar did not restrict his breathing. He did not stir now when she touched him—the drugs had him firmly in their grip. She needed only to lift an eyelid to confirm that he was quite insensible. Coming atop the first strong dose, the second draught would keep Tristan out for many hours, probably straight through till the next morning.

Once again, she had sadly miscalculated. Night had only begun to fall when, all at once, Tristan sat up, then stood and tried to walk away from the fire. There was no guessing where he thought he was or intended to go, through the haze of madness and mandrake. His eyes were open, but their focus did not shift—Tristan was not awake. Casting off the wool bag, he had fumbled as a man just waking might have been expected to.

At least he did not seem violent. Elisena waved Polassar off and led Tristan back to his place. She settled him on his bedding once again. When she had him safely there, he seemed to sink back into a deeper sleep, but she could hardly trust her casual observation of his condition and she was afraid to probe deeper for fear of provoking him, as she had done that morning. What ought she to do with him, then?

The drug doses had plainly become less effective as a control. Tristan was apt to try to wander again at any moment; he'd need to be watched closely to guard against that. It was too soon to dose him again without risk of poisoning him with the mandrake or driving him more mad than he already was.

Reynaud realized that as fully as Elisena did and his suggestion that they bind Tristan was not meant unkindly, despite the snarls it drew from Polassar. They were all worn and desperate for rest, none of them reliable guards for a man from whom no rational action could be expected. Reynaud said only that.

Polassar looked willing to finish the choking Tristan had been interrupted at. His hands twitched in time to his words.

"Put a rope to him, sorcerer, and there won't be enough left of you for a carrion crow to make off with! That I swear."

"You want him to wander off the side of the mountain next time?" Reynaud asked politely. "I don't want to hurt Tristan, Polassar, but I won't let him kill me either—or himself, which seems the more likely."

Polassar made no reply, but his knucklebones went white with his restraint.

"Look at him," Reynaud invited, gesturing at Tristan. "We can't keep drugging him unconscious. Outside of a few bruises, there's nothing the matter with Tristan bodily. He's healthy enough to throw the drugs off now. A heavier dose will only poison him. We're helpless, so long as he's in that state. We can't carry him up here, and he certainly can't climb, not like that."

"Why not craft up that pretty mare of yours, sorcerer, if you're wearied of honest walking? A horse might be useful to us now."

Reynaud shrugged. "Perhaps. Though, considering the trails up here, I rather doubt that. The matter is academic. It's also not possible—the spell requires juniper smoke, and we've no wood of any sort. Ambere's magewood warms our bones, but beggars my sorcery. I'm sorry."

Polassar cursed at what he took as mockery. Reynaud

turned away from him, as from an argument ended to his satisfaction. "Elisena—"

"You'll not touch him, I tell you!" Polassar's huge right hand swung Reynaud about in a swirl of cloak and bruised the man's shoulder to the bone. Reynaud winced delicately.

"I wasn't speaking of rope, for the gods' sake!" He twitched free in annoyance. "There are other ways to restrain him—"

"No." Elisena said flatly.

Reynaud looked at her askance. She had not joined Polassar's quarrel, and he had taken that for agreement.

"Reynaud, you can't put a Binding on him. Especially *you* can't. The state Tristan's in, I can't begin to guess what the result would be, but it surely wouldn't be good. If Tristan fights even me, whom he trusts, how do you expect him to respond to *you*?"

Reynaud lifted his shoulders, spreading his hands in resignation. He might not understand Tristan's rage, but he remembered it clearly. "We have to do something, Lady."

Elisena's crystals jingled as she brushed her hair clear of her face, closing her eyes with weariness as she considered again what her thoughts had never been far from.

"I know, Reynaud. But I think he's beginning to recover a little. Tristan may be over whatever happened to him and only suffering from the drugs now. Their hold on him may have worn off, but there are other effects to consider. It's very possible." That possible might be true as well was all Elisena dared hope. No more would she permit herself.

"We've got to let Tristan be, if we want him alive—so no more magic, no more mandrake. I will keep watch over him, and that will do."

"Lady, you need sleep just as much as any of us—"

"Then we'll share out the watches, sorcerer," Polassar rumbled with finality. "Put him in the middle when we settle to sleep, so he won't slip past us all if the watcher dozes." His tone was firm. "Then, come morn, or as soon as he's got wit enough to walk between us, we'll go on. 'Twill shake the cobwebs out of his brain, I'll hazard."

* * *

Elisena had risen early, with work to do before the others stirred. She was not such a fool as to expect Reynaud to surrender his arguments and she could not forestall him without first gathering some answers. The last stars were still bright in the sky when she began her quest. When she had finished, they were gone out like blown candles, but the dawn showed plainly the blade lying beside Tristan, even to the rough stitches where Polassar had mended the scabbard.

The blade lay quiet finally. She had thought to use it to heal Tristan again—and had been rebuffed. Before she could even attempt her craft, the sword had twitched and hissed like a snake at her touch, then had sheathed itself violently, cutting at the mittens on her hands. Elisena mended the slashes clumsily as she kept a watch on both Tristan and his weapon.

What the sword's behavior meant, Elisena could not guess and was too exhausted to try. She knew better than to touch it a second time; and though she mourned the loss of its possible cure, she spared it little further thought. What strength she still had, she must husband for a harder task—answering what she'd do should Tristan not be better when he awoke.

If the sword's reaction had astonished her, then it had also left Elisena with nothing to feel but chagrin over a failure which had probably come about from lack of sleep. She thought it well that no one else had seen, or there would have been more quarrels with Reynaud—unnecessary, as it chanced.

Nor had there been need for the lost sleep, or any of her worries, in retrospect. Tristan woke at nightfall, himself again.

At least he only lay blinking at Elisena as she bent over him, slowly schooling his eyes to focus on the objects about him. He made no angry outcry and no attempt at further mayhem. Elisena refrained from questions and kept her relief hidden as well, lest it alarm him. She spoke but a few soft words to soothe Tristan, as she propped him upright and fed him a bowl of warm broth.

By the time she had given him the last drops, there was color in his face again beyond the tint the fire lent it, and the drugs had plainly worn off. Little trace of them

remained in Tristan's eyes, none on his voice when at last
he spoke.

"All right. Where is he, then?"

Startled, Elisena dropped the horn spoon into the
wooden bowl. The thump it made as it struck served as
a question, at least to Tristan.

"Reynaud," he explained bitterly, staring at Polassar's
cloak tented above him. "Where is he?"

Elisena sat frozen, wondering if she'd been left with
wit enough to restrain Tristan if he yet proved violent,
grieving wildly that she should still need to do so, and
cursing the hope that had left her so vulnerable.

She kept her voice casual, as she hoped to keep Tristan
calm, but the effort cost her much. She could not speak
gently while she sought to master strong feeling. Perhaps
it was better to ignore the emotion.

"Reynaud's with Polassar, cooking supper. Do you want
more broth?

"More broth?" Tristan looked as baffled as he was.
"What does that have to do with Reynaud?"

His eyes had gone wide, whites showing all around.
Elisena put a hand on his shoulder. "It's all right, Tristan."

"All right? What do you mean, all right?" He didn't
sound soothed.

Polassar heard the difference between honest argument
and Tristan's former delirious shoutings. He heaved a sigh
of relief and continued his clumsy chopping of dried beef
into the stew pot. Trust the wizard to come out of this
quarrelsome. He'd be right as rain in moments and as if
naught ill had ever befallen him. The lady's spell must
have worked betimes. Polassar stayed where he was, confident he'd not be needed except as cook.

Reynaud also sat silent, as if he did not hear every
word—hardly able to relish the argument as Polassar did.

The look in Tristan's eyes was the product of the outrage flaming in his heart, but Elisena failed to read it
accurately. The pressure of her hand on his chest increased
markedly.

Familiar words seemed to have scrambled their mean-
ings, Tristan thought. He could hear Elisena's words when
she spoke to him, but it didn't seem that she'd comprehended what he'd asked. It was as if she didn't know
what had happened to him. How could that be? He'd told

her all of it, all about Reynaud . . . A chill ran down Tristan's back, as if he felt Channadran's frosty bedrock through all the warm bedding he lay on. His heart misgave him.

"Be quiet and listen to me now," Elisena said, maddeningly calm. "I don't want to have to dose you again—"

He had again that sense of not connecting. It scared Tristan and made him angry. The fear might keep silent, but the anger had a voice. And he'd finally realized what the aftertaste lingering in his mouth was—a taste that stayed even through the beef broth.

"Why? Are you afraid of getting the dose too high? Whose idea was the mandrake, anyway? Reynaud's?"

Reynaud forebore to cringe, but his eyes were too hooded for the fire's light to reach.

"Mandrake?" Elisena repeated stupidly, as if they were having two separate conversations. Tristan tried again to break through to her. He sat up.

"Did you think I couldn't taste it?" He discovered that he still could and he wiped at his mouth. "Toadstools, that stuff's *poison*—"

"So I'd hardly have fed it to you without reason, now would I?" Elisena asked matter-of-factly. "Listen to me, Tristan. I know you're confused. That's quite natural after what happened to you. But—"

Tristan broke her control once again by simply ignoring what she said. "All that's confusing *me* is Reynaud walking around loose after he tried to kill me! How do you explain that?"

Elisena sensed rather than saw Polassar's head lift by the fire. Good! He'd be ready should she need him, but would otherwise keep a tactful distance. And there was no danger that Reynaud would interfere, she thought. Elisena turned her whole attention back to Tristan.

He was watching mistrustfully, as she was sure he had been doing every moment while she thought. He looked upset and was still badly shaken. Though better, he was hardly well yet. He needed rest and quiet—and he wasn't going to permit that treatment; he wouldn't let matters lie. He had lured her too quickly into a heated exchange she had not intended and should never have permitted.

She had gone appallingly soft. But with luck, there was still time to mend matters. Elisena took Tristan's hand.

"Tristan, after you disappeared, we searched the whole night for you. The icefall blocked the way we'd seen you go, and there was a sorcery there as well, so we combed the whole ridge, every crack and crevice, because that was the only way we could hope to find another way in, or be there if you found a way back to us." Elisena's poise had returned to her. She felt confident again, sure she'd be able to calm and convince Tristan of the truth.

"Reynaud found you just after dawn and dug you out of the snow, half-frozen. He called to Polassar and to me, but we were some way off. It took us a while to get to you. By then Reynaud had revived you."

Tristan's gaze was stony, but he held his tongue, and it might be hoped that he was listening.

"It's understandable that you were confused then, that you kept struggling as you'd had to while you were getting free of the ice, and that you kept on fighting Reynaud. That wasn't your fault, and he doesn't blame you for it. But you have to let go of it now. You can't let resentment and jealousy twist the simple truth of what happened. It's not like you."

"Whereas dropping an avalanche down on me is precisely like Reynaud," Tristan said. "Particularly when you admit that there was no one close enough to witness his doing it."

Elisena looked at him steadily. "You are hardly the best judge of what happened, Tristan. I am telling you the truth. You fought against Polassar, too—and me. You fought us like a man possessed of demons. I don't suppose you remember *that*?"

Tristan blinked. "Fought *you*? No. I remember that there was some sort of spell, but that certainly wasn't you. It was Reynaud—"

"Reynaud was nowhere near you. You don't remember that very well either. After Reynaud pulled you clear of the ice, after you nearly managed to strangle him, it was Polassar holding you back—and me."

"You think I don't recognize a spell when one's thrown at me? Of course, he'd make it look like someone else was doing it—" Tristan spoke almost by reflex, his mind barely working in the cold that had settled over him. Why would Elisena say such things and lie to take Reynaud's part? He'd told her himself what had happened, just as soon as he was able to speak. Why had Elisena chosen not to believe him? Had Reynaud tainted her with his clever words, with the explanations he'd surely had ready in case he was caught at his treachery? Tristan felt himself being buried again, only this time he could not see the ice, but could only feel its shriveling chill.

"Tristan, there was no spell! Don't you think I would know that? It was chance that Reynaud found you and not Polassar, but he saved your life just as surely, for all of that. Truly." Elisena put her hands on Tristan's shoulders and spoke more gently after she discovered how he was trembling.

"It isn't your fault, and I'm not surprised at any of this. You were buried in that ice for hours, alone in the cold and the dark. You nearly died. That would give anyone fantasies. But you've got to let go of them now. Reynaud, dragons in the ice, Blais—those were only nightmares, don't you see?"

"You think I was just hallucinating?" Still the horror closed in, icier yet, and Tristan couldn't force more than a whisper through his throat. He wanted to scream.

"It's likely. A common side-effect of mandrake, remember? I was sorry to give that to you, but there was no other way to calm you. And you wouldn't have lasted long without it in the state you were in when we found you."

"But I *told* you—" Tristan's voice failed in the middle of that desperate cry. He'd told her, yes, but she didn't remember, or chose to put it down to mandrake-ravings. "I can prove what I said before, about what happened. I *can*. I—"

Hope flared so fast, he wanted to weep. Blais' box. *There* was a proof Elisena couldn't deny. Neither her drugs nor his ordeal would effect its reality. Tristan reached for it eagerly. He'd prove he wasn't mad—she'd have to accept what he told her, Reynaud or no. He opened the pouch attached to his belt and still lying at his side, where his own magic box shared its home with his master's.

The other box wasn't there in the pouch where he'd left it, nor in his pack when he demanded that be brought, nor in any of his pockets—and there was nowhere else to search. Disbelieving, Tristan ransacked every suspected location twice or more, throwing gear everywhere. He kept at it even after he realized that Reynaud would have taken it. By then he was more than trembling; he was shaking as if with a fever-chill and weeping with frustration. Elisena's eyes were wet as well as she turned away to steep the sleeping-herbs.

She had put a dollop of honey into the mug along with the tea, but, if Tristan noticed, he gave no sign of it.

"Thomas can tell you," he stated flatly, sipping only when he saw she would force him to drink otherwise. "Even if Reynaud took the box, Thomas still knows what happened. He was there. He knows." Tristan's voice grew stronger as he realized that he still had a valid defense against the hallucinations Elisena alleged and Reynaud's treacheries. He shouldn't have lost control earlier—there was no reason for such despair. Elisena would believe Thomas.

"Where is he?" It was odd that he hadn't seen the cat about yet.

The expression that crossed Elisena's face was uncertain, forcing Tristan to choose its meaning for himself. Why should Elisena be loath to answer his question? Unless—no, her silence couldn't mean what he thought it did! Cold squeezed Tristan's heart again, bringing tears back to his sore eyes.

"*No—*" he said, and dropped the mug, his hands going limp. The tea flowed over the wool bag until it found a way to the ground and snow it could soak into. Tristan went on whispering denials senselessly and so didn't hear those Elisena spoke until she had seized both his hands and pulled them away from his face.

His stricken expression smote her. How had she not realized how he'd take her silence? She'd only meant to forestall yet another tack of argument, one that revolved around poor Thomas as the last one had centered on whatever proof Tristan had expected to find in his pockets. But instead of sparing them both that, her efforts had only whiplashed Tristan with grief when he could least afford the hurt.

At least what he feared wasn't another truth he had to accept. Elisena jerked at Tristan's shoulders to get his attention, shifting so that he could see past her and spot the well-wrapped bundle lying close by the fire. It was too long a while before she knew that Tristan comprehended the sight or her hastily chosen words. His shoulders untensed.

"He's all right, isn't he?"

"Yes." Elisena rubbed at Tristan's hands, which seemed cold even to her own, gloveless in the mountain air.

"I want to see." Tristan tried to climb out of the wool bag, but Elisena had little difficulty in stopping him.

"Not now. Let him be till morning. He was really shaken around, as badly as you, almost. And he's asleep now, anyway. He hasn't been properly awake since Reynaud dug the two of you out. Wait till morning."

Tristan, dry-mouthed, remembered how Cheris' boot had sent Thomas tumbling. He thought how the cat's thick fur could hide serious injuries. He met Elisena's eyes, over the rim of the freshly refilled mug.

"You checked his ribs?"

"Yes. And gave him potions to keep him quiet while they knit." She thought it wise not to mention that Reynaud had really done most of the tending. "He'll be all right, Tristan."

"Good. Then he'll tell you what happened," Tristan said with grave certainty.

But in the end, Thomas offered no corroboration, and Tristan asked none of him. He held the cat gingerly beside the breakfast fire, inspecting the healed ribs for himself despite Elisena's disapproval.

The cat lay on his chest inside the warm wrappings, his paws folded back into his fur so that he was all but legless. His eyes were shut and his ears relaxed.

"Thomas?" Tristan asked softly. He had his questions ready. Even through the fog Elisena's sleeping potion had left on him, his resentment of Reynaud's lies burned. He'd have his satisfaction soon, and it would be sweet, as well as keeping all of them a bit safer.

He didn't know what they'd do about Reynaud. It was late to banish him from the group. Maybe Polassar could offer some solution. Tristan didn't care what, just so long as Reynaud didn't continue to walk about free while everyone assumed that he, Tristan, had lost all his wits past hope of recovery.

Thomas stirred, and cried softly. Tristan bent closer. He saw a slit of green between just-parted eyelids, and the tip of Thomas' pink tongue came out, to brush Tristan's fingers with just a hint of moisture. Then the cat went back to sleep.

Potions had been given to keep Thomas quiet while he healed, Elisena had said; probably not so different from the befuddling medicines she'd been giving *him*, Tristan thought—potions which she admitted confused reality and brought strong dreams as real as life but likely to be contrary. Tristan wanted to groan. Why should he think that Elisena would believe Thomas now, any more than she had believed what he'd already told her himself?

Tristan never asked his questions. It began to seem safer not to. He and the cat had been through an ordeal together under the ice—but what he remembered, what Thomas might recall, what was real and what only dream, Tristan could no longer say with any semblance of certainty. His clearest present thought was a doubt, and that directed at himself.

Heart's Winter

TRISTAN FELT JUST SLIGHTLY BETTER THAN HE HAD upon waking. He ached all over and was sick to his stomach—that probably was the gift of the fierce headache he also had. But it had taken a long time for any of those troubles truly to bother him—the same long time it had taken for a strong dose of poppy to wear off. By the time it finally did so, he had been walking—and with much help, climbing—for several hours.

He dimly recalled a lecture from Polassar as they set off at dawn—something to do with his being shaken till his brains rattled like peas in a shriveled pod if there were any more nonsense from him. Tristan could remember that he'd felt both guilty and misjudged, but his feelings seemed to be at some distance from the rest of him, and he could not clearly understand why he'd had them at all.

After the morning, he had only widely scattered memories of events—a rock face here and there, a dazzle of sunlight, and the touch of hands that had boosted him when he faltered on a difficult climb. Then they'd stopped making him move, and someone had put food in his hand. Tristan saw that he'd eaten a few bites of it, but he couldn't remember how it had tasted.

He set his nibbled meal down and used his freed hand to rub at the back of his neck. Most of his headache was centered there, as if he'd been carrying his head at an unnatural angle and had strained something. He sat so for what felt like a long while, sad and wondering about that, wondering what it was he didn't want to remember and couldn't quite forget. He'd have called the feeling lone-

liness, but with his friends all about him, how could that
be?

Then Tristan remembered—everything.

He'd been in a fog all morning, incapable of climbing
on his own, but that was not—or not alone—why there'd
been a hand always at his elbow and eyes watching him.
His companions were ever alert for a relapse of suspicious
behavior on his part. The least misstep made them wary.
Tristan glanced up, and the eyes that met his dropped
hastily, almost with embarrassment.

After that, there was no question of his finishing his
meal—his stomach was full up, hugging tight around the
lump of lead that he'd somehow swallowed and which
might explain why his throat also hurt so.

The situation was, once he became aware of it, unbearable; but Tristan said nothing. Isolated as he was by his
companions' mistrust of him, he still didn't want to risk
making matters and the distrust worse. That adjustment
left him with a beaten feeling that went hand in hand with
his lingering confusion.

At least his mind was his own again—till that night's
camp and his next sleeping draught—but his thoughts
were such that Tristan wished they could belong to someone else for a while and that his dinner had included a
mouthful of merciful poppy or even mandrake.

He'd been reckoned well enough to travel. That was
something, even if without much meaning. In their supply
situation, they could not afford to tarry long in one spot,
and Ambere's birds must have been nagging at them to
move on for all the days that Tristan supposed he'd delayed
them.

Something other than birds tugged at Tristan as they
went on and made him search his memories till his brain
felt sore. Round and round he went with them, trying to
decide if he'd been an utter fool or was perversely ignoring
a vital warning that only he had been gifted with. One
question bothered him with a particular relentlessness.
Had the whole incident under the ice been a carefully laid
trap of Nímir's? If it had, then Elisena ought to be told
again all that he could remember of it. She'd need every
scrap of information to make her guard strong enough to
protect them all and safeguard their vital mission. But
Tristan was loath to speak of it to her. When she opened

the subject and even pressed him on it, he refused to answer her.

His intransigence hurt her. Tristan saw that and was pained to see it, but the pain did not move him from his position. Her doubt cut him equally deeply, even while he was none too sure of the truth himself. So, stubbornly, he said only that he'd seen one of Ambere's birds under the overhang that day and had gone in hoping to rescue it.

He refused to back down or elaborate. After a while Elisena had to let him be. Which was what he wanted, wasn't it? Let the whole matter, unpleasant as it was, be forgotten.

But something about it still bothered Tristan. Where one trap was set, often there were others, placed before every way that the panicked prey might choose to run. Sometimes that first trap was meant to be found, so that the prey might think itself out of danger, and become unwary.

He was assuming there'd truly been a trap, but Tristan knew he had no proof of one, and could hope for no proof beyond his own shaky memory. That memory came after he'd been buried nightlong in ice and rock, been buried yet again, and then dosed with a powerful poison. Tristan didn't know which bothered him most—Elisena's supposition that he'd hallucinated thoroughly enough that he couldn't recognize the memory for such—or his own terror that he *hadn't* imagined any of it, that the nightmares had been all too real.

"He'll come around in time, Reynaud. It's been but a few days—"

Reynaud offered an enigmatic smile, one of his best.

"I am not troubling myself over what Tristan thinks of me. I've known that for a long while and I probably deserve his opinion. Whatever happened has only prompted him to be more open about his feelings."

"But something troubles you?" There was time aplenty for Elisena's questions. The camp was quiet. Tristan and Polassar were both safely asleep. And Tristan was certain to stay so.

Reynaud played idly with a rope end, rolling it between his elegant hands. "I'm tired, is all. It's weary work climbing with a man who's a thousand leagues off till at least sun-high, and not much better after."

"I don't like drugging Tristan either, but a little poppy to put him to sleep is still better than setting a watch on him all night. And it won't be necessary much longer, I should think."

"Hoping for a spontaneous cure, or are you finally listening to me?"

"We've been through this, Reynaud," Elisena said sharply. She would not justify herself to him.

"Without concluding it. It has been days since we spoke of this last, and though Tristan may be calm *now*, there's been no other change to render the subject invalid. We are fast approaching the day when each and all of us will find our utmost strength required. I do not think Tristan will recover on his own that quickly—if at all." Reynaud sighed. "If he hadn't refused your questions, I might think otherwise. But he's doing more than lying to you—he's keeping the truth from himself with even greater diligence."

"I don't find that surprising. He's in no shape to face it. And I won't have him badgered, Reynaud. It's not as if he'd permit you to treat him, whatever you have in mind. So let's not risk a setback by trying for a cure for what's hardly a life-threatening condition."

"A life-threatening condition *yet*." Reynaud fidgeted. "Elisena, this has to be said. You told me that once in Kôvelir, when Tristan was under stress, he was vulnerable . . . Nímir found a way into his mind and led him a long while. We have to consider that it could happen again."

"The same could happen to any of us, Reynaud. I'm sure Tristan has thought of it from time to time—I will not torture him with that either." Her expression matched the determination of her words.

"I don't ask that, Lady. Only that you remember it."

Elisena nodded, hesitantly. She had not forgotten for a single moment, but she would not gift Reynaud with that knowledge. Just the thoughts provoked pangs of guilt. Revealing them, especially to Reynaud, would be an outright betrayal.

"I could be wrong, of course." Reynaud at last left off teasing the rope and began to coil it efficiently. "There's an easier explanation for Tristan's reluctance to talk about what happened, and simple is always best. He just can't say that things might have happened other than as he remembers them. He won't admit that he really doesn't *know* what happened." A twist secured the rope's end to the coil. "That would not surprise me, if it were so. A good wizard must be very self-willed. Tristan certainly is, for all he's been brought up to be politely diffident. In Kôvelir, it's truly said that wizards are not easy patients." He looked directly at Elisena once more. "You've a job ahead of you, Lady."

"I can bring him around, Reynaud, never fear. He's always listened to me before."

Reynaud regarded her somberly. "I doubt you've ever asked anything of Tristan that he didn't want to give, whether he realized it or not. I warn you—that makes a difference."

Tristan made a small noise in his sleep. It was not a loud sound or one low enough to be construed as a moan, but it woke Elisena easily, as she slept close by him.

She raised on one elbow and looked down at him. Though close to her side, Tristan's sleeping posture seemed to put him miles away from her, behind the wall he'd thrown up to guard himself. He was turned away from her, as if he feared to turn to her—the same feeling Elisena got every time she tried to speak with him, shown with his body now rather than merely his eyes.

He lay face-down in the wool bag, his arms flung up to either pillow or shield his head. He moved one hand as she watched, his expression shifting. Tristan looked as if he were trying to escape something, some terror that pursued him even into sleep, where he ought to have been most safe.

Once she could have helped him gain safety with a touch of her rings or even her bare hand. Now, Elisena thought, Tristan would wake at the lightest brush of her fingers, and then she'd have to confront the look in his eyes once again, that lost look which she couldn't fight her way past, try as she might.

Dreading to face it again, staving off feelings of cowardice, Elisena told herself that Tristan needed even fitful sleep more than any comfort he'd now accept from her. She lay back and snugged her wool bag about her neck, wondering how she expected to find sleep around the leadenness that had settled in her chest. Skilled with herbs as she was, she knew of no remedy for such a pain—others' or her own.

A fold of blanket had brushed Tristan's face and pressed lightly against his nose and mouth. Even that was enough to make Tristan wake screaming, certain that he was being buried under snow again, suffocating.

It was a long time before he calmed enough to recognize the snow as a dream, and by then there was something more than memory and worse than nightmare pressing in on him.

Tristan looked about in horror at the ring of eyes that surrounded him, all their expressions revealed like lightning flashes, curious, sympathetic, or sardonic, shifting and multiplying unbearably in his mind.

There was no escape from the humiliation or from the tears he couldn't stop, except back into sleep, and that seemed impossible. Tristan fought for breath—difficult to do with his nose and mouth once more buried in the wool bag.

Associations of smothering were no less pleasant awake than they had been asleep, but Tristan needed to bury his head, to hide his tears and shut away the pitying glances he saw whenever his uncovered eyes snapped open. Finally he completed the journey into oblivion, exhaustion helping him the last bit of the way as he pulled the welcome blackness around him. By that time, Tristan felt as if his heart had been scalded away.

His journey back to normality was no less perilous a way to tread than the trek into Channadran itself and as likely never to end. Tristan might as well have been sleeping still when the next day's climb commenced, and that might have been thought some comfort after his bad night, but it was not. For the first time, Tristan was utterly weary of his state and wished that his thoughts were his own again, all the day. It seemed to him hours before the cold air tasted sweet rather than stale to him. Breathing did him no more good than if he'd drunk seawater to slake his thirst.

They had paused for a meal before his head even began to clear—time had passed uncommonly slowly. Tristan's thoughts, once they began to return, seemed silty. Maybe he *hadn't* found sleep on his own, after his dream. Elisena might have given him something to drink, to ease or shorten his distress. Tristan couldn't be sure he'd remember it.

Once finally clear, his head began to ache. Tristan gritted his teeth against the pain, hoping that it might pass sooner for having had no heed paid to it. He fed Thomas the rest of his meal, or such tidbits as he knew would tempt the cat's small appetite.

He stuck to his resolve not to trouble Thomas with questions he knew couldn't be answered, for once sure that his motive was humane and nothing more complicated. Thomas batted delicately at Tristan's fingers for a while, then went back to sleep, nestling against Tristan's jacket.

When the march resumed, Tristan refused to relinquish Thomas back to Reynaud's carrying. He was scrupulously polite about it, but firm. He didn't realize it, but he was watched with far less anxiety after that—there was little danger that he'd misbehave while he was in charge of Thomas' welfare. No one thought him so mad as that. Tristan walked with his slow thoughts, no trouble to anyone.

Elisena watched the firelight playing on Tristan's sleeping face, finding hollows in his cheeks. She sadly traced the lines that staring into sun and wind had put at the corners of his eyes. Bearded, he'd look as old as Reynaud.

And he was thin. He wasn't eating much of anything. Once she might have coaxed Tristan, tempted him with sweets, or simply ordered him to eat, but now even the gentlest persuasion seemed like to breach the fragile balance Tristan had managed to strike. She doubted he could forgive another intrusion, or that she could bear the look in his eyes if she should force the issue. Tristan kept his hood raised most of the time, and, Elisena thought, not alone for its warmth. Its folds would also serve to hide his gaunt face—would let him hide, period, so he need meet no man's eye.

Tristan didn't eat. She didn't sleep. Neither of them was very wise. Elisena was filled with guilt and shame, and a part of her perversely wanted to blame Tristan for the feelings, as if that could salve her conscience. She wanted to accuse him of a mistrust to match her own—of lack of faith.

But she could not do that with any honesty. Tristan had never questioned a single one of her decisions, however perilous. Probably it had never even occurred to him that he should.

And in return for that unshakable loyalty, she drugged him with neither his knowledge nor his consent and watched him more closely and with less trust than she'd have offered a confessed thief. She had left him alone, literally and metaphorically, in the cold. Still, he offered her neither reproach nor complaint, but kept to himself as if all the wrongs were his and her sternness only too well deserved. Tristan expected no better treatment than she gave him.

It was small wonder that her conscience should hurt her. Elisena shut her eyes and felt tears burning between her lids. She was failing Tristan yet again, despite all her resolve, for surely she could have been gentler with him, even under the necessity of saving his life. If she'd offered him the slightest comfort, he wouldn't be lying alone now, genuinely afraid to turn to anyone save Thomas.

What had happened to Tristan had hardly been his fault. She might at least have let him know that.

Oh, he'd heal, given time, of all but that sadness in his eyes. He might come to seem quite like his old self soon. He was closer to it every day, at least on the surface. Only in Channadran, there was neither the time nor the warmth necessary to effect the deeper healing that he needed.

She'd let Tristan down cruelly, with all her good intentions flying as bravely and as uselessly as banners.

The love, Elisena thought miserably, the love that made these rings and the greater love that linked them . . . what's become of it? How much of it have I let Tristan see? He holds his heart out for anyone to look at or to trample. He doesn't stint or try to spare himself, while I have learned my lesson, the wisdom of holding back, of saving myself, only too well.

Cruel winds blew through Channadran, but their puissance was blunted, a thing beyond Channadran's experience.

Deep in the cottony darkness that henbane and poppy brought in place of sleep, Tristan dreamed. He dreamed, though he didn't remember it once his extreme need was past, of white birds flying upon a wind that was not cold beyond freshness—a wind that smelled of salt and the wide sea. Beyond the wind, he heard the ceaseless, calming beat of waves upon a shore.

Tension left him. His clenched jaws relaxed, no longer needing to lock shut against his screams.

Remember, a voice nearly familiar admonished. *There is a light to counter darkness and other powers than the Winter King's. Sleep, healing, are neither of them beyond your reach. You did me a service, to take my heart in charge. The promise I made you then, I do not recant. You, I do not forsake.*

For a moment, half waking, Tristan had a disconnected thought that his life was not being twisted without purpose. There was somehow a reason just beyond his grasping fingers, an answer that said he was twirled thus and so as fluffy wool was drawn out and twisted into a strong thread that would not break under the stress of the loom. Much must the wool endure, before the cloth is done.

Tristan's eyes began to open, and his brow creased in concentration. It was no use. The realization, whatever it was, slipped away like rain through his hands, leaving only a trace of salty wetness that was gone altogether when he woke in the morning light.

A vague sense of comfort remained, a tantalizing taste nearly remembered and quite impossible to place. Tristan clung to the comfort, determined not to question its source. It had been too long since he'd known anything like rest—he would not willfully destroy his fragile calm by attempting to dissect it.

And dream-gold or not, it had inspired him with a strong resolve which did not fade away. While Polassar gathered gear and apportioned it out, Tristan got hold of his sword and belted it carefully on.

It belonged to him and to no other. The only way Tristan knew of proving that he was still fit to carry it was to do so. He might also need a weapon. If he'd seen what he thought, he had best be prepared for what must follow. If he was mistaken—well, what further harm could his friends' opinions as to his sanity possibly do him?

Tristan's fingers felt like so much wood a-dangle at the ends of his arms, and his sight was so drug-blurred that watching what he was doing was futile, but he managed the task of fastening the sword belt all on his own. He looked up from its completion to see Polassar grinning with approval, then accepted the man's hand in getting onto his still-wobbly feet.

As a first step back, it was something more like a limp. Practically, it was less even than a gesture, but it seemed to have some small value as a symbol. That night, Tristan refused the tea Elisena offered him. He got a measuring look, but no argument.

He slept badly, suffering tedious dreams which were only scrambled versions of the day just past, tiring him more than the reality that had spawned them. Tristan hardly knew what to make of a clear head the next morning, or of climbing when he wasn't as good as asleep. The mountainsides seemed sheerer. The days and the nights both stretched unbearably. The air was colder, or perhaps drier—he had nosebleeds often. But Thomas was better, and Tristan was glad to be alert enough to appreciate that.

The cat batted away the bit of sweet Tristan had been plying him with, his claws out enough to prick any fingers they caught.

Enough. Cats can't even taste sweet things, so you're wasting it on me. There are limits to the amount of cosseting even I can absorb. Can't you cheer up? Misery's really not all that fond of company, you know.

Storm Warnings

IT WAS GOOD TO HAVE THOMAS BACK; BUT IN SPITE of the comfort that brought, Tristan's mood stayed mostly leaden. Thomas, sated with food, slept. Tristan sat staring into the fire, though the flames had no pictures to show him. His fingers moved slowly in the cat's fur.

Elisena came to sit beside him, but the moment was awkward, too strained for reconciliation. Any sympathy she offered only added to Tristan's distress. And he suspected that she was only putting off sleeping until she saw him safely bedded down. He resented the continuing lack of trust which that hinted at. It was worse than Polassar's heavy-handed pretense that nothing had changed between them. Tristan thought he preferred Reynaud's careful maintenance of aloofness to either of the other solutions. It certainly seemed to him a more natural reaction.

Tristan had thrown a wall up somewhere just behind his eyes, Elisena thought; if she spoke to him, he'd answer, conversing naturally enough, if warily. And then, after a moment, he'd retreat back behind his barrier. He seemed grateful for kind words and small considerations, but he was never expectant or trusting of them. To see him still so cut Elisena to the heart. It was a pain she was helpless against, despite all her care to avoid it.

The days went on, days of cold and climbing—always climbing. Tristan was watched less overtly, though not less carefully nor less frequently. There was nothing for him to do but accept that quietly as a consequence of his own folly. Tristan thought sometimes that he would almost rather have broken his other leg than everyone's trust.

Mostly he tried to keep his mind as numb as the cold kept his feet.

His eyes were bothering him again, too, though now the heavily overcast sun couldn't be blamed. The wind carried confusing eddies of snow, flinging the stuff in his face; after a day of peering through the mess, Tristan's eyes often burned with weariness, and his lids itched. It was a nuisance no one else remarked on, so he said nothing and dosed himself with hawkweed unobtrusively.

The food drops were becoming more substantial. Now they always received slightly more than they needed to eat in a day. Mostly the surplus was dried stuff which was light to carry and would keep well. Ambere was probably preparing for the possibility of his birds being storm-grounded and unable to reach them for several days. Even though the dried food weighed as little as food might, their packs grew heavier; in the thin air the loads were hard work to carry. How matters would stand once they were even deeper into Channadran, no one liked to forecast.

They were plainly nearing the limit to which the birds were able to penetrate. Some days their guides did not land at all, but dropped their sacks as they swooped over, and there might be a perilous climb to be made before the rations were secured. Tristan searched the vista ahead constantly, wondering how the company would choose their direction when they no longer had their guides. It would not be by listening to *him*, he felt sure.

The days were marginally longer as they went higher since there were fewer peaks left above them to block the sun. All the same, those shadows that touched them seemed to settle in Tristan's bones. He felt as if he'd been cold his entire life; he was too used to it by then to shiver at less than the worst gusts of icy wind.

Food was dropped at sun-high, allowing the birds full time to return to Am Islin by dark. Normally, those with supplies landed near Elisena, if they landed at all, whatever the order of march might be at the time of their arrival. The eagles were apparently wary of Polassar's clumsiness, and wary of Reynaud altogether. Tristan thought he could guess why, but did not dwell on his suspicions. This day, however, one of the eagles back-winged to land in the snow at his own feet.

It carried no bag of provisions in its talons, but bore a small sack on a short thong about its neck, the sort of bag a token or message might be carried in. Tristan looked from the bag to the eagle and back again. They'd had no direct word from Ambere through all their journeying. His birds directed them and gave them food, but no more than that. If Ambere had chosen to communicate with them more closely, Tristan was hardly sure that he should be the one to receive the message. He scuffed his feet in the snow uncertainly, not wanting to make a mistake.

The eagle opened its beak and made a small noise, as melodious as the creak of a gate hinge, obviously directed at him. There was no mistake, then. The bird had come to him.

Tristan still hesitated. The cords that held the bag were knotted very short; plainly the bird could not loose itself from its burden. Did it expect him to do the task, then? Would it permit his touch? Tristan looked at the heavy, curving beak and the hot yellow eye above it, trying to be sure he truly understood. The eagle repeated the odd sound.

Tristan stepped forward, still cautiously, but the bird held very still while he unpicked the knot. It did not even take to the air at once when he had the bag safe in his hands. It did back off a good pace, though, looking relieved to have the contact over with.

The bag in his hands was light, so light that Tristan wondered if it were empty. It was no load at all for one of Ambere's eagles—why had the bird carried just this and nothing more? A message could have been added easily to a larger load, or rolled into a hollow quill and tied to the eagle's leg.

The bag's top was laced tightly. Tristan undid the fastenings, his fingers clumsy from being long inside mittens. The top popped open. A familiar chirp greeted him.

While Tristan stared, Minstrel wriggled out of the bag, perched upon his wrist and vigorously preened his somewhat matted white feathers, running his beak hard along the flights, stabbing and picking at the softer fluff upon his breast, reaching over his shoulder to attend to his back.

"Minstrel? But how did you—" Something white still stuck up out of the bag's top—a scrap of thinnest parch-

ment with a few words hastily scribbled upon it, blotted as if the writer had not allowed them to dry before tucking the missive into the bag.

"I will not be party to any living creature's misery," Tristan read, almost in a whisper. "Cherish this one well, for he loves you better than you can deserve or know."

Minstrel cockily chirped agreement with that. Squeaking with delight, he spied a spot where Tristan's sleeve had ridden up to leave a gap between it and the mitten and began to nibble the skin bared there. Tristan didn't mind the pricking. He watched the little bird till his eyes misted with emotion, then hastily turned his attention to the woolen bag Minstrel had arrived in. It would have to serve the bird again, he thought. Minstrel would need more than his feathers to protect him against Channadran's cold.

He was not the first to have thought of that. The bag was in fact a snug cage, crafted of dense-woven cloth, lined with warmest eider down, and ribbed with springy whalebone so that no weight could crush it. Tristan probed inside with his first finger and discovered a deep pocket in one side, full of seed, and a second on the other which held a tiny crumb of damp sponge. Minstrel looked on proudly as his traveling home was inspected, then chirped impatiently for Tristan's attention.

Tristan took his finger out of the bag and began stroking Minstrel's grayish-blue head feathers with it. "I can't believe you did this. You were *safe*, simpleton."

Minstrel raised and then settled his wings, a gesture as eloquent as a shoulder shrug. Tristan wiped his eyes again and hung the bag carefully about his neck. Minstrel hopped onto Tristan's shoulder, then inside the raised hood, where he'd be warmer, and began to sing.

In a way, that bright song was a greater victory than any they'd dreamed of winning when they set out. No bird had sung in Channadran within generations of memories. Snow cascaded down the sides of a distant peak, in helpless fury at the challenge. Minstrel but sang the louder and then bit at Tristan's ear.

Minstrel's return put heart into each of them, though Polassar strove not to show any pleasure in the bird's songs. Perhaps his distaste was genuine enough—Minstrel was inclined to greet the dawn rather promptly; and in the chill air, the shrill sound was impossible to escape, even with a wool bag drawn close about one's ears. Tristan knew that only too well, but wasn't about to complain of it.

They sorely needed the hope a birdsong could offer them. Snow squalls hit at least once every day; though those seldom lasted more than a few minutes, those minutes were unbearable. They huddled helplessly among the rocks wherever they'd been caught, breathing snow that the air was thick with and torn by winds as fierce as a wolf pack. Ambere had warned them that wind would increase with elevation and he was not proved false. The snow was far from the worst feature of the storms thrown at them. The cold shrieking among the rocks was worse; that turned drops of sleet to daggers of silver.

They tied strips of cloth across noses and mouths to keep out air so cold it seemed to freeze their lungs. But breath froze almost at once upon the cloth, producing a coating of ice that made breathing hard in the thin air. Tristan's mouth seemed to be continually open as he gasped for the little ice let through. His teeth ached, and the ice seemed to intensify the cold. There was no escape from the misery and no dispensing with the cloth, either.

Cruelest of all, the constant wind set Tristan's ears aching until he wept unashamedly at a pain which was bad enough at times to send him staggering. He wanted nothing more than to lie still and wait for the agony to ebb, but that hope was false, a delusion that could kill him if he gave in to it. Tristan kept walking, if not always with great energy. He pulled wool out of the lining of his boots and stuffed it into his ears. It helped keep the cold out. At night, he dosed himself strongly with camomile tea; by the time he woke, warmth had vanquished the pain, at least till later in the day.

Wool stuffed into his ears could muffle cold and some sounds, but it blocked neither completely enough. There were voices in the wind like those of the Winterwaste. Sometimes at night there were also lights to be seen among the rocks, and tumbled stone and snow feigned to be castles, impossible outposts of safety. Like the lost voices crying for help, they were traps, but cunning enough to tempt even the supremely wary. Tristan supposed that would be because lights, warmth, and fellow humans were

exactly what he and his companions longed most desperately to find. That longing granted the cold mirages
their terrible power. It was too easy to believe in them.
Cold-numbed wits left hearts free to see what they chose
to. Even Reynaud seemed nearly taken in, as he gazed
with longing at the distant lights.

It was possible to fight the visions off, but never easy.
The effort produced a mental exhaustion that mated too
well with bodily weariness. Tristan learned to keep his
eyes away from the vast reaches the magewood fire did
not illuminate. If he woke in the night, he did not sit up
to look about, nor did he watch the stars.

The voices he closed out by silently rehearsing every
song and ballad he could recall. It helped pass the lonely
hours, but the technique's success was marginal otherwise, and Tristan thought it might be a while before he
could appreciate a bard again.

Idiot. As if you'll ever get the chance. Thomas, calm
by some effort of will beyond human reach, purred loudly
near Tristan's ear. The warm sound smothered what the
doleful ballads had not, and Tristan gratefully slept. He
did not stir again till the clatter of camp being broken
disturbed him and sent him yawning and shivering into
yet another day.

Their trail had grown confused in the rough weather,
difficult to find and harder to keep to through all the fresh
snow. The birds could not stay with them for more than
a few moments each day. Sometimes, unguided, they went
very wrong and needed to retrace considerable distances
the next day when the error was detected. The ropes iced
up, and one broke, though fortunately while Polassar was
testing it before a climb, when it harmed only their nerves.
Double-roping was bulky and slow, but quickly became
an accepted necessity.

Reynaud spliced the wrecked rope in the evening and
made a close inspection of all the others, saying spells
over doubtful spots. Polassar looked as if he'd trust the
splicing a lot farther than he'd trust the magic, but he
didn't refuse the service. Keeping company with wizards
was working a change on the man, albeit a shallow one.

All the gear needed attention, as the constant cold
weakened it. Tristan had needed to repair his scabbard

twice, for the thread he'd used didn't keep the rent in it closed long with the blade bumping against it as he walked. He must, he thought, have caught the thing on sharp ice while he was trying to get out of the snowslide, and the memory of the leather ripping had been transmuted by the mandrake dream. Even a very extraordinary blade couldn't cut its way out of its own undamaged sheath, however battle-eager such a blade might seem when drawn. What a fancy he'd had!

He was glad it was night again. The firelight was kinder to his eyes than daylight, or else he simply didn't have to look so far to see the things he needed to do. By day's end Tristan had found his eyes to be very tired, playing him tricks, and the matter was starting to worry him. It was not the first day he'd been so troubled. No one else had complained about a return of the snow blindness, and indeed the sun seldom shone. Yet just that afternoon he'd tripped and nearly fallen while trying to step over a ridge of ice that hadn't been there at all; it wasn't the first time that had happened, either. Unless the problem got worse, it was only an annoyance, but he'd have dosed himself with hawkweed again, if he could have done so without inviting unanswerable questions.

Tristan said a spell to sharpen his bone needle so that it might easily pierce the scabbard's leather and began to make small, neat stitches. His eyes were tired, but there was no blurring of his sight to hinder him. Maybe it was only the thin air that bothered him, then, or the nagging earaches. Either might also render him clumsier than usual. His eyes might be fine.

Tristan tested that comforting theory continually on the next day's march, sometimes convinced and sometimes unhappily not. He discovered he could see Ambere's birds with perfect clarity and could even distinguish the she-eagle from her mate, though the differences in the feather markings were subtle. He could see the rocky slopes all around him clearly, even in sunlight. Perhaps he'd imagined the whole problem, then. It would be no great wonder, concerned as he still was with appearing as normal to the others as possible, knowing they still watched him. It was a strain. He'd become extremely sensitive to detail and painfully self-conscious. He ought to be drinking tea of valerian and clover for his nerves.

That settled to his satisfaction, Tristan's mood lightened appreciably. He moved along at a good pace for the rest of the march, listening to Minstrel, talking cheerfully to Thomas. His occasional glances into the distance and his continual checks of his vision were mere habit—he was barely seeing the things he looked at and was critical no longer of the quality of his sight.

Then, at midafternoon, it hit him again. There was no warning.

The air was as still as it ever was. In the cold, their own forward movement produced what felt like a breeze. Beyond that, however, Tristan could *see* a wind moving toward them. He took the sight for a swirl of cloud at first, but he'd never seen one move so swiftly. That speed was deceptive. The wind coiled lazily, light as the faint feathers of a drop of ink sinking into a bucket of water and dispersing as it went. The movement became so faint that Tristan thought he'd blinked it away, a momentary aberration.

He hadn't. It was back, closer. Tristan rubbed his eyes then, despairing, disappointed.

The wind was still there. Closer. It had moved a lot nearer while his eyes had been closed. Now it was less dispersed, more purposeful-looking. It looked as if it were some sort of vapory snake, coiling to strike. That was absurd, and Tristan tried with all his might to will the hallucination away. Maybe if he refused to see it, react to it—

The wind came closer with a rush, striking. It took all Tristan's strength to resolve not to hurl himself flat on his face to get out of its path. Then he saw that its aim was too high, over all their heads, and he took his hands away from his ears, hoping no one had seen his reaction and relieved that he hadn't given in further. Still the movement drew his eyes. He looked up. He could do that without arousing suspicion.

The rock above was festooned with icicles like fangs. The sun must shine sometimes, then, long enough to raise the temperature appreciably, or such shapes of ice would never form. The strange wind whistled among them. Its sound began the precise instant that Tristan thought he saw its first tendrils move among the icicles. The timing was unmistakable. As he still watched, one long finger of air curled about the longest icicle.

Tristan stood still, disbelieving. The icicle was already dropping, falling faster than it should have done by itself, as if it had been *hurled*—before Tristan had done more than widen his eyes. Like a sword of ice, the icicle drove toward Reynaud's unsuspecting back, just yards in front of Tristan.

It seemed to Tristan that the blade fell faster than he could hope to react. He thought the snow had melted and refrozen about his boots to hold him in his place, so slowly did they answer to him. Any sound that came from his dry throat was muffled by the cloth over his mouth. He couldn't give a warning, and he seemed to move impossibly slowly, almost imperceptibly, while the ice crashed silently down.

He knew he could never hope to be in time, but Tristan threw himself forward. His boots slipped in the snow, treacherously robbing him of most of his forward motion, and his shoulder hit Reynaud across the backs of his knees instead of the higher spot Tristan had been aiming for. Thomas yowled with surprise. Reynaud toppled sideways without time even for a curse, and the icicle thudded against the rock and snow barely an inch from his face. The great blow was misstruck, but not by much.

Tristan pushed himself up and felt Reynaud's feet slip forward as the man sat up in the snow, away from him. He didn't know whether to expect an angry question or a blow and wasn't prepared to fend off either. He was shaking with reaction, and his knees were too weak to let him try to stand, but at least he hadn't quite managed to knock the wind out of himself. That was an improvement, surely.

He finally risked a look at Reynaud, when no word seemed to be forthcoming, just as Polassar wheeled around and started back toward them. Reynaud's eyes were wide, and there was blood on the man's left cheekbone—the slashing ice had fallen that close. That shock, more than the fall itself, was probably what kept him silent.

Reynauud's fingers reached out and brushed a fragment of ice lying atop the snow. It was thicker than his arm. He glanced up, his eyes traveling slowly to the high spot the ice had fallen from. The gap was plain. Reynaud shivered.

"One more thoughtful guest-gift," he remarked, much steadier than he looked. "My thanks."

Thomas jumped out of the pack, fur and temper both badly rumpled. He stalked through the snow, till he was close enough to give Tristan's chin a hard swat with a paw that shook with reaction. *I thought we'd agreed that you wouldn't do this sort of thing anymore. I should have known a nap wouldn't be safe.*

Minstrel poked his head out of his nest and began shrilly scolding the cat.

Tristan shook his head. He was still trying to understand what he'd seen—and was still failing. In any case, they'd have to deal with this new danger. How best might they protect themselves? He got to his feet and began to brush the snow out of his clothes. It occurred to him that if he opened his mouth about what he'd seen, he'd be offering just one more proof of his mental instability. Tristan wasn't sure he could afford that.

It had been a trick of the light, surely. That, and coincidence that the ice fell. Maybe he'd *heard* the ice let go, without realizing it. Tristan could feel the beginning of a headache, which he tried to will away without the slightest success.

Meanwhile, he heard himself making some sort of explanation to Elisena and Polassar, a lie relating how he'd seen the ice starting to fall through pure chance. The words were automatic, touching him not at all. Underneath, Tristan's mind was otherwise busy. There followed a lot of conversation, in which he apparently took a sensible part, but Tristan couldn't remember any of it five minutes later.

It wasn't possible that he could have seen what he thought he'd seen. There had been no dust in the air, and what he'd seen was dark, not white as wind-carried snow would have been. The only thing he could possibly have seen was the wind itself—and that was impossible. It *had* to be a hallucination. Tristan kept staring nervously around as they climbed onward, ready to see another gust of wind and expecting worse sights. He was relieved when night fell.

As if it happened fresh to him that instant, Tristan

remembered the ice-lizard, cut in two by his sword. Tristan's supper cooled in front of him. He felt again the shock of the lizard's blood spattering across his face, even as his body seemed to go cold all over. Ice-lizard's blood was said to be poison, and there were other legends about it listed in the grimoire. He'd read them, along with much else. The things weren't common where sane folk—even wizards—could expect to encounter them. It was said, though, that a drop of the blood on the tongue could make a man able to understand the speech of animals and birds— someone not already a wizard, that must be.

That was swallowed blood. What might it do, then, in a man's eyes? Tristan knew he had wiped the stuff away at once, else it might have burned or blinded him. Still, a single drop might have got in. Could such an accident cause a man to see the otherwise invisible—the wind?

That assumed the ice-lizard to have been real. Imagined blood from a nonexistent lizard would have done nothing to him.

Your mind's going like a butter-churn tonight. What's the matter?

"What makes you think anything is, Thomas?"

Oh, there's plenty wrong. We're here, for one thing, instead of on decent, level ground somewhere warm. And I don't need to be able to read minds to see something's bothering you. You've taken that grimoire out and then put it away at least a dozen times tonight.

"I'm sorry." Tristan put Minstrel to bed in his furry cage, then put the book away one last time, lacing the pack shut after it. "There. Happy?"

Oh, simply ecstatic. I wish you could say the same. Then maybe you'd show some sense and go to sleep, instead of staring at the fire all night. No wonder your eyes hurt you.

Tristan started. He hadn't thought Thomas knew anything about that. Certainly he hadn't complained of it to the cat. He'd been careful not to.

It's pretty obvious, Thomas said complacently. *And catnip is very good for restlessness. I might spare you enough for a cup of tea.*

Tristan didn't expect that the single herb would help all that much, but surprisingly it did, and he slept for the rest of the night. It was well he finally got some rest, for the next day was worse than the previous one. It saw what would surely be their last food drop. The skittish eagles never even landed, but dropped their bundles into a not very handy snowbank and departed. Minstrel sang a farewell after them with more than a touch of pride, but a few moments later he crept back into his pouch to warm himself and there he stayed for the rest of the day.

Tristan still saw movement where there was nothing capable of it. He ignored the impossible sights resolutely, if nervously. The trouble would pass, surely. He clung to that thin hope rather desperately.

Therefore, when the sudden fluttering came at the edges of his vision, just at sun-fall while they were making camp, he was amazed to see Reynaud turning toward the sight and to hear him exclaim at it. It took Tristan a stunned moment to realize that there actually must be something there.

The something was a bird, Tristan discovered—a crow, its normally glossy black feathers reduced to bare tatters. It was a wonder the creature had ever reached them—it could hardly have flown a further hundred feet. Now it was grounded and could not even stand, but flopped in the snow, its torn wings flapping in a futile attempt to support it.

The crow's beak opened, and it made a croaking sound. The end of its tongue was slit so as to make a fork there—that was done to help a bird shape human speech, Tristan knew. He put his hands out to the crow, though he doubted there was much he could do for it. It was either injured or tired almost to death; in either case it looked past recovery. Its dark eyes closed, shutting out the world as mortally sick birds did just before the last of their strength failed them.

Elisena, beside him, was reaching into a bag of herbs. Tristan wondered what good she could hope to do, unless she thought to ease the wretched creature painlessly on its way. No bird would show sickness until it was literally dying. This one was past even Elisena's healing.

His fingers touched the maimed feathers and felt the heart beating raggedly beneath them. Or was that only the wings again, struggling against his touch? The crow's eyes and beak opened. This time, it managed speech.

"Beware," the bird croaked, then died.

A HeRo's Duty

AMBERE'S MESSENGER HADN'T LIVED TO SAY PRE-
cisely of what they were to beware, but they had possi-
bilities enough to worry over. The four debated long over
which way to proceed and settled on a direction, choosing
it finally because that way looked the most hostile. Guide-
less, it was the best they could do, but no one was easy
about the necessary choice. A promise and a price, Elisena had said so long before. The prices in Channadran
were too high, Tristan thought bleakly.

Fog or clouds lay in the deep valley they had just
climbed up out of, and the peaks around them were separate as islands in a misty sea. Tristan stood beside Polassar, trying to map out their day's journey while they had
a good vantage point, drawing comfort from the sheer
solidity of the man in the face of so many uncertainties.
Polassar might be somewhat lacking in imagination, but
that left him with fewer worries to torment him. Tristan
envied Polassar that.

"We'll take yon ridge of snow, I think. I vow 'twill be
better footing than the rock there." Polassar pointed, so
that his direction was clear.

Tristan nodded. The rock thereabouts was all scree
slope, slithering about alarmingly underfoot. The snow
ridge actually offered a safer path, though hitherto they
had clung to bare rock whenever possible.

Polassar took no offense at Tristan's rather abstracted
agreement. Indeed, the man seemed to match his mood.

"See aught you could put a name to, Wizard?"

Tristan had been looking long and hard, but the answer

didn't come easy. "Nothing I can name, no—" There was no wind, at that moment.

"Yet there's something. As that ill-omened bird told us?" Maybe Polassar wasn't so lacking in imagination after all. "You feel it no less than I do, Wizard. A doom's on us. It makes itself known now, 'tis all."

Tristan shook his head at him. Maybe the man was right, but what did it help, dragging fears into words? "Polassar—"

"Nay, 'tis true. We've gone unscathed too long, Wizard. We've used our luck to the last crumb. This isn't luck holding, now—'tis but an enemy waiting till he's certain-sure of us, till we're right betwixt his hands, till the crushing will be cruelest."

Allaire's name was not upon Polassar's lips, but her image stood in his eyes, as well as his heart. Polassar had a lot to lose, too. Tristan put a hand on his friend's arm. He should, if he'd been thinking in friendship at all, have ordered the man to stay home, glad as he'd been when Polassar had insisted on coming. Crogen seemed so long ago.

That sorrow must have shown on his face—or something did.

"I'd not trade this place with any, Wizard. It's my due, and no other's." Polassar chewed his moustaches a while, a sign of thought unaccustomedly deep, for a man who preferred action by nature. "Nay, 'tis no duty. Lassair has stood alone and could do so again, at need. Nor is it a boast of friendship, though there's that between us. Neither of those should be enough to bring a man here—but how else can I keep this foul thing from coming at my lady again? I'd have her able to sleep at night, Wizard, and not taking fright at every chilly breeze and thinking she hides it from me behind her smiles."

Tristan wished he had some comfort to offer, but his tongue clove to his mouth when confronted with the lies his brain proposed. He thought of Crogen so far away—thought of it safe and warm and at peace, as if by thought he could make it so, though he knew no wizard born or made could wield the power to work so much by thought alone. Calandra was home, and it must be still and ever the same as when they'd left it. To think otherwise was madness, and there were plenty of other thoughts fit to send them mad.

They'd return home, someday. They each kept up that fiction, even—in a burst of wild optimism—partaking of exceptionally frugal meals to save food for their journey back, until they could reach Ambere's birds once more. That was not as difficult as might have been expected. Whatever allure dried fish and venison had once possessed had long since faded away, and the small squares of journeybread were dry, no matter what manner of tea they were washed down with. Reynaud magicked his portions into the semblance of puff pastries, saying that what fooled his eye could fool his belly as well; but Tristan had no use for such empty artifice, and apparently Reynaud found little either, for he soon stopped the practice.

They kept a sharp eye out for icicles when they were near cliffs and for thin lips of snow when they walked the ridges. They learned to cross faces of cliffs by cutting steps and following precisely in each other's footsteps, grateful that they'd been schooled in the use of ropes on lower, easier slopes.

They were vigilant for ice and stressed rock which might not bear their weight, or for exposed slopes where sudden wind gusts might sweep a man into a very deep grave. They never thought, even Tristan, that they might not be alone in Channadran.

Having just ascended a precipitous slope, they were resting, a luxury become necessity in the thin air. The ledge was wide and it sheltered them from the wind, so they began setting down their packs to sit in comfort for once. Tristan was only half-free of his when the first of the four armed men popped up among the rocks. The pack kept him from leaping to his feet as quickly as he tried to—in fact he nearly tumbled over. Minstrel fluttered wildly, caught away from the safety of Tristan's hood and unable to regain it.

There was surprise enough just in seeing strangers, but Tristan's eye took in the weapons, too—swords for three of them and a battle axe for the fourth. He gained his feet at last, grabbing for his own weapon.

Polassar had reacted even more swiftly, as if he'd been prepared all day for the moment—or all of his life. He didn't bother with his sword, but swung his ice axe handily. He missed his stroke, but the man had to jump back, and tangled with the man next to him in doing so. Unhappily, neither fell.

Four to three would be terrible odds. Tristan tore his sword out of the scabbard and jumped to get in front of Elisena before any of the men could close in on her. He tripped over his own pack and went down on his face—luckily, as it chanced, for steel whistled close over his head as he sprawled. The axe, he thought. Tristan struck out with his blade as he got to his knees, a necessarily shortened stroke, but he hit something, anyway. Somebody tugged at his belt—he realized that Elisena was drawing his dagger, to second her own.

He recognized her purpose in an instant, as a blinding flame came from over his shoulder. His knife was brass, and Elisena could work a magic with it as she could not have done with a steel sword. One man was unlucky enough to be blinded by the flash and never saw Reynaud's thin rapier leaping forward to transfix him. That left three.

The fight was a mess, worse than when they'd met the knights of Westif. Tristan was unhappy to discover that he'd been singled out by the axeman. He ducked under a slash so close that it trimmed a tuft of fur from the edge of his hood. Backing hastily, he bumped against Elisena.

Thomas ran under his feet, nearly tripping him, but Tristan hadn't time for a curse before he understood the cat's strategy. A banshee wail in a man's ear could prove a useful distraction. It bought Tristan's sword a fleeting opening, and he was fast enough with his attack to take proper advantage of it.

He had to be. Even dying, with Calandra's sword hilt-deep in him, the man might still manage one last stroke with that axe. Tristan went in low, hitting as hard as he could. His momentum was sufficient to throw the other man off his balance, even though the blade somehow slipped in without touching spine or ribs, meeting no resistance Tristan could push against. The axe flew wide, and Tristan sprawled atop its former wielder.

He picked himself up in time to see Reynaud, feigning a fall, attempt to dispatch his second opponent from one knee. His sword thrust missed, but that didn't matter and might even have been part of Reynaud's ruse. Reynaud's left hand was already on his dagger; with a touch and a word he sent it winging into his adversary's heart as if into its own sheath. No help was needed there, then.

Polassar had lost his ice axe, its shaft chopped in two. He hurled the splintered bits contemptuously in his foe's face and reached back over his head. Grabbing the hilt of the longsword, Polassar drew it and started his stroke in one movement. The mighty blow clove through the white-clad swordsman as if through heavy cream.

The man fell, and the sword's point hit rock a pace in front of Polassar's wide-planted feet, jarring his arms. Something worse jarred his senses. The warrior in white vanished, though a suspiciously large bank of snow lay to each side of Polassar's blade. Brown bones poked up out of it, and the hilt of a sword, gilded and jeweled. Polassar stared and made his favorite hand-sign against evil.

"Wizard? What are they, then?"

Minstrel gave a questioning chirp, almost like an echo, as he settled on Tristan's shoulder.

Tristan turned to examine the man Reynaud had killed. He was just noticing that a thrust through the heart hadn't produced nearly the outflow of blood that was to be expected, when the body began to dissolve under his fingers. He jumped back with a yelp of surprise. In seconds nothing remained of the body but a few ragged tatters of cloth and a heap of moldering bones. Even the man's sword had fallen away to rust.

"Nímir reanimates the dead," Reynaud said colorlessly.

Tristan backed away another step, fighting sickness, thankful he hadn't eaten since dawn. He shouldn't have gotten so *close*. Thomas, a more reasonable distance off, agreed with him. Even the battle-hardened Polassar was looking pale. Reynaud only moved in for a better look, seeming not the least upset. He called Elisena closer for consultation, looking sober and sincere, as if he were lecturing in Kôvelir, not fresh from killing two men whose bodies behaved so arcanely. Tristan took the moment to catch his breath and realize that, against all odds, they were none of them so much as scratched. He was suddenly terribly glad of that. The slightest cut from one of those polluted weapons—he didn't like to think about it.

"These aren't like the others, the ones in Westif," Reynaud said. "I think these were dead to begin with—and obviously for a very long time." He prodded at the rags with the tip of his sword, lifting them for inspection by any who cared to look. Tristan turned his eyes away. The small cowardice was less embarrassing than being ill.

"They won't quicken again?" Polassar asked anxiously.

Reynaud answered seriously, with no hint of mockery, that he thought not. "There are limits to all power, however great. There's not enough left of this poor clay to use again, even for the Cold One. It will have been difficult for Nímir to collect these—not many folk come here, and he would use the best weapons available to him, this close. If these are a true indication of what the best was, we needn't fear that particular trick again." Reynaud let the rags fall back in a gesture almost like the closing of a dead man's eyes. "I wonder what far-famed hero this may once have been?"

One of the men had worn a ring of heavy gold on one hand. It still lay among his scattered fingerbones, the ruby it was set with bright as a drop of new blood. Tristan could see, among the rags and tatters of his clothes, shiny threads which must once have been most costly embroideries. He thought of wizards and princes disappearing into Darkenkeep and wondered. Reynaud could well be right.

Not all of the corpses were bare, picked bones. The fourth one was nearly as fresh as if the man had been truly living but moments before—only the smashed-in hole in his skull showed that he could not have been. Cold had preserved him, Tristan thought, recalling the frozen rabbits the eagles sometimes brought and also the man frozen into the very walls of Darkenkeep. This warrior must have died falling into a crevasse in the glacier, down deep where sun and wind hadn't reached him. The ice had kept him safe, though quite dead. His clothing, also well preserved, was antique, the runes chased along his sword older than any Tristan had ever read. He might have been in the ice a *very* long while.

Tristan felt eyes on him and thought them Thomas', the cat having crept closer as his curiosity overcame his distaste. Tristan looked up, ready with a jibe. Sanity demanded a swift lightening of mood.

His heart had scarcely blood enough to pump. It all spilled away into his boots, in a cold rush.

Not three yards away, come out from among the tumbled rocks that had hidden him from all their sights, a fifth man crouched over a gleaming sword. His face was thinner than Tristan remembered it, creased and burned by sun and wind, lined with pain and cold, and bearded, too. There was no mistaking him, though, however he'd been changed or transformed. The same recognition that was in Tristan's astonished expression could be read plain in Galan's one remaining eye, narrowed against the sun as it was.

They seemed to hang in time, suspended by their locked gazes. Tristan could feel his own heart beating raggedly— it was the only movement between them. Nímir had not after all lost his best tool, and the Winter King could have chosen no better weapon to scale Channadran's heights and collect the hideous band of once-men while waiting with nearly infinite patience for his drink from the cup of revenge.

There were shouts, not so distant as they sounded to Tristan. Galan had been spotted by someone else. But Polassar and Reynaud were both too far away—only a moment's run, but a moment Tristan correctly guessed he did not have. Galan lifted a lip in a sneer, showing teeth as white as any hunting-cat's.

"This is going to be a great pleasure," he said conversationally. "I was promised many such when I took service, but I had not expected they would commence so soon or taste so sweet." His blade shifted restively in his fingers.

That betrayed him. Galan struck before his lips were done shaping the words, but Tristan was warned, at least peripherally, by the finger movement. He leaped back and to his right. The jabbing blade, its aim spoiled, only grazed his left cheek. In the cold, Tristan didn't feel the cut, just the warmth of the blood running. Continuing his reflexive move, he backed another long step, only to come jarringly against rock. He'd gone the wrong way, though it had seemed the only direction open to him, and trapped himself against the cliff side. Tristan cursed himself grimly. At least he'd bought time to get his blade up.

Galan's sword licked out like the hungry, questing flame

of a funeral pyre. Tristan kept his own blade still, waiting. It took more nerve than he'd ever thought he had, for all that he knew it was the right tactic. If he moved after Galan's blade, he'd be too easily deceived. His world narrowed sharply to the stark simplicity of a fencing match. Where Polassar and Reynaud were, what they were doing or trying to do, Tristan neither knew nor cared. Just staying alive, moment to moment, occupied his whole attention and it must continue to do so.

The ice beneath his boots was slick, often melted and wind-polished. He must be careful how he moved and he dared not lunge. Tristan's mind registered those statistics dutifully. His retreat was limited to inches and could not be considered. Flat against the rock, he'd not even be able to draw his arm back without risk of knocking the blade from his own hand. That was still another factor carefully added to his calculations.

Tristan remembered how Blais had once set him with his back to a wall for his fencing lesson—so that he'd learn to defend himself without depending on retreat—and then attacked him for a solid quarter-hour. It had been a good lesson—attack was far easier than defense, and recklessness was an asset to it. You had to be faster and surer to defend successfully. Galan's blade slid in again, testing. Tristan let his blade meet it that time and pretended to try a bind which he knew he hadn't room to execute, so Galan would have to back up to get away. The contest began in a weaving of steel.

Three times the blades met, and Tristan gained a single step with each meeting. Having won that much ground, he could move more safely and did, riposting at every opening that looked reasonable to him. Imperceptibly, the battle shifted. He was no longer constrained to pure defense. He could and did consider plans beyond meeting Galan's next stroke with a sufficient parry.

Tristan attacked toward Galan's blind side—constantly and forcibly. Each attack was beaten off. Tristan expected that. It was part of his plan. Galan dared not let anything from that side pass in the hope that it was but a feint. He must treat those attacks seriously and so must see them, which was awkward for him, since he'd lost the eye opposite his sword-hand. Always he turned his head slightly as he made the parry.

Tristan expected that movement and relied upon it, but he did nothing to exploit or deceive the action yet. Let Galan think him cleverly stupid, continually attacking what ought to be a soft spot long after Galan had proved it wasn't. Then, when Tristan finally *did* feint that way, disengaging to come in the other way . . .

He dared not try the trick too soon. Galan had to be half expecting such a tactic. Tristan forced himself to hold off a little while longer, varying his attacks slightly so as to lull even the strongest suspicions. He must make it look as if the variations were the deceptions, and the blind-sides the true attacks.

The air was too thin to play the game as long as he felt he needed to. Tristan's breath sobbed through his raw throat as he endlessly thrust and parried, not quite loudly enough to mask Galan's beginning laughter. He kept hammering away at the closed line, long after the most persistent fool would have given it up, wondering now what would happen if he *did* get through when he wasn't expecting to, cautioning himself to be wary of Galan's ripostes, which were quick and true. Tristan was almost always in reach of them, pressing his attacks as he was, and only vigilance would protect him.

Now, surely! His wobbling legs wouldn't let him delay any longer. Tristan feinted hard to Galan's left—then, dipping his point under the offered parry, lunged in real earnest.

His point was a finger's width from Galan's chest when Tristan's right boot slipped. He might still have struck home from sheer momentum, but just then Galan realized that this time his parry would not find the other blade. He swiftly reversed his stroke, slamming his fist and the sword's heavy pommel into the side of Tristan's head. The blow shoved Tristan farther off balance than he already was, and he slid right past Galan because he could do nothing else. The fall put him in the clear, but only if he could get back to his feet before Galan caught up to him. Tristan rolled over and heaved himself up, just in time to be knocked flat again as Polassar vaulted past him.

The shove, meant to put him out of harm's way, jarred the last of his breath out of him, and Tristan had his fingers bruised again when they got trapped between the ice and the sword hilt he refused to let go of. He was sorely tempted to stay down, as he fought dazedly for air.

Indeed, he wasn't up long. Tristan regained his feet once more and lunged after Polassar, only to run smack into the wall of solid air that Elisena was trying to interpose between the combatants. It was invisible, of course, and totally unexpected. Tristan rebounded off of it and sat down hard, his sight blurring and drawing in at the edges. It was a moment before the grunts and cries roused him, and he moved again to lend what help he could.

Elisena made a frustrated noise and gave up trying to get the spell in front of Galan, letting it drop before Tristan could tangle with it again. With so much steel waving about, magic was too dangerous a tool. Her rings were hot, blazing from fruitless efforts.

Polassar had reached Galan. There was no fancy swordsmanship now, but a brief and brutal scrimmage beyond anything Tristan would have had strength for. Polassar's first headlong rush bore Galan back, and then they strove together almost like wrestlers, blade pressed to blade as they matched their strengths. They were too close for even shortened blows with swords. Galan drew his dagger as he leaped back to break the press.

Polassar's sword whirled down to strike the blade from Galan's hand. The dagger buried itself somewhere in the snow, and Galan ignored his bloodily flopping hand. His sword strokes were no weaker for the pain of his injury, and he seemed oblivious of it. His smile never left his white lips.

Having fought a while already, Galan should have been nearly too weary to stand. Certainly he should not have fought so freshly. He was twice wounded, too—a cut to one leg had sent him to his knees moments before. But where Nímir's other tools had fallen away to nothing in their defeat, this one yet held his life and with it the strength of his madness, a hate that would burn till his body was consumed as utterly as the others had been. When Galan was dead, he'd be dead, but while he lived he could do nothing but continue his fight.

Wild as beasts, the men strove against each other. Tristan sought vainly for some opening, some help he might give, and found none. He had no qualms about taking Galan the coward's way—from the back—but the fighters shifted too rapidly. He never had a clear stroke. He was far too apt to hamper Polassar if he got any closer than he was, and that left him too far away.

And then there wasn't time to try. The shoving match broke up again. There was a release of the blades, a rejoining of them, and then both swordsmen found themselves too close to the cliff edge. Still locked, they went over.

The drop was only about ten feet, less than half again Polassar's height. Tristan went down it nearly as heedlessly as the other two men had, only jumping instead of falling. He landed badly, sprawling forward onto knees and hands, but in one piece. Thomas, leaping with more care and foresight, landed on top of him. Tristan scrambled to his feet.

It seemed his haste wasn't needed. Polassar was dragging his sword out of Galan's body, and by the way he tugged at the thilt, his thrust must have gone deep indeed. Tristan began to smile with relief, forgetting his own battering and the new aches he'd just gotten for himself. One knee pained him when he put his weight on it, but it didn't seem to matter much.

Polassar was on his feet as well, wiping blood from his sword hand rather carelessly across the front of his padded jacket. He looked down as if only just noticing what he'd done. Tristan saw the tufts of down, some of them bloodied, drifting through the air, even as he realized that he saw too much blood for it to have come from Polassar's hand even if the hand itself had been cut instead of merely spattered with Galan's blood. He realized that and knew what it meant, but still was not fast enough to catch Polassar before the man tumbled over.

Polassar's sword, stuck point-down into the snow, stood upright a moment longer than its master did. It toppled unnoticed past Tristan as he flung himself onto his knees again beside Polassar.

Tristan called Polassar frantically by name, terrified when he got no response, his fingers plucking at the edges of the chest wound, trying to hold them closed against the outpouring blood. He saw, incredulously, what must have caused the hurt—Galan's flung-away dagger jammed point-up in the ice, its whole blade stained red. Galan had missed falling on his own knife by chance and inches. Polassar had not been so lucky.

Tristan was desperately thankful that while Ambere had not managed to convince Polassar to leave his armor behind, Polassar had finally given in to the demands of the climb and left his mailshirt behind at one of their camps. Had the man still been clad in cold iron, even the little spells of healing Tristan's fingers were now scrabbling through would have been useless.

Where were his herbs? He needed knotweed, dried plantain, and shepherd's-purse, to stop the bleeding. His spells were making no headway alone. Tristan didn't have the slightest idea where he'd left his pack, but Thomas would know. He sent the cat after the medicines, never even looking up from his futile work.

He had nothing even to press over the wound to staunch the blood that way. The cloth of his jacket was heavy and wouldn't tear. Tristan tried, swearing, but only managed to tear his own fingernails, so that a little of his blood mixed with Polassar's. It seemed an eternity since Thomas had gone.

Blood kept welling up between his fingers, despite all his efforts. Polassar's chest heaved as the man drew a deep breath, making the situation worse. There were bubbles of air in the blood—the blade must have pierced a lung. That was very bad indeed, Tristan knew.

Polassar's eyes were open, watching him. If the man was in pain, there was none of it to be seen on his face—only a sort of mild surprise. He tried to speak. The effort brought pink foam to his lips and started a cough, which was the last thing the wound needed.

"Don't try to talk," Tristan said, alarmed. "Wait for Elisena. She'll be here soon."

She was a better healer than he was, by far. Surely— Tristan remembered the drop he'd hurled himself down so blindly and felt his heart turn over in his chest. Elisena might be some while finding a way to reach Polassar, though he didn't doubt she was trying. He shouted for her and reached for the only things he had left to work with—his magic stones.

He didn't know what to try. His mind was shockingly barren of spells.

A tendril of wind brushed past Tristan's fingers, over Polassar's chest. Ice tinkled in the silence, falling down the cliff side. Only Tristan heard the black laughter behind the sound, but that one time he doubted neither his senses nor his sanity. His eyes were wide open, streaming tears. He knew what had happened, saw Nímir's ruse plainly. Polassar saw it, too, when recognition was futile. Tristan bowed his head. Feelings of uselessness and a longing to contribute something to a fellowship—he'd known them himself and seen them in Polassar. How had he not also sensed that they could be used to bait a trip?

Polassar's fingers clenched on his arm, so hard that Tristan thought they'd meet at the bone. He looked down at his friend. The man was speaking, but not above a whisper—Tristan had to watch his lips carefully, as well as listen.

"My lady—you'll know what to say to her? She's passing fond of you, 'twill come easier—"

"It's not that bad," Tristan lied, fooling not even himself. "Try to stay quiet."

Polassar paid him no heed. "It's not a bad way to go. I've seen worse ends and expected them, here. Taking yonder scum out with me ought to count for something—fair passage paid in the Underworld. I'd have thought there'd be more hurt, though. Or be that your doing, Wizard?" He looked at Tristan's still blindly magicking hands. "I'm beholden to you for that. 'Tis only cold, summat."

"Hold on. There must be *something* I can do!" Tristan had nearly had the wound closed once, but his concentration had broken before he could seal it properly. With all the blood, his fingers were slippery, and he couldn't draw the edges tight together again. Tristan's thoughts raced with spells, but they were mostly random or nonsense, and his shaking lips mangled the words of those he did try.

"When my son's born," Polassar said calmly, "and when he's old enough, you teach him how to use a sword. No magic tricks, mind. Just plain, honest bladework. I never knew you were so good at it till today." Regret crossed Polassar's face. "I took your kill from you, Wizard. I shouldn't have done that. You had him fair."

"Teach your son yourself," Tristan said with false asperity. "I don't intend to let you die and stand your place as a fencing master. Your son will probably be even bigger than you are, and I'll get bruised black before he learns any kind of control." The tears dripping down his face contrasted with the jest. Tristan hadn't known they were there until his throat started to ache and he tasted the salt in his mouth.

"Mark you," Polassar whispered, his fingers cold in Tristan's and bloodied, like the rest of him. "You're not to teach him any witcheries. Your pardon, but 'tis not a fit calling for an honest man. Do but give him my sword and stand by him, and he'll have all he needs. I'll be content."

"*Polassar*—"

The broad chest heaved once more under Tristan's hands, and then did not rise again. All Polassar's breaths had not been deep ones—plainly they hurt him more than the lack of air did. Now, the change was subtle but obvious. And no next breath came.

"*No*—" Tristan whispered, and the word that began as a protest ended as a sob. He sat back, stunned by the suddenness, the finality of it. Elisena stood beside him at last, breathless as Polassar, her bag of medicines in her hands, her help too late, and her comfort unwelcome.

Absolution

ELISENA KNELT SWIFTLY AT POLASSAR'S SIDE, IGNOR-
ing the agonized look she got from Tristan.

"What do you think you're doing?" he asked furiously.
His face was a mask of tears and blood from the forgotten
scratch on his cheek, though that bleeding had nearly
ceased. "He's *dead*. There's nothing you can do now."

"Don't be silly. No one bleeds to death that fast." Elisena had mostly recovered her breath. "He's fainted, that's
all." She began to unfasten Polassar's clothing.

"Leave him alone!" Tristan shoved her hands away.

Elisena looked at him, saw how he was shaking, and
made an effort to keep her tone gentler than her words
must be. "Tristan, I don't have time to deal with you now.
If Polassar's going to live, he needs my help and all my
attention. Go over there and wait, or I'll have Reynaud
take you."

Ordering him so hurt her worse than if she'd had to
strike him, and Elisena nearly sent Reynaud after Tristan,
anyway, though he complied wordlessly. Tristan staggered blindly toward the cliff, uncaring of his direction or
danger, but Minstrel fluttered in his face till he finally
turned, and Elisena cast him ruthlessly from her thoughts
thereafter. There was no help for it—if she could not save
Polassar, Elisena doubted that Tristan would ever trust
her again. Distractions or pity would not aid her in the
battle.

* * *

In an hour she had done all she might, little as that finally seemed, and then she could think of Tristan again. She went to him.

Reynaud had cleaned him up and doctored the cut on his face with a scrap of cobweb to staunch the blood. Tristan's eyes turned to Elisena blankly as she sat beside him. Reynaud might have drugged him with something, which would account for his dazed look. Elisena hoped not. That would be a further wounding, and Tristan was battered enough. She was mildly surprised that Reynaud had been able to get near him at all, much less treat him.

"It was as bad as you thought," she said gently, hoping that Tristan could hear. "There was a lot of damage. I've closed the wound, but Polassar lost a great deal of blood. He can't travel. We dare not move him. The strongest magics I dare use have barely kept him alive."

Tristan's expression was still nearly blank. His movements as he turned toward her were mechanical; if he rejoiced that Polassar was indeed still alive, it didn't show. Perhaps he didn't believe the tale. It was hard to be sure. He might just be floating on a sea of poppy.

"Listen, then. This is what I've done. I've crafted a shell of air and magic over Polassar, drawing on the power of the rings. It will keep the cold and the snow off him. It will keep him alive, even with no one to tend him. When so little life is left in a man, the final spark can be quite amazingly stubborn. If we take him with us, Polassar will surely die—as perhaps he might if we stayed here with him. This way, he lives till we return, and we'll have more options then. That's his only hope—a slender one, but it's no worse than the one we've all of us shared since we set out."

Thomas regarded her from Tristan's side. Tristan himself still said nothing. Elisena hoped it was safe to leave him again with the cat to watch him. She went after Reynaud.

She found him going through Polassar's gear, sorting out the things they'd need which Polassar would not. Reynaud bundled up the remaining objects to be left beside Polassar. A golden arm-ring flashed amid fabric.

"You heard?" Elisena asked him.

"I saw, rather. If we can't take Polassar with us, then it's the best thing for him." Reynaud shrugged, then went on. "Maybe the best thing, period. Where we go, there's work for only one sword, and we all knew from the first that it wouldn't be Polassar's. He's never been comfortable around magic. He's better not having to watch it, wanting to help and not able to."

He knotted the last thongs savagely hard; then, thinking better of it, he loosened them slightly, so the bundle might be untied, even by a wounded man. "Tristan blames me for what happened, because I did nothing to help Polassar. Likely he's right, but I couldn't slide a spell between them any better than you could."

"He blames himself, too," Elisena said. "He's hurting, Reynaud. He strikes out at anything near."

"I know. How could I not see?" Reynaud did other, utterly unnecessary things to the packs, fidgeting. "I antagonized Tristan the very first time we met. Do you remember? Who could have known then? But I've managed to do the same—or worse—every time we've spoken since. It was irresistable, he always rose so delightfully to any sort of baiting. Now he takes every word I say for mockery, and who can blame him? Not I." He picked up all the packs but Elisena's, which he suffered her to take. The load must have been heavy, but Reynaud gave no sign of discomfort. As a penance, it wasn't much, but he might not have intended it as such.

Tristan was by Polassar, his face composed. For all his quietness, Elisena still hardly liked the look of him. She'd forgotten to ask Reynaud if he'd dosed Tristan with anything, but if they'd argued as they must have, Tristan would hardly have taken anything unless it was forced upon him. He might be far from himself, but he wasn't drugged.

Wrapped in his cloak, his sword put by his hand, Polassar looked ready for his burial, despite Elisena's assurances. Her magic was invisible. It was hard to accept that he was still living. Tristan stood looking down at his friend, then turned away.

His glance fell on Galan's equally quiet body, still lying where it had first fallen. One good push with his boot sent it rolling over the edge and down the cliff. Tristan looked as if he felt better after that, though the alteration was slight. He took his pack from Reynaud when it was offered to him and put it on carefully. Minstrel, silent on his shoulder, stepped quickly out of the way of the straps.

"I wonder if he followed us all the way here?" Reynaud asked, looking toward the cliff edge. "Or was he just set to wait along the way we'd have to come? You'd think the birds would have seen him."

Incredibly, it was Tristan who answered him, not even turning to face Reynaud at first.

"We could have been waiting for *him*," he said bitterly. "We could have been, if it hadn't been for my pride. I ask pardon of you, Reynaud, for the things I said to you a little while ago. You couldn't have saved Polassar, once the fight started, but I could have, if I'd only spoken sooner."

Tristan went on, haltingly, before they could begin to question him, and spoke of finding Cheris in the caverns, the fight between them, and the bargain with Nímir Cheris had claimed. He didn't look at either Reynaud or Elisena as the story straggled forth. That seemed to make the words a little easier to drag up. Easier, but not less painful.

"I didn't tell you. You already thought I was seeing things, and I was afraid that, if I insisted, you'd think I was crazy. Then, in a little while, I wasn't so sure of what had happened myself and so I let it go."

Thomas stood staring at him, amazed, though no one but Minstrel noticed.

Tristan finally made himself face Elisena and lifted his eyes to hers. "I tried, anyway. It didn't work very long, and so I knew what I'd seen had to be true, even if I didn't think I could convince anyone else of it. I knew. I should have been ready for this. If Cheris could come here and be kept waiting for us, why not Galan? He disappeared just about the same way Cheris did, into Nímir's winds. I never wondered about that at the time—we all just assumed he was conveniently dead, even though we never found his body. What could have lived through that storm? Such blind, stupid complacency! And I fell right into the trap—because I was *afraid*—afraid of what you'd all think, too proud to risk it. If I hadn't been, if I'd spoken up instead of locking it all away and suffering nobly, we could have posted watches and stayed on our guard. This wouldn't have happened."

Tristan turned away again blindly, before Elisena could

stir or deny the blame he'd heaped on himself. Reynaud's stance interrupted the first movement she did begin to make. He stood stock still, face white as if he bled from some hidden, mortal wound.

"Lady," Reynaud whispered, strickenly. "He *was* right. All the time. He wasn't imagining any of it."

"What do you mean?" Elisena hardly cared. She only wanted to get past Reynaud to Tristan. She did not want the weight of Reynaud's words entangling her and holding her back.

"That morning I was looking at the slope and I saw what we couldn't make out in the night, a spot where there might have been an opening in the rocks under the snow. Every test I tried said that I was right about it and that it was there, but there was snow over the whole slope, and I was weary of digging. I didn't want to risk magic there a second time, but I thought I could uncover it more easily another way." Reynaud's words tumbled crazily. "It was simple—just a loud shout, really. At the right moment, you can make an avalanche anywhere here, just by raising your voice. I wasn't ready for the scope of it, though. The slide almost caught me, because I hadn't thought to put any controls on it."

"So, you uncovered the opening. What does that have to do with what Tristan's talking about or his thinking you were trying to kill him? If you hadn't brought the snow down, we might never have found him—"

Elisena meant to argue only long enough to get clear of Reynaud. She wanted desperately to get to Tristan. He was bending to pick up Thomas, his shoulders drooping, even when he straightened up again. She didn't have to see his face to guess his need of her. She dared not be too far away again. Tristan had grown too used to that.

Reynaud's fingers were claws on her arm, holding her back. "Don't you see yet? He said he was in there most of the night, digging. There was an opening there. There were probably dozens of them; that rock face was holed like a wormy apple. It took him all night, but Tristan found an opening and worked his way out. Then, just when he'd finally got clear, I came along and brought half the mountain down on him!"

Reynaud dropped her arm at last and stood staring at Tristan's back. "And then, when he protested, as anyone might be expected to do, we told him that I'd saved his life and that he must be mad to think otherwise. We let him know that every word he said would only further prove our point. We healed him with poisons and asked him questions whose answers we wouldn't have believed. You wonder that he's withdrawn as he has? By the Council of the Nine, what did he dare say?"

How much Tristan had heard of the exchange was anyone's guess. Certainly he looked surprised enough when Reynaud dropped to his knees in front of him, black cloak falling careless as a shadow onto the trampled snow.

"My lord, I don't expect you'll believe me, for I've given you little cause to trust my word, but I swear I never saw you that morning. Not till after the slide, when I was searching for the opening I thought I'd uncovered. I swear that on my life."

Tristan stood a while bewildered, looking for the trap, quivering like a deer surrounded by hounds and hunters and about to go down. Then a longer, slower shudder went through him.

"It wasn't your fault," he said dazedly, looking at Elisena over Reynaud's bent head, and it was impossible to say which of them he was absolving, or if he meant the speech to include them both. "I believed it, too. I thought you must all be right—"

The relief that he felt was so intense, so unlooked for that Tristan thought he'd faint, but he found that he couldn't even smile; he was too worn with emotion and loss. He made to raise Reynaud to his feet, then staggered and had to be steadied himself. It was all he could do to take Elisena's hand, but he didn't need to expend his small reserve of strength to maintain the grip—or the emotion that flowed through it. Her hand was warm and alive in his, and it felt as if she never intended to let go of him again.

The snowslide came while they were still in plain sight of the spot where they'd left Polassar. It had to come then, or the cruel irony of the gesture would have been lost on them. The slide began with a familiar deep rumble, just to draw attention to itself, and continued visually as the snow began to slip down the long slope.

The disaster proceeded slowly, as if to underline their

helplessness. A wave of snow seemed to pour forever down the mountain side behind them. When it was done and the last of the white powder had been hurled high in a cloud and had settled back again, the ledge where the fight had ended and the bright blue dot of Polassar's cloak were both gone, vanished and lost beneath many hundredweights of snow.

Contrasted against the vastness of all Channadran, it was more of a slap than a studied attack. Tristan, who'd thought he was beyond feeling any more pain, discovered that he'd deceived himself. He cried out sharply and tasted blood in his throat. The mountain air had an edge like sword steel to it. Yet his face still wore a look of resignation. He had not expected the snowslide, but it had not surprised him much.

Elisena was saying calmly that they need not despair. Polassar was no worse off than he had been prior to the avalanche. Buried he might be, but the spell she'd laid over him still held and still kept him safe. If anything, the snow would keep him safer. Tristan didn't know if that was true. It didn't matter to him; he barely seemed to listen. He watched the sky, a set to his jaw, and saw what he had expected and hoped to see.

He saw the black tongues of wind circling above them, certainly the very same winds which had but lately rushed over the face of the snowfield, pulling the snow free of the mountain side and sending it hurtling down. Tristan saw where the winds came from—or at least knew, by extension, for he saw where the winds went when their task was done. And so he knew which way he had to go.

They needed no birds to guide them, after all. By fortune, they had not strayed much from the true way, even while moving blind. The three of them stood upon the sloping shoulders of the very peak whose head was hidden by the seething, swirling blackness that the winds had just rejoined.

A Last Great Deed

NO ONE QUESTIONED TRISTAN'S ABILITY TO LEAD THE final stage. It would not have mattered if they had—Tristan would have gone on alone. He didn't need to. He merely described what he saw, and the three of them set off after it, with no backward glances. Having the journey's end in sight made such fateful resolve easier, somehow.

Powdery snow chirped under their boots. Minstrel answered it bravely, though he was too well swaddled for any but Tristan to hear.

Night came, like a curtain dropped, surprising them all. They slept just where the darkness found them on the slope, with no chance to make any sort of camp. Spreading their wool bags among the rocks, they wedged themselves in as best they might. There was no level ground, nor was there a way to put the bags close to each other—once they laid their heads down, they wouldn't even be in sight of each other.

It would be their coldest and loneliest night yet. They each felt the loss of Polassar keenly, and being unable to huddle together would make matters worse in the night. No one was eager to bed down and lie alone watching the cold flames of the stars that pressed down from above. Tristan spread out his bag and crawled inside reluctantly, making room for Thomas—then discovered that the cat was nowhere to be found. He sat up just in time to see Thomas' tail vanishing after the rest of him into another bag.

Tristan stared, disbelieving. Thomas had gone to Reynaud?

Tristan had only seconds to waste on a jealousy that later shamed him. There was a movement on his other side, and then Elisena slipped nimbly beside him into the bag as he turned his head. She tried wordlessly to lay her own bag over top of the one they shared for its added warmth. Pressed close as they were, it was difficult, and Tristan lent a hand to his side. Their fingers brushed, and their eyes met again. The crossing glances were like the caress of fingers.

There was no need for any of them to be alone after all that night. With Elisena's head resting against his shoulder on the spot where Thomas was most wont to lie, Tristan wished a blessing on the cat, though he didn't quite know whether for tact or kindness. Kindness, he decided, glad as he'd never thought to be that Reynaud was not lying altogether alone in the night, either, but at least had another warm creature near him.

Tristan woke to find Channadran wearing all the beauty it could ever hope to claim. The slopes, lit by the just-risen sun, spread literally at his feet. Just out of sleep and still sleep-trusting, Tristan didn't find the sight dizzying. The snow and ice upon the rocks sparkled like a king's ransom of diamonds, and it was possible for a moment to fancy them just that and forget both their freezing coldness and their danger.

Below, dawn lit the edges of clouds, gilding them, while the rest of the world was a pink-brown fog, warm and glowing, shading to nut brown in the farthest valleys. The mountains, their sides ribbed with ridges like the grain of wood, seemed almost benign guardians of the scene.

For the moment, Elisena still slept, the sun warm upon her face. Tristan was startled to see small green leaves springing from a crack in the rocks just above her head, and the stalk of a flower uncurling above the snow. He recognized the furled bud and the thick, rounded leaves. He had known that the cyclamen was a mountain plant, but he had never seen one flowering white before.

Elisena had come awake and was watching him, though she'd made no sound. One hand crept out of the wool bag and touched the bud Tristan was staring at. The flower, released, opened at once, its perfume rich and exotic upon the air.

Her lifetimes of bondage to Nímir had taught Elisena a blind courage and lessoned her superbly well in that virtue. It was a courage well able to proceed in the face of vast peril, loneliness, and uncertainty—even of a paralyzing lack of knowledge. Her ignorance of the precise nature of the deadly battle they faced was no less deep than Tristan's own, but her hope was unshatterable. She moved ever ahead of him along the wildly wavering line between the darkness and the bright light of foreknowledge; and still she could smile at Tristan, as if the two of them sat beneath an arbor of cherry blossoms in Esdragon, safe in the sun.

Shocked by his scarcely grasped realization of her plight, Tristan took the hand she groped toward him with, seeking to lend strength where he had so often drawn it. Her rings shone between his fingers like dew drops. The clasp lasted as long as it could—moments only. The sun climbed higher.

All of them felt the closeness of their goal, though only Tristan could actually see that nearness. The climb looked hard, but the day's light should see them there, probably but a little after sun-high. When they'd eaten a scanty meal, they cached all the packs. There'd be no need to burden themselves with such things on their last climb. If they were so lucky as ever to need them again, the packs would be easily recovered. Reynaud left his sword as well. It would not be needed, either, so close to the peak.

There was little space for dread, little time to pay attention to fast-beating hearts or late-come doubts. The rock above was sheer, and they had to resort to elaborate ropings to get up it. Polassar's strength and skills were sorely missed, though Reynaud was clever enough at rigging the ropes about them all.

They felt as small as gnats on the rock face. There was no direct route up. A vertical crack gave passage for a while, providing easy footholds; but when it gave out, they had to work crabwise for more than a hundred paces until they reached another crevice they could use. Minstrel was sent up to scout the route. Following him, using metal pins, they fashioned anchors for the ropes, then chipped footholds into the rock.

Working at that, Reynaud missed his footing and fell as far as the rope would let him. All that held him up was Tristan's fingerhold, and Tristan tried hard not to remember that it was also all that held *him* up. He thought his fingers would take root in the rock—and would have been pleased if they had—before Reynaud had clawed his way back to secure footing.

They went on wordlessly, as if speech had been left behind with the packs. Trust for the person at the other end of the rope had become too implicit to require comment.

They gained a ledge at last, a shelf deeply cut by the crack they'd ascended. Tristan scrambled to the top, then overbalanced till he nearly fell. He'd had a foot on each side of the crack and had made the mistake of looking between his legs. He could see straight down to the floor of the valley below, with clouds trailing over it. Reynaud's arm dragged him over to the relative safety of the narrow ledge. Elisena popped up next, made the same error that Tristan had, and both men grabbed her.

Panting, they sat at rest for a while.

Can I open my eyes yet? Thomas asked.

Reynaud gravely assured the cat that he'd missed the best part of the climb. Thomas hissed disgustedly.

Journeybread and sweets were passed around. The journeybread was tough, though nourishing. They chewed in silence a long while. Minstrel ate some crumbs and then climbed back to the warmth of his bag. Reynaud stirred himself enough to gather the ropes in, coiling them to unroll smoothly at his word when they were needed again.

"How much farther do you make it?" he asked.

Tristan tipped his head back, looking up the cliff above. It sloped back more than the bit just below them had, making for marginally easier going. Whether faster, too, he couldn't tell. He'd send Minstrel up to be sure there was nothing unseen up there to block them. Maybe he could also send Thomas up the lower part, dragging a cord which they could use to haul a rope up.

Guess again. Thomas rolled over onto his back, feigning utter exhaustion.

The spot where the winds swirled most thickly was still well above them. Two more stages to climb, at least, Tristan thought. He started to say as much, replying to Reynaud's question.

As with the attack from Galan, there was no warning, and they were no better prepared than they'd been then. Tristan heard a loud *sniff* beside his left ear and saw all Thomas' fur suddenly stand on end, though the cat was still lying on his back. Tristan turned his head automatically to see what the sound had been, even as Reynaud and Elisena were also beginning to sense something, judging by their beginning questions to each other and to Tristan.

Small wonder that they were confused! Reynaud and Elisena saw nothing and felt only a breath of cold, foul air. Thomas could see nothing either. It had always been Valadan who'd given warning of the Hounds, sensing them, although he could not see them, either. Tristan thought he might well be the first person ever gifted with that special sight—but if there was any distinction in that, he couldn't appreciate it.

The Hound looking over his shoulder had the eyes of a slug and a mouth like a lampfish, all long needle-teeth that meshed when the mouth was closed. The mouth was not so closed. It drooled messily and lolled a gray tongue.

The Hound had only holes for ears and not quite the proper number of legs. Its body was thin, hinting at great swiftness, its hide covered with what looked like rotting fungus, mostly gray with a tinge of green. Tristan thought it understandable that the unseen Hounds were mistaken for wind. Swirls of leaves and dust always revealed their otherwise invisible presence, flying ahead of them as if lifted by wind gusts. Not even dead leaves could bear to be near such a beast and fled any threatened touch.

Tristan didn't blame them. He himself responded as anyone confronted with such a sight would surely have done—he lost the journeybread he'd just swallowed and whatever was left of his breakfast as well. He didn't see Elisena flinging ring-bearing hands up to form a shield about them and didn't know when the thing at his elbow was thrown back outside the protecting circle. Just when he thought he was done being sick, he looked up and saw more of the beasts circling around them, trying the barrier, and his emptied belly heaved again so hard that he nearly fainted.

Several heartbeats passed before he dared open his eyes again. This time Tristan confined his looking to Elisena and to Reynaud, who was augmenting the binding she'd laid upon her spell. Tristan was never so glad to see Reynaud at work. If ever a spell needed to stay unbroken, this one it should be!

Thanks to the cliff behind them, leaving Elisena no need to craft a wall to guard their backs, she had been able to fling her shield high enough that they might all stand straight, and wide enough that they had room to work without tangling arms. Tristan got unsteadily to his feet. Neither Elisena nor Reynaud spared him a look. The Hounds were hurling themselves against the barrier, subjecting the spell to a continual testing which wizard and witch could feel if not see.

It was impossible for Tristan to say whether only one or many of the Hounds prowled. Sometimes a single body would seem to sprout two heads, yet what appeared otherwise to be two beasts owned no more legs than a single one did. After another bout of nausea, Tristan stopped trying to count the things. Plainly, the Hounds did not obey natural laws and could not be viewed on a normal level.

"There's no reason to think they *can* be killed, Reynaud," Elisena said tautly. "Even with Tristan's sword. Nímir channels too much of his power through them."

"They can hold us here till we starve, if we don't try!" Reynaud countered tensely, his hands still flashing with spells. "He won't send them elsewhere—we're the most pressing danger to him. There's nowhere he could need them worse than here!"

Tristan could see thick yellow saliva dripping down the fangs of the nearest Hound. He turned his head away.

"Can we try to move the wards?" he asked. "I can tell you where the beasts are."

Elisena glanced at him, realizing for the first time that he could see the Hounds. The expressions crowding across her features would have interested Tristan greatly—at any other time.

"It won't be easy," she answered. "How will we climb, keeping that sort of watch? And they'll just follow."

"If we can stop Nímir, they'll stop, too," Tristan guessed. It wasn't much to pin hope on; but having come so far, he wasn't minded to be stopped within sight of the end. Besides, their situation was hardly likely to alter for the better. Aloft, the winds swirled more lazily, seeming to watch him as he watched them.

"Better than waiting for them to find a way in," Reynaud said.

Dogs can't resist chasing cats, Thomas offered. *And if they thought I was going for help—*

Tristan grabbed the cat up roughly by the scruff of his neck, locking his fingers in the thick fur. "You even *try* that, and I swear I'll come back from the dead to make the rest of your nine lives as miserable as I've made this one!"

Thomas blinked greenly at him. *Point taken, I think. If I said I was only joking, would you let go of my neck?*

Instead, Tristan put his left arm under Thomas' paws, so that the cat was cradled instead of dangled. "We're staying together, you daft animal," he said fiercely. "No noble sacrifices, if you please. I—"

Automatically, he was looking at his other companions as he spoke, meaning the words equally for them. Elisena was busy at the spell still, considering the variance she'd have to work if they were to move the fringes of the barrier as they'd need to, climbing upward. Reynaud was drawing something in the snow with his silver dagger, making great flourishes that scraped down to the bare rock and interspersing those with the most delicate movements of the sharp point upon the topmost crust of the snow. It was some sort of ward, Tristan thought, that Reynaud had thrown up as Elisena cast her spell, and the two were now one.

Reynaud might have interwoven his magic with Elisena's, but Tristan knew his own part in whatever came next would be only that of a lookout, for a magic so finely tuned and blended would not accept another power into it, any more than water would blend quietly with oil.

He had been watching for several seconds before he realized what Reynaud was *doing* with the ward—and by the time Tristan recognized what he was seeing, there was only a split-off instant left in which to act, too brief a time for him to do more than cry out.

Deliberately, graceful as Kitri the dancer, Reynaud drew a boot toe across the ward-line, breaking it and inviting the Hounds into their circle—into his trap.

He'd laid it cunningly. Tristan saw the beasts—squeezed into a single creature as they slipped through the narrow space—springing for Reynaud. Reynaud stood ready, his silver dagger agleam with some manner of puissant spell, stabbing for the Hound's throat as if he could see it as well as Tristan could.

The rush of the attack bore Reynaud over backward, but his grip never loosened as he fell. He was hanging on for life itself and knew so. The dagger drove deep, twisting, flaming, molten, while Reynaud's left hand clutched the beast to him, even as its struggles dragged him perilously near the boundaries of the ledge. His black cloak draped the Hound, showing him its shape, and he held the creature somehow where it was, preventing it from falling free to escape him.

The Hound howled. Its tail and its paws curled about Reynaud like fingers of wind, trying to take his breath so that he could not complete the speaking of the incantation he'd been reciting all the while. It had thought of the tactic too late, probably too long used to being invincible—a failing it shared with its master.

Reynaud laughed gaily, amazedly, as if something pleased him. Then there came a great flashing and flaring of power, like nothing Tristan had ever imagined. He had little enough time to wonder over it. The blast caught him, and Tristan was hurled from his feet. His head hit the ice, and a darkness came crashing down over Reynaud's laughter.

He dragged himself back to consciousness, aware of some threat, though the pain in his head kept him from remembering more distinctly what it was that he dreaded. Tristan pushed himself to his knees, seeing double the usual number of fingers on the hands in front of him. There was a shrill, bothersome ringing in his ears. He tried to shake it away, which was not a good idea. He felt sick. Fear still nagged at him, sharper than the pain. Tristan opened his eyes again.

The snow and ice had melted away for some little distance about Reynaud. In spots, the very rock had a melted look. Of the Hounds there were no signs, unless a greasy smear of ash meant something. Reynaud lay on his back beside it, as limp as if he'd had every bone in his body broken to jelly.

Tristan couldn't quite manage to stand, so he crawled to Reynaud, feeling the rock growing warmer under his hands as he got closer. Reynaud's eyes were open when Tristan got there, though the man's thin mouth was twisted with pain till he spoke.

"Sorry to spoil your lecture to Thomas," Reynaud whispered. A smile ghosted about his lips then. "I may be the only one of the fellowship who got what he came here for. That's one creature of Nímir's that will serve him nevermore. And I needn't trouble over living out a life tedious with anticlimax, either. Don't look so sad at my good fortune, Tristan."

The magic signs on Reynaud's clothing glowed like a king's melted crown, all gold and winking rubies. Their light was blinding at first, hurting Tristan's eyes, but it was swiftly fading from the edges in. Curls of smoke rose up from the designs as they vanished. There was a stench of burning hanging in the air—but not from Reynaud's damaged clothing.

Tristan bent over him as he had over Polassar, with a horrible sense of events repeating themselves, an endless catherine wheel of pain from which he could find no release. Reynaud's dagger was gone, and the hands that had used it were black, smoking stumps, with the finger bones somehow still holding together. The spell had been difficult to work and wield, with fingerplay paramount even while the knife was plunged in. Reynaud had worked it well, but he would never work another.

Tristan's head reeled as the blood left it, but he held onto his senses, knowing that, if Reynaud could bear the pain, he must at least bear the sight. He searched for medicines in the pouch at his belt and found only the silver butterfly box, with a dab still remaining of its precious ointment. The salve was a simple one, meant to deal with nothing worse than scrapes and bruises, and would work even less well on Reynaud, as it had not been patterned for him, but it was all Tristan had to work with. He'd have to try it.

He drew off the lid, but Reynaud shook his head at him.

"Don't waste it. There's little feeling left, and it will do me no good."

Tristan felt tears on his cheeks. He remembered how he'd striven without success to help Polassar and knew that this was somehow worse. Futility was as bitter as the lingering taste of sickness in his mouth.

"Reynaud, *why*?"

"Why? You're the last should ask me that. Didn't you feel it yourself, when you had the Guardian of Darkenkeep under your sword? The joy of striking back, just for once, and knowing an enemy's been hurt? Maybe you don't remember—Elisena told me you almost died yourself, and that clouds the memory." Reynaud paused, considering. "It's not what you're thinking. I was careful not to be lured, as Polassar was. Nímir may tempt to suicide, but this was my own choice." He stopped again, catching breath or thoughts.

"Say, then, that there are few great deeds left for a wizard, and I'm proud. I wanted to claim my portion before all were gone. That's not the whole truth—nothing ever is, I've found—but it will have to do. It won't sound well in a song, though. See what you can do about that, if you ever hear of any." Reynaud smiled again, apparently at the absurdity of a bard's trying to deal with their present situation. Certainly it was unlikely that any bard would ever come to hear of it.

Reynaud looked down at his clothes, moving his eyes only. The sigils were nearly all faded, leaving a dust grayer only by a little than his face. Reynaud could no longer nod his head; he had not strength for that, but he shut his eyes, accepting.

Tristan gathered himself for another attempt at healing. His head was clearer, though it pained him still.

"Don't you dare die!" he ordered Reynaud, crooking his fingers over the man. "I've had enough last wishes thrust on me. I won't take yours, too!"

Reynaud's eyes opened again. He grinned, or at least jerked the corners of his mouth. "All right. I absolve you of the song. But do not try to hold me. I don't wish to live like this, even if you could arrange it, which I doubt. The result would be unpleasant for both of us—and, as

I said, anticlimactic. The story ends here. You can't stretch the last page of it."

"You can't die! Not *now*! Not when there's just a chance I might start to understand you!"

"You mean to say you never did?" Reynaud whispered. "That the mystery has been so successful? That's extremely flattering, but it's still no reason for me to live— only for you to. See you do so."

Reynaud smiled one last time, a mere flicker across his old-young face. His eyes shut again as his lips slackened.

the Final Confrontation

"HE TOLD ME HE WAS THE ONLY ONE OF US WHO GOT what he wanted," Tristan said. He held Elisena's elbow to steady her as they stood looking down at Reynaud. Elisena straightened, moving gently away from his support as her own legs grew stronger, but not letting go of his hand.

"Let us prove him wrong, then."

Tristan got the rope anchored securely with his first cast. His mood was such that it seemed impossible he should miss and need to try a second time. Indeed, he was able to loop the rope so that he could bring both ends to the ground and charm the two sides into a ladder, a fine application of his craft such as he'd seldom dreamed he'd be capable of. He wished Reynaud could have seen.

When they'd climbed, they left the ladder where it hung. They needed to go no higher. For all purposes, they'd reached the mountain's top. Above, there was no more rock, only a piled ridge of snow which changed moment by moment as the circling winds played with it. Tristan was breathing hard from the exertion of climbing, but there was no substance to the air. His lungs ached emptily, a different ache from the one in his heart.

He put Thomas down upon a waist-high rock. Removing Minstrel's bag from around his own neck, he tied its thongs carefully about Thomas'.

"Wait here a while; if we don't come back, try to go down the mountain. If you can get far enough, Ambere's birds will take you home."

No.

"You don't need to be afraid of the eagles, Thomas. They won't hurt you."

Thomas lashed his tail. *I am not afraid. I'm just not going.*

"Allaire will need Minstrel, I think. It's not fair to keep sending him back, if I take you along. I'm trusting you to see he gets home. Do that for me, Thomas?"

That's a low trick. I thought better of you.

Tristan was leaning close over the bag, his lips moving almost noiselessly as he bade farewell to Minstrel. There was a fluttering from inside the bag—angry, Tristan thought. He looked at Thomas, smiling wanly.

I'd say good luck, but if you had it, I doubt either of us would be here.

Tristan ran a finger over the cat's head once, then turned and was gone. Thomas' tail twitched restlessly. He bent his head to his chest, peering awkwardly at Minstrel. He saw a bright, bold eye and heard a brave chirp. It spoke assent.

Stealthily, Thomas got up and crept after Tristan.

They were high up, but not too high to be still among clouds, Tristan discovered—clouds of ice crystals, he saw as he and Elisena passed through. Like broken needles, the bits hung in the air about them, obscuring all but the closest objects. Elisena spoke a word softly and touched one of her rings with another. The crystals ceased to settle upon their clothing. She held her hands loosely, gloveless and ready. Tristan drew his sword.

Visibility was still dangerously poor. Tristan took his crystal in his left hand and lighted it, aiming its beams low to pierce the gloom before their feet, so that they would not step blindly into a crevasse. He opened his mouth to ask Elisena what it was they were looking for, then thought better of speaking. Within the cloud, the mere sound of their boots scuffing upon the snow was loud. Speech seemed a fearful risk. Tristan felt that each ice crystal was an eye, trained like an arrow upon them.

Elisena's head was up, and her hood was flung back. The pendants in her hair swung gently with her stride. Her thoughts, whatever they were, were beyond him by then, Tristan knew. For that reason, too, he forebore to speak, lest he damage her concentration at some perilous moment. There was little else he could do at that stage to aid Elisena's quest. His own moment, whenever it was, was not yet.

Welcome, children.

The commonplaceness of the voice startled them both, far more than the suddeness of the sound. They had come, after all, expecting to find something—and anticipating it to be dreadful, fearful beyond comprehension. A normal voice, however disembodied, was so far from that expectation that it stopped them in their tracks. Tristan's heartbeat accelerated jerkily.

Your persistence is quite astonishing, the voice went on softly. *You have endured a great deal to reach a spot which most other mortals would endure a great deal in hope of avoiding. I am as much surprised as impressed.*

Tristan looked wildly about, searching the gloom both high and low. He could see nothing but the ice crystals in any direction. There weren't even any of the dim, bulky shapes that had proved to be upthrusts of rock when he'd approached them earlier. Yet the voice was close—it sounded as if it was right in his ear.

Your struggles on your way to me have amused me vastly, children. That is a rare accomplishment. You deserve the fate you have won—I would have stopped you long since, but for the entertainment you have provided. Wizards are few now. It has been a long while since I have played with one.

For Tristan, the meaning could not have been clearer had Nímir named Blais directly. His anger flared, and he found his voice.

"We haven't come to play."

The words seemed rash, spoken aloud. Tristan felt Elisena stiffen beside him.

So? the voice breathed, begetting ice crystals in Tristan's blood. *Do what you have come to do, then.*

Tristan felt his sword's point lift, then dip, as if the eager weapon were somehow confused. It plainly wanted to strike as it was meant to, but there was just as plainly no target in sight. Unless—there, was that a slight darkening among the crystals? A cloud within the fog? Tristan brought his blade up and stepped forward a pace.

The crystals parted, shimmering darkly. The colors

flashing from them were haunting and familiar. Tristan shook his head, certain he heard laughter.

He stood still, fighting the sword's wish to be slashing wildly in all directions. The blade was no less confused than he was. Nímir might require a physical focus to affect anything other than their minds—but he had cleverly chosen a form impossible to combat. Clouds could scarcely be threatened by steel—they'd only flow together again behind a slash or thrust, unharmed and unaltered.

Well?

Elisena made motions for what must have been a descrying spell. Tristan saw the flicker of her rings at the edge of his sight, like lightning just over a horizon. But though she said the spell truly, nothing was revealed by its agency.

Did you think, then, that since you have won so far— and since you, little wizard, have even earned a second manner of sight, that I would unveil my face to you? That you would be granted some sort of cosmic knowledge? Is that what troubles you, then? You are mistaken in what you think you deserve—and impudent.

Elisena, unperturbed, continued her spell-casting.

Such impudence, then, should receive what it asks. Behold!

The ice-crystal cloud swirled apart as if thrust aside by a giant hand. That was the last thing Tristan saw.

He has left you, Lady. You used that tool too long to a purpose it was never meant for and now you have at last broken it. His spirit fled into death rather than face another hopeless battle.

Elisena knelt beside Tristan's too-still form, not daring to draw a breath herself, her lungs in sympathy with his. She tried to make her fingers reach out to touch him and search for the blood-beat at his throat, but she could not move. A struggle raged within her—the need to touch battling the standing order to hold back and stay still. Movement might break a fragile peace and loose a deadly spell.

Her old, safe habits were strong, dearly learned. They shaped her reactions, rather than the other way around. She must withdraw before she could be hurt—must hold herself at a careful distance. The tactic had always served her well. Why did she now see it as failure and weep that she could not seem to leave off using it?

She looked again at Tristan's still face, unable to say whether what she felt for him was love or only compassion for a tool too long and cruelly misused. Was there even a difference between the two? Tristan's defenselessness made her ashamed, even as she shored up the barriers that should have protected them both. Tristan would have rejected her weapon, without the least thought for himself.

You doubt his death, this ultimate desertion? Is this then the first time he has tried to escape your cruel plots? The first time death has seemed a fairer choice than life? Think again, my child.

Elisena stood trembling, assaulted by truth—and doubts. *Could* what had been so long broken be mended strongly in so short a time as there had been? Tristan had his habits to fall back upon, too, as strong and as fatal as her own. His road had been hard and perhaps longer than his life.

Never once had he looked back to say, "Witch, what have you led me into?" His eyes had been wide open all the time, seeing all, even when he couldn't hope to understand it, accepting, and choosing to risk trusting. And what sort of guide had she been? Elisena swallowed back a wail of grief, tasting bitterness in her mouth.

Love is a vulnerability, as you learned long ago. What you love and can be separated from puts you at risk. He's left you in the only way he could.

An egg is whole, perfect, and secure, Elisena recited to herself. But unless it cracks and splits, the bird within will never hatch, and the egg is made a symbol of death rather than life. Nímir's pursuasions were too glib. They woke her sense of caution fully.

There was more at issue than she was given to see. The danger on the surface was perhaps less deadly than what it might veil. Elisena forced a smile onto her lips.

"O Father of Lies, you do urge too sweetly to your viewpoint. Am I a child to think that night has come because my eyes are closed? I had an oath sworn to me by this man. I do not lose my faith that it is kept, simply because you confuse my sight."

There was a sound like a crystal goblet smashing, and the cloud of ice dropped down again, veiling all.

Tristan was lying on his back, or else he was on his face and something very solid was lying on top of him. He was cold all over, but the back of his head, his shoulders, and the backs of his legs felt the chill worst. Tristan opened his eyes, oriented himself, and sat up carefully.

He felt nearly as ill as he had after Reynaud had destroyed the Hounds. His sword lay in the snow beside his hand. Tristan wrapped his fingers around its hilt and felt a portion of his strength return, even if only in his imagination. He looked around, suddenly frightened for Elisena—whatever had befallen him might have harmed her, too.

She was nowhere to be seen.

Tristan leaped to his feet, heedless of any injuries he might have suffered, not caring that he hadn't the least idea of what had struck him down and thus couldn't avoid a second attack. *Where was she?*

He was answered as readily as if he'd shouted the question.

You're all alone now, little wizard. She's left you. She fled while she could. She's a bit better practiced with her weapons than you are with yours, you see.

Tristan stared about him, disbelieving. "No," he said firmly. "What have you done with her?"

You do not believe she has gone? Look, then.

The cloud of crystals swirled apart again, and Tristan flinched, but he was shown only the ground and the single set of scuffed footprints there, leading back alone the way two sets of footprints had come. He knew a pang of doubt.

Elisena wouldn't really have left him, surely? There was no answer that time, save the utter silence of the place. It was so quiet that Tristan thought he'd have heard another person breathing half a league off.

How long had he been lying senseless? He was so cold that it could well have been several hours. He must admit that possibility, not having the least idea what had happened after that flash of power. Could Elisena, then, have thought him dead?

Ah, but even then she wouldn't have left him—

Consider Allaire in Darkenkeep. Was it only hours?

Your mind is full of moonbeams, and you have slept long, a voice that sounded so like his own voice whispered subtly. *You love her, so you conveniently forget the other times and the other risks taken by you at her word. What did she risk? You failed her this time, and she's left you behind, like a bit of broken crockery. If you think, you'll see that there's nothing so new about that.*

Tristan's throat ached. He didn't doubt that, if she'd gone, Elisena would have had her reasons, perfectly logical ones, but still it hurt. Couldn't she have waited for him? He considered his plight, cast alone in the middle of Channadran, and knew he would never have used her so, no matter what had befallen.

Nor would she have used him so! Deep inside him, something stirred, and struggled to surface.

Why do you find it so difficult to doubt her, when she found it so easy to mistrust you? The voice inquired.

Tristan was seared by memories of the awful days after the avalanche—memories he'd been willing to let drop, though he had not forgotten them. Those memories were hard to ignore no matter how strong his resolve.

Tristan shut his eyes on them, but found that gesture futile. He was not seeing with his eyes, for all that his tears burned between his lids like acid. He knew again his shame and the injustice of the accusations. The pain was sharper than when the hurt had been fresh. Nímir's question was more than apt. He hadn't been treated at all fairly. And that time was not the first. And yet...

Risks—what do I know of her risks? Tristan insisted to himself. *She'd never tell me. What risks are there for Elisena that I know nothing about? I can't judge what she's done.* He held his eyes shut on the tears, unwilling to let more of them fall, lest they be misinterpreted. He could die, but not full of self-pity like that.

"O Father of Lies," Elisena said from by his side. "Can you still think to play at this old game? Do you judge either of us so easily shaken from all we've vowed that you can serve us both with the selfsame guising? A few illusions and cobbled tales of betrayals will not rid you of us."

Tristan's heart leaped with astonished joy. He'd never expected such an instant reward—or indeed any reward at all—for the tiny crumb of his faith. His terror of being abandoned melted away, though it left him hollow, and his knees were trembling as if they might not hold him up much longer.

Somewhere, far off, there was a crash as of ice breaking or being shattered. It was a peeved, angry sound.

Thomas crouched behind a snowdrift, wondering how much closer he dared to go. He was as much afraid of Tristan's notice as Nímir's. Minstrel stridently ordered him onward.

Baggage-carrier to a bird. I'm glad my mother can't see me now.

Minstrel's reply was scornful and brief.

"As Tristan has said, O King of Winter, we are not come here to play your games. Forgive us, but we decline your sport." Elisena lifted her hands. On them, her rings blazed.

She began to draw the magical shapes of them in silver fire on the air and she wrote them huge, beyond mistaking. First she chose a crescent and star, and her spell began to grow. All at once the light of a full moon was washing over Tristan, bathing him in silver. Its loveliness filled him and shored up his quivering legs. Standing straight, he watched the moon pass through all her phases and saw the little star that dogged her side as if tethered there. He knew that star was free, bound only by its own will. Appropriately, this first sign was that of Partnership. He looked toward Elisena.

As if day had come, Tristan saw next the graceful swirls of clouds in the air between them—great piles of newly shorn fleece drifting benignly above the green fields below, their shadows dappling the ground. The soft shadow passed into the sea, where Tristan saw flashes like the rainbow of colors hidden within the whiteness of a pearl and felt the peace of waves sliding ceaselessly in toward a golden-beached shore. Then there was the silver slither of falling rain and streams running to the sea, watering the gardens of the land as they went, joyous and generous.

Upon that land, all manner of plants were springing, their fine roots mingling and joining, till all Calandra was one in its life, a great tangled binding spell, linked to the throne at Crogen, where another stone winked with a blue deeper than that of the summer sky.

There came just the merest hint of a snickering laugh.

Across the warm face of the land, a dagger of ice slashed. Half Calandra died at once. All that lived there was frozen to powder, and the Winterwaste was born. The knife paused, hovering over a tiny, straw-thatched cottage.

It could be spared, the voice suggested. Tristan stared at his home, full of golden memories.

Father of Lies, Elisena had named Nímir. Would Nímir next offer to give Blais back? Tristan told himself that he'd long ago renounced his home and knew it to be true. What he wanted was not within Nímir's power to grant. But the offering of it might be a first sign of weakening. He had read somewhere that Nímir's greatest power was the divining of the deepest wanting in a man's soul. That power might be a weapon trotted out now in desperation—or at the first twinges of it.

If so, Nímir was too late at using the weapon. Tristan had long before learned that he could never hope to go home in the way Nímir offered. As a lie, it wasn't in the least convincing, and as a bribe, it was useless.

Before Tristan's face, a row of hearts glowed upon the air. A gentle warmth enveloped him, a sense of love and belonging that had naught to do with the past. Then he saw a twist of silver, which shaped itself into a circle of flames like a hearth-fire. Tristan could scry pictures in that fire, and in the crystal which glinted in its light. There was hope therein, and the peace the other rings had promised.

Admit the truth. You are only here because it has simply never occurred to you that you could go home any time you chose to.

Tristan looked down at the sword he held before him. The shapes of Elisena's rings were laid like runes along the whole length of the blade. They were signs of life, every one of them symbols to confront Nímir with the one thing he dared not face—the truth of life, which continued despite all advice against it. Twist and turn as he might, Nímir could not escape those signs. They blazed before his face, silver-white against the darkness.

What do you fear so greatly here? Have you come to any harm, save what you have yourselves invited by your intemperate actions? You were not forced to come here.

Elisena drew the sign of the tenth ring in the air. It felt solid and real to Tristan as it slipped onto his sword, exactly as it had been the day he had placed it upon Elisena's finger so long ago, when it had been freshly remade. As the sign slipped past those of the other rings, their lines broke, reformed, and rejoined, till all the surface of the blade was covered with one vast interlocking design of life and magic, more complex and profound even than the roots within Calandra's magic-laced soil. Tristan beheld the sight with awe, seeing the long-dead High Mage's greatest work at last fulfilled. He had never known what to expect. The sight beggared imagination.

The sword glowed as it had at the moment of Tristan's crowning, when it rested in Crogen's throne—and the blade hummed as well, a sound of eagerness. Its investiture was nearly complete.

Elisena wrote the signs, the truths her rings had borne safe for all her lifetimes, in stars across the night sky overhead. And when Nímir sent a wind to freeze Tristan's eyes shut so that he should not see their magic, Minstrel promptly sang the signs in crystal notes beyond any his throat had ever known. So much for leaving the canary safe with Thomas, Tristan thought, but he had no leisure to think of the bird beyond that, except in gratitude.

Cold descended. In the chill air, sound shattered and was no more. Silence fell, but Elisena wrote the signs once again painstakingly upon Tristan's heart.

There were not many of them that she needed to write afresh. She had but to trace what already was to be read there. The sword began to lift once more. It knew its target now, and the goal was well within its reach.

Elisena had forged her weapon and cast it at evil's heart. But as that weapon left her hands, so, too, did its protection. She stood alone, vulnerable, wide open to attack for the first time. And the attack came with the speed of thought.

Tristan turned, as Nímir meant he should, to see Elisena struck down in a whirlwind of sleet—struck down as every other thing he'd loved in his life had been. It was so swift that she never had time to make a sound.

"No!"

Tristan saw Elisena fall silently and saw the light of her rings go out. Now, Tristan knew, he was truly alone in the night.

That did not surprise him or dismay him much. Part

of him had been ready for such an end since he had seen
the avalanche bury Polassar, and that part ruled him then.
The other parts of him, the best parts, the parts that had
dwelt in the flickering intervals of daylight he could
scarcely remember, were all burned away. Tristan stood
in the dark, waiting.

*Run away, little wizard. Make haste, and perhaps in
my mercy I will let you go.*

Tristan did not think mercy was a word Nímir knew.
It would be another trick. It didn't matter.

*I owe you much punishment for slaying my Guardian.
That was an evil deed and a debt long owed. Yet your
struggles to reach me have diverted me pleasantly. The
two debts cancel one another. Lay down your sword and
go.*

Go where? To the edge of the nearest cliff, to cast
himself over? It came to Tristan that Nímir paid his debts
very promptly—in fouled coin. He knew already that he
had no reason to live one heartbeat longer and that he
had no home to make for. But it would amuse Nímir much
more to let him live than to strike him dead.

A promise and a price, Elisena had prophesied. Very
well. The price *was* the promise now and it was not at all
heavy to Tristan. There was but one way. Nímir would
never kill him outright—unless Tristan still looked to be
a threat. It was the only way Tristan felt sure he wouldn't
be tricked again. But he'd have to make it look real...

There would be time for only one stroke. The sword
had been ready before, so whatever it had wanted to strike
at must have been very near. It still would be. Tristan
peered through the gloom and the tears blurring his sight,
sword held ready, vainly seeking a target. As if it had fled
the sword, the ice cloud was gone. The air was still. But
the ground before Tristan was littered with crystals of
snow and ice.

A mere pace ahead, one crystal stood out, glittering
brighter than its fellows with strange, dark colors. Cold
past imagining breathed out from it—cold and a terrible
fear that drove all life away from it and destroyed all that
lived, for so it protected itself from life, which alone could
harm it. Recognizing it, Tristan smiled with his cold-
cracked lips.

The crystal was tiny and helpless-seeming. Almost he

might have been moved to pity it, but the hate it hurled at him was too strong to breed such thoughts. The crystal wanted none of his pity. It simply wanted him dead and frozen into harmlessness. Tristan was staggered and dismayed by the singlemindedness of the thing. For one moment, that held him still—and then memory came flooding back. He could hate, too. He had reasons—plenty of them.

There was no need for him to aim his stroke. The blade leaped gladly, pulling his arm along after it. Tristan did not think for one instant that he would reach the crystal, but he knew Nímir would never risk his succeeding or count upon his failing in the attempt.

He was right. Even as Tristan moved, Nímir played his last card. He froze Tristan's heart, stopping it between beats.

Tristan felt a sudden painful coldness spreading through his chest, as if he'd been pierced by an arrow of ice. Then a numbness spread outward into his limbs. His fingers lost strength, and the sword dropped from them. Tristan's sight darkened, and he fell forward like a puppet with its strings slashed, to lie beside Elisena.

Tristan's heart no longer beat. But in a box of ambitiously carved wood, hidden deep in a leather pouch that now lay crushed under Tristan's hip, a tiny pink stone gave one twitch, then another. It moved upward in the box, bumping against other stones as if to beg their aid.

It won none, but the stone did not cease moving. Instead, it began to pulse strongly and regularly. As it did so, there came a faint sound from the box, like the sighing of the sea—or like the wind beyond the walls of a high tower.

Tristan woke from a dream of Am Islin rising above the green waves and discovered that the sighing he'd heard was his own breath between his barely parted lips. He could only open his eyes a little way. Frost was thick upon his lashes.

Toadstools, couldn't he even manage to *die*? Tristan's disappointment was such that it woke a flame of anger in his chest, as warm as if he'd taken strong drink. He must try again, then—but he wasn't sure he was alive enough for that.

He was lying on his face with his arms flung out before him. He was only inches from the crystal, though it might have been on the moon, it was so safely beyond his reach. Tristan tried to lift his sword again and found that his fingers refused to obey him. There was frost spreading over them and over everything he could see, thickening as he watched helplessly. Tristan knew a last flicker of perverse hope. Perhaps he wasn't quite done with the business of dying, but he was well on his way.

It was written that dying men, if given time, might review their entire lives. Tristan didn't know if that was true, but it seemed he might have time to find out. At the least, he could entertain himself by calling back one spot of light to take with him into the darkness. Elisena—

Hanging against Thomas' chest in his cage, Minstrel stirred, his feathers rustling.

Now, a remembered gentle voice spoke into the canary's mind. *As you never sang before . . .*

Minstrel's throat began to vibrate softly, as if he had learned the art of purring from long association with Thomas. Then the bright notes began to break free and shattered the air. Minstrel forgot himself, forgot green eyes and the tang of salt air. His song was one he had sung long, long before, in what seemed to him the morning of the world . . .

Tristan couldn't call Elisena's face to mind, somehow. Instead, lifted by bird song, there rose before his eyes another memory, bright as all his childhood had seemed to be . . .

Tristan saw the toad, the one he'd assumed Blais had magicked, squatting on the sunny cobbles by the cottage door. It hopped away at his approach, and he followed after it eagerly. He'd thought all toads were his master's work, after he'd seen Blais make one from a stone and a spell. Blais must be a very busy man, Tristan thought, to have made so many toads while still conducting the vast remainder of his fabulous affairs. Soon enough he'd have help, apprentice Tristan promised himself—starting with the toads.

Tristan remembered the spell Blais had used. He had a flawless memory for words and gestures then, and he paid close attention to the things that fascinated him. It was a gift that Blais had not so far suspected he had. Nor did Tristan know the language the spell was spoken in, beyond recognizing that it was not the common speech he and Blais used together. Still, he reckoned the sounds would be enough, without the understanding. He remembered them and the gestures.

Tristan had cast the spell perfectly, though he didn't know that, any more than he knew, at five years of age, what would happen to a real, unmagical toad exposed to that spell.

The toad almost made the transformation to a salamander, but its flames consumed it. Alarmed, Tristan tried the only quelling spell he knew—the one which Blais used to stifle the fire at bedtime. The two magics meshed no better than did water and oil. The backlash hit Tristan like a lightning bolt. He never even saw it coming.

Hours passed before Blais found him hiding in the reeds by the stream, and he greeted Tristan's ensuing fever with no great surprise. Children often ailed mysteriously. The boy didn't speak a word for days, but Blais was not much concerned. Even when he was well, Tristan was mostly a quiet child.

At length, Tristan began to mend and to take an interest in his world again, even in magic, as Blais began to train him in it. The boy was clumsy at his tasks, which puzzled Blais. He'd thought he had sensed something more than talent in Tristan, early on, and had planned to nurture it carefully. It was hard for Blais to believe that he'd been so mistaken, or that Tristan had grown out of his early promise. Well, the boy learned, at any rate, in the ordinary way. Tristan had much patience, if little reliable skill.

Tristan let his breath out with a long sigh as the old, old guilt dissolved away like dried blood at the touch of herbed water. To discover finally his deepest secret *now,* when it didn't matter at all . . .

He wished Thomas could have been there to share it. The cat was the only one who might have understood. All these years, he had hidden from his guilt and from the fear of further punishment when his crime was found out, all over a child's mistake! If he hadn't been carrying the load of it, he might have become a wizard indeed, and things might have ended very differently for him.

Tristan's mouth crooked at the irony of it. He'd finally learned the cause of the block that had plagued him and blighted his career—and now it was utterly irrelevant! He would have laughed aloud, but that would, he thought, have been painful. His smile deepened. Pain was only to be dreaded if there was the promise of it continuing a long while. He needn't fear *that,* of all things.

Tristan knew one final flash of his old stubbornness. His sword had fallen from his hands, though it lay between them, and he wanted it back. He might never have been a wizard, Tristan thought, and he might not be worth the killing, but he was still Calandra's King and he would die as was his right, with the sword in his hands—or one of his hands, if that was the best he could do. Surely his failure did not forbid that to him.

His sleeve was frozen to the ground. It was all Tristan could do to lift his fingers, and the sleeve kept him from moving them more than the little length they gained when he straightened them out. He was able to touch the blade, but he could not close the fingers around it to take the sword into his hand.

Tristan sighed at the failure. He was close enough to see every notch upon the steel, every pit where rust was beginning to take hold, and the last faint silver traces of the signs of Elisena's rings. He could see how sharp the blade's edges were. He remembered Dickon's pride in the care he'd taken of the sword while it had been in his possession. The boy's zeal had put an edge beyond belief on the old blade. Tristan had never needed to whet it since. But in the struggle the sword was meant for, never a blow had been struck. He was glad Dickon couldn't know.

One last time, with the little that remained of his strength, Tristan stroked the blade, seeing in his mind Calandra and all his friends, most of whom were dead by now or would be soon. Tristan's hands were so white with cold that he didn't feel the sword's edge cut him, slicing deep as his first finger trailed down the blade. It was a little while before the gash began to bleed, and there was no sensation from the flow. Tristan's eyes were closing with the weight of the frost on their lids, and he did not see the red blood flowing.

Welslin's heart still beat dauntlessly, and the cut bled

slowly, but freely. A tiny, twisting trail of blood trickled inexorably toward the crystal.

Something arrested Tristan's peaceful drift toward oblivion. At first it was no more bother than a pebble under a sleeping mat, but it proved just as impossible to overlook. Giving himself up to death had seemed to Tristan a fair enough plan—when it had been working. It no longer was.

Tristan squeezed his eyes more tightly shut, dimly aware that the agony he tried to close out was far from physical. He could not, after all, lose consciousness of his memories, recent or far past. They stayed with him and became more demanding as his will weakened. He saw Elisena toppling into the snow, watched again the avalanche bury Polassar, and beheld Reynaud's burned hands. He felt the aching, empty place that had been carved out of his heart when Blais died. His thwarted hopes for real wizardry stung him. Even the memory of one frost-blasted rose in a garden back at Crogen returned to him, so clear that he could sense the texture of the blackened petals.

There was nothing he could do about any of it and no redress he could make. All hopes were vain. He'd *failed,* finally and totally—if not particularly spectacularly. Tristan's misery welled up till flesh seemed barely able to contain it and it must surge free, though it burst his heart in the process. What would Welslin's heart do then? Tristan wondered. Would he never be able to die of his grief, but be prisoned so in Channadran forever?

His tears found a way free first, somehow still warm enough to unseal Tristan's eyelids. But for what was building, they were not adequate release. Tristan turned his eyes to sight along his fallen sword toward the gloating crystal that had settled before it, all too safely out of any reach he was capable of.

In Tristan's mind, sudden resolve took shape, swelled, and crested.

There was no fingerplay or whispered spell, but the sword skidded through the trickle of blood until the hilt rested against his fingers. The physical contact was slight, but sufficient. At the touch, light flashed down the sword's length—and beyond, terminating at the ice crystal.

The light was so brilliant that the crystal was lost to

Tristan's sight. It had been enclosed in a coffin of fire, a box which collapsed and pressed inward upon it at once. An anguished scream rang through the bones of Channadran.

The mountain shuddered, but the beam of light held steady. Something even brighter seemed to weave within the beam—the life-signs Elisena had laid onto the blade, leaving the sword and flowing toward the crystal.

The crystal began to steam, but even that escape was cut off as the vapor was enclosed and pressed back upon itself by the walls of fire. The screams cut off, though the ground quaked yet more violently.

Tristan refused to note the distraction. He held to his unplanned, unvoiced, and unfingered spell, watching as the box of fire tightened until it was a scintillating point so small as to seem leagues away. He let the last of his misery seep into it, yielding it all up.

The pinprick of blinding light exploded and left behind only darkness.

Daybreak

Tristan awoke to the sound of water dripping.

At first, the steady plopping sound was comfortably below the threshold of his awareness, but after a few moments it became annoying, and he opened his eyes, hoping to discover the source of the nerve-tweaking sound. His lids lifted easily, though Tristan wasn't able to appreciate that yet, or even be surprised at it. All he saw—which didn't begin to explain the sound—was Thomas, so close that he looked blurry. The cat was crouched down and seemed to be licking at something.

Tristan must have made some slight sound, because Thomas raised his head and looked at him.

That's a nasty cut you've got yourself there, he said. *It will be a while before your fingerplay's up to even your abysmal standards.*

Then Tristan noticed that all of his clothes were soaking wet. In fact, he was lying in a puddle. Remarking faintly on that, he tried to sit up, or at least push himself up off of his face.

Careful, now. I got the bleeding almost stopped, but it needs binding. Don't go knocking it into anything.

When he moved, his right hand suddenly felt as if it had been plunged into flame, so Tristan didn't have to ask what Thomas was talking about. The first finger of his right hand was bleeding. It was gashed deeply and looked as if it might require sewing to close the edges of the wound. Thomas jumped onto his lap and began to lick at the gash industriously once more.

That didn't seem to help much. Thomas looked up

between licks, blood all over his whiskers and his chest. *Look, handy I may be, but I'm a cat. There are limits to what I can do. You're going to have to find something to wrap around this.*

Tristan rubbed his free hand across the bridge of his nose. He had a terrible headache. When he let his hand fall again, it hit and then slid off his leg, and his fingers splashed when they reached the ground. He noticed the wetness again, but this time it captured his whole attention.

"Thomas? What's happened?" Tristan looked around, his sight blurred as if, for some reason, he was learning to use his eyes again. Nothing would come clear, but he didn't seem to see the whiteness he'd expected. And the water—there shouldn't be water here, in Channadran! It ought to all be frozen—

Thomas had finally managed to rip a part of Tristan's jacket's lining loose. Feathers spilled out, but at least he'd gained a scrap of fabric for a bandage. *Here. See if you can tie this. How do I know what happened? I'm not going to try to explain to anyone how you saved us all just by cutting your finger on your own sword. I'll leave that fun for you. It ought to make a great ballad.*

"What are you talking about?" Tristan couldn't tie the bandage, so he just held it in place with his left hand. The finger hurt less if he held it tightly, he noticed. His mind was thick as treacle.

Something the matter with your eyes, or are your wits still scattered? Oh, I forgot—it's just dawn. You'll be able to see more in a bit, when there's more light. Be patient.

He'd have to be, Tristan thought. He used the time searching for his most recent memory. That seemed a sensible course. Nothing he dredged up suggested any logical reason for him to be napping in a puddle, though, hurt finger or no. Thinking wearied him. Tristan dozed, sitting in his puddle. When he opened his eyes again, it was because the first rays of the morning sun were touching his face, startlingly warm.

At first, he just blinked and yawned. Then the dazzle was gone, and Tristan forgot all about his sleepiness.

All around him, there was water, running, dripping, and pooling upon the level spots. The morning sun struck rainbows from every drop. Nowhere was there the least vestige of snow or ice. Above, where the snow peak of the mountain had been, there was only pale green sky. All around, where the fangs of ice had dripped from the rocks, drops of water hung. When they grew too round and heavy, they fell, causing the dripping Tristan had heard when he first woke.

Mouth open, he looked at Thomas. The cat sat regarding him inscrutably. After a moment of that, Thomas got up and stepped aside so Tristan could see past him.

The sword still lay upon the ground. Tristan's first concern was about the water; the blade must be rusting already, and he should fetch the rags and the oil— The thought stopped. Beyond the sword, though only by a little, was the spot where he'd seen the strange ice crystal.

Memory flooded back, so sharp that Tristan cried out. He made himself open his eyes and saw that where the crystal had been, only a blackened spot remained, as if there'd been a burning there. There was nothing in view to prove it, but Tristan knew that the melting of the ice had begun there and spread outward.

Like sun-dazzle, more memories flickered just at the edge of his reach. Tristan remembered straining hopelessly toward his sword—just a flash again, before his mind slammed shut on the pain, refusing it. That flash was more than sufficient. Tristan shuddered as Reynaud's doubted words about his potential came back to him.

Indeed, he had got around his block well enough when he had to. Words and fingerplay seemed to be quite unnecessary. The will was what mattered.

There was a key in that somewhere to the treasure of a great discovery. Tristan wasn't sure what manner of discovery, precisely, but it felt close—close as the spot where the crystal had been. He leaned forward, fingers out, ready to explore.

I wouldn't. Thomas said. *I really wouldn't. I wouldn't even look at it again. Turn around.*

From behind Tristan, Minstrel chirped excitedly.

Thomas cocked his head at the sound. *Oh. Already? Yes indeed, I'd turn around.*

Tristan did as bidden, wondering what Minstrel could possibly be doing that Thomas thought worthy of anyone's attention. In the sun, every surface glittered, and a mostly-white bird was hard to spot. Minstrel cheeped helpfully to give him direction.

And then Tristan was turned around, on his feet, and moving swiftly. Minstrel left his post upon Elisena's shoulder, so that Tristan was able to lift her up just as her eyes opened.

At first, she didn't seem to know him. Tristan inspected her hands, dreading that he'd find them as blackened as Reynaud's, all ash and melted, twisted silver. Her fingers were whole, though, and unmarked. The rings glowed softly.

She didn't seem to be hurt at all, but Tristan remembered how he'd felt when he first awakened—and it was no hardship to hold Elisena close to him and to feel her heart beating strong and true against his own. Tristan realized that he was thirsty and thought Elisena surely must be also. He used his good hand to carry water for them both, cupping it under a stream running merrily down through the rocks nearby.

That water was as wine to him, clear, pure, and full of joy. Tristan was amazed to discover the little glossy flowers of buttercups springing up at the edges of the puddle where they sat. Among the rocks there were yellow poppies, and anemones. The whole rock-rimmed world looked washed and new.

A hand, silver-ringed, reached up to brush his face. Tears sprang to Tristan's eyes, but they were tears of a happiness such as he'd never thought to know.

"I thought I'd lost you," he said.

"If you're trying to, you won't manage it by setting me in a puddle," Elisena murmured. "I'm not a sugarplum. I won't melt."

Her lips, under his, tasted sweet enough to give the lie to her words.

They made their way down the mountain side, and a film of green spread before them down the slopes. With the ice gone, the fearful way was almost easy. Water, prisoned as ice so long and joyful at its release, had smoothed the mountain side and prepared it for their feet. Days of rough climbing had become walks to be accomplished in hours, with only a few steeper spots remaining to be scrambled down.

When at last they came to the level where the glacier had been, they found only a broad valley, green with grass and dotted with iris-fringed pools. The warm sun lifted the water up into great billowy towers of cloud, but there was moisture aplenty left upon the ground to nourish flowers. They could not walk a step without trampling something fair. The plants sprang up behind them unharmed, flowers blooming thickest where Elisena and her shining rings had passed. Minstrel flew in formation with bejeweled dragonflies.

The mountains of Channadran, so long held under Nímir's unnatural spell, were rebounding with a counter-magic force of their own, compressing days into minutes and seasons into days. The marks of Nímir's long mastery were already almost gone.

Elisena's magic flowed naturally from her, without any conscious effort on her part—if she was even aware of it as anything more wonderful than one breath following another. Tristan had worked no spell of his own, not the smallest firelighting. He had needed no magic, but he was startled when he came to think of the matter. Was he a wizard any longer? The little gift he'd had might have been burned out of him, up on the mountain peak, despite the apparent lifting of the block that had kept his magic mostly beyond his control all his life. It might be gone altogether, and Tristan thought he'd hardly regret the loss. He could look upon it with relief—as a burden set down at last, to let him stand upright.

A stream sparkled suddenly among the fringing grasses. They halted to consider it, Elisena's hand twined with Tristan's. The air was warm from the sun, and Tristan supposed he wouldn't mind wetting his feet, but there were stones that promised him a way across dry-shod, if he was careful. At worst, he could make use of them to help Elisena over the stream. Thomas had already gone bounding over.

Tristan stepped out onto the nearest rock and felt an utterly unexpected, totally familiar wrench at the pit of his stomach. His balance was startled away, and he wind-milled his arms frantically, while Thomas and Elisena both laughed at him, and Minstrel flapped and fluttered. He slipped off of the mossy stone, landed ankle-deep in the cold, running water, and began to join in the general mirth.

No, he would not have been glad to lose the magic, but he could admit that only once he was sure that it hadn't gone from him after all. Walking was a squishy prospect till his boots dried, and Tristan's wide smile as he hiked puzzled Thomas greatly. Truly, humans thwarted the understanding of cats.

Tristan woke next morning to find tiny blue forget-me-nots pillowing his head and briar-roses arching over him for a roof. He didn't mind the thorns of the roses, but he disentangled himself with some care before sitting up. Spatters of dew flew flashing through the morning air. Elisena, ringed by white anemones, slept on undisturbed.

Wind stroked the tall grass as Tristan might have stroked Thomas' fur, drying it. Not all the grass tossed to the wind, however. A long trail of it was bent, only slowly springing upright again. The track stretched over the horizon, mostly straight and only wavering where it crossed the stream that ran nearly hidden between banks thickly grown with lilacs. Tristan traced it, turning his head, sleepily curious.

The grass ceased to bend only a few paces off—where Valadan stood knee-deep in the irises. His eyes, with all their deep-set, flashing colors, regarded Tristan as the horse deliberately chewed the mouthful of flowers he'd just plucked neatly. The purple blossoms hanging and nodding on their stems from the side of his mouth gave him an amused look.

You sleep soundly, King of Calandra. It is well I came. It is a weary walk back to Crogen, even through such a happy land as this is become.

It was not, however, the prospect of being spared a footsore walk that got Valadan's mane soaked with joyful tears as Tristan hugged the horse's neck.

Forgive the delay, Lord. I could have reached you far sooner, but the others have only mortal speed.

From far off, a whinny was heard. In a moment, horses appeared over the horizon. Tristan knew them—Elisena's gentle mare and Polassar's irascible roan.

Dickon will be glad to have you back, Valadan observed, reaching down for another mouthful of tasty flowers. *Being the son of a practical farmer, he can deal with a crafts-*

man like Jehan well enough, but Crewzel's complaints and Kitri's attentions have begun to distract him.

Tristan's eyes widened as he looked back at the stallion. Jehan and the others had been far from his thoughts for a very long while. "I didn't think—I don't even know how long we've been gone."

Long enough, Valadan answered gravely, taking no note of his master's confusion or possible embarrassment.

It could have been months or years. Tristan wondered if the difference really mattered and decided that it didn't. He laid his discomfiture aside. Channadran cast a new spell now, and while they made their way out of its influence, many worries might be safely deferred—as many more could be forgotten altogether, a new habit to be quickly learned.

Valadan wore neither bridle nor saddle, but neither control nor comfort demanded such things where Valadan was concerned. Tristan didn't think they'd need their remaining gear much longer either, but he thriftily made a bundle of it all, with straps around it so he could manage it easily one-handed as he rode. His finger had been neatly stitched and thickly bandaged. He was clumsy because of that, but otherwise not much troubled by it.

Elisena stood at his elbow, awake and quietly stroking Valadan's nose. The stallion lipped at her hair, setting the crystals ringing like wind chimes.

The mares arrived, whinnying greetings to Valadan and jostling for pride of place beside Elisena. Valadan's ears went back as he snorted a warning to the roan, whose hip had almost sent Tristan tumbling as she cantered indiscreetly by.

Tristan caught his balance and made sure his feet weren't in any danger of being trampled, but he never left off staring at Polassar's roan mare. If Valadan had brought her, then— His heart leaped wildly, joyfully, acknowledging a hope he had forgotten he held to. There was better than a chance, then, that Elisena had been right and that Polassar might yet live and be healed.

They would, he guessed, be able to reach the spot where they'd left their friend by nightfall. That was a journey he was glad to have eased—and speeded. Tristan didn't pause to wonder how Valadan had so surely found them. He had perhaps finally learned not to question those things that weren't apt to have an easily given answer.

Huh! Thomas interjected. Tristan raised an eyebrow and continued with his gear-bundling.

The Winterwaste is a meadow now, Valadan remarked to Elisena complacently. *Darkenkeep's roof fell in.* Minstrel settled between the stallion's ears and began to sing a counterpoint of celebration to the news.

Tristan heard the shout just as he was finishing the last knot he intended to use on the packstraps—knotting with only one hand was too awkward for him to care if he made less than a proper job of it. He looked up as the sound was repeated. For days he and Elisena had heard no human voices save each other's.

Danger no longer dwelt in Channadran. Tristan had grown so accustomed to that state of affairs that he hardly remembered to wonder as he straightened and turned to face the sound. It wasn't till he made out the gaudy blue cloak, brighter than any of the flowers that spotted the valley, that Tristan let the pack fall unheeded to the ground. Nor did he stoop to recover it. He stood still one moment more, scarcely breathing—and then he began to run toward Polassar.

"I tell you, Wizard, I thought I'd drown for sure! 'Twas like being on the sea's bottom! I've not been properly dry since—"

Tristan grinned, thinking of the torrent of water rushing down the mountain side, awakening life wherever it went. He remembered the taste of that meltwater, like sunshine in his mouth. Polassar, of course, would never believe that mere water could release a man buried in a slide of ice and rock, could carry away the stones, and could fill a battered body with life, healing it. Water drowned you, that was the only truth that Polassar knew. If it was a lesser, obvious truth, that could be superseded, Tristan wasn't going to tell the man that yet. He wanted to savor his own joy a while longer, and an important part of that joy was listening to Polassar grumbling over how they'd abandoned him and left him all alone, foodless and shelterless, in the dampest spot in the kingdom.

One might hope that coming back almost literally from the dead would work profound changes in a man. Tristan was happy to hear that it apparently hadn't changed his friend. Polassar was sober a while when told about Reynaud and puzzled a bit over the rent in the front of his own jacket, but only a moment later he said Allaire's name like a fragment of a song remembered, and then he was all haste for getting home to her—wasting no more time on the unhealthy hobby of serious thinking. He was already riding off toward Calandra and his lady when Tristan swung up onto Valadan's broad back.

Tristan debated asking Polassar to change course, not that he was likely to be obeyed. But perhaps they ought to consider returning by way of Am Islin? Tristan touched the belt pouch where Welslin's heart nestled. She might, perchance, be expecting it back.

Minstrel, perched atop Valadan's forelock, turned to fix him with one dark eye. His throat feathers vibrated softly, and the canary sang so quietly that Tristan felt the notes more than heard them. They seemed not to be sounds at all, but images rising up in place of the meadow and the distant mountains before his eyes.

Am Islin soared white through gleaming fog, with silver gulls circling and crying about it. No windows showed upon its shaft and no door, either. It was closed to Tristan, and perhaps it always would be.

Minstrel didn't know why that should be. He was, after all, only passing a message. A task had been completed, a prophecy fulfilled, and a tale spun to its end. Something of all of that, and more, was in his song, and all of it utterly final. Tristan nodded sadly, accepting, even though he could not understand.

On to Calandra, then! Tristan settled himself on Valadan's back and took a last look back at where he'd been.

There was a great deal of fertile land at the feet of the mountains—not to mention the former Winterwaste which they had yet to see. That land that would require settlers and homesteaders. It was land where Calandra's life could begin afresh. There had been names attached to this place once, Tristan thought, before Nímir. Elisena probably knew what they had been—he'd have to ask. Names would matter. One of the King of Calandra's next tasks would be the coercing of folk to migrate in. But the King would not be among them. Tristan knew it would be some time before he'd be truly easy at the sight of Channadran, even changed as it was. He cheerfully saluted the mountains in farewell.

And in the action, he stopped as still as if he'd been frozen on the spot, despite the bright sunshine all around. The peak they'd so lately descended was snow-capped already—as were the tops of all its neighbors. The flowery meadow in front of him shimmered. Tristan thought he might be about to faint.

Polassar, several horse-strides off, halted and looked back.

"Wizard, enough of your dawdling! What's amiss now?"

Tristan tried to speak. He thought he'd failed, but a word or two must have come out of his closing throat. At least, Polassar seemed to understand.

"*Snow?* There's always snow atop mountains! 'Tis cold up so high." The matter settled, Polassar turned the roan and began to ride once more.

Tristan rubbed his eyes, trying to grind away his memory of flowers blooming at the top of the peak. *Not a magic that could last,* he thought. Of course Polassar was right. And he was tired to his very bones, despite the wonders that the healing waters had done for him, no less than for Polassar. He'd been walking for weeks, not eating or sleeping very well except for the past very few days. He was exhausted, surely that explained...

Tristan looked behind him again, and the smokelike tendrils were still there, where he'd seen them. Faint against the snow's dazzling whiteness, they coiled closely about the peak, before a distant snowfall hid them from even Tristan's sight. Clouds closed in.

They'd have snow in winter as well, Elisena was saying matter-of-factly. That they must accept. But it would be a natural season, a necessary fallow time for the land, very different from the winters Tristan was accustomed to. He might even learn to relish the change in seasons.

Tristan hardly heard. There was an awful suspicion blooming in his mind, and he wasn't quick enough to twist away from it successfully. He tried, with all his might, but the maneuver failed. He knew! Elisena knew, too, and had known all along, Tristan saw that as his eyes met hers. He'd gone along these past days rejoicing like a child, never seeing that she held some corner of herself aloof from that happiness.

Even so, Tristan felt compelled to speak, as if eyes might lie while lips might not. His voice was falsely light. "Nímir's gone for good. We can go home now."

He knew her answer, even before he'd finished speaking.

"Gone? But evil will always grow, so long as it is allowed fertile soil. A purge may alleviate symptoms, but it seldom cures the disease."

Tristan heard her out calmly, finding it hard to believe that he was not weeping or trying vainly to close his ears and mind to Elisena's words and their implications. Their victory was empty and hollow, as he'd perhaps known all along. There was a taste of sickness in his mouth.

He remembered the thing that had looked like a crystal of dirty ice and tasted again the fear and the hate that had poured from it. It was a thing that had wrecked a kingdom and laid nearly a whole land waste rather than suffer the touch of any warm, living thing. Its fear was stronger than any evil.

Such could not be destroyed, Tristan realized, beginning to sense the scope of it, though his mind skittered away from wholly grasping it.

"Not destroyed," Elisena told him. "But defeated."

"Was all this in vain, then?" he asked her. "All the lives, the pain, and the loss? All for *nothing*? A dream that could never live?"

Tristan felt himself drowning in bitterness. Nímir would return, probably stronger than before. Who knew how many times? And the fight would be all to do over, with no better result waiting at its end. Tristan's head fell against his chest as he heartily wished that he'd died upon the mountain peak, still ignorant and believing that victory was possible.

Something moved before his eyes. The silver of Elisena's rings shimmered, beckoning and promising that where old worlds fell, new should arise and be wondrous fair. Tristan beheld towers, tapestries, flaring torches, jewels aglow, and fruit trees heavily leaden; he heard songs as lovely as the sea and sad as time—and children's laughter.

There were tears in Elisena's eyes, but her voice was quiet and firm. "Come home with me, Tristan."

He looked back again at Channadran, trembling, trying to draw back from the sword edge of his despair.

"Nothing we could have done would have stopped him forever," Elisena said. "Even the High Mage who made the rings must have known that. Nímir will seep back, little by little, as men permit him to, and it's for others to choose then, not us. We have planted a seed and ensured a warm space for its growth. For the rest, I am content to wait. The matter's out of our hands. Will you wait with me?"

His eyes drank desperately at hers for comfort.

"What was done was well-done," she assured him. "And if it lasts for but ten thousand summers, will you grieve that it could not be forever?"

Tristan did not answer, though he continued to look at Elisena for a long while.

Polassar had halted again, halfway to the horizon. When they caught up to him, Tristan thought, Polassar would likely roast his ears for this dallying.

Tristan spoke to Valadan and headed downhill—toward home.

And so it ends in a beginning, Valadan said.

Living happily ever after is hard work, Thomas observed, mostly to himself.

About the Author

SUSAN ELIZABETH DEXTER was born in July of 1955 and has always been delighted that NASA should schedule such important events as Moon landings and the telecasting of *Viking* Mars photos on her birthday.

She was born in western Pennsylvania and has spent her whole life to date in that area, except for shopping trips to New York and side trips to World Fantasy Conventions. She had an uneventful education until high school, when she enrolled in a three-year commercial art course at a local vocational-technical school. She has been employed as a fashion illustrator, layout and free-lance artist for the past several years.

An interest in illustration led her to adult fantasy, via its many award-winning cover designs, but the roots of her interest go far deeper. In childhood her main literary interests were fairy tales and horses, and as she grew up she moved into historical fiction and the occult. From there the next step was logical, and she's still unsure at what exact point she crossed into Fantasy.

Her interests include omnivorous reading, fencing, herbs, macramé, weaving, soft sculpturing, and fine arts. She loves Richard III, Fafhrd and the Gray Mouser, unicorns, canaries, King Arthur, carousel horses, books, pizza, birds of prey, wolves, and silver rings.

From the lairs
of darkness
comes...

THE DARWATH TRILOGY
Barbara Hambly

27 million Americans can't read a bedtime story to a child.

It's because 27 million adults in this country simply can't read.

Functional illiteracy has reached one out of five Americans. It robs them of even the simplest of human pleasures, like reading a fairy tale to a child.

You can change all this by joining the fight against illiteracy.

Call the Coalition for Literacy at toll-free **1-800-228-8813** and volunteer.

**Volunteer
Against Illiteracy.
The only degree you need
is a degree of caring.**

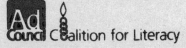

Ad Council Coalition for Literacy

LV-3